The Falls
Murder at Niagara

Larry Elin

Library of Congress Control Number: 2025909400
ISBN-979-8-9988740-0-0

Cover design by Larry Elin, created using Photoshop, Printed in the
United States of America

DEDICATION

To Wallace L. Popielinski 1943-2022
Dear Brother and Motorcycle Companion
Role Model and Moral Compass
Vietnam War Hero

In 1970, Americans were confronted daily by the war in Vietnam, the antiwar movement, the draft lottery, draft dodging, draft deferments, civil rights, voting rights, school integration, women's rights, gay rights, sexual liberation, recreational drug use, and a raft of minor revolutions that challenged social, political and religious norms. These topics dominated the news, were the center of every political debate, watercooler chat and most dinnertime discussion. Everyone picked sides, and more often than not the conversational conflicts pitted young people against their parents, college students against veterans, whites against Blacks, workers against businessmen, progressives against conservatives. It was, to say the least, a target-rich environment for a murder mystery.

Many of the people and situations in this novel come from my own life. Not the murders, of course. They are fictional. I was finishing my freshman year in college in May, 1970, when the Kent State shootings occurred. The Ohio National Guard shot and killed four student protesters at the university. The National Student Association, known simply as NSA, organized antiwar demonstrations at college campuses all over the country, including mine. Although there were plenty of students who supported the war, or whatever our government said and did, and there was a strong ROTC presence, the overwhelming majority of my peers boycotted classes. Including me and my professors. My college shut down. Classes ended for the year. Students went home two months early. I got my summer job back at the Bethlehem Steel plant.

Everyone in my circle avoided the military draft with college deferments until graduation. Then, we all generally knew whether or not we'd be called up based on our draft lottery number. If it was high, no sweat, if low, go to grad school, get a medical deferment, become a conscientious objector, or emigrate to Canada. Avoid military service at all costs. This drove a wedge between all the guys with no alternatives and those of us with plenty. Ah! More grist for a murder mystery.

I call this novel *The Falls* because the murders take place at Niagara Falls, where many draft dodgers first went before continuing on to other parts of Canada to make a new life. But the title is also a metaphor for all the lives that collapsed because of that decision. As you will read.

As in my debut novel, *The Cinder Drop*, the venue for *The Falls* is Lackawanna, New York, a hardscrabble city that hosted old-fashioned, rust-belt industries like steel and auto making, Great Lakes shipping, coal-burning, railroading, grain storage, flour milling. A blue-collar utopia for white folks. For Blacks, not so much. Even I considered foregoing college and enjoying a union job at Bethlehem Steel for the next thirty years. Good pay, great benefits, union protections. I'd have a house, a car, and could send my kids to college if that's what they wanted. But that war! The draft! College was a safety blanket. I curled up under it until graduation in '73.

In *The Falls*, I incorporate as much of this history and its environment as I can to paint the victims, the crimes, the motives, the perpetrators, the investigators and all the innocent people who surround them. I hope you enjoy the story and are immersed in the time, place, and all the characters, dead and alive.

A word about terminology: The novel is a murder mystery, but also has an important subtext involving the racial tensions that very much defined that time and place. For that reason, characters and scene descriptions necessarily include race identifiers. An author describing the same today would probably use terms such as "African American," "people of color," or "BIPOC" to describe a person who is non-white, and "white" for whites. But research shows that in 1970, news stories, government documents (such as the U.S. census), and everyday usage, the term "Negro" was still common. The term "Black," either by itself or with "Person" or "Community" was just entering the lexicon. For the sake of authenticity, I have used both terms, and have put them into the mouths and thoughts of characters depending on the speaker and the context.

PROLOGUE

Hale Ramsay has kept his brand-new Pearson Wanderer 30 at the Niagara-on-the-Lake Marina all summer and finally has a chance to take it out. If it wasn't foul weather, it was some kind of drama at the theater — not the kind on the stage — or at the hotel or at the restaurant he owns. But today the sun is shining and all is well up on King Street. Today he'll enjoy a maiden voyage on his prized sailboat with a particularly beautiful maiden as a first mate: Shaina Ford. Blonde, blue-eyed, long legged, and built like a Barbie doll. She's wearing a two-piece swimsuit with an almost invisible long sleeve shift, a big floppy sun hat, and brand-new white boat shoes. She's sitting, legs crossed, in the cockpit behind the wheel, smiling, admiring him through giant sunglasses. Aware she's watching, he scurries around on the deck, pulling up bumpers, stowing lines, wrapping sheets around winches, preparing the halyards to hoist the sails. He keeps looking over at her and she wiggles her fingers back.

He has planned everything perfectly down below. The cabin is stocked with beer, wine, champagne, plenty of food, clean sheets and towels, and a little pot in case she likes to get high. He hopes so. He does.

The dockhand, Timothy somebody, walks over and unwinds the bow and stern lines from their cleats on the dock. He holds them taut so the boat doesn't just drift off. Hale will fire up the engine and then motor out into the Niagara River, put the bow into the wind, and hoist the sails. He thinks Shaina will enjoy keeping the craft pointed upwind while he shows off his muscular, tanned biceps, cranking the halyard, raising the main. It's going to be glorious.

He checks to see that the throttle is in neutral, pulls out the choke, turns the ignition key, and the twenty-five horse-power engine starts to turn over, but suddenly stops.

"Crap," he says, good-naturedly. He looks over at Shaina, who pouts in a cute way. He tries again. Same thing. But a third time is the charm, and the engine sputters for a moment, then springs to life and idles smoothly. *Not bad*, he thinks, *for an engine that's just been sitting there for two months.* He lets it warm up for a minute, then signals Timothy to toss him the stern line, which he piles down in the cockpit. He'll reverse out of the slip, while Timothy walks down the dock alongside the boat.

Timothy will toss the bow line up at the last moment, and they'll motor out to the river.

But when he pulls the throttle into reverse, the engine makes a clunk sound and just stops cold. It's like the propeller is frozen in place.

"What the hell?" Not good-naturedly.

Back into neutral, no choke now, turn the ignition, sputter, shudder. It's trying to fire-up but struggles. *Goddam*, thinks Hale. *Brand fucking new boat.* For a moment, he's torn between worrying about his investment in the boat and his investment in Shaina. It's going to cost him some money for mechanical help and he probably won't get laid. He tries it again and again but the engine won't start. He thinks he has to eliminate causes, and the first one is to make sure the propeller shaft isn't fouled or, God forbid, bent. He'll have to go in the water. He tosses Timothy the stern line, and the hand ties off the boat to its dock cleats again.

"Will you need help?" he asks.

"Maybe. Can you stick around? I'll get into my swim trunks and inspect the shaft and prop."

Hale makes a quick change in the cabin while Shaina looks on. Her expression is genuinely sorrowful and understanding. She may already know that sailing is, in equal measure, fixing shit and filling the sails with the breeze, keeling at ten degrees, carried along silently at six knots.

Hale flips the stainless-steel ladder over the transom and steps down into the river. The water is warm but smells more oily than fishy. *Cigarette boats*, he thinks, *the mortal enemies of real sailing*. He slips on his swim goggles and lowers himself completely into the water. A second later he sees the problem.

A human body is tangled grotesquely around the propeller and the shaft. Wedged in tight. It could be a man, but the body and its clothing are mangled and chewed up. It has long dark stringy hair that swirls around in the gentle current. Its right hand is extended in his direction and looks like it's waving at him. Hale just stares at the apparition until he needs to surface for air.

When the call comes through the switchboard at the Lackawanna, New York, Police Department, it takes Sergeant Decker, who runs the front desk, a moment to clarify for the caller who it is he is trying to reach.

"Officer Tom Baldwin is now a detective sergeant," Decker says.

"Then I must have an old business card."

"He's in, I can put you through. Can I have a name and what you want to talk to him about?"

"I'm Inspector Henri Paquette of the RCMP in Niagara Falls. This is about a body."

"In Canada?"

"Yes, I'm afraid. We need help identifying him, and he was carrying Detective Baldwin's card. Nothing else. I thought, maybe they knew each other?"

"I'll put you right through, sir."

Baldwin picks up on the first ring, and Decker explains who and what and patches Paquette through.

Baldwin is pushing thirty but fit as a teenager. He was a basketball star up at Hillcrest College in Buffalo in the early '60s, and still works out every morning. Pushups, knee bends, a leisurely 5K jog. Often dribbling a basketball. Around the back, between the legs. He's the only Black on the Lackawanna force, and one of only three in all of Western New York. He's still learning the ropes as a detective, a rank he's held for fifteen months. But he's a quick study and has worked several big cases. Big for Lackawanna, anyway. Helped his boss take down a major mob drug operation, find the killer of a teenage girl, solve the murder of a Catholic priest, and put away a whole family of petty thieves.

"This is Detective Baldwin," he says, and pushes away a pile of reports and prepares to take notes. "I understand you have a body that you need to identify. Can you describe him?"

"It appears he went over the Falls, so he's pretty bunged-up," says Paquette. "He was found wrapped around a propeller. But he's white, maybe twenty, long brown hair and brown eyes. A starter beard. I'd guess about five-ten. Medium build. Dressed like a hippie."

"Could be almost anybody," says Baldwin. He's thinking about the college students he met while working the priest murder last year. The boys all looked like that. A pause. "Does this happen often? Somebody goes over the Falls?"

"About ten times a year. Most of them suicides. Now and then an accident. This looks different, though, and I'd rather show you than explain it. Any possibility of driving up here and taking a look? It would be a big help. We'd like to get an ID and notify family."

"Today is good," says Baldwin. "I'll clear it with my boss and I could be there by three this afternoon. And where is there?"

Paquette gives him an address and directions to the Mountie detachment in Niagara Falls. Baldwin has been in that city many times, so he has no problem charting the location.

"There's one more thing, Detective. This is the third body we've recovered in the river since May. Same general description, same condition. But the others had some form of identification and they were both Americans. One from Baltimore and the other from Akron, Ohio. We contacted their families and they collected the boys. If this is a third, it's an unhappy pattern."

"Suicides?"

"Or murders. The first two, their parents told us those boys had no reason to kill themselves and to come all this way to do it. Plus, three identical accidents don't make sense either."

"I'll be there as soon as I can."

Baldwin is meticulous. Always has been. It's the quality that got him where he is despite rampant and palpable racism in the department, the city, and society. He has to be twice as good to be the equal of his white coworkers. He quickly categorizes the reports and case files that are scattered over his desk, making three piles: right away, later, and tomorrow. Right away consists of just one case that won't go away. It's a local civil rights violation that he has no jurisdiction over and he can't get the FBI or the Justice Department to pay any attention to it. One reason it's high on his priority list is that it is high on his wife's.

Sandra Moore is an investigative reporter with the *Lackawanna Beacon* and has been following and writing about the Martin Luther King Homes, a housing development for "Negroes and Puerto Ricans" that was slated to be built in Lackawanna's Third Ward. The Third is a white, middle-class enclave

4

and the residents there have put up a relentless fight to keep the Negroes out. Almost two years have gone by and one obstacle after another has delayed it, and most recently crushed it. Everything points to discrimination, but the mob is probably involved, too. It was before. It has a lot of money at stake.

A year ago, the Federal Department of Justice became co-plaintiff in a lawsuit against the City of Lackawanna over the King Homes. It joined the Negro nonprofit, called Better Homes Now, and the Catholic Diocese of Buffalo and a group of Protestant and Jewish congregations, who were outraged that the city would stoop to a racist position. Standing in the way of a housing development for the poor. The coalition won that civil rights case, and that should have cleared the way for the development to get built.

But now, the DOJ is disinterested and has moved on, leaving the Negro nonprofit to fend for itself against powerful forces: banks, businesses and almost every white person in the city. The banks just refuse to finance the housing but have no problem making building loans for any number of questionable alternatives. Mainly, anything proposed by the local mob through its shell companies: "legitimate" construction businesses. For the umpteenth time, Baldwin calls his contact at the FBI in Buffalo, Agent Doug Reynolds.

Reynolds is the new Special Agent in Charge – the SAC – of the Buffalo field office. Reynolds comes across as a hard-ass and by-the-book, which should be the good part. But he's also a devotee of J. Edgar Hoover and the director's blatant racism and misogyny. Wrong book. To Reynolds, everybody who doesn't look and think like him is a commie. That includes Baldwin. They don't get along.

"The day wouldn't be complete without a call from you, Baldwin," says Reynolds. "Lemme guess…the banks are colluding with their favorite customers, the mafia, to prevent Negroes from living in nice houses."

"Yes sir, that's why I'm calling," says Baldwin.

"It's not our problem," says Reynolds. "Don't call me again about this. We got real work to do."

"I'm calling you about a federal offense. I can't pursue and prosecute this myself. The FBI and the DOJ should be all over it."

"Don't tell me what we should be doing," says Reynolds, dismissively. "I told you this before. The country needs warm bodies in Vietnam and the antiwar movement is draining them away. I'm focused on draft dodgers and deserters, and there are plenty of them to snatch, especially in this neck of the woods. They come to Buffalo and cross into Canada at the rate of two hundred a month, and that's a low estimate. My job is to round them up."

"I'm going to keep trying," says Baldwin.

"Answer's always going to be no," says Reynolds. "Every single time you bother me. And you want the truth, Baldwin? Even if I had the resources, I wouldn't lift a finger to help a bunch of nig... Negroes... move into a white neighborhood."

He hangs up, loudly.

Baldwin stares at the receiver for a second or two, marveling at how little progress the civil rights movement has made in Federal law enforcement. A couple of years ago the FBI invested thousands of man-hours compiling a vast file on Martin Luther King. Now it won't lift a finger to investigate the mob, or the city fathers of Lackawanna, New York. It's obvious that the FBI and the mob are on the same page as far as Black people are concerned.

Baldwin's next stop is his boss, Chief James Plishka. Plishka took over a year ago and has struggled to rebuild the department after almost a quarter of its cops either quit or were run off. They had been part of a cabal in the LPD that reported to the corrupt mayor, Angus Brophy. They took bribes, harassed the mayor's opponents, even vandalized Baldwin's home when he got a promotion. The department is still shorthanded, and top-heavy with rookies. Plishka spends a lot of time teaching and mentoring. He waves him in when Baldwin appears at his door.

"What's up, Tom?"

"I've been asked to identify a body for the Royal Canadian Mounted Police, up in Niagara Falls. Okay with you if I disappear for the rest of the day?"

"Why you?" asks Plishka

"The man had my business card and no other ID. There's a chance I met him, dealt with him on some level. That's all I know."

"A crime involved?"

"Unknown. But the inspector up there has some suspicions that he didn't share with me," says Baldwin. "He did say that this is the third body the RCMP found under the same circumstances. He suspects foul play."

"It wouldn't hurt us to make nice with the Mounties," says Plishka. "Sure, go. But don't take your gun. They don't like them up there."

It takes Baldwin an hour to make the drive up to the Mountie detachment in Niagara Falls. The route takes him over the Peace Bridge, which crosses the Niagara River within a few blocks of downtown Buffalo. On the American side there are no official guardhouses or checkpoints on the way into Canada, but somebody put orange traffic cones on the bridge to form a slalom, slowing traffic down to a single lane crawl. Posted here and there along the route, right up to the official national borders halfway over the river, is a painfully obvious FBI presence.

The agents peer into each car very carefully. He sees one with binoculars, while another jots down the license plate number, and a third snaps a picture of each driver and whatever passengers they can focus on. Most of the drivers stiffen, sit upright, try to look innocent, trustworthy, not worth the trouble. But a convertible full of college girls revs its engine while the coeds flip off the agents, howling with laughter. The men smile, wave back, but look carefully at Baldwin. *Who are you?* they wonder.

Paquette's directions are good and Baldwin has no trouble finding the detachment headquarters a couple miles west of the city. A modern, low-slung building with ample parking in the middle of a grassy park. Paquette greets Baldwin at the door. He's a tall, solid fifties. Close-cropped black hair and a small, trim mustache. Gray suit. His language is proper and his accent slightly French. He gives him a quick tour of the office.

He introduces Baldwin to five constables, who are busy with paperwork, taking phone calls, pulling files. They all glance up, nod, then go back to business. The place is neat, clean, and organized like a military unit, which is its heritage. Now it's like the FBI.

"We have a short drive to the morgue," says Paquette. "Shall we?" and he motions for Baldwin to follow him out to his car. Once seated, Paquette hands Baldwin the business card they found on the body. "How we found you."

It's spent some time underwater: faded, crumpled, falling apart. Baldwin sees it is one of his patrolman cards, which he often gave out if he wanted someone to get back in touch. Looks like it worked, but not the way he'd hoped.

The morgue is in the basement of a large, gray, granite municipal building in the middle of downtown Niagara Falls. In fact, you can clearly hear the Falls' thunder just a block away: A loud, endless roar accompanied by a cloud of mist rising from the gorge a hundred and fifty feet below. Looks like city offices and maybe the courthouse up above.

Oddly, the building with corpses in the cellar is surrounded by restaurants and businesses that cater to the twenty million tourists they get every year: A Madame Tussauds Wax Museum filled with lifelike versions of famous people. Dwight Eisenhower is right out front on the sidewalk, reaching out to offer you his hand. Next to him, Josef Stalin, pointing at you with a sinister smile on his face. Adversaries in life, pitchmen in death. Not without irony, the attraction next door is Ripley's Believe It or Not.

Paquette and Baldwin enter through a rear door, walk down a flight of stairs, and are met at the foot by the coroner, whose name tag says Silas Griffin. He's probably shown Paquette quite a few bodies. They appear to have a well-worn professional relationship, exchange a few words about a

7

previous case, how it turned out. He beckons them to follow. Down some dark, slightly damp-smelling corridors to a double-door entry.

Inside is Griffin's workspace. Here it smells like chemicals: one might be chlorine bleach. It or something else in the atmosphere stings the eyes. An entire wall consists of ten stainless-steel doors. Each is about three feet square, arranged in two rows of five. The rest of the walls are lined with cabinets and sinks. In the middle of the room is a steel table with gutters along the edges, faucets and drains. Two bright lights hang from the ceiling directly over the table. There's a body on it, covered with a plastic sheet.

"Here's your man," says Griffin. He pulls back the cover, exposing the head. Baldwin steps closer to see. The face is disfigured. It looks like he had been beaten with rocks, then sort of chopped up with a sharp instrument of some kind. But Baldwin recognizes him. He swallows hard and steps away.

"I know him," says Baldwin. "First name is Alan. I'll have to make some calls to find out his last."

"How do you know him? Suspect? Victim? Anything like that?" asks Paquette. "And is he American or Canadian?"

"He's an American, I think," says Baldwin. "I met him last year while investigating a murder in Lackawanna. He was a college student whose professor, a Catholic priest, was killed. And a classmate was killed as well. I met with the whole class and they helped with information. Nice kids."

"Somebody didn't like this one," says Griffin. "Most of the damage to his face that you can see? That was all post-mortem. He didn't feel any of that. What killed him was a blow to the back of his head that caved it in." Griffin gently rolls the body to its side and points at the back of Alan's skull. "Blunt force trauma. Vicious. Angry. I've seen many wounds inflicted during a fight, but this was beyond the beyond. This boy was murdered."

"Not drowned?"

"No. No water in his lungs."

"Time of death?"

"His body was found on August 3rd. He'd been in the water at least four days. July 30 is my best estimate."

"What kind of weapon did that?" asks Baldwin, pointing at the wound.

"A tire iron could've done this. A crowbar. A heavy pipe. Maybe one of your baseball bats."

"Inspector, you mentioned two other bodies, similar circumstances?" asks Baldwin.

"Some similarities, yes. All three were found in the Niagara River, all three went over the Falls, all three are about the same age. This first two did drown, however. They, too, had similar damage to their bodies from falling one hundred fifty plus feet and getting pounded into the boulders at the bottom. They turned up in different places below the Falls. Alan here was carried almost all the way to Lake Ontario and his body collided with even more junk. Tree trunks, rocks, maybe a collision with a boat. He was found wrapped around a propeller."

"I can guess what concerns you," says Baldwin. "The first two looked like accidents or suicides, but this one is clearly a murder. You're wondering, maybe the first two were, as well? Just better disguised?"

"Precisely."

"So, you'll be looking for things that tie the victims together?"

"Beginning with where they were killed," says Paquette. "They were found in Canadian water but could have been thrown into the river above the Falls on the American side. Your Alan could have been beaten to death almost anywhere and dumped into the river. Where these boys were killed establishes jurisdiction. We can cooperate on determining that."

"I will find out who Alan was, where he was from, what he was last known to be doing," says Baldwin. "If you give me all the information you have on the first two victims, I can look for things that might connect them."

"Bonne chance, Detective. If they were indeed murdered, we might have a serial killer out there who isn't finished."

Back at the House, the local nickname for the Lackawanna police station, Baldwin reports to Plishka, tells him everything that just happened up in Canada.

"So, you knew this kid?"

"Yeah, but not well. I met with him and the others in Father Martin's class when we were investigating his murder. He just blended in with the other boys. I don't even know his full name."

"Got a way to find out?"

"I'll start with Angie McIntyre. Works for the State Department now," says Baldwin. "She and Sandra have stayed in touch since the investigation."

In June of 1969, Martin Goezina, a Catholic priest, was found murdered at the Bethlehem Steel Plant. As part of the investigation, Baldwin questioned the students who were in Goezina's class at Buffalo State College. Alan was one of the nine students, and Angie was Goezina's teaching assistant. She became a big asset in finding out what really happened and helped Baldwin's now wife, Sandra Moore, write news stories about the killing.

"You said they found two other bodies, Americans, in the river?" asks Plishka. "What's that all about?"

"I got their info, autopsies, all that stuff right here. Haven't had a chance to look at it yet," says Baldwin. "There may be some personal connections between them all that'll turn up. Right now, it's just age, sex, national origin and Niagara Falls."

"Let me know if you need help," says Plishka, "but I don't know who's available. We are still way short-handed."

Baldwin carries the paperwork he got from Paquette to his office down the hall. It had been Plishka's office for more than twenty years, but everybody got a promotion last year and moved to new spaces. Baldwin painted his and decorated it with basketball mementos from his playing days at Hillcrest College. There's a basketball from the NIT championship signed by his teammates. He has his wedding photo, pictures of his mom and dad, a few photos from his and Sandra's honeymoon in Paris. He had made it his refuge. Not a small feat for a Black detective in a very white department.

He opens the file and studies each sheet as he removes it. He settles back and reads carefully, occasionally jotting down a note to himself. Things to check up on, delve into, people to call.

On top is the report on Dominic Styron, age 23, born May 16, 1947, in Akron, Ohio. White, black hair, brown eyes, six feet tall, one hundred seventy-five pounds. There's a picture of him clipped to the corner, probably a high school graduation portrait sent up by his folks, not the one from the coroner's gurney. He was ruggedly handsome. Employed in Akron at the Goodyear Tire factory. Family reported him missing on May 22, 1970. He left work that day and disappeared. There are notes from Paquette's interview with the family. Styron had always been upbeat, popular, optimistic about his future prospects. Decidedly not suicidal.

Paquette had made a notation that if there was one thing that had the family worried, it was Styron's friends. They were described as countercultural, hippie types. Their son's girlfriend, Ashley Lange, "led him astray" into a group of antiwar activists. Parents were mainly worried about drug use, getting in trouble with the law. Her picture is in the file, too. Dark curly hair and brown eyes, perfect teeth, a pretty face. A note says that she disappeared before Styron did, but she was known as a drifter who would turn up anywhere, anytime.

Styron's body was found in the gorge below the falls on June 2. A New Yorker riding in one of the Maid of the Mist tour boats, the ones that take their customers close to where the Falls crashes on the boulders in the gorge, got sick and when he leaned over the gunwale to puke, he saw the body suspended just below the surface. It was determined that the boat was in Canadian water, and the police from that side of the border recovered the body.

Baldwin thinks about Alan and his classmates. He had met them at Goezina's apartment, where they had held classes, right near the Buff State campus. It is a hippie enclave. Dope smoking going on all around, serenaded by the Grateful Dead and Santana. There were spent joints, still secured in roach clips, in the ashtrays. Is dope a link? Hippieness?

The other possible connection, or at least similarity, is the antiwar activism. Baldwin isn't privy to Alan's feelings about Vietnam, but he was in college and that's where most young people get radicalized. He did know that Alan and his classmates were advocates for social justice, world peace, cultural change on a national and global scale. *Something to explore*, he thinks and makes a note.

The next report is on Jaime Roesler, age 20, born February 2, 1950, in Baltimore, Maryland. White, brown hair, brown eyes, five-six, one hundred forty-five pounds. His graduation photo shows a boy who looks younger, almost baby-faced. His hair hangs over so much of his face that only his button nose and large eyes peek out. There's a gleam in his eyes and his grin is mischievous. His shirt collar is too big, like it might have been his father's dress shirt, and his expression suggests that it's all part of the joke.

The report says he worked as a server in a clam bar but didn't show up one day. He just disappeared without a word. This was June 28, 1970. He didn't own a car, but the Greyhound station is within easy walking distance. No one there remembered seeing him, selling him a ticket, watching him board a bus. Just poof! Gone. A week later a dog-walker found him, washed ashore along the Niagara River in Canada, about five miles north of the Falls.

Paquette's notes about Roesler were a bit circumspect, as though he were trying hard to not write down exactly what he suspected. But the code is there. Roesler was possibly a closeted homosexual. Nobody said it, but clues were all over the place. Effeminate looks, behaviors, interests. Paquette seemed to think that this could have led him to contemplate suicide, but his parents insisted that Roesler was the happiest kid in the world. He played the guitar, was a terrific artist, was taking acting and dance lessons. Nobody who is thinking about offing themselves does that much joyful stuff. There wasn't any mention about drug use or political activism. Baldwin doesn't see anything to connect the two drowning victims with each other. He decides to call Angie McIntyre. She'll know about Alan.

"Tom! It's great to hear from you! How's Sandra? We haven't spoken in weeks." Angie sounds really pleased that he called.

"Sandra is doing fine!" he says. "Finishing up several stories. Union issues at Bethlehem, student unrest at the high school. Obsessed with the Martin Luther King Homes charade, acting like a civil rights bullhorn as much as an unbiased reporter. I think she's a little conflicted on that one."

"She's doing the right thing," says Angie. "We can talk more about that but you're calling for something else?"

"Yes," says Baldwin cautiously. "I'm calling about your old classmate, Alan."

"He's in trouble?"

"He's dead."

There's a long silence. "How?" Angie whispers.

"He was found by the Canadian police, in the Niagara River," says Baldwin.

"He drowned? I remember he was a pretty good swimmer in high school. All Western New York. What a tragedy!"

"No, Angie, the coroner says he was struck in the head and murdered. Probably dumped in the river. I am so, so sorry to tell you this."

Baldwin can hear Angie inhale, choke up, and let out a long breath. He remembers telling her that her professor, Father Goezina, and her young friend Sarah Simpson had been murdered, too. Now here he is, a little more than a year later, calling to tell her the same thing, about someone close.

"We've been here before, Tom," says Angie. "Are you calling once again to ask for help? Because I'm in."

"Yes."

"What do you need?" she says readily.

"Whatever you can tell me about Alan. We don't even know his last name, who to contact."

"Crowe, with an e at the end," and she goes on the tell him everything about Alan.

They were both from West Seneca and grew up just a few houses away. She's five years older than he is, but her sister is the same age and the two were friends. Alan was an athlete – a swimmer – and wasn't a particularly good student but got into Buffalo State College and suddenly changed. His grades exploded. He took an interest in everything when he got into the college culture, especially when he took Goezina's course about revolutionary movements in Central America.

Alan's interests extended wider, to civil rights, feminism, the peace movement, poverty, labor movements. He had been unaware of geopolitical intrigues, revolutions and wars, social upheaval, but got educated. He became spellbound by the world outside little, parochial West Seneca. He couldn't get enough of it. He loved it.

"How many college freshmen do you know who use the word 'hegemony'?" asks Angie. "Alan was well on his way to becoming a big shot in the Popular Democratic Movement. If he were Black, it would have been the Panthers."

"Did he have any enemies?"

"Like everyone on the left side of the political spectrum, he probably had antagonists. But he was only what, twenty years old? Who could he have possibly pissed off enough to kill him?"

"Any idea who he was hanging around with? Like, anybody else from the class? Anybody who would know what he was up to lately?" asks Baldwin. "His political and social activism is one thing, but a lot of violence is done over money or a lover. Did he owe anybody money? Have an affair with somebody's wife?"

"I can't imagine it, but I don't know. These days? Anything is possible. I've been away for a year and he wasn't in my circle. But his parents might have an idea. My sister might even know something. They stayed in touch. She's in college in Boston. I'll give you her number."

14

Baldwin writes it down.

"I should have asked you how you are doing, Angie," says Baldwin.

There's a long pause while Angie gathers her thoughts.

"I love DC, love my job, met a nice guy," she says, and sighs, "but I am getting disillusioned about our foreign policies. I'm working in the Bureau of East Asian and Pacific Affairs, so I'm privy to a lot of the decision-making about Vietnam, Cambodia, Laos. We get a briefing every week, and it's always the same thing. It's, I think this is the right word, myopic. They look at the world through a soda straw. Very confrontational and militaristic. Very little talk about ending the conflicts peacefully. It's all about winning. Everybody here is a veteran of World War II or Korea, and they approach this conflict the same way. To a bunch of men with guns, everything looks like a battlefield, and success looks like dead enemies."

"You sound despondent."

"Yes, that's how I am right now. A bit hopeless. Maybe things will change. Nixon promised he'd end the war so I guess I'll give him a chance. Otherwise, I might quit. Do some peace marches."

"Don't quit. I speak from experience. Better to agitate from the inside," says Baldwin.

Baldwin calls Angie McIntyre's sister, Fiona, who's attending Boston College. The payphone rings in a dormitory hallway, a girl answers, and she finds Fiona for him. He manages to catch her between classes.

"Hello?" She sounds just like Angie.

Baldwin introduces himself and explains why he's calling. He carefully explains about Alan. He knows they had been childhood friends, but there's no getting around the shocking truth. She bursts out crying. Baldwin can hear the receiver bang against the wall, hanging by its cord. Another girl's voice is trying to comfort Fiona, he can hear that, and he imagines hugging and consoling going on. The other girl comes on the line.

"Listen, I'm sorry, but Fiona can't come back on. She's...she's too distraught."

Baldwin gives the young lady his name and contact information.

"I wrote it down and maybe she'll call back, but it might take a while."

Now Baldwin has the much more difficult contact to make: Alan's parents. It's after five, and they might both be home. He heads down to Plishka's office to see if he'll go with him or arrange for another to act as a grief counsellor. Plishka listens to Baldwin's report and decides to tag along. They take Plishka's new chief-mobile, a long black Buick.

The Crowes live on Bayberry Avenue, a solid middle-class neighborhood in West Seneca, across the way from the new Southgate Plaza. It takes them only a few minutes in light traffic to get there. The lights turn green every time they approach one. Baldwin hopes it's a sign.

Every house is a split level, built in the late fifties. There's a Chevy station wagon in the driveway when they pull up and park behind it. They can hear a young boy inside the house yell, "Mom, somebody's heeerrre!"

By the time they get to the front door, Mrs. Crowe and a kid about nine are standing in the doorway. Mrs. Crowe is mid-forties, a little plump, blond turning gray. She was once a beauty and is aging well. She looks worried because even though neither is wearing a uniform, they ooze cop.

"Mrs. Crowe?" asks Plishka. "Can we have a word with you?"

"Is this about Alan?" She has an expression that says she expected it.

"Yes ma'am," says Plishka. "I'm afraid it is." He holds up his badge and Baldwin follows his lead. They both tuck them away.

"Is he in custody?"

"Uh, no," says Plishka, looking over at Baldwin, who looks surprised. "This is different. Can we come in?"

She hesitates for a moment, then puts her hand on the young boy's shoulder. "Honey, can you go over to Brian's house and watch television until dinner?" The kid practically flies out the door past them and skips down the street. "We never let him do that," she says, and holds the door open for them.

Plishka introduces himself and Baldwin. She's surprised that the Lackawanna police are making an official visit. Plishka tells her that they got handed the case.

"Is your husband home?" he asks.

"He's walking the dog. Should be back in a few minutes."

"We'd like to wait for him," says Plishka.

She leads them to the living room and they take seats opposite each other, Mrs. Crowe on the couch.

Plishka has always had a sympathetic face. Sad brown eyes that sometimes seem half closed. When he purses his lips, she can tell the news is worse than she thought. She takes a huge breath and lets it out slowly. Her mouth forms an O, and her eyes get misty. She pulls a Kleenex out of her pocket. Her mother senses have kicked in.

At that moment the front door opens and a brown and gray dachshund scampers through to the kitchen on his short little legs. You can hear him dive into his food bowl. The pup is followed by Mr. Crowe. He's Plishka's age, fit. He's wearing a sweatshirt and blue jeans, running shoes. A knit watch cap with a Navy logo embroidered on it: an eagle grasping an anchor in its talons. He seems to grasp who the visitors are immediately, and slowly walks in and sits next to his wife. He nods at the two cops.

"You caught Alan," he says.

"No," says Plishka. "It's not that, I wish it was." He introduces himself and Baldwin, then goes on. "Alan's body was found by Canadian authorities in the Niagara River. Downriver in Niagara-on-the-Lake. This happened just yesterday. The identification was made by Detective Baldwin, here. We are very sorry."

The parents are dumbfounded. Their eyes drift to Baldwin. Simultaneously one asks if he's sure, and the other asks if he knew Alan.

"Yes, and yes," says Baldwin. "I met him a year ago."

18

"How?" says Mr. Crowe. "An accident? Did he drown?"

Plishka and Baldwin look at each other, and Plishka nods at him. Go ahead. They have to know.

"The coroner in Canada believes that he was struck on the head hard enough to kill him, and then his body was carried over the Falls, then down river towards Lake Ontario. That's all we are confident about so far," says Baldwin, as softly and slowly as he can.

Plishka and Baldwin watch as two more lives come apart. The Crowes look at each other incredulously. Mrs. Crowe's lips are trembling, and she falls into her husband's outstretched arms. They spend a couple of minutes whispering to each other, 'Oh my God, sweet Jesus.' Some of it sounds like a prayer, but mostly it's shock: 'Dead, killed, our boy.' Then they grow quiet for several minutes.

"What happens next?" asks Mr. Crowe softly, without looking away from his wife, trying to be strong.

"You will have to claim the body. We can check for you and let you know when and where. What sort of documents they may require. We could go with you," says Baldwin.

"Thank you," says Mr. Crowe. "We'll wait to hear from you. I'll give you my work number."

"Will there be a time when we can ask you about Alan?" asks Baldwin. "We are beginning an investigation now. There is so much we need to know." Baldwin thinks they may need time to accept the news, but they surprise him.

"Right now," says Mrs. Crowe, firmly. She sits up, wiping away tears, a determined look on her face. "If somebody killed Alan, we need to find out who. They need to be punished. What do you want to know?"

Once again, Plishka nods at Baldwin to proceed, to ask the pertinent questions.

"You didn't seem surprised that two cops came to the door. Can we start with that? Was he getting into trouble?"

"Trouble found him," says Mrs. Crowe. "The draft lottery. His birthday is July 17, number 98 in the Vietnam War sweepstakes. He was notified to report for induction."

"He was a student, wasn't he?" asks Baldwin. "Didn't he have the deferment?"

"He dropped out of college after finishing his sophomore year, this past June," says Mr. Crowe. "He said he had work to do and couldn't split time with school. His conscience wouldn't permit it." Crowe shakes his head in frustration.

"Work? What kind of work?"

"All that stuff he studied under the murdered priest, Goezina. Social justice, antiwar, anti-racism," he says. "He became a member of the counterculture, or as he called it, the resistance."

"When did you last see him or speak to him."

"About a month ago. He came home and we had dinner together," says Mr. Crowe. "Had our typical argument about the war. He really did not want to go, to get drafted. I think maybe I talked him into not dodging it. He didn't want to disappoint us."

"He said he'd go for conscientious objector status," says Mrs. Crowe. "That would've been okay with us." Mr. Crowe nods yes.

"You said that he came home for dinner. From where?"

Mrs. Crowe says, "Alan had a large circle of like-minded friends. Antiwar activists, hippies. They have an organization that's part of a national movement. This local group is like a chapter of the bigger one. Alan was spending all of his time with them, even staying over at their place all the time. He pretty much lived there. It's in Lackawanna, the First Ward."

"That's the Negro community," says Baldwin. "Are they all Black?"

"No, all white. That's just where they all work," says Mr. Crowe. "On civil rights stuff, education, labor law, housing. You name it."

Plishka and Baldwin look at each other. They both realize that may give them some sort of jurisdiction, if Alan was killed there.

"What's the name of the group?" asks Plishka.

"Popular Democratic Movement," says Mr. Crowe. "The PDM."

"Radical. They get into trouble with the law from time to time," says Plishka, "Is that why you thought we were here?"

"Yeah," says Mr. Crowe, "I thought maybe a big drug bust or something. Trespassing on government property. Burning a draft card. They do that kind of stuff, too. But not this, not him getting killed." Mr. Crowe shakes his head, his expression is complete disbelief.

"Tell us about his network of friends and acquaintances," says Baldwin. "From high school on."

The Crowes take turns talking about their son, finishing each other's sentences, sometimes correcting the other. In high school, it was almost entirely about swimming. He was an exceptional athlete. One-hundred-meter freestyle, four-hundred-meter relay. It seemed like he never lost. His teammates admired him, his coaches loved him. For a couple, he made their careers. He didn't have any enemies, but he did disappoint quite a few swimming competitors. The other boys took it in stride. Actually, it was their parents who got angry. There was one swimmer whom Alan beat in an Olympic qualifying meet in 1968. It ruined the kid's chance to go to Mexico City and his father threatened Alan, came at him like he was going to beat him up. Meet officials pulled the guy away.

"Should we track him down?" asks Baldwin.

The Crowes exchange a glance and decide it was a spur of the moment tirade. The guy was an asshole, who always did that when his son lost. But Baldwin takes his name down, anyway: Brian McGee from Orchard Park. His son is Michael McGee.

"I know him," says Plishka. "He's the deacon who passes the collection basket at church on Sunday. Active in everything in town. Scouts, little league, volunteer fireman. Ran for the school board. You name it."

"Does he need anger management?"

Plishka nods, sits back. "Yeah, he can be a butt. Screams at the umpires, who are also firemen. Nobody pays any attention anymore. That's just him."

They rule him out.

"There's more for you to know," says Baldwin. "Two other young men have turned up dead in the Niagara River. Both are about Alan's age. One is named Dominic Styron and the other Jaime Roesler. Do those names ring a bell? Did Alan ever mention them?"

"No," says Mr. Crowe.

Mrs. Crowe shakes her head. "Were they murdered, too?"

"We don't know. Just suspicious. Three young men, weeks apart, same venue," says Baldwin. "I'm hoping to find anything that might connect the men to each other, or to someone else."

In the end, they get no motives and no suspects from Alan's folks. He was a popular, thoughtful, respectful young man who just got drafted. Then someone killed him, but why?

Plishka and Baldwin get the Crowes' permission to examine Alan's room. Upstairs over the garage, with the other two bedrooms and a bath.

It had probably been Alan's room his entire life. The furniture dates back to the fifties. A single bed, a small writing desk, a lamp with Davy Crocket on the shade. Ten swimming trophies line a shelf over the bed. All of the posters and framed pictures feature swimmers or in a couple of cases, divers. Some are action shots and others are group photos. Him and his buds.

The room is a time capsule of Alan's high school years. There's nothing to suggest that he was a college radical, or ever in college at all. Nothing political, no mementos from Buffalo State. To Baldwin, it looks like Alan sanitized his room, maybe to hide evidence from his parents or some imaginary law enforcers who might come after him. Though not, he thinks, for the reason they are.

Plishka and Baldwin drive back to the House and discuss next steps: Find out how to get Alan's body to his parents if they have jurisdiction over the investigation. If they do, retrace Alan's steps since he was last seen alive, take a close look at his friends and activities.

"We're stuck with this until we can determine why and where he was killed," says Plishka. "I think we start with the PDM. I wonder where their hideout is."

"A house full of white college kids in the First Ward? They shouldn't be hard to find," says Baldwin.

"The PDM is in the news every day. They organize all the antiwar demonstrations, mostly on college campuses." says Plishka. "If I were them, I'd be up near the colleges in Buffalo, not down here in Lackawanna."

"We'll have to find out why that is," says Baldwin.

"I really don't like them," says Plishka. "Burning draft cards, vandalizing government offices. It's un-American."

"True," says Baldwin, "but these guys aren't violent so far. They don't blow stuff up like the Weathermen, they're mostly a pain in the ass. That whole generation is about, 'make love, not war.' Who can argue with that?"

"If they want us to love commies, then I argue with that," says Plishka.

"Still, they got to be our first stop," says Baldwin. "They can help us with a timeline at the least, what was he working on, maybe what he finally decided to do about induction, did he finally make some enemies."

"They aren't friendly," says Plishka. "We're the pigs, after all. They'll be uncooperative. Stonewall us."

"We might have to be creative," says Baldwin. "Maybe some sort of backdoor move."

"Sounds to me like you want to go undercover, infiltrate the dope-smoking, free-loving radical left."

"It's one of those rare moments when being Black will open a door," says Baldwin.

When they park the car in the motor pool behind the House, Plishka hands the keys to one of the rookies, Samantha "Sam" Simpson. She will gas it up, clean it up a little, get it ready for the next trip.

Simpson's sister, Sarah, was murdered last year and she helped Plishka and Baldwin find the killer. Once she got a taste for law enforcement, she enrolled in some night courses in criminology, and aced them all. Then Plishka got her into the police academy where she excelled in every area, including handling a gun. She is a natural marksman, so good that she shamed most of the male cadets. And she caught the eye of the instructor, Jack Weidner. They've been an item ever since. They spend a lot of time shooting at things and hitting them. Plishka hired her right out of the academy, and she is now the only female police officer in Western New York, and maybe anywhere else.

"Your time is coming, Sam," says Plishka.

"I hope so," she says. "I don't want to become irreplaceable doing this stuff," holding up a tin of car wax and a rag.

On the way into the station, Plishka tells Baldwin that he'll handle the Canadian authorities, says it's all bureaucratic crap that he's supposed to do, anyway. He'll arrange for Alan's parents to do whatever they have to do, and for the body to be returned.

"Just go find the radicals and what they know," he tells Baldwin.

Desk Sergeant Decker has a message for Baldwin, that Fiona McIntyre called, and she's ready to talk. She's waiting for him at her dorm. Baldwin jogs up to his office and calls her back. Like before, someone else picks up and locates Fiona in her room. A minute or so passes.

"Hello, this is Fiona. I'm okay now, I can talk."

"Again, I am so sorry I called with that news," says Baldwin. "Were you close?"

"Since we were riding tricycles," she says. "He's the first boy I kissed, when we were, like, twelve."

"Has your relationship been romantic?"

"No, it's been more brotherly-sisterly since junior high. We gave each other love-life advice, celebrated victories, consoled each other when there were breakups," she says, and pauses a beat. "We loved each other as fellow humans. I know that sounds nuts, but that's where we got to."

"It doesn't sound nuts."

"How did he die?" she asks, an octave lower, and Baldwin imagines that a tear is running down her cheek. He tells her what the coroner told him, that his injury is consistent with being murdered, and that's how they are handling the investigation. He tells her what he learned from Alan's parents, about getting a low lottery number, trying to figure out what to do next, about the Popular Democratic Movement. He tells her his first inclination is to believe that all his social activism is a motive for someone to kill him. It's not unprecedented, the Ohio National Guard shot down four kids just a few

24

months ago. On the other end of the line, Fiona is very still.

"Fiona?"

"Yes, here, I'm…thinking something," she says. "Give me a minute."

Baldwin can hear her breathing, a little cough, then she's back.

"I'm going to tell you something because it might have something to do with this, but you have to promise me that you will never tell anyone or put it in writing. His parents must never know."

"I can't ignore any criminal activity," says Baldwin.

"It's not criminal. It's deeply personal."

"Then okay, I agree."

"Alan was gay."

A rush of thoughts invades Baldwin's brain: A homosexual, antiwar draft-dodger? A radical, leftist, activist queer in the Army? The only thing missing is he's not Black. There are what, a million people who'd hit him in the head? Baldwin thinks that Alan was faced with three choices and all of them were bad: Get inducted and try to navigate being gay in an Army that doesn't want homosexuals; admit to being gay during the medical exam and jeopardize all of his relationships; finally, run for it.

"Okay, I understand. That will help in our inquiries. It's another lens to see things through, and I'll do my best to keep it confidential. But Fiona, if it turns out to be a mitigating factor, like a motive that leads to an actual suspect, or the killer, it will come out."

"I understand, totally. Thanks."

"What can you tell me about his circle of friends? And did they know or care about his…did they know about him?

"In high school, his friends were all jocks. Nice guys, but not serious, not great students. Today, all his friends are college-aged, educated, mostly white but a Black here and there, wandering through. They all live together in a sort of communal thing in a big house in Lackawanna, in the First Ward."

"I heard about that. That's the Negro Ward."

"Yes, but they are working on civil rights issues. Anti-racism policies, poverty, voting rights, housing issues, like that. Not just Vietnam, which, by the way, affects Black folks way more than white ones. And no, they either don't know or don't care about him being gay, as far as I know. The group is accepted there in the Ward. The neighbors consider them like allies."

"Did you meet them? His friends?"

"I visited Alan once during my summer break. We had dinner with his parents, then drove over to the commune. I got introduced to maybe eight or ten of them?"

Baldwin is surprised. That's a big number.

"Your impression?"

"Cultish. There's the stereotypical charismatic leader, whose name is Adrian. He looks like a golden-age Dutch painter's idea of Jesus Christ. You know, handsome. Blond and blue-eyed, bearded, long hair, thoughtful. He acts like a guru, surrounded by followers. There are a bunch of female admirers. Braless, brainless, stoned all the time. They sing along with the Arlo Guthrie and Bob Dylan songs playing on the turntable. There's a couple of recent babies, who they named after Tolkien's elves. A fair number of males who are there partly because of the politics and mostly because of the females. Alan was popular with them. Both sexes. Of all of them, Alan seemed to be the most focused on the reason they were all together – protest and social change. If Adrian gets arrested or dies of an overdose, Alan would have been chosen to take over."

"If I marched in there as a cop and asked for them to help me find his murderer, do you think they'd help?"

"Nope. They are programmed to distrust you. You are the establishment, the pig, and we're only three months removed from Kent State, two years from the Democratic convention in Chicago, one year from Woodstock. Sorry, but you know what I mean. In fact, when they find out Alan is dead, that he had been murdered, who do you think they would suspect?"

"Us."

"Uh huh."

Baldwin thanks her, gets a few more names, the address of the commune, promises to keep Fiona in the loop.

Now he has to figure out how to penetrate the protective layer of leftist suspicion and anger. He could order a raid and haul them all in. There would probably be enough dope to put them all in Attica for a decade. But that would not solve the murder, and maybe two others. It's a quandary.

Baldwin reviews what he has on the three victims, and again, other than age, sex and race, can't see much of a connection. Two of them may have been gay, two may have been hippies. One was a blue-collar Midwesterner, another an athlete, and the third a waiter on the coast. Only one had attended college. Except for the Falls, where their bodies were found, nothing connects all three. That's got to be something because so far, it's the only thing. FBI Agent Reynolds told him that hundreds of young, draft eligible young men are crossing the border into Canada every month. Could that be what brought the two out-of-staters here? If so, what got them dead? The U.S. government wants them back alive and the Canadians are welcoming them. None of it makes sense.

Baldwin gets home to the duplex he and Sandra share with his parents, on Buffalo's east side. His parents, Reginald and Ethel Baldwin, live on the ground floor and have for more than twenty years. The newlyweds live upstairs. Sandra has been home for an hour and has dinner ready. A hearty beef stew. Potatoes, carrots, onions, celery and cubes of beef, all swimming in a thick gravy. Marriage has definitely been an upgrade in the meal department, not to mention in every other phase of life. They hug for several minutes, exchange whispered love.

Sandra and Tom met last year when he was investigating two murders and she was reporting on both for the *Lackawanna Beacon*. It was love at first sight, literally. They still joke about falling in love at a picnic table in the middle of a pot-holed parking lot, surrounded by abandoned, vandalized industrial buildings. A metaphor for the world around them.

During dinner, they rewind and play back their workdays. Sandra had spent most of the afternoon at the Lackawanna Board of Education, where a public forum was held about the decrepit condition of the Roosevelt Elementary School, which is in the First Ward. The sixty-year-old building is falling apart, and members of the city's Southern Christian Leadership Conference – all Black – had asked the board to build a new school. Instead, it looked for a cheap alternative: It passed a contentious $20,000 bond issue to pay for a renovation plan. At the same time, it's building a brand-new elementary and middle school in the city's Third Ward, the all-white neighborhood.

"About ten people spoke to the board during the comments period. All of them pleaded that the old school be torn down and a new one built," she says. "They all had the same message: We won't have equal education until we have the same modern classrooms the white folks have."

"I know how well that went over," says Tom.

"The board shined them on. Said they would consider everybody's concerns, discuss it in committee, that sort of thing. But it's a done deal. There will be a study, and then nothing."

"This is déjà vu," says Tom. "Last year the city lost that case over the King Homes project, but they are still fighting it. They must figure they can do it again over a school building."

"And why not? They'll get away with it. The Justice Department is off the case. It won't take a side on this one, even though it is clearly a violation of the Civil Rights Act," says Sandra.

"I know, I called Reynolds at the FBI today and got the same answer about the King situation. He told me that draft resisters are the DOJ's and FBI's top priority. And coincidentally, I'm now investigating the possible murder of one."

"What?"

"You might remember him. Alan Crowe. One of Goezina's students."

"Vaguely," she says, looking off to one side. "He was murdered? My Lord, that's three from the same little class?"

"I know, hardly seems possible," says Tom.

Tom tells her the whole chronicle: Seeing Alan's body up in Canada, talking to Angie, visiting his folks, getting more info from Fiona, and finally about the PDM group in Lackawanna and his need to get their cooperation. He doesn't mention Alan's sexual orientation. "And here's the thing, he may be one of three victims. I'm looking for any connections between them besides their demographics."

Sandra steeples her fingers and looks at Tom with half-lidded eyes. "They were at the board meeting today," she says.

"Who was?"

"The Popular Democratic Movement," says Sandra, raising her eyebrows. "I interviewed a few of them for my schoolboard story. Now you've given me another story to talk to them about."

Tom sits back in his chair and his mouth falls open. It takes him a moment to recover. *What were the chances?* He wonders. "Can you tell me about them, or would that violate your duty to confidential sources?"

"Yes, and not at all," she says. "They want me to tell the world about them. Practically begged me to get it right. It's publicity they crave. Making news is their whole reason for being. They want to move the world with their message."

"Was there a guy named Adrian?" he asks.

"Very magnetic. When he walked in with his entourage, the room came to a standstill. The board member who was speaking, a white woman in her forties, stumbled all over her words. Star-struck. The recording secretary simply stopped taking notes. So did I," she says with a grin.

"Should I be jealous?"

"No, sugar, he's not my type. He is tall and handsome, but not dark enough," she says with a wink. "And I knew exactly what he would say when his turn came up, it's the same script over and over. They stand with the poor and exploited, they want society to change, they support what the Black folks want, they'll work towards that end, and on and on."

"Sincere?" asks Tom.

"There's no money in it for him so, probably. I kind of hope they're sincere, but what exactly can they do? Organize protest marches?"

"Sometimes those work. Remember Selma." Tom says. "We marched, the Alabama State Police beat us up, and the federal government stepped in, mostly on our side."

"This time, it's more convoluted, Tom. Think about it. We have at least two examples of the City of Lackawanna blocking the progress of its Black citizens." She holds up a finger. "One, they are doing everything they can to block the Martin Luther King homes." She holds up a second. "Two, they refuse to replace an elementary school that is shedding bricks into its parking lot because it's where the Negro kids go. All that, and we cannot get help from the Department of Justice to stop them. Instead, we get help from the very people that the DOJ is going after: the PDM."

"Good point."

"I don't think you'll get anywhere with them, the PDM, as a cop," says Sandra. "Talking to the police about anything isn't in their playbook."

"It'll be challenging. I agree. I got to figure out a way to get their trust."

"I'll be talking to them for my story," she says. "They treated me like an asset. I know they'd answer my questions. I might find something out that will help you later."

"I can't ask you to do police work," says Tom.

"I would be doing reporter work," Sandra says. "Alan Crowe getting murdered is a big story and I want to write it. If your instincts are right and there were two others, that's huge. If the local chapter of the PDM has information about Alan, maybe the others, it's my job to go get it."

"Get your story, I'll do my investigation." says Tom. "Maybe, hopefully, we get the same results."

In the days that follow, the Crowes arrange for Alan's body to be delivered to a funeral home in West Seneca, and for his obituary to be published in the Buffalo Courier-Express. His viewing will be on this coming Friday, and the funeral on Saturday. Angie McIntyre notifies the cohort from Buffalo State College and expects all of them to show up. Fiona notifies the PDM members whom she had met, and they promise to spread the word. They expect that a large number of First Ward folks will attend, show their love.

Baldwin spends time researching the Popular Democratic Movement. He wants to know who he'll confront when he questions them. A Political Science professor up at Buffalo State College helps him with that. He finds out they've been around a long time, at least ten years, and grew out of a much older organization called The League for Industrial Democracy. They are radical idealists who want to transform society by eliminating racism, inequality, poverty, militarism and on and on. He's onboard with most everything they want but can't see them taking down the country's stakeholders. Not in this lifetime.

On Wednesday, two days before the event, Sandra's first short article about Alan's murder appears in the *Lackawanna Beacon* and is later picked up by other papers and radio and TV. Tom Baldwin is sought out for interviews and comments. His voice and face are everywhere. If he had hoped to go undercover to investigate the PDM, that's done. His cover is blown, and Sandra essentially tells the radicals that law enforcement is on the way. He decides the best time and place to make their acquaintance is at the funeral home. Everybody will be on their best behavior, he hopes.

Local Activist Found Murdered in Canada
Lackawanna Police Investigating
By Sandra Moore

LACKAWANNA, N.Y. – The badly beaten body of former West Seneca High School swimmer Alan Crowe was discovered by

Canadian authorities on August 3, in the Niagara River. The coroner in Niagara Falls, Ontario, Dr. Silas Griffin, believes that Crowe was killed with a blunt instrument, and then dumped into the river above the Falls. His body was found entangled with a boat propeller in the marina at Niagara-on-the-Lake nearly 15 miles downstream. His death is being investigated as a murder by Lackawanna Police Detective Thomas Baldwin, who was acquainted with the victim and made the initial identification. Baldwin said that the police have no suspects at this time but are pursuing various leads provided by friends and family. "He did not seem to have any enemies, so his violent death is surprising and shocking to those who knew him," said Baldwin.

Among those whom the police will question are members of the Popular Democratic Movement. Crowe was an active member of the organization and lived with other members at a home in Lackawanna's First Ward. The PDM, as the group is commonly known, is part of a national antiwar, pacifist movement, but is also working on civil rights, voting rights and anti-poverty issues. Adrian Foster, the leader of the local chapter, told this reporter that they would cooperate with the police but had no information that would help the investigation. "It is unthinkable that anyone would harm Alan, but there are violent establishment forces out there that are threatened by our work. It would not surprise me to find out that he was martyred," said Foster.

The rest of the article talks about his swimming exploits in high school and his popularity among his teammates and schoolmates at Buffalo State College. Sandra ends the piece with the irony of Alan having been one of Martin Goezina's students. Goezina, she reminds her readers, was the Catholic priest who had been murdered a year earlier. One of his other students, Sarah Simpson, had also been murdered on the same weekend. It was a class, she ruminates, that seems to have been cursed.

Fairview Funeral Home is on busy Center Road, right next door to the Presbyterian Church where Alan's funeral service will take place on Saturday. It's rather grim to call a funeral home "trendy," but Fairview is busy every day. Its parking lot is huge and usually full. There can be five different viewings in tasteful visitation rooms simultaneously. The city installed a traffic light at its entrance to ease traffic in and for the long lines of flagged cars on their way out to the cemetery.

Tom and Sandra decide to go in separate cars, to avoid drawing attention to their relationship and so each can leave whenever they need to. Baldwin sees his wife pull into a parking spot and finds one in another row. They arrive at the entrance at about the same time, where small groups of mourners chat in low voices, smoke cigarettes, glance around to see who else is there.

On one side of the wide sidewalk that leads to the glass double doors are Alan's college classmates. Six very sad-looking twenty-somethings. Boys who have managed to squeeze into suits they haven't worn since the high school prom, girls in long peasant dresses and teetering on high heels that might belong to their mothers. Several give timid waves to Baldwin when they recognize him. He gives them a little salute. Everyone says hello how are you, how terrible, he'll be missed. One of the boys, Pat, a chain smoker with braces, leans into Baldwin's ear and whispers, "Catch the fucker." Baldwin looks him in the eye and says, "You bet."

Sandra has already walked inside and Baldwin finds her talking to someone who could only be Adrian Foster. She was right. He is impressive. Six feet tall, maybe one seventy-five, tanned. He has long blond hair parted in the middle, a nicely trimmed beard and mustache. He's dressed in what looks like a baggy, east Indian Kurta pajama. Sandals. Give him a guitar and you have a Woodstock star. Surrounding him are three women, all very pretty, hippie clothing, flowers in their hair. They seem to be trying to crowd Sandra out, prevent her from getting too close to their yogi, as though she might have some secret sauce that they don't. Sandra motions to Tom to come over.

"Adrian, this is Detective Thomas Baldwin. He's investigating Alan's murder. Detective, this is Adrian Foster who was one of Alan Crowe's friends."

The two shake hands. When Baldwin gets close, he thinks Foster smells like incense. Or maybe hashish. The women seem to study Baldwin's face very carefully, as though they are wondering why a Black guy would ever become a cop. Adrian wonders the same thing.

"Excuse me for saying this, but you're the first Black police officer I've ever met," he says.

"I'm the first Black cop anybody has ever met, at least in this part of the world," says Baldwin. "It can be...challenging."

Adrian smiles. The women smile, too. Maybe the ice is broken?

"I'd like to step inside, give my respects. Will you all be here when I come back, like ten minutes? Could we talk?" asks Baldwin.

"It's a closed casket, not what I'd call a viewing," says Adrian. "Somebody out there is vicious."

"Yeah, I know," says Baldwin. "Wait for me, okay?"

Adrian nods once and steps back, melting into his followers.

Inside, Baldwin follows the signs and directions from funeral staff to the room where Alan's coffin is surrounded by dozens of bouquets and flower arrangements. A few of them are enormous. Mr. and Mrs. Crowe and Alan's young brother are seated on one side, taking visitors one at a time.

About thirty or so Black folks are already through the line, and are studying the pictures, news stories, swimming trophies and other items that reconstruct Alan's short but eventful life. Baldwin recognizes many of them, and they, him. Raymond Jakes, a First Ward barber and head of the Negro non-profit that's trying to build the King Homes, steps over to him.

"Somebody keeps killing our white friends," he says to Baldwin.

"It does seem that way, Mr. Jakes." Baldwin wonders if that is, in fact, the case. He'll have to ask Foster and the others what they were doing on the King Homes project and if there had been any threats. "I'll get in touch with you and we can talk."

"Come get a haircut, young man," says Jakes, and he moves away.

At that moment, the line in front of him has moved on and he's next to offer condolences. Mrs. Crowe introduces him to Alan's young brother, Davey, who seems oblivious to what's going on. He knows it's serious, solemn, sorrowful. But he's not sure if he's on the same page as everybody else. To a nine-year-old, death is an abstraction, and with a closed casket, it's imaginary. More than he can comprehend. Probably better that way.

"Thanks for coming, Detective," says Mr. Crowe. "I read that you are investigating. Anything yet?"

"Just the preliminary things," says Baldwin. "Lining up interviews, creating timelines, looking for motives and opportunities. Suspects. It's difficult with a victim like your son, who seemed to have no conflicts with anybody."

"I'd like to talk with you about that. I've been giving it some thought. Before all this," and he gestures toward the casket. "I heard some things at the VFW. Just random comments about draft dodgers and resisters. Emotional stuff. Some of it angry. I had similar thoughts, myself, about patriotism. I don't want to believe anybody would act on those feelings, but people can surprise you, you know?"

"Yes sir, I do."

"Call me next week?"

"Yes sir, I will."

Baldwin steps over to the displays and looks carefully at the photos, hoping something or somebody pops out at him. Maybe somebody with an expression or body language that looks unfriendly. Maybe someone who looks like a jealous boyfriend or girlfriend, an adversary. But everybody looks perfectly delighted to be in a picture with Alan. Somebody or another has his or her arm around Alan, even kissing him on the cheek, holding up an index finger or a peace sign.

"Like I said, everybody loved him."

It's got to be Fiona McIntyre, thinks Baldwin without turning. And it is. Baldwin extends his hand and they shake.

"You met the hippies?" she asks.

"Just the big honcho. I am hoping to talk to them in a minute or so."

"They just left, but they asked me to tell you to come by the house on Monday, around noon. You have the address."

"Huh," says Baldwin. "That's gotta be progress."

"I know," says Fiona. "I'll bet they are kind of conflicted. You're a cop, but a Black one. What do they do with that?"

"We'll find out on Monday."

On Monday, Baldwin's to-do list includes speaking with Mr. Crowe about the VFW and visiting the PDM commune at noon. But he also has an idea that he wants to bounce off Chief Plishka. It might be harebrained, but sometimes those are the best kind. He heads down the hallway at the House to the chief's office.

Every time he makes this stroll, he's reminded of how dismal the place is. The Lackawanna Police Department is housed in an ancient brick building on Ridge Road, on the far eastern edge of the city. More than forty officers serve in the force, crammed into spaces meant for half that many. Electricity flows through wires that are stapled to the interior walls, water flows through pipes that hang from the ceiling. Everything has been painted a million times with the same awful, grayish green color. It's the color that results from mixing leftover paint from every conceivable hue that isn't green.

There's a proposal at city hall to build a new station with modern police accoutrements. Like working toilets, a locker room with a shower, maybe two locker rooms: a second one for female cops. An up-to-date phone system, a boiler that works in the winter, maybe that new thing called air conditioning. Enough parking for everybody. But the city is broke, has prioritized education, at least for the white kids, and is reluctant to raise taxes on any of the many industrial giants that employ almost everybody. They would all hightail it for another town, state or even country.

Plishka's secretary, Maureen, types away at her desk outside Plishka's office. She points her thumb over her shoulder and Baldwin closes the door behind him, takes a seat.

"What's up, Tom?"

"Well, first, thanks for taking care of getting Crowe's body out of Canada," says Baldwin. "It was a big help to me and the family." It's always a good idea to praise your boss when you're about to ask for something.

"No problem," says Plishka. "What are you about to ask for?" He's been there.

Baldwin smiles. "Remember we talked about the PDM and how difficult it might be to get their cooperation?"

"Is it?"

"Actually, no, not yet. I've been invited to come over there and talk to them at noon today," says Baldwin. "I'm thinking they might open up to me."

"How did that happen?"

"They seem befuddled about having a Black cop want to talk to them about their friend's death. You know, it's natural to say no to a cop and yet, for them at least, not to say no to us Black folks."

"Interesting dilemma for them," says Plishka. "So, what's the problem?"

"They might not really open up. They might hide stuff, thinking I'd bust them for drugs, or their political activity. I dunno. They might send me off in the wrong direction, play me," says Baldwin. "I'd like to have a backup plan ready to go."

"A raid?"

"No, no, no," says Baldwin. "I'm thinking we get one of our own people in there, undercover. Infiltrate. Watch them from the inside for a period of time, gain their trust. If they are on the up and up, no foul. But if they are concealing something that would lead us to Alan's murderer, then we might break the case."

"Some of our guys might blend in a little," says Plishka, "but realistically, they would make them in a second. Cops work hard at getting the cop look, and now they can't peel it off. Plus, they'd have to grow some hair and a beard."

"I was thinking of Simpson."

"Hmmm," says Plishka. He looks up at the ceiling, contemplating that. He knows that Sam Simpson can handle just about any situation. She already helped apprehend her sister's killer, and that was before she became a cop. She's smart, tough-minded, physically fit. She'd win a gunfight with Billy the Kid.

"The leader, a guy named Adrian Foster, has a squad of hippie girls around him. I thought he'd take one look at Sam and wave her into the fold," says Baldwin.

She is cute, thinks Plishka, *and in the right age range.*

"She'd love it," says Plishka, "and I think she'd be great."

"That's a yes?"

"That's a let's ask her. She's out on patrol with Diaz right now, but we can radio them in." And he orders it up. Decker contacts them, and she and her partner make it back to the House in fifteen minutes. Sam appears at the door.

Sam is a young-looking twenty-four. Like, sixteen. Black hair, hazel eyes, pale complexion. Many citizens she encounters while handing out parking tickets or stopping traffic at a school crossing think she's a Girl Scout. She's had to contend with a lot of doubters and more than a few bullies. Her boyfriend, Officer Jack Weidner, has been training her in martial arts so she won't have to shoot any of them right off the bat. Instead, she could fracture a windpipe.

"Sir?" she says.

"Come in, have a seat."

She pats Baldwin on the shoulder and sits down next to him.

"Sergeant, why don't you explain your idea to Officer Simpson."

Baldwin tells her the background: a murdered activist in Canada, possibly draft resisting, a member of PDM, their possible smokescreen, his hope to get info from the inside, his belief that she's the one to do it. "It's hard to tell what these people are really all about," says Baldwin. "They are strident, politically active, and might actually be doing some good things. But they are also anti-everything including, maybe, being truthful with us."

"You want me to assimilate, observe, report back."

"Exactly, for however long it might take to find out whatever they know about Alan Crowe's murder and aren't telling us."

"What if I have to smoke some dope or drop some acid to earn their trust?"

"Whatever doesn't kill you will make you stronger," says Plishka. She takes that as an okay. Then he adds, "Just don't tell me about it."

"When do I start?"

Baldwin looks at Plishka, who shrugs and says, "You're in charge, Detective."

"I think you should go home and get packed," says Baldwin. "Imagine *antiwar protester* while deciding what to take and how to dress. And use a backpack for your stuff. Create a backstory for yourself. You're from somewhere else, hitchhiking around, going from one hippie settlement to another. Whatever you think you can convince them of."

"A new name?"

"What's your horoscope?" asks Baldwin.

"Gemini."

"That's who you are. They love that crystal-gazing thing. And appropriate, since you'll have a twin...you."

She smiles. "Should I take my piece? Badge?"

"Well concealed. You may need them both."

"When do I show up there?"

39

"I have an interview with them at noon today. We don't know how cooperative they are going to be. If I think, for whatever reason, that they are blowing smoke and do have information we need to solve a murder, then you'll be sent in. So be ready to ring their doorbell at dinner time."

"And if they aren't blowing smoke?" she asks.

"Then we'll stand down."

"This has got to be the first time in history that a cop is hoping for a house full of uncooperative witnesses," says Sam.

Baldwin heads back to his office, hoping he's done the right thing with Sam. If anybody can meld into the Popular Democratic Movement it'll be her, he's sure of that. But if that's what got Alan killed, then maybe he better rethink it and add some kind of protective layer. He decides to call Reynolds at the FBI and find out what they may already have on the group. He thinks he probably should have done that first.

"I not going to share any information with you," says Reynolds.

"I'm only asking if you have eyes on the PDM in Lackawanna," says Baldwin.

"What the fuck do you think?" asks Reynolds. "Of course, we do. Why would you even ask that?"

"I'm investigating the murder of a young man from West Seneca, whose body was found by Canadian police floating in the Niagara River," says Baldwin. "He was part of that group."

"Alan Crowe. I read about him and your investigation. What's he got to do with us?"

"He may have been helping draft dodgers, if not one himself. He may have been on your radar. If he was, I thought you might have information that would help me find his killer or killers."

"First of all, Baldwin, if he was helping draft dodgers, we aren't saddened by his death. When I read that he was a member of the PDM, I pulled his file." says Reynolds.

"And?"

"Like I said, I'm not in a sharing mood. But, in any case, we're trying to stop them from running off to Canada, not kill them."

"Do you know of anyone or a group that does want to kill them?"

"Part of me wishes there was," says Reynolds. "But everything we've heard about and investigated so far turned out to be bluster. Shouting matches at protest marches, sometimes a fist fight or pushing scuffle. First amendment rights seasoned with a bloody lip. Most people want these guys, the ones who are skipping town after getting called up, or who are burning their draft cards or vandalizing Selective Service offices, they want them to go to jail, or to Vietnam. That includes me. And no, we haven't found anything like a vigilante group."

"You said you're watching the PDM here. Do you have anyone inside?"

"Can't answer that one."

"Man or woman?"

"Can't answer that one."

"Confidential informant or special agent?"

"Can't answer that one."

"Anybody there now?"

"Listen, Baldwin, the whole idea of a clandestine operation is that it's probably not happening. But we want the bad guys to think, *maybe*," says Reynolds.

"Okay," says Baldwin, "if I was to put someone inside the group to gather information that might help our murder investigation, would that person be mucking up something you are already doing?"

Reynolds stalls a long time before answering. "Since I cannot say we are doing anything, I obviously cannot answer that question."

"They might wind up arresting each other," says Baldwin.

"Life sucks," says Reynolds. "But if we did have someone in there, I would probably be inclined to tell them not to arrest anybody or cause any bodily harm."

"I could do the same, if I had any plans to infiltrate the group," says Baldwin.

"Alrighty, then," says Reynolds as he hangs up.

Baldwin and, he suspects, Reynolds as well, is now faced with a dilemma: Having maybe two undercover operatives living in a house full of anti-establishment radicals, and they don't know each other. Unless one or the other or both are really bad actors. At least the FBI supposedly has eyes on the place. Maybe they'll see a problem before it becomes one.

Baldwin pulls out a business card where Mr. Crowe has written "Call me." He sees that Crowe's first name is Kevin, and he owns a camera store in the new shopping plaza. He decides to drive over there and talk in person. It's only a couple miles away.

The Southgate Plaza is the biggest retail development the area has ever seen. Anchored by three huge department stores, the long spaces in between are filled with dozens of smaller establishments. It forms a gigantic "L" shape hugging a parking lot for hundreds of cars. He finds Crowe's Camera, parks nearby and walks in, activating a bell on the door.

The store has glass display cases and shelves on the walls behind, full of cameras, tripods, nylon and leather cases and shoulder bags, film, and some vests and jackets with zippered pockets that photographers wear to carry all their gear. On a shelf high above and running along three walls are antique cameras, some dating back to the eighteen hundreds. Baldwin tries to remember the name of that Civil War photographer who would've used one of those. There are photographs everywhere, blown up and framed, of pretty girls, athletes, families, babies and dogs. Baldwin remembers being taught in a psychology class at Hillcrest College that babies and dogs can sell anything.

Crowe steps out from a room in the back. He's wearing a black armband and looks totally spent. Like he's aged ten years since they first met. "Mondays are always slow, so coming by works," says Crowe.

"If a customer shows up, I can shop for something," says Baldwin. "I've been thinking about getting a camera for some time now."

"Find Alan's killer and I'll give you one," says Crowe. "C'mon in the back till the bell rings again."

He leads Baldwin to the small back room, which is piled high with inventory. But there's a desk, filing cabinets, and a guest chair. There's a workbench with small tools and one of those large magnifying glasses mounted in an armature. A dissected camera under it. "Have a seat, Detective."

"Thanks," says Baldwin as he eases into a chair opposite Crowe. "You had something you wanted to share that might help?"

"Yes. I couldn't say much at the viewing. Not with my wife right there. Busy with the mourners and some of the men from my VFW post. I didn't want anything I'm about to tell you get overheard and maybe misunderstood."

"I understand."

At that moment, the bell rings out front. Crowe holds up a finger, like, wait a sec, and steps out to the store. Baldwin overhears one of those conversations he's come to expect, live with.

"Mr. Crowe? You okay?" says a voice. A male one, sounds husky.

"Sure. Fine. Why?" says Crowe.

"Well, I saw a Black guy come in here and not come out," says the voice.

"I have a guest," says Crowe.

In a low voice, almost a whisper, "A welcome one?"

Crowe answers with an edge, "I invited him. So, please leave."

Baldwin can hear the bell again, and Crowe returns. "Rent-a-cop," he tells Baldwin, and rolls his eyes.

"They're trained to profile people," says Baldwin. "I get it a lot."

Crowe looks genuinely embarrassed. "Where were we?"

"VFW."

"I'm in Post 947 over in East Aurora," says Crowe. "There's about forty active members, mostly WWII and Korea, and maybe five guys from WWI. All branches. We get along good, work on projects together. Do a lot of drinking. Squeeze into our uniforms and march on the Fourth."

"My father's in the American Legion Post up in Buffalo," says Baldwin. "The Black one."

"Good for him," says Crowe. "The Legion does good work, too."

"So, what does all this have to do with Alan?" asks Baldwin.

"The whole purpose of the VFW is to promote patriotism and to take care of veterans and their families. So, we are all true blue. None of us like what we are seeing with the antiwar movement," says Crowe, "but some guys are extremely angry. Maybe capable of violence, I don't know. I'm worried."

"Against Alan?"

"Against anybody."

"Who are these guys? Anybody who we should keep an eye on, talk to?"

"Two guys who lost their sons in Vietnam," says Crowe slowly. "They get red-faced angry while we're watching the news at our bar, when the student protests come on, or when they hear about returning vets getting booed at airports. I mean, we all get pissed off at 'em," and his voice sort of trails off.

"But it's escalating?"

"One of them says he's going to kill one of 'em, and the other one says let him know when and where."

Baldwin sits back. "That's serious. You know these men well? For a long time? Are they capable of that?"

"Decades. We go back to '45. We've been through a lot. Hitler, Hirohito, Korea, the Cold War, Cuba, and now Vietnam. I bet all of us would enlist if they'd let us. We love this country so much." He glances up at a portrait of John F. Kennedy that he's got up on a wall.

"Are they capable of murdering somebody? Your son? Anybody?"

Crowe lets out a long breath, like he'd been holding it. He looks like he might cry and does wipe his eye. "I don't want to believe it, but I don't want to, I don't know how to say it, ignore the possibility. Three dead boys including Alan?"

"Tell me who they are."

Baldwin sits in his car in the parking lot outside the camera store and reads his notes. If he remembers anything else he wants to add it now, while it's fresh. He adds a notation to his conversation with Kevin Crowe. *The man thinks his friends maybe killed his son.*

He wrote down the names of the two veterans that Crowe is worried about: Harry Johnson from Elma and Daniel Fredricks from East Aurora. Johnson is the one who made the threat. Baldwin will look them up when he gets back to the House. He checks his watch. He has to get all the way back to the First Ward and visit the hippies. When he looks up, he sees the security guard staring at him, arms crossed, a menacing expression on his face. He looks like the guy who gets into a lot of bar fights. His nose goes off in three directions before ending near his upper lip. Close-cropped hair, jutting chin, pumped biceps. Baldwin cocks his head and stares back at him defiantly until the guy looks down at the sidewalk, spits, turns and walks off. Baldwin starts the engine and pulls away.

It takes him almost an hour to get to the hippie house on Swan Street, right in the heart of the Ward. Traffic was bad and then a freight train loaded with coal was parked on the tracks over Ridge Road near the steel plant. Stood there for twenty-five minutes before pulling away very slowly. A daily occurrence. Folks in the First Ward don't make appointments outside it without having three exit options.

The First Ward is snugged up against the fences surrounding the Bethlehem Steel plant, a gigantic industrial powerhouse that employs over twenty thousand men. Smoke, dust, and grit from the plant have rained down on the Ward since 1903, so the homes and businesses are nearly black with soot. You know what color a house is only after a very windy, rainy storm. About five thousand colored folks live there and just a handful of whites, not including the dozen or so members of the PDM.

Baldwin parks out front. The house is a duplex, probably dating back to 1920. It's ramshackle, with a sagging porch, weedy yard, cracked concrete walk. It might have been yellow, once. The neighboring houses are about the same. But the hippies have tie-dyed sheets hanging in the windows, stand-ins for shades. A small gang of young Black kids on Frankenstein bikes race by, lots of laughter and good-natured insults for each other.

There are two VW vans in the short driveway. Somebody is working on the engine of one of them. Swearing, clunking. "Fucking fuck," he says.

"Hello," says Baldwin.

The guy untangles himself from the engine compartment, rubbing a bloody knuckle. "You the cop?" He's a long-haired 20-year-old, red bandana, shirtless, barefoot, bell-bottoms, holding a wrench in the damaged hand.

"Uh huh," says Baldwin. "Adrian at home?"

"Right inside, man, just walk in." And he goes back to work. "Fuck," he says as he bends over the engine block.

Baldwin steps up on the porch and lets himself in. He's immediately assaulted by about five different aromas. Spaghetti sauce, incense, marijuana, baby poop and BO. The living room is a bedroom for at least five people, or ten if they doubled up, whose mattresses and bedding are scattered about. Piles of sheets, pillows and clothing here and there. Full ashtrays, empty wine bottles, a few dishes from the last meal. Three cats wander from one to the other licking whatever remains. They scatter when Baldwin comes in.

In the dining room, a pretty young woman sits at the table and nurses a baby from a swelling breast. She looks a little familiar to Baldwin but he can't place her. She smiles at him and points to the back of the house. "He's waiting for you."

Adrian's in his office, what was once a bedroom. It's clean, orderly, professional. Big desk, work lamp, comfy chair. There's even a bouquet of flowers in a tasteful oriental vase. It could be your accountant's home office. Except on the wall behind the desk, there's a portrait of Mao.

Adrian looks different than he did at the funeral home. He's wearing a tee-shirt from the Woodstock music festival from last year and cutoff jeans, white tennis shoes, knee socks with red stripes. He's got a white, elastic sweatband on his head. Maybe he was playing a few sets this morning. He has that preppie look that you never lose when you move away from Greenwich, Connecticut or Cambridge, Mass.

"Thanks for coming," says Adrian. "I know you must be busy."

"Thanks for being available," says Baldwin. "And I am."

Baldwin sits down opposite Adrian, on a love seat. It's very cushy, and he sinks in. Wonders how to get out of it. But he knows why it's there. He has to look up at Adrian.

"We are all still in shock about Alan. Have you made any progress? I'd love to tell the people that you have."

"I have some folks to talk to, but nothing to call progress."

"Who?"

"Well, you, to begin with," says Baldwin. "As far as I can tell, you all might have been the last people to see him alive. When was that, exactly?"

"We put our heads together and discussed it. It was the end of July, around the 27th or 28th."

"The coroner says he died on July 30, a Thursday. Any idea where he would have been or who he would have been with on that day? Did he have any routine?"

Adrian sits back and looks at the ceiling. It looks like he's thinking, maybe trying to remember. Or make something up. He hasn't earned Baldwin's trust yet and he thinks probably the latter.

"We are working on several projects here in the Ward and our people go off alone or in groups just about every day," he says. "So, I cannot pin that down. Nobody reports to me or asks permission. It's very ad hoc."

"Did Alan have a pet project?"

"Two that he focused on, that I'm aware of. One is the Martin Luther King Homes project. He's been meeting with the Better Homes Now people, the people trying to build it. He was helping to write grants, apply for mortgages, find attorneys who'd work pro bono." He takes a breath. "The other has to do with our antiwar activities. We are all part of that effort. Demonstrating and pamphleteering at companies that do business with the military. Organizing sit-ins at the university. Like that." He looks at Baldwin. "Everything within the law."

Baldwin has no reason to doubt that, or to believe it. He just acknowledges that he heard it with a nod. "How did Alan get around?"

"He had a car. A beater. A maroon Pontiac Tempest. Maybe a '62. Rusted fenders. Bald tires. Burns oil."

"Is it here?"

"No. He must have driven it somewhere the day he disappeared."

Baldwin jots that down. *Find car.*

"Did Alan work with anybody here, on his projects?"

"Aries and Jamal were with him on the Homes. On and off again. They had their own passions. Aries is around but Jamal isn't. You can catch them both in the evenings. They haven't seen him since the 27th or 28th, like the rest of us." Baldwin makes a note to talk to them. "As far as we know, he wasn't doing anything on his own on the antiwar effort. There isn't much an individual can do." Adrian says the last thing with a pang of regret, that their cause is impossible.

47

Baldwin decides to take a chance, ask a loaded question. It can be effective to ask surprising questions, out of the blue. "As part of your antiwar activities, are you helping draft dodgers cross the border into Canada?"

"If we were doing something like that, we'd be helping people break the law, and I just told you we don't do that," says Adrian, with a bit of an edge. "And our organization actually doesn't want people to emigrate. The national has made that clear. We need resisters here, resisting."

"Are there any mavericks in your organization, someone who'd maybe go rogue, drive a guy across?"

"No. Why are you asking?" Again, he sounds annoyed.

Baldwin is asking because in their own way, all of them are rogue.

"Because two other young men were found by Canadian police in the Niagara River. They may have been murdered, too," says Baldwin. "They came from out of town, out of state. They may have been emigrating. They would've come through this area. I'm trying to establish if there is any common denominator between Alan and them. Alan got drafted. He was facing induction. I'm wondering if he headed for Canada."

Adrian looks genuinely stunned. It takes him a bit longer than it should to recover, to answer the question, to move things along. Two more dead guys seem to have surprised him, taken him off-script.

"We haven't seen or heard about any draft dodgers. Emigres," he says quietly.

"Okay, then what about Alan? What were his plans?"

"He was going to claim conscientious objector status," says Adrian, "and he would have gotten it. We have a lawyer up in Buffalo who helps. He would have wound up mopping floors in a Quaker hospital somewhere."

Baldwin wonders if he would have gotten the exemption because he was gay. Does Adrian know this? Not the time to play all his cards, he decides.

"What do you think happened, then?" asks Baldwin. "Insanely popular, hardworking, big-hearted murder victim."

"I think somebody targeted him for what his beliefs were. They made an example of him. You should focus on people who have something to lose if they build the King Homes, or if we win over hearts and minds and end the war. People who are invested in the military industrial complex either emotionally or monetarily or both."

Baldwin has to admit that he's got a point, but if you want to direct a cop in the wrong direction, you might give him something else to sniff around for. He thinks that Sam should pay a visit soon, maybe get her own sense of direction.

They chat a little more and smooth things out. Turns out they both majored in psychology in college. Adrian, no surprise here, went to Princeton.

They discuss a couple of textbooks they both used. By the end, they are friendly again. Adrian probably presumed that Baldwin had to play cop, but he had to come around because he is after all, an ally. Adrian says that if he has more questions, he can come back in the evening when everybody is home. Like Aries and Jamal.

Adrian walks out with him, and they stop to study a large poster of Huey P. Newton, founder of the Black Panthers, hanging on the wall near the living room. There's a large, well-used votive candle on a shelf in front of the picture, as though they revere him. He wears a leather jacket and a beret, sits in a big wicker chair surrounded by African shields, a zebra pelt on the floor. In one hand he holds a spear and in the other a long hunting rifle. He has a menacing look on his face.

"The women you met at the funeral?" says Adrian. "They all think you look like Huey."

10 THE COMMUNE

Baldwin doesn't know what to think about everything that's happened so far. Too many possibilities and none of them conclusive. No suspects, no motives, no means, no opportunities, just a murder victim. Maybe three. He has added more to his workload but not to his progress. He has a couple of veterans to locate and question, he has to find Alan's car, he has to talk to the two PDM members who worked with Alan, and Mr. Jakes wants to talk to him. He drives back to the House, prepared to contact Sam and get her ready to join the commune. Get some answers.

She's waiting for him in his office. Baldwin does a double take. Sam had cut her long dark hair into a pageboy and dyed it platinum blonde. Now her eyes look huge and she even more petite. She looks amazingly like Twiggy.

"Your hair," he says.

"A disguise. Lots of people in Lackawanna know me, but not anymore," she says, smiling. "What do you think?" She opens her arms and spins around, showing off her costume. Samantha plays the part, the consummate flower child. Bellbottoms, frilly peasant blouse, bamboo sandals. She looks like the model for the next Led Zeppelin album cover.

"You might want to tone that down just a little, Sam," says Baldwin. "These folks are more on the work-ethic side of things." He sits down at his desk and takes out his files and notes.

"Less Haight-Ashbury, more Army surplus?" she asks.

"In the middle somewhere," he says. "What's your backstory going to be?"

"I'm from Westchester County, out by New York City," says Sam. "Dropped out of Skidmore after one year to fight in the revolution. Been traveling around, haven't found the right fit, heard about Martin Luther King Homes from a brother I met in Syracuse, thought I'd check it out."

"If they ask questions? Like, who was your favorite professor?"

"Hincklin, English Lit. I did my homework."

"Here's what you have to study before dropping in on them." He hands her the reports on Styron and Roesler. "Their leader, a guy named Adrian Foster, says nobody ever showed up at their place. He said they don't want people skipping town. He said this, that their fight is here. They actually don't want people to leave."

Sam opens the file and glances at it.

"These are the other two Niagara River floaters?"

The characterization, coming from Sam, makes Baldwin wince, but he nods.

"You think they came here to cross the border? Dodge the draft?"

"It's possible," says Baldwin. "Reynolds said everybody heads here, crosses, then makes for Toronto. He's been trying to gather them with a very leaky net. I'm going to contact their families and see if they had been called up, like Alan was."

Baldwin tells her everything he's got on Alan, what he was working on, his big win in the draft lottery and trying to get CO status. "I'm going to show up there to question a couple of members who worked with him. Maybe this evening. A woman named Aries and a male named Jamal. You should find out what you can about them. And remember, you and me are strangers to each other."

"Who are you, again?" she asks.

"Oh, there's an important detail," says Baldwin. "There might be, and I'm guessing probably is, an FBI informant already embedded in that group. Don't know anything about them, so watch for any kind of tell. If you find out, get in touch with me."

"How do we communicate?" asks Sam.

"Find the nearest phone booth, call Decker, leave messages." says Baldwin. "And make them believe you have a boyfriend somewhere. Ask them for loose change, as though it's a long-distance call. It'll help with your cover."

How does he think of these things? wonders Sam.

When she leaves, Baldwin arranges for Decker to find out from the Department of Motor Vehicles what Alan's license plate number is, and to put out a BOLO, a be-on-the-lookout for it.

Sam goes home and changes some of her disguise. Now she's wearing bell bottoms, a blue work shirt, a worn pair of black Converse All-Star high-tops and a red bandana. She looks more like a traveler. She packs a few things in an Army surplus backpack, including her .38 and badge down at the bottom. The clothes at the top come right out of her laundry, a bit smelly, needing a wash. She thinks it will discourage anybody from poking around and convince them she's been on the road. Her boyfriend, Jack, sees her off and fights the urge to go with her. A big hug and a long, drawn-out kiss. "I'll be fine, right down the road," she says.

"I'm more worried about them," says Jack. "And I like your hair."

She takes a city bus west on Ridge Road and walks the five blocks down to the house on Swan, arriving at about five. She sees what Baldwin saw: rundown house, VW buses. But now there are two couples sitting on the steps, passing a joint. One of them cups it when she shows up. Paranoia runs deep, as the song says. They study her squinty-eyed as she smiles at them from the street.

"This must be the place," she says cheerfully, and walks up towards them.

Sam is instantly appraised by the two young men. They look delighted. They both get up and one of them slips her backpack off, the other one holds out his hand. The one with the backpack looks impressed that she carried something this heavy around. She hopes he doesn't drop it. A round could go off.

"Welcome!" he says. "I'm Jim, this is Peter."

"I'm Gemini," says Sam. "Looking for the local PDM, you them?"

"We are," says one of the women. "I'm Aries and this is Amber," pointing at her friend, who steps down and offers her a toke on the doobie.

"Just what the doctor ordered," says Sam, as she takes a little pull and hands it back. The smoke curls out of her mouth and up her nostrils. She looks like she's done this before. The ice is broken.

"You need a place?" asks Jim.

"Yeah, is there room at the inn?" asks Sam, as she glances up at the dump.

"We'll make room," says Peter, slinging the backpack over his shoulder and heading back towards the house. Everybody follows, asking questions, where you from, how'd you find us, what's going on back in civilization? Sam has already made most of this up, but also had a long conversation with an aunt who lives in Westchester and knows some stuff about what's happening in New York.

"We're shutting down Columbia, City College, NYU, a bunch of others. They won't be able to open in the fall, not without some concessions," Sam tells them.

"Divestiture," says Adrian, who stands at the door with a toothy grin on his face. "I'm Adrian," he says, "Welcome to the fold." Sam thinks that Baldwin nailed it. He looks at Sam with what can only be described as hunger. Sam feels like a piece of chocolate cake. This guy is assembling a harem whether the PDM ends the war or not.

53

"We want them to unload their investments in the military industrial complex, to stop doing research for them, to get rid of ROTC," he adds.

"They gotta stop murdering babies," says Amber, and Adrian smiles at her.

The group flows into the front hall, and Sam looks around for her backpack. Adrian notices. "Peter took your bag up to the room, up the stairs and on the left."

"Well, thanks," says Sam. "I'd like to take a shower if that's alright?"

"That's upstairs, too, Gemini," says Amber.

"Call me Gem," says Sam. "Everybody does."

"You can use my soap and there's towels and things in the hall closet. Take what you need, Gem."

Everybody smiles, greets her as she moves for the stairs. Three others wave from the living room and dining room and tell her their names as she makes eye contact. Sue, Ann and Jamal, the only Black so far. They're all in their twenties, healthy looking, even fit. A childhood of comparable privilege. Maybe summers in Nantucket? The Hamptons? It's clear that none of them had to pick up after themselves. The place is a mess. It's all she can do to not start cleaning. *Act like them*, she says to herself, *fit in, be a slob*.

She takes a long hot shower and puts on the same clothes she arrived in. Clean underwear, though. She goes barefoot down the stairs to the living room, where she can hear Adrian talking, a few soft voices asking questions, more Adrian. He stops just as she gets to the arched entry. She's pretty sure his last words are "…were never here."

The group is assembled in the living room, which looks like it was picked up and pushed to the walls to make room. Adrian's in a straight-backed chair on one side, facing ten others who form a half circle on the floor and in overstuffed chairs, a battered old couch. Two of the ten are kids. One is about two, the other a newborn. One sits on his mother's lap. The infant is asleep on her mother's chest.

"Okay, that's about it," says Adrian. Most people get up and stretch, start off to wherever. A few remain where they are, light a cigarette, pick up a conversation. One of the men reaches down and walks off with the two-year-old. Maybe it's his dad.

"Every evening, after dinner, we have a family gathering like this," says Adrian to Gem. "If you're staying, join us. Get involved."

"Okay, I will."

"What would you want to get involved in?"

"I heard about the Negro housing thing. King Homes? I'm interested in that. Civil rights issues," says Gem.

"That's perfect, we just lost our main guy working on that," says Adrian.

"Jamal can bring you up to speed. He's in the same room you are."

Gem wanders around, hoping to get better acquainted with her new housemates. Find out what they're all about, what they're working on, did anybody have an issue with Alan. She moves from room to room, plants herself among the small clusters of three or more. She figures if two are together, they might be a couple who want some alone time, so she bypasses them.

One small group consists of Amber, Jim and Peter, who are together on the front porch, just like before. Passing a joint, giggling a little. Down below, head in the rear engine compartment of one of the VW vans, is Ryan. They watch with some amusement as a litany of curses waft up at them. Every other word is some version of fuck. He's struggling, and has been for some time, trying to replace some important engine component. It's unclear whether he's done anything mechanical before.

They all seem delighted that she's stopping by and hand her the joint. She takes a toke, holds her breath, exhales. It hits her almost immediately. Her brain feels like it's taking a lap around her skull, in a pleasant way. Jim says something like, "Tijuana Red."

They hear a metal-against-metal sound. Like a clang. Ryan says something that's a bit garbled but might have been, "Fucking about-fucking-time, you fucking bolt." They all crack up, not because it's all that funny, but because it's really good grass. Gem doesn't think she'll learn anything from this group. In fact, she'd probably get too high and they'd learn too much about her, so she moves on.

Inside, two members of a small assembly animatedly argue about something some German philosopher had written and what he meant by it. Nietzsche? They're all sitting on the floor, cross-legged like sitar players. The two-year-old is hoisted up on the shoulders of his dad, hands on his forehead, weaving back and forth to Brubeck on the hi-fi. Five-four time for the toddler. A dead hash pipe rests in an ashtray in the middle of the group.

There's some chest-beating about intellectual superiority, Ivy League rankings, Nobel Prize-winning professors, jockeying like that. If you can't win on merit, win on privilege. The two who are watching seem amused, not taking sides. They don't notice Gem, who hovers over them for a minute. She had also read *Human, All Too Human: A Book For Free Spirits* and discussed it with Sarah, her murdered sibling. She is pretty sure they both got it wrong, so she moves on, down the hall.

In the office that Adrian calls his own, he and Ira are playing chess. They look up from studying the board when she peeks in, and they both wave her over, but just as quickly get back to their game. From appearances, this is what they do every night after the meeting.

55

"Do you play?" asks Adrian, not taking his eyes off the board.

"Yes," says Gem. "My sister and I…" and thoughts about Sarah bubble up. Sarah was much better and clobbered her regularly, but she was working at it, reading some books, practicing with her dad. "It's been a while," she finally says.

Ira says, "After I demolish Adrian, I'd like to play you."

"Me, too," says Adrian.

"Mind if I watch?"

They both say, "Sure," simultaneously. Both know she's sizing them up, watching their strategies, tendencies. Spying on them. She is, of course, spying, but it's not about the chess.

It takes twenty minutes, and Adrian wins. Ira takes it well, smiles, stands up and says, "Rubber match tomorrow."

"That'll be the fifteenth rubber match in two weeks," laughs Adrian.

"Yeah, well…" and Ira heads out.

Adrian begins putting the pieces back on the board and Gem slides in opposite him, helps out. "This is the most perfect game," says Adrian, caressing a rook before placing it down.

"I agree," says Gem.

Adrian smiles. "And what makes it perfect for you?"

"To play it well," says Gem, "only requires knowing how the world works. My sister taught me that."

Adrian crooks his head to the side.

"The pieces represent how the world has organized itself," she says in response, exactly what Sarah told her. "We have precisely this hierarchy, this class system, in every social, political and economic society." She points at the pieces as she recites their positions, strengths, abilities. "Kings and queens, religious leaders, military leaders, and financial institutions, all lined up along the back, protected by the little people, the pawns." She goes on to explain how each piece moves relative to its power within the system, just like in the real world. "It's no accident that typically, the only pieces left on the board are the king and his captor, often a newly crowned queen. A pawn who has used her wiles to get to the other side and put herself in the exact location to win."

"Want to win at chess, play politics?" asks Adrian.

"Yes. That's about it," says Gem. "And play people who are better than you."

Twenty-seven moves later, Gem checkmates Adrian's king.

Baldwin uses the phonebook to locate Harry Johnson in Elma and Daniel Fredricks in East Aurora, the angry, possibly homicidal members of the VFW. He copies their addresses and phone numbers in his notebook and starts thinking of how best to approach them. Crowe had filled him in on their backstories, and that'll be a help getting prepared.

Johnson is in his early fifties, was a Marine and fought in the Pacific: Guadalcanal, Iwo Jima. He participated in some of the bloodiest battles of the war. Came home with two purple hearts and a bronze star. His son, Ronny, an only child, followed in his footsteps and enlisted in the Corps right after graduating from Frontier High School. He was killed in Vietnam in 1968, buried at Arlington. Johnson is a master plumber and works for a company that builds or refurbishes motels and hotels all up and down the east coast. He's gone a lot. No wife in the picture.

Fredricks is late forties. He has a car dealership in East Aurora. Married, no other children. He was in the AAF during WWII, what's now the Air Force. Fought in Europe. Or rather, flew over Europe in a bomber. Crowe said that Fredricks beat the odds by surviving twenty-five missions. His son wasn't as lucky. Daniel Jr. was drafted while working at the steel plant and was killed just six months ago, after only eighty-seven days in 'Nam. Two of his letters arrived home after his body did.

Two patriotic Americans who were willing to make the ultimate sacrifice with their own lives, but not, perhaps, with the lives of their sons. Or maybe it's the other way. They are willing to lose their sons to a cause but will not tolerate others who won't or can't. Baldwin, who majored in psychology at Hillcrest, tries to understand what might be behind, or underneath, the outrage that the two men expressed at the VFW, among their friends. Crowe told him that none of the dozen or so men at the post that evening disagreed with them. *That*, thinks Baldwin, *is very bad news*.

He has to get this right, so he decides to think it through more, maybe get Plishka's advice. Plishka is a war veteran; he'd have some perspective.

But it's dinner time, so he decides to return to the PDM house and get that business done.

At Swan Street, Baldwin catches the same scene that Sam did. Two couples on the front porch, maybe smoking dope. Cigarettes for sure and passing a bottle of Ripple around. This time, though, one of them is Sam posing as Gem, blowing smoke rings from a Camel. Baldwin recognizes the others from the wake, but never learned their names, so he uses the opportunity to boost Sam's story. He walks up and introduces himself. He turns to Gem. "I'm supposed to be talking to Aries, is that you?"

"No, sir, my name is Gemini," she says with a smile. She crunches her eyes into what might be a double wink.

"She's new here, Officer," says Amber. "But Aries is inside and I can get her."

"That would be great," says Baldwin. Amber pops up the steps and goes inside, Gemini steps back. Observe, don't participate. He scans the others, the two men. One is Black, who averts his eyes. Won't look right at Baldwin. Seems odd. *We're brothers*, thinks Baldwin. *I'm the kinship cop.*

"I'm Jamal, the other one you want to talk to," he says to the sidewalk. "Adrian told us to expect you."

The other guy simply says, "Ira," but instead of shaking hands, he sticks his hands in his pockets and eyes Baldwin suspiciously. Ira is mid-twenties, skinny, hair and beard all over the place. He's wearing a black Hot Tuna band tee shirt, raggedy bell bottom jeans and he goes barefoot. It looks like he may have never worn shoes.

"Thanks," Baldwin says to Jamal. "I need some help from you. You might know something important, something that'll help solve Alan Crowe's murder."

For a second there, it looked like Ira was going to protest. "We don't help the pigs," or something like that. But in his world, the word "murder" isn't in the lexicon. He only hears it on TV, mostly on crime dramas or the local news. He clams up. Depending on where he comes from, Jamal might know a lot more about it. Both of them are now looking at the ground. Baldwin wants to get things started.

"Jamal? Can we talk about what you were working on with Alan?"

"Okay."

"Let's sit down."

There are a few old bridge chairs and an aluminum beach chair up on the porch, and they take seats. Ira tags along quietly, and if Baldwin had to guess, this is the guy who doesn't trust any cops, Black or white. He's probably going to monitor the situation, and maybe interfere if he thinks the heat is getting too pushy.

Baldwin knows what he's after. He wants to know if they had run into any trouble with anybody while working on the King Homes project. He, himself, had. A year earlier the FBI had uncovered Mafia connections and payoffs involving the mayor and others in Lackawanna government. Baldwin and Plishka had been threatened by the mayor and his small army of corrupt cops. Then a mafia underboss had been murdered. So, violence surrounding the housing development for Negroes isn't unusual. He's looking for motives and suspects, and this is the right place to start. The obvious one. He begins by finding out all he can about Jamal, where he comes from, why he's here, and finally what he's been doing.

Jamal is a sophomore at Howard University, the famous HBCU in Washington, D.C., majoring in Political Science. His father is a professor there, his mother works at the Library of Congress. For him, this was the best way to spend the summer. He could have gotten an internship somewhere in the government, maybe working for a congressman or at an agency. But this kind of work, "in the trenches," as he puts it, is more satisfying. "You can see results immediately," he said.

Jamal is upper-middle, maybe even privileged class, and Baldwin is pretty sure that "murder" isn't in Jamal's glossary, either. Jamal has probably backpacked in Switzerland.

"Alan was the lead on this," says Jamal. "He'd been active on it for more than a year, knew everybody, knew the history, had the relationships."

"Such as?"

"With the folks at the non-profit, Better Homes Now. Mr. Jakes, mainly. Alan was helping them write grant applications, apply for mortgages. That's pretty much what I was doing, too. I'm a good writer."

"I'll be meeting with them soon. Who else?"

"He met with people at the Diocese of Buffalo pretty often, to keep the land sale deal going. They have been very patient, waiting for Mr. Jakes to pull the money together." The Diocese was selling the land to the Negro non-profit to build on. The City of Lackawanna was standing in the way.

"Monsignor Turney?" asks Baldwin. They are well acquainted. Turney and Baldwin had worked closely on the Goezina murder investigation.

"That's him," says Jamal. "Nice man."

"Yes, he is. Who else did you meet with? Any unfriendly relationships?"

"Well, just about everybody else is unfriendly," says Jamal. "None of the lending institutions want to have anything to do with us. I think they shit-can our paperwork the minute we hand it to them. Then there are the white folks from the Third Ward. They show up at every city council meeting to complain and protest. Property values, crime, the usual doomsday grievances if us Negroes move in. And, you know, the city itself. Constantly adding more and more paperwork, permitting, requiring guarantees, and so on. Legal fees alone are a burden for the project."

"Alan was working on all that?"

"He was, and he was good at it. A college dropout who could easily pass the bar exam. He worked hard to learn this legal stuff, and he had a gift for it."

A lot of this is about money, thinks Baldwin. *Always a strong motive for murder.*

"Any help from the Department of Justice, or the FBI?"

"None that I'm aware of. Alan didn't mention it," says Jamal. "And besides, we wouldn't want their help."

They talk a while longer, and Jamal gives him some names of people who were regulars at the city council meetings. The most outspoken, the angriest. Baldwin thinks he'll look into them. He'll ask Sandra if she knows who they are. She goes to those meetings.

"Did any of you ever get threatened?"

"Not physically," says Jamal, "but we all felt intimidated. At those council meetings? Where all the white folks would show up? Most of them looked like ordinary housewives and factory workers. Shouting, getting red-faced. But watching every time, from one corner or near the door, there would be these men who looked more menacing."

"They made you nervous?"

"Yeah. They looked like and acted like mob enforcers, like you see in movies. I thought, you know, one bad mistake and I wind up wearing cement overshoes." As soon as he says it, he realizes that's pretty much what happened to Alan. He looks heartbroken. Alan was a friend.

This info doesn't surprise Baldwin at all. The local mafia was behind the original attempt to stop the King Homes. They had a financial interest in surrounding developments and the King Homes would have rendered them worthless. It looks like they are back, while the FBI has moved on to apprehending draft resisters. Baldwin will attend the next city council meeting.

"So, with Alan gone, who takes over for him?" asks Baldwin.

"I guess me and Aries, but I'm heading back to school in a month," says Jamal.

"I'll be up and running by then," says Gem. "I'll help Aries."

At that moment, Aries shows up on the porch for her turn with Baldwin. "I'm sorry it took so long," she says. "I had to put Arwen down for sleep. She's so finicky this time in the evening."

Baldwin does a double take. Aries is Ashley Lange, Dominic Styron's girlfriend from Akron. Baldwin glances at Gem for a second, and she arches her eyebrows. *Yeah, I know.*

It takes a minute for Baldwin to reorient himself. He could not have imagined that Dominic Styron's girlfriend would turn up in Lackawanna, and with a child. He decides not to reveal what he already knows. Test her honesty or lack thereof. Aries, whose real name, Baldwin and Gem know, is Ashley Lange, has long, brown, very curly hair and brown eyes. She appears to be in her mid-twenties, slightly chubby, and with the swollen chest of a breastfeeder. She seems comfortable and ready to talk.

Jamal says something about having things to do and waves goodbye. At some point Ira had disappeared, too. Probably satisfied that Baldwin wasn't going to bust anybody. Now it's just Baldwin, Aries and Gem.

"How old is she?" asks Baldwin, while Aries settles into the beach chair opposite him.

"Two months," says Aries with a proud smile.

Baldwin and Gem realize that Styron died around the same time that his daughter was born.

"That's nice, congratulations," says Baldwin, with a bit of sadness that he hopes doesn't tell. "Can we talk about Alan Crowe and your work together?"

"Uh huh, but I don't know what I can tell you that would help you find his killer. Everybody loved him here."

"What about out there?" Baldwin asks, gesturing towards Lackawanna and beyond.

"There's tension and conflict, but that's with all of us, not just Alan."

"Let's start with you, then. Do you mind if Gemini is here? I don't."

Aries looks at Gem and says, "We'd probably go through all this eventually." The women smile at each other.

Baldwin gets her life story, or what she wants to tell him about. Born in Columbus, Ohio, went to Ohio State, got radicalized, joined the Popular Democratic Movement, and traveled around planting new chapters at colleges around the state, coordinating communication between them.

Toledo, Cleveland, Kent State, Bowling Green, Akron — *ah*, thinks Baldwin, *there it is* — then Lackawanna. Things are not good with her parents; they have pretty much given up on her. No contact, no love. They're on the other side politically. "They know about Arwen, but don't care." She's downcast when she says it.

"Why did you come here? It's off the beaten path."

"Different work, more what I want to do," she says.

Baldwin crooks his head to ask, like what?

"Civil rights. It was all about the war on those campuses, and it's the right thing to do, for sure, but I was a big fan of Dr. King, and now here I am, working on a housing development named after him."

Against his better judgement, Baldwin is beginning to like her. He steals a glance at Gem and thinks she does, too. A genuine friendship might develop between the two. Might be good, might be bad.

"Alan was the lead on that project, helping Mr. Jakes and the non-profit?"

"Yeah, I'm sure Jamal filled you in. He'd been working on it for a year and was making progress, I think. We got some applications finished."

"You mentioned conflicts?"

"The city obstructs, mostly with burdensome paperwork. The white people stand in the way with racist attitudes, demonstrations, media attacks," she says.

"Is that all? I'm not sure if there is a murderer in there somewhere," says Baldwin. "There have been paperwork and arguments for ages, nobody gets killed." *Unless you're a Negro, and it's Mississippi*, he thinks.

Her eyes drift to the right and she bites her lower lip, like there's more but she's not sure if she should say what it is and if this is the time.

"What else, Aries?" asks Baldwin.

She pauses, clasps her hands on her lap. "I saw somebody threaten Alan, kind of."

"Kind of?"

"It was at the end of a city council meeting. During the meeting, Alan had spoken and brought up about three legal challenges that Better Homes Now – the Negroes – could make to what the city was doing. It caused a commotion. The white people started yelling, the councilmen started whispering to each other, putting their hands over the microphones. He had hit a nerve."

"Remember what the challenges were?"

"Legal stuff I didn't understand, but it would be in the minutes, if they kept any."

Baldwin jots that down in his notebook. "When was that?" he asks.

"End of July."

That coincides with when Alan went missing.

"What was the threat?" he asks.

"There are two or three men that always attend the meetings, but don't act like they are emotionally involved, not like the regular white citizens. More like, I'd describe it as professionally involved."

"Jamal mentioned them."

"One of them stood up at the end of the meeting, when everybody was pushing chairs away and leaving, and he blocked Alan's path. Poked his finger in Alan's chest and said something low, right in his face, like, 'Keep it up and see what happens, you fucking faggot.'"

Baldwin writes all this down.

"This is far more information than you alluded to, at the beginning. Far more serious. Why were you thinking of holding this back?" asks Baldwin.

"I didn't want to out Alan," she says, her voice cracking a bit. "But if that's why he was killed, then I thought I better tell you."

"Most of the time that 'faggot' stuff is just an insult. It doesn't mean Alan was a homosexual," says Baldwin.

"But I knew that he was," says Aries. "And if they did, too, then maybe you have a suspect. A motive."

"You did the right thing, telling me this," says Baldwin. "What did the man look like? Do you know his name?"

"No name. That's the only thing he or any of them ever said. But he was taller than Alan, heavier, bulkier, like a weightlifter. White, of course. About forty-five or so. Black hair, porkchop sideburns. Honestly, Officer, I thought he looked like either a cop, the military, or the mafia."

Baldwin thinks about that, and she's right. There is a typecast that fits all three in civilian clothes.

They talk some more about the housing work Aries had been doing with Alan and whether she is prepared to take over. She says that she has a steep learning curve, she's only been around for a few months. She's got a baby. Jamal is leaving soon. She feels overwhelmed. Gem says she'll be her support, help out all she can. The two women reach out and take each other's hand. Baldwin thinks they may have lost a good cop. *But if the Black folks get a housing development out of it, well...*

"I have to ask you just a couple more questions, then we'll be done today," says Baldwin.

"Okay."

"You said you came here to work on civil rights issues, but this organization here, in Lackawanna, does antiwar activities, too. You and Alan participate in that?"

Aries hesitates for a moment or two, as though she's parsing through what she can say about that. The FBI isn't watching them help the Negroes get a mortgage, but it's probably watching them do sit-ins at Selective Service offices or carry placards and block traffic at the GE plant. They all imagine that the FBI has a fat folder on each of them full of pictures taken from a mile away.

"All of us, including Alan, are part of the antiwar movement. We have exercised our first amendment rights to speak, to assemble, to petition the government. Nothing we've done here is illegal," she says, stridently. She's been on the front line.

"I'm not here to give you a hard time about that," says Baldwin. "I'm investigating Alan's murder, and so I'm looking for reasons why someone would want to kill a young man who you say everybody loved. Did he get any threats for his antiwar activities?"

"All of us have," says Aries. "If he was killed for being antiwar, then it was a random act. There is no reason to single him out. One of us keeps watch all night long to make sure we don't get firebombed. Or shot at."

"It's that bad?"

"We think so. There's a saying, Detective, goes like this, 'Just because you're paranoid, it doesn't mean you aren't being followed.' It's like that for us."

Dinner is in the fridge when Tom gets home, so he puts the casserole in the oven. Sandra is curled up, eating a bowl of popcorn, watching *Dragnet* on TV. The original series with Jack Webb, in glorious black and white.

"Until I met you," she says to him as he plops down next to her, "I thought all detectives had zero personality, like these two." She points at Joe Friday and Bill Gannon.

"I hope I didn't disappoint," he says, as he digs into her bowl.

"Not at all. You gave me a whole new perspective," and she kisses him.

"That's the exact term I would use to describe what's happened on my case, today," he says.

"Tell me."

He tells her about his interview with Kevin Crowe, Jamal, and Aries, and embedding Sam in the PDM. There are those two VFW men, about a hundred angry homeowners, and three goons that may be mafioso. Now he's got some actual people who made actual threats to Alan's life, with motives behind them. He'll have to investigate means and opportunity next. To top it all off, the girlfriend of another Niagara River victim worked with Alan, on things that might have gotten Alan killed. All in one day! But he tells her he's got to make some sense out of it. Too many loose ends.

66

"Tomorrow morning, I'll make a visual aid for you," says Sandra.

Baldwin knows it'll be one of her famous thought diagrams. It's how she pulls all the loose threads of a story together. Charting bits of knowledge, or even hunches, on a piece of paper is her way of taking notes. She puts things that are "knowns" in circles, things that are "known unknowns" in squares and "unknown unknowns" in triangles. She connects them using either solid or dotted lines, depending on the dependencies or connections between them, with arrows on the end. An unknown killer would be in a square, connected to the known victim in a circle with a solid line, an arrow pointed at the dead guy. If there is some sense that the killer was hired, he'd be connected to the unknown unknown, shown in a triangle, with a dotted line. The object of the exercise is to investigate doggedly and turn everything into a circle: a known.

"Where will you put the threatening mobsters?" he asks.

"In squares. They are known unknowns. I've seen those men at the meetings that I've covered," says Sandra. "They do look creepy, like they are watching closely who does what. They give off vibes like it's their job, not their passion. Like they were sent there by their boss. The mysterious boss will be in a triangle."

"Do they do anything besides watch?"

"A little. More than once I'd see a councilmember look out at the crowd and gradually focus in on one of those men, and they would give a little nod, or maybe a head shake. Like, giving direction. But real subtle. I'll connect the mysterious men to the city council with a dotted line."

"I never thought of the mafia as being subtle," says Tom.

"Maybe it's not them," says Sandra. "Maybe those guys are just control freaks sent there by some developer, protecting his investment."

Just then on the TV, Sergeant Joe Friday says, "Just the facts, ma'am," to a housewife he's questioning.

Sandra's diagram is waiting for Baldwin when he sits down for breakfast next morning. She'd left it for him with a love note by the coffee pot. He studies it while peeling a hardboiled egg, buttering a piece of toast and sipping the morning brew.

In the middle is a circle with Alan's name. Surrounding Alan are other circles, some squares, and a couple of triangles: knowns, known unknowns, and unknown unknowns. They are the mysteries that must be solved. A square called "killer" is connected to the inner circle labeled "Alan." There's lots of space to add more geometry as he uncovers more people and clues.

Just then the phone rings.

"Hi Ricky," says Sam.

"Ricky?"

"My boyfriend, the angry leftist militant who is probably making pipe bombs in the tenement apartment back in Brooklyn."

"Do you actually know anybody like that?" asks Baldwin.

"No, but I read about one in a crime novel I just finished. He died in a hail of gunfire with NYPD, but the hippies don't know that part."

"Keep them in the dark," says Baldwin. "What have you got for me?"

Sam tells him what she learned in the half day she's been there. It turns out that Dominic Styron is Arwen's father, but there is no indication that anybody there at the commune knows that he is dead. Aries didn't mention him by name but said her boyfriend back in Akron, Arwen's father, is active in the antiwar movement. His birthday is May 16th and he had a very low draft lottery number, number fifty-five. Last she knew, he was trying to figure out what to do about getting drafted. He was looking into CO status. That's how Sam made the connection. She had read his file, knew his birthday. Sam said it was devastating for her not to tell Aries anything about Styron.

"She's oblivious," says Sam. "Her lover and the father of her child has been dead for two months. The last time she heard from him was back in April, before he took off. He told her he had to keep moving and would contact her when he's safe."

"Is she worried that he hasn't communicated with her since then?"

"Somewhat surprised, but not worried," says Sam. "Hippies are constantly drifting around, melting into new towns and new groups, then moving on again. That's her lifestyle, too. I could wake up tomorrow and find out she left for San Francisco. She probably pictures him settling into a safety net on a pot farm in Oregon."

Baldwin tries to imagine that life. Sounds a little like the underground railroad, but with no particular goal and nobody in pursuit.

"That means that Styron and Alan had something in common besides Aries. They were both called up for the draft, looking for a legal way out. Anything else?" asks Baldwin. He's feeling miserable about all of this. One tragedy piled on top of another.

"I spent a little time with the others, observing them, and had about an hour with Adrian. I beat him in chess. He took it well and wants to play again. But all we talked about was philosophical. Sarah would have liked him." Sam pauses for a minute, thinking about her. "I'm just trying to blend in. I think it'll take a while to gain everybody's trust, become part of the apparatus."

"Yes, my advice at the beginning is to do exactly what you're doing," says Baldwin. "Become one of them. Good work so far. What does today look like?"

"Babysitting."

Tom adds a circle to the chart and connects it with a solid line to Styron's circle, puts "Aries" inside. Then adds "+Arwen."

Baldwin decides to call Raymond Jakes next, whose circle is connected to Alan's, and who said he had some important information. Hopefully, something about the murder case.

"Mr. Jakes. It's Tom Baldwin."

"I'm glad to hear from you," says Jakes. Baldwin can hear the low murmur of conversations in Jakes' barber shop. Some background music from a radio, a buzzing electric razor.

"Good time to talk?" asks Baldwin.

"Can you come on down here? Better in person," says Jakes, "And I got some heads to trim."

"Twenty," says Baldwin, and he heads for his car.

Baldwin drives through the white, middle-class neighborhoods of the Second and Third Wards, teeming with small but neat homes and businesses. Pride-of-ownership nice. Everything in order. Flower beds, mowed lawns. Then he crosses five railroad beds, littered with industrial detritus, garbage, abandoned vehicles and twisted, unrecognizable junk and enters the First Ward, the Negro community.

The steel plant owns most of it and rents it all out, like a feudal lord. The homes and businesses are crowded up against the fence surrounding the blast furnaces and towering smokestacks. The residences are constantly under the soot, ash and grit raining down. Rarely is there anything people can call fresh air.

Baldwin pulls into the parking lot of Jakes' and Bake's Hair Emporium on Steelawanna Avenue, bouncing up and down as his tires dip into and out of the potholes. They make a thump sound. Three other cars are tucked into parking spaces. It's a local institution, been there for decades. Old, scarred red brick with large picture windows filled with commercial ads, announcements for church and community socials, and signs asking young men not to loiter. A tattered canvas awning hangs over the front door.

Everybody gets their hair trimmed and their chins shaved at Jakes', but today it's not that crowded and Baldwin gets seated right away. He's needed a cut, and a shave would be nice. Two other men are in the chairs and one is waiting for the barber whose unfortunate nickname is Dagger. Must be his routine. Once a man knows how to cut your hair just right, you stick with him.

Baldwin takes the seat, gets the apron and the paper neck wrap, and relaxes. Jakes tells him everybody already knows everything he's going say. They talk about it every day. No need to hide anything. Baldwin nods, sure. Maybe others know some things that'll help.

"Tell me about Alan," says Baldwin.

"He was the second coming of Father Goezina as far as the Dr. King project was concerned," says Jakes. One of the other men says, "Amen to that." Baldwin looks up at the wall above the mirrors in front of him. There's a framed portrait of Goezina with a black ribbon draped over it. It's right next to a portrait of Martin Luther King.

Goezina had been the lawyer for the Diocese of Buffalo and sued the City of Lackawanna because it rezoned the land the diocese wanted to sell to the non-profits. He was murdered before the case went to court. Fortunately, the big federal civil rights trial ended in favor of the Black folks. But when Goezina died, momentum on the project died too.

Alan resurrected it. Started showing up at every city council meeting, always came with legal arguments that got the council frazzled. It's like he was always a step ahead of them. He wasn't gaining ground, but he was stopping the city in its tracks. And the best part was that he was working for free and the city had to pay some lawyer. They were feeling it in the painful place, their pocketbook. *Motive*, thinks Baldwin. *Of course, money.*

Jakes goes on to describe the same threesome that Jamal and Aries had. Big, quiet, dangerous-looking men. Intimidating, without saying or doing a thing. Somehow, they're in control of the meeting. Who can talk, what they say, what they vote on. "Those men seem to be in charge, or working for the man who is," says Jakes.

"Did they show any special interest in Alan? See anything? Hear anything?"

"Well, yeah. When Alan would get up and talk, he's the one who made sense. They didn't like that. They got annoyed. They would glance at each other, like, what we goin' to do with this guy? Just a gut sense they ain't right," says Jakes. "I mean, I don't think they're even from around here, don't live in the white wards, don't know their way around. Why they coming to those meetings?"

"What makes you think they're strangers?"

"After a meeting a few months ago, first one I seen them at, I was leaving late, dark outside. Them three was standing on the sidewalk, lighting cigarettes and having an argument about how to get to Elmwood Village from here. I mean, who doesn't know where Elmwood Village is?"

Elmwood Village is a very affluent neighborhood in Buffalo. Baldwin knows that one wealthy resident, Vincent Falco, is a mafia underboss whose territory includes Lackawanna. He owns a legitimate construction company that builds housing developments all over Western New York. He also controls drugs, prostitution, and loan sharking. He is capable of murdering anyone who would threaten his businesses and probably has. Never been arrested for anything, though. He would have a financial interest in seeing the King Homes project sink. He may have put those wiseguys to work making that happen.

And it not only makes sense for Vincent to be behind the three interlopers at the council meetings, but also eliminating Alan Crowe. His late father, Carmine Falco, was suspected of putting the hit on Father Goezina, whose lawsuit threatened both his legal livelihood in Lackawanna and also his illicit ties to city government. When the FBI started investigating Falco for the murder, he and his wife turned up dead in their own dining room along with three other people. A little housecleaning by the capo. Then Vincent took over all his father's enterprises, including the ones threatened by the proposed Negro housing. He also moved into his father's mansion in Elmwood Village, maybe the place the goons were trying to find. Baldwin thinks he has yet another lead, and a way to follow up on it.

The other men in Jake's Emporium pitch in with more anecdotes and stories about Alan, the help that those white hippies were providing the community, hopes for a new elementary school, and so on. One of them does drop a bombshell, though. Says his nephew Quincy got drafted, a notice to report for service in the Army, would've gone to Vietnam. He decided to hightail it for Canada. Had heard they were welcoming draft dodgers. Some local white hippie helped him out. Got him all the way to Toronto, and the folks up there got him a job.

Adrian told him that they weren't doing that, but here it is. Baldwin isn't really surprised to find out Adrian might be shining him on, and he's happy that Sam is in there, infiltrating. Of course, the hippie helper could have been a loner. There are a lot of them, including up in Canada. Baldwin had read news stories about the large and growing community of American draft resisters up near the University of Toronto. The thing that caught his eye, and his imagination, is that they are all clustered around an area anchored by *Baldwin* Street. One reporter estimated two or three thousand young men and their girlfriends and wives live there. Maybe that's who helped Quincy out. It could be a lead.

"Are you in touch with him?" asks Baldwin.

"I can be," says the customer. "His ma is my sister. They talk."

Baldwin gets the man's contact information and arranges to get Quincy's phone number. He assures the man that he is no threat to Quincy, who is safe in Toronto. Nobody can touch him there. What Baldwin doesn't say is he wants to understand this modern-day version of the underground railroad. Is this where the lives of Crowe, Roesler and Styron converge? Were they all riding that train?

Baldwin has a thought, and calls FBI Agent Doug Reynolds when he gets back to the House.

"It's still no, Baldwin," says Reynolds, thinking it's about the King Homes again.

"This is different. I'm looking for Crowe's car."

"We can't help you with that, either, unless he was kidnapped. Even then, I'm not sure we want to help."

That makes Baldwin wonder if that did not, in fact, happen. Another theory.

"You took a picture of me, I saw your men on the Peace Bridge," says Baldwin. "How long have you been doing that? Taking pictures of bridge crossers."

"Several months. Actually, more like six. We are doing the same thing up on the Rainbow Bridge."

"If I gave you a description of the victim's vehicle and the plate number, can you check your photo gallery? See if he's in it? If he drove it into Canada, and not back, then he may have been killed there. Maybe his car is still there, full of evidence."

"Why would I do that?" asks Reynolds. "I don't care that he was killed, how he was killed or where he was killed. He was a fucking commie!"

"You told me that you're interdicting draft evaders," says Baldwin, appealing to Reynolds' self-interest. "Crowe might have been doing that. Helping them. Wouldn't you want to know that? See how they operate?"

Reynolds is silent for a moment, maybe weighing the pros and cons of helping to find the killer of somebody who he would have arrested.

"We have tens of thousands of photos, no wait, closer to millions. Most of them honeymooners, families. Pretty ordinary and very boring. Or gross. It's amazing how many people pick their nose while driving. The most interesting one was a car full of what looked like nudists. I can't even tell you how many prints were requested. Somebody ordered one for Hoover. So far, the whole photography effort has been a waste of time and film. The upside? Kodak stock is up."

"Can you? It could break my case open and justify your photo op. You'd get all the credit."

More silent contemplation by Reynolds. Baldwin can't tell what motivates the guy. So far, it isn't law enforcement. Self-interest? Ideology?

"Since you put it that way, then okay, but it will take a very long time, maybe forever. It will help if you have a time frame."

"July 26th to August 3rd," says Baldwin. He thinks the range would have to include Alan, if he indeed went to Canada to meet his end.

"Okay, that's helpful. Probably only about a quarter million cars that week."

Baldwin gives Reynolds the car description and tag and arranges to send him a picture of Crowe to compare with the photos they have. Reynolds has only one person to help with this. It might take a week. Or forever. "I can't promise anything. This won't be her priority."

Baldwin has two more things to put into motion. He calls Lieutenant Abe Zubricky at the Buffalo Police Department. Zubricky was part of the big drug bust in Buffalo last year, the one that eventually took down the mafia boss, Stefano Maglione. They became comrades and friends.

"Zubricky," he says, when he picks up.

"Lieutenant, It's Tom Baldwin down in Lackawanna."

"You've decided to enroll at BPD?"

"No sir, but I always appreciate your encouragement."

"Then it's something else."

"Yes," says Baldwin. "I'm investigating the murder of a young man who may have gotten himself into Vincent Falco's crosshairs."

"My favorite goombah," says Zubricky.

"I have no proof of anything, but three men who may be associated with Falco were seen threatening the victim. I want to follow up on that, see if they work for Falco, go on from there."

"You want me to watch Falco's house? See if there's some coming and going?"

"If it's possible," says Baldwin, then adds, "Maybe a phone tap?"

"We'd need a warrant, and we'd only get one with reasonable cause," says Zubricky. "We'll have to watch and wait. Maybe they'll shoot somebody in the front yard."

"Understood."

"What do they look like? Got names for them? What kind of car do they drive?"

Baldwin gives Zubricky what he has, which is practically nothing. Three big white guys, maybe from out of town. He'll go to the next council meeting and see for himself.

"Picture would help," says Zubricky. "But meantime, we can stake out the house, take our own pictures, work it backwards."

"Yes, please."

"We'll start tonight," says Zubricky. "I'd love to nail that sumbitch for something."

Baldwin takes the stroll again down to Chief Plishka's office. He waits while the chief finishes up with some other officers. Sounds like a teachable moment. He can hear Plishka calmly tell a rookie how he fucked up, how it happens sometimes, and how to get it right next time. He hears the "Yes, sir" and "Thank you, sir" and watches the young men, one of them Black, leave the office in a hurry. They survived and want to get off the battlefield quickly. Baldwin peeks in. Plishka is weaving a piece of paper into his typewriter.

"Writing them up?"

"I'm putting something decent in Jones's and Harris's files. They caught a car thief."

"But..."

"Chased him goin' ninety through a residential and business neighborhood. The guy crashed into a liquor store. Luckily, doesn't open till noon. If it had been a drugstore, well, could have had casualties. As it is, the business is closed and the car is totaled."

"The thief?"

"Mercy Hospital. Fourteen years old," says Plishka.

"On a school day."

"Yeah," says Plishka. He just shakes his head. "What's next..."

"Can you take a moment to give me some advice?" asks Baldwin. "It's about the Crowe murder."

Plishka motions Baldwin to have a seat and leans forward on his arms.

"Kevin Crowe, Alan's father, heard some members of his VFW Post talk openly about killing antiwar demonstrators and draft resisters. I have the names and addresses, phone numbers for both of them."

"He didn't think it was just a drunk guy's fantasy? Those guys get plowed at those Posts, say all kinds of things they can't remember in the morning."

"His son is murdered. I think we owe it to him to follow up, just check them out."

Plishka admires Baldwin's sentiment. Reconsiders it.

"So, what kind of advice do you need?" asks Plishka.

"There are two complications. First is, how do I approach them. I'm a Lackawanna cop investigating the murder of a kid from West Seneca that happened in Niagara Falls. They'll wonder what the fuck I'm doing talking to them. Plus, I'm Black."

"Second, they both lost sons of their own in Vietnam. They are both veterans like you. Patriots. I'm imagining they're deeply conflicted about the war, the cost in lives, the war resistance by privileged kids, while theirs went off and died. I guess I wanted to ask you if you could put yourself in their position?"

Plishka had never thought about it, losing his son Robert in Vietnam. He's only sixteen, has two more years of high school, will probably get a college deferment. But now he does roll it around in his head. What if he lost Robert in that war? How would he feel? The emotions that he entertains for a few moments are heart-wrenching.

"Tom, this is your case, your investigation, and I don't want to mess you up," says Plishka. "So, if you don't agree with me on this, just say so."

"What do you think?" asks Baldwin.

"That maybe I should check them out, first, for both your reasons."

That's a surprise. Baldwin never considered asking the chief to talk to those men, but it makes perfect sense. Plishka will empathize with them, and they with him. The three have so much in common. Plishka will be able to commiserate, communicate, and bond with them in ways he would not. If they are capable of doing harm to Alan, or anyone else, Plishka will know.

"I'd appreciate your help on that. Yes sir, you should meet them, first. See if I should follow up."

They spend the next ten minutes transferring the information Baldwin has on Johnson and Fredricks, and Plishka makes plans to go to the VFW Post on the night when they are regulars. Best to talk to them in their natural habitat. He'll call Kevin Crowe and tell him what he's doing and when. Maybe Crowe should avoid the Post that evening.

Then a fourth thing comes up. When Baldwin gets back to his office, there's a note from Sergeant Decker at the front desk. Some guy, who described himself as the barbershop man, called and left a name and address and phone number for his nephew in Canada: Quincy Taylor.

Like most draft dodgers who emigrate to Canada, Quincy is in Toronto, in a neighborhood bulging with American ex-pats trying to make a new life and avoid killing and possible death in Vietnam. There is an entire ecosystem of supporters, housing, job placements there. Baldwin could call the young man but thinks it might be best to interview him in person.

Quincy booked for Canada to avoid induction, and he knows that American law enforcement would have stopped him if it could. He's probably suspicious of American police and won't be cooperative, or even available. Then he wonders if Canadian authorities would even allow him to drive up to Toronto and conduct an interview. He phones up Inspector Henri Paquette.

"Detective, I'm glad you called," says Paquette.

"I've made some progress, Inspector, and I want to report that to you, and I have two requests."

"Let's get started," says Paquette.

It takes Baldwin almost fifteen minutes to brief Paquette on everything that's transpired. As he goes along, he realizes that he actually has made some progress even though he has no one suspect. In fact, he has too many to look at: veterans, mafioso. He tells Paquette about the PDM commune and the woman whose boyfriend was Dominic Styron. Same commune Alan was a member.

"So, there is some concrete connection between two of the river boys," says Baldwin. "They were both facing induction, both had no intention to serve in our military, both knew at least one woman in Lackawanna."

"And both died," says Paquette.

"Yes, there is that," says Baldwin. "There is a young man, an American draft dodger, now living in Toronto. He was helped by someone described as a hippie to get to Canada. Could be the PDM folks, or any number of others, even people in Canada. Can you see what I'm interested in?"

"You want to know if this young man was assisted by the same people who Mr. Styron and perhaps Mr. Crowe knew?"

"Yes, something like that," says Baldwin. "I would have some questions for him about who helped him and how. What is involved in me going to Toronto to interview him?"

"A mountain of red tape, most likely followed by a polite no," says Paquette.

"I was afraid of that."

"Our countries disagree about your draft resisters," says Paquette. "We don't consider them criminals, but you do. I'm guessing that my government would regard your visit as an attempt to lure him back to face your justice, or to obtain evidence that would incriminate others."

Baldwin agrees. There's only one option left.

"Can I talk you into interviewing him," he asks Paquette.

"Because…"

"He will trust you. I don't think he'll ignore his host. You are trying to find out how maybe three other young men just like him died at the border. Why wouldn't he answer your questions? You are no threat to him, and he could assist you solving a capital crime."

"I have to be very careful, Detective, because we cannot help you apprehend and prosecute anyone who is helping young men come to Canada, even if it's because they are avoiding military service. Especially if they are doing that. It's our country's policy."

"Then just ask him questions that may lead both of us to the person or persons responsible for perhaps three murders," says Baldwin. "All I would want to know, because of where my investigation has gone so far, is who, in general terms, helped him, and did he ever feel threatened?"

"Give me his contact information," says Paquette. "I'll arrange to meet him, get details of his personal experience. But I cannot give you any names, nothing that would lead to arrests or even questioning of individuals."

"Can you ask him if he knew Alan?"

There's a pause. "Okay, that would be alright. Alan is dead. And now that you open that door, I'll ask him about Styron and Roesler. You just never know. The world is small."

"Sometimes the world seems tiny, Inspector."

It wasn't Baldwin's intention to subcontract all the work out, but that's how it is. Simpson is infiltrating the PDM commune, Plishka is questioning the VFW men, Zubricky is watching the mafia boys in Buffalo and Inspector Paquette of the Mounties is tracking down a draft dodger in Toronto. It's an international affair. The whole law enforcement world is looking for Alan's car, especially some lab tech at the FBI, pouring over a million photos of people crossing the border into Canada. The advantage is that all of them can work simultaneously, in parallel.

Still, he feels deflated. He wants his own boots on the ground. He has one more possible motive to explore: Alan's sexual orientation. There's a lot of prejudice out there towards homosexuals, and he should explore that possibility. Did he cross paths with a hater? And on the other end of the spectrum is love, and the damage that comes with a breakup. Obsession, jealousy and revenge are often motives for violence and murder. Did Alan have a lover? A jealous one? A jilted one? Where does he start? He decides to call Fiona McIntyre, who told him that she and Alan confided in each other about their love interests. Maybe he confided about being harassed or threatened as well.

As before, a young woman in Fiona's dorm answers the pay phone on the wall and tracks her down. A minute or two passes before she picks up.

"Fiona, It's Detective Baldwin."

"Something to share?" asks Fiona.

"Not yet. Soon, I hope. I've got one more thing to look at right now. Something you can help with."

"Me?"

He's not sure if Fiona will be willing to help with this or not. It might mean revealing the names of other gay men.

"It's time for me to examine Alan's relationships with other males."

"You think I can help with that?"

"You might be the only one who can. When we first spoke, you said that you and Alan confided with each other about your love life. I thought he may have told you about bad experiences, breakups, anything that may have left somebody angry or vengeful. Maybe something dramatic and scary? Something more than a broken heart?"

Fiona is quiet for a minute, probably mulling this over. Baldwin knows that she doesn't want Alan's homosexuality to become common knowledge, even after his death. He suspects that she may not want to violate the privacy of Alan's lovers, either.

"I know this is hard," Baldwin says, "So, let's start at the beginning and take it in baby steps."

"Okay, good."

"When did it start? Changing his sexual preferences."

"That's the wrong way to put it," she says. "The wrong way to ask the question. Being a homosexual is not only about who to have sex with, any more than being straight is. It's about how you see yourself. It's about your identity."

Baldwin is slightly embarrassed. He should know better. They covered this in a psychology class he took at Hillcrest. "You're right. Sorry. And of course, thinking about it differently will help me understand Alan better, and his relationships."

"Thank you, Detective. Glad you get it."

"So, when did he begin to…see himself?"

"Middle school," says Fiona. "I was the first and only kid in school who could tell that something was going on with him. He was comfortable confiding in me that he thought he might be different, possibly gay. Then, later, he determined he was, and we talked about it as the years went by."

"About his self-awareness?" asks Baldwin.

"At first, it was about his inner conflicts, his difficulty reconciling with them. We were both young, just entering puberty, nobody was actually having any urges, much less acting on them, even heterosexual ones. We were only, like, thirteen years old."

Baldwin knows fourteen-, fifteen-year-old parents.

"When did he begin to have feelings towards other boys? Like a crush or something?"

"That began a few years later," says Fiona. "At first, he was really mixed up and afraid, didn't want to believe it was happening to him. He was in a deep funk for a couple of years in high school. He was very good looking and tons of girls were falling all over themselves to get close. They all thought they were the one who could make him happy. And I was having feelings for him, myself. Because I had fantasies about getting married to him when we were little. My puppy love for him never ended." There's a pause before she adds, "He took me to the prom."

Baldwin hears her sniffle. He is sure that she is crying, and he waits it out.

"What was really hard for him," she says finally, through a tear and a sigh, "was being in the locker rooms and showers with boys he liked as friends and might have been attracted to physically. But he fought a little war with himself and repressed that. The swim team was all these great-looking, strapping jocks. But he never acted on it, kept his secret, and took it to his grave."

"Where did he find the companions that he told you about?"

"Here and there. He told me that it isn't hard to identify another gay man. He was approached from time to time, tried to settle into a quiet, secret, but meaningful relationship, then things wouldn't work out."

"Is that where you came in?"

"Yes, how to handle a breakup. Sometimes how to initiate a breakup."

"He's the one who wanted to breakup? Why?"

"In the three instances that I know of, it's because the other boy wanted to be out with it," says Fiona. "To hold hands, to be explicit. Celebrate. Alan wanted to survive high school, stay on the swim team, maybe make the Olympics, go to college. He thought he couldn't do any of that if everyone knew he was gay. He thought the news would also destroy his parents."

Baldwin thinks that he was probably right about that.

"Did he succeed in keeping his secret?"

"You were at his funeral, you saw who came," says Fiona. "Every member of his high school swim team, another handful of guys who he beat, and streams of girls who had crushes on him showed up. If he had been outed, it would have been a very small, quiet affair."

"The boys he had encounters with," says Baldwin. "Did any of them show up, that you know of?"

"One boy, yes. I'm pretty sure that he stayed closeted. He was really a mess at the wake and funeral. Probably still in love."

"Did any of the breakups turn ugly that you know?"

Fiona gives it some thought. "From what Alan told me, only one seemed to end with really hard feelings. The boy was very hurt and got angry. Threatened Alan but never followed through. But it was years ago, I'm sure that boy just moved on like we all do."

"Threatened?"

"Not physically," says Fiona. "He said he'd tell the world about them."

"But he didn't."

"No, he used it as a threat, as leverage to get Alan back and when it didn't work, he just finally let go."

"Do you remember his name?" asks Baldwin. "It's a lead. I should follow it up somehow."

Fiona is silent for a moment, again, then a little cough. "He was another swimmer. A competitor. They seemed to take turns beating each other."

"A name?" he asks hopefully.

"His name is Michael. Michael McGee."

Baldwin flips back a few pages of his notebook and finds that name. McGee was probably the kid who Alan beat in an Olympic trial, and his father went ballistic. The Crowes know them both. So does Plishka. There's a possible motive for the father or the son or both to get violent with Alan.

"Any idea where I could find him?"

"He is swimming in college, somewhere, most likely," she says. "He is good enough in the pool to go anywhere, and probably got as far away from his father as possible."

"They didn't get along?"

"Father is a bully and a homophobe. Sometimes he would humiliate Michael after a loss or a bad time."

Bad combination, thinks Baldwin. If he is a violent bully and a virulent homophobe, hitting your son's lover with a tire iron would be within bounds. "How do you know he hates gay people?"

"He always shouted stuff like, 'Stop swimming like a faggot!' to his son. He used slurs like that. Sometimes he'd call the kid who Michael beat a faggot. Pretty disgusting."

"Did he know about Michael and Alan?" asks Baldwin, jotting notes as fast as he can.

"Don't know. You'd have to ask Michael, I guess. Or his father."

Baldwin decides to start with the former.

The McGees live in Orchard Park, Plishka's hometown. Baldwin heads down to the chief's office.

"I was going to call you," says Plishka. "I'm going to the VFW on Wednesday, hope to meet our angry vets."

"Great, thanks. Have you figured out how you'll handle it?"

"With empathy." says Plishka. "And it won't be hard. I'm a vet and a father, too. I see their point of view. Of course, if they acted on it, I will handle them differently. Either way, I'll put it back on your plate. I've got a department to run. What about you, where are you on this case?"

"I've just learned something new about that McGee guy from Orchard Park," says Baldwin, "and I have to tell you something about Crowe that wasn't relevant until now."

"Alright, what?"

"Alan was gay, but in the closet. He had relationships with other men, several that ended when he thought that he'd be outed."

Plishka knows how that changes everything. The curtain rises on a whole new landscape of motives and suspects.

"Where does McGee come in?"

"His son was one of them."

"Ouch," says Plishka. "McGee doesn't strike me as someone who would tolerate having a queer son. Not him. He has a macho male self-image. He reeks of testosterone."

"What would a guy like that do if he found out?" asks Baldwin.

"You're the one with a psychology degree, what does Freud tell you?"

"He's dead, too," says Baldwin. "But I could ask some former profs up at Hillcrest what they think."

"Good. Might help with questioning him, assuming you might have to."

"I'm going to start with Michael, if I can track him down," says Baldwin.

"He's at Cornell," says Plishka, "breaking swimming records."

Baldwin looks at him quizzically.

"He's in the Orchard Park weekly paper all the time. Local-boy-makes-good stories. He's All-Ivy, probably going to be an All-American. Every once in a while, his father is quoted, taking credit for his accomplishments."

"Fits the profile," says Baldwin. "He sounds like one of those men who lives out his own fantasies through his son. If I had to guess, he never amounted to much when he was a teenager, or maybe ever."

"I can't help you with that," says Plishka. "He does piss people off. His wife left him years ago. Just disappeared. Town gossips say she ran off with one of his friends, but I never bought that part of the story."

"Why not?"

"He doesn't have any friends."

"I'm driving out to Cornell tomorrow," says Baldwin.

"Good idea. The old man would be a dead end."

Beth Egan had always wanted to be an FBI agent, but the Bureau is still an all-male club, so she took the job that was offered: filing clerk. Her rationale was that if it gets her closer to the work of Elliot Ness and J. Edgar Hoover and the men who caught Soviet spies and members of the Gambino crime family, she's all in.

It's a good civil service job with benefits and a pension plan. Her work puts her in the midst of investigations of all kinds. Mafia loansharking, Ponzi schemes, insider trading, counterfeiting, an occasional kidnapping. Paperwork coming in, new reports getting written, meeting minutes that must be taken. She sees it all and has learned plenty. It's busy and kind of exciting, even though it's other people's experiences. She gets to write it or read it and find the proper place for it. She is the only female among about twenty men, but nobody ever hits on her, she's never faced any of that sexual innuendo thing that she's heard about. She hopes it is because these men are all decent, and not because she is about ten years older than most of them.

Her father is an avid photographer, and she got very good at it from a young age. She knows her way around a camera and the darkroom. F-stops, apertures, shutter speeds, ASA. She knows all the technical jargon and how to use it. But her dad also taught her about framing the shot, the rule of thirds, composition, depth of field, color theory. Capturing the moment. He taught her about photo editing. The art of photography. Her photographs adorn her parent's house. She won some awards. But nobody ever heard of a female photographer who made a living at it. Well, maybe Leni Riefenstahl, but she was a Nazi.

When the FBI office in Buffalo initiated the photo shoot at the Peace Bridge and the Rainbow Bridge in an effort to spot draft dodgers, she volunteered to help. She wanted to practice her craft shooting with a long lens, getting just the right framing, exposure, and white balance. She wanted to capture the moment when a subject looked up and noticed her. Maybe put up a hand to hide his face. The FBI had other plans. They put her to work developing film, making prints and filing photos. All in a dark, underground bunker.

The photos are taken by untrained agents. They can shoot at paper targets at Quantico, grouping bullets into what would have been a bad guy's face, but they cannot shoot pictures. They suck. Day after day she develops and prints the worst photographs ever taken. *What a horrible waste of perfectly good film*, she thinks. After six months looking at absolute crap, she wants to cry.

But during this time, watching tens of thousands of photos slowly appear in a stainless-steel bath, another thing started to happen in her brain. She began to see patterns on the prints and magically record them somewhere in her memory. Things like this: Every morning at eight the same black pick-up truck crosses the Peace Bridge with just a driver. He's about forty, mostly bald, and his left arm is pink because of the way he hangs it out the window. Another: Peak crossing times, those with the greatest number of cars, goes from 10 am to 12 noon, except on Fridays, when it peaks at 3 pm to about 9 pm. It's the same on both bridges. There are other cars and trucks that seem to have a routine, as though the driver works in Canada but not every day. She recognizes and remembers having seen certain drivers more than several times. She can't help it. She sees these patterns and they lodge in her head.

On Tuesday afternoon, her boss, Special Agent Douglas Reynolds, suddenly appears at the door of the makeshift photo lab, which the bureau hastily built in the underground parking garage under the Federal building. Reynolds is pushing fifty, fit, Marine haircut, Aryan. She's not enamored. He looks like and acts like aggression. His chest is always pushing out against the tired buttons trying to hold it in.

"I have a new assignment for you, Egan."

"Sir?"

"I need you to study about two-hundred thousand photos that you have already filed away," he says.

"Sir?"

"You will be looking for a particular vehicle, possibly driven by a particular individual, possibly accompanied by an unknown individual," Reynolds says. "Up for it?"

"Part of an investigation, sir?"

"A murder."

Egan can't suppress a smile. "Yes sir. What am I looking for?"

Reynolds spends the next twenty minutes explaining the crime, the victim, his car and what might have happened: Alan Crowe might have driven across the Peace or the Rainbow Bridge in his Pontiac Tempest with the person who later bashed his head in.

"Call me the minute you find something," he tells her. He gives her Baldwin's number in Lackawanna and tells her to call him if he is not available. "But only in an emergency."

Beth Egan is so excited she almost wets her pants. She can't believe her luck.

"How long do I have?"

"How long will it take?"

"Do I focus on this and not the undeveloped film coming in every day?"

"No, you do both."

Egan does the calculus. Two jobs, both time-consuming. One might solve a murder, the other might nab a draft dodger, who she secretly hopes gets away clean. Then she finds a solution.

"I'd like your permission to bring in an assistant."

"No budget for that," says Reynolds.

"He'd work for free," she replies.

"Free is good. We'd have to clear him, do a background check and drug test. Who is it?"

"My dad."

The next morning, Bruce Egan joins his daughter at the photo lab. He has spent his entire life taking photos, developing film, making prints. He could do the darkroom work blindfolded, but still delights in seeing the image take shape on the paper. He jumps right in. He immediately sees what Beth does. The pictures are technically atrocious. But many of them are hilarious. Slice of life, candid camera stuff. A toddler being held up so he can pee out the window; a guy wiping bird poop off his windshield while steering with his knee; a newlywed couple rear-ending a station wagon while they smooch. He can't wait for the next roll to develop.

Beth has her instructions, what and whom to look for on prints depicting a one week stretch of bridge traffic back in late July, early August. For economy, every roll of film was developed and contact-printed on a single sheet of photo paper. Thirty-six images on an eight and a half by eleven sheet of glossy paper. Each image the size of a 35 mm negative. About one and a half square inches. The size of an Easter Seal.

Beth uses a loupe, a small handheld magnifier that she can rest on the print and peek through to inspect each image. It blows the image up. She puts the loupe on the first image of the first contact print and presses her eye to the lens. It's the front grill of a dark blue, late model Chevy, with a man's face behind the steering wheel and a woman laughing in the seat next to him. Pennsylvania license plate. Not Alan Crowe, not his car. She moves down to the next image. Nope. Then thirty-four more nopes and she puts that print aside and begins inspecting the next one.

After about twenty prints, she is getting into a rhythm. She knows that she is not there to look at cars and people but to look for a particular car and a particular person. She keeps that image in her head and scans the contact sheets speedily. After fifty prints, she is only looking for the color maroon. Crowe's car was a maroon Pontiac Tempest. Reynolds had given her a Pontiac sales brochure from 1962 so she could identify the shape of the grill. She looks for that chrome shape in front of a maroon hood. Color and shape. After seventy-five prints, she is holding up the contact print and scanning the whole tableau all at once. No maroon, no bother. What had started as a few seconds per image becomes maybe ten seconds per page.

Every once in a while, she has to rest her eyes, stretch, get a drink of water, check up on her father, who is having a ball. He's laughing at how bad the pictures are and says the same thing she thought, "What a waste!"

At noon, he emerges from the darkroom and says he's going out to get lunch for them both. She directs him to a pizza place across the street. "It's not great but it's fast and cheap."

"Two out of three ain't bad," he says. "Pepperoni?"

"Yes, sir," she says absentmindedly. She spotted some maroon. Maybe the tenth time today. She zeros in on the picture with her loupe. Blinks a couple of times and presses her eye to the print. Wrong grill, wrong plate number, but she's getting more confident that nothing maroon will get by her. She's been at this for nearly four hours and has scanned almost two thousand images. She's not sure if she'll get faster or slower over time. Her eyes will get blurry and tired, her mind will drift. Best case, she'll finish in twenty days. Worst case, forty. Unless she sees the car and Alan Crowe and maybe his killer before that.

She takes a deep breath, sips some water, and picks up the next contact print.

Baldwin and Moore have breakfast together on Wednesday. Sandra has an early morning interview set up at the steel plant about some sort of environmental infraction, so she darts out right after the last sip of coffee. Tom does the dishes, puts on his suit and tie, fills a thermos with what's left in the percolator, and heads down to his car, parked in the driveway behind his father's station wagon. As always, there's a note from his mother under the wiper blade. "Have a blessed day," with a little heart. He kisses it and slips it into his pocket. A talisman that will ensure that he does, indeed, have a blessed day.

The drive to Ithaca takes almost four hours on two lane roads through farm country and then the Finger Lakes winery region. Every now and then he's slowed down by a piece of farm machinery being towed by a tractor with a top speed of ten. Twice he is slowed by a horse-drawn Amish buggy. Top speed about five. It's okay, though. It's good to slow down, look at the scenery, admire God's creation. He has time to contemplate, and he has a lot to contemplate about.

With Seneca Lake, one of the magnificent finger lakes in central New York, on his left and tall goldenrod and purple aster meadows on his right, alive with monarchs, he heads south on Route 14. He's headed for Watkins Glen, then he'll go east to Ithaca and Cornell University.

Sailboats skim silently over the shimmering blue, pristine water, a flock of swallows glides silently over the meadow. They turn on a dime, en masse, as though hitting an invisible wall. He feels the same way, hitting a wall. On his mind is Alan Crowe, the young man everybody loved, who was bludgeoned to death by one of a growing list of possibilities.

Did Alan anger the mafia because of his work on behalf of Negroes in the First Ward? Did he earn the wrath of super patriots because of his work with draft resisters? Is there a homophobic serial killer out there? A scorned lover? And how does Canada play into all this? Niagara Falls?

Outside of Watkins Glen, Baldwin is pulled over by a county sheriff's deputy. He seems to have emerged from behind a tree blind and followed Baldwin for a mile or so, then turned on the bubble and tooted the siren. Not a long, drawn-out siren, just that little high-pitched "Whoop." Baldwin pulls well off the road on a gravel patch used by long haul drivers to eat lunch. It's littered with sandwich wrappers and paper cups. He rolls down his window, turns off the engine, puts both hands on the wheel.

The deputy starts off by asking Baldwin if he knows why he was stopped. Baldwin tells him no, he doesn't know why. He wasn't speeding and there were no stop signs, lights, or other rules to break. The cop asks for Baldwin's license, registration and proof of insurance, which he hands over, followed by his badge and ID. The deputy looks surprised and perturbed.

"Why didn't you say you're a lawman?" asks the deputy, handing everything back, not really looking at any of it but the ID, which tells him Baldwin is a detective. He does a double take on that. *A Black guy is a detective, in a big town, and I'm busy stopping poorly located Negroes and local, underaged teenagers with illegal beer?*

"My profession isn't why you pulled me over, is it?" replies Baldwin. "I didn't think it should matter."

"Yeah, well, I mean, you know, it's a professional courtesy," says the deputy. "We don't ticket brothers in blue."

"Just brothers," says Baldwin, as he puts everything back in his wallet and pockets. The cop doesn't get the pun, at first, then looks embarrassed, maybe a little defensive.

"Why did you pull me over?" asks Baldwin, though he knows the answer to that. DWB. Driving while Black. Not the first time. Baldwin wishes he had kept track of all the times he'd been pulled over for being a Negro where he shouldn't be.

The deputy blinks a few times, takes a step back and appraises Baldwin's car, a shiny green Plymouth Roadrunner. A muscle car with few rivals. Zero to a hundred in a heartbeat.

"We've had trouble with drag racing in this vicinity, on this stretch of New York 14. I just wanted to get some intel, take some names, have some leads if we get more reports, complaints. But that's not you, sir." He doesn't look convinced of his own explanation. "Drive safe, have a nice day."

He gives Baldwin what looks like a salute and retreats to his car. In his rearview mirror, Baldwin sees him take what looks like a deep breath. He lets the cop pull out and pass him by before getting back on the pavement and continuing on to Cornell.

Baldwin had set up a meeting with Michael McGee at his fraternity house, Delta Phi Psi, on a tree-lined street bordering the main campus. All of the sprawling stone mansions are fraternity or sorority houses, one after the other, dating to the late-nineteenth, early twentieth century. They look stately, left over from a previous, more genteel past. Stained glass windows, tall double oak doors, stone arches holding up carports, or what would have been buggyports when built. Inside are oak paneling, teak chair rails, tasteful wallpaper, music rooms with grand pianos, Persian carpets, dark-stained bookcases stuffed with volumes that haven't been read in many decades, if ever.

Within all that grandeur today are raucous beer parties laced with pot and other illegal substances, music by the Stones and the Grateful Dead bellowing out of Bose speakers the size of refrigerators, dizzy girls donated by the sororities, and crazy drunken games involving diving out of second floor windows into blankets pulled taught by rugby players. Most of that will start shortly after Baldwin leaves, but the pot smoking has already begun. Baldwin catches a whiff as soon as he opens his car door in the crushed stone parking area out front.

Michael McGee waits for him on the top step of a wide granite staircase that leads to the front foyer. He looks like the consummate Ivy Leaguer. He's handsome, tall, broad shouldered and narrow waisted. Auburn hair with a Princeton cut: a Bobby Kennedy look. He's wearing a blue button-down dress shirt, khaki trousers, and a red windbreaker with the words "Cornell Swimming" stitched over the left breast. He bounces down the steps in his penny loafers and extends a hand to Baldwin.

"Michael," he says.

"Tom," says Baldwin, wanting to keep it friendly, informal.

"I thought we could talk in the garden," McGee says.

"That would be fine," says Baldwin.

McGee leads him around the side of the manse, following a blue slate path framed with ivy and cedar. It smells wonderful. In the back, an expanse of terraced lawn steps down towards Cayuga Lake off in the distance. A powerboat the size of an ant speeds along, leaving a wake behind.

The grounds are idyllic. Stone benches here and there under oak and maple trees. Clumps of lilac bushes that would be blooming purple or white in the spring. A small orchard of apple trees that are hung heavy with green fruit, ripening in a month or so. It feels like they're above it all and could launch themselves over it if they wanted. They land at a round stone patio ringed with flowers past prime, yellowed, begging to be thinned. They sit on a low red brick retaining wall. The cobblestones at their feet are littered here and there with cigarette butts, a crushed beer can.

"You said you were investigating Alan Crowe's murder."

"Yes," says Baldwin.

"How can I help with that? We were competitors in high school. Then, he went one way and I came here."

"Well, that's why," lies Baldwin. "I'm looking for suspects. Motives, means, opportunities. I am looking for any reasons at all why someone might want to hurt Crowe. I thought, competition?"

"Okay, but swimming?" says McGee. "It's a sport. Somebody wins, somebody loses, everybody moves on to the next meet. Nobody kills over it. Besides, he stopped swimming years ago."

"Maybe, I hope you're right. But let's explore it for just a minute," says Baldwin. "You two had many of the same competitors. He can't tell me about them, but you can. Was anybody who you and he swam against, were any of them crazy? Vengeful? Did he ruin anybody's life?" Baldwin hopes that McGee will reflect on himself and maybe his father, because the question was intended to apply.

McGee weighs his answer, looking at the butts on the ground in front of him. He sticks his shoe out and crushes one of them into a smudge of tobacco and mangled rolling paper. "Swimmers are pretty chill athletes, compared to, let's say, football players," says McGee, quietly. "None of us are going to make a living at it." He smiles to himself. "Well, maybe as lifeguards or high school coaches. That's about it."

"So, nothing at stake, really," says Baldwin.

"Well, in my case, I get accolades, trophies, write-ups in the paper, All-American honors, maybe a spot on the Olympic team. That's not nothing."

"But what you're saying is a swim meet doesn't rise to the level of murder."

"No, it doesn't," says McGee. He targets another butt with his other foot. Baldwin lets a moment pass.

"Nobody would've killed Crowe because he beat them," says Baldwin, more as a statement than a question.

"No. Just about impossible. Can't imagine it," says McGee, quietly. If nothing else, these questions seem to be forcing McGee to imagine a dead Alan Crowe. A sadness descends on McGee. He folds his hands between his knees. Another pause. Longer this time.

"What about the emotional side of things. Was Alan Crowe close to anybody? Did he hurt anybody's feelings because of that?"

The question catches McGee off guard. Baldwin watches as he shrinks into himself slightly. His shoulders rise up while his head slumps down, like a turtle in a defensive posture. There is a long silence that, by itself, suggests that they were close, and he was hurt.

It takes McGee a full minute to answer. "Yeah." He wipes a tear that forms under his eye. He uses his whole palm. "We were close."

"He was a good friend," says Baldwin. Not a question.

"Yeah." A cough, another tear.

"More?" asks Baldwin.

McGee glances over at Baldwin, perhaps debating whether he can or should trust this man. Should he come clean? Would it help with the investigation? Can he help catch Alan's killer? He reaches a decision, looks off into the surrounding trees.

"Yeah…yes. We were more than friends."

A long moment passes

"I am aware of Alan's orientation. His friend Fiona told me. She mentioned you, too. So, thank you for your honesty," says Baldwin. "It must be very difficult."

McGee hangs his head and begins to sob quietly. He puts his face into his hands.

"We were far more than friends, but it ended suddenly and badly," says McGee. "I had such feelings for him, and he did too, for me. I wanted to shout this out to the world, to tell everybody and to hell with them if they don't approve."

"Alan, not so much," says Baldwin.

"No," says McGee, quietly and sadly. "He had ambitions and goals, and coming out like that would fuck it all up. I was selfish, I see that now. I made some threats, hoping to keep him, but that is no way to keep a love going. I see that now."

McGee retreats into his memories, some of them torture him.

Baldwin feels compassion for this man. Baldwin can see that this admission, this coming out, even this sadness is therapeutic. If something good results from this trip to Cornell, this is it.

A minute passes. McGee looks over at him. "I wanted to go to his funeral." There's another tear in his eye that he wipes away.

"But…?"

"I was dissuaded," says McGee.

"Why? By whom?"

"My dad."

"Why?"

"He said it wouldn't be a good look."

Baldwin tries to unpack that remark.

"The only reason he would have thought that is if he knew, or suspected, that you and Alan were more than competitors and more than friends. Does he know that?"

"He has known about my homosexuality for about a year, has suspected it for much longer. He could see that I had no interest in girls back in high school. Couldn't figure it out. They were throwing themselves at me. He told me I should have fucked all of them."

"Did he know about Alan?'"

"Yes, because I told him."

"How did that happen?"

"He confronted me. Subjected me to his 'faggot' tirade after I lost an event to a guy at Brown. My only loss that year," says McGee. "I was just sick of it. A whole life of that shit. It would take too long to go through the whole thing but basically, I told him I am queer. I asked him how that makes him feel, that his son is both gay and an All-American. He's straight and is a nothing. An angry, loud-mouth asshole. Somewhere in there I told him that Alan is also a gay man who has made something of himself. I told him that's what I love and admire about Alan. I told him Alan is a role model for all of us, meaning gay men."

"How did your father react?"

"He told me I was a liar. He said I was just getting back at him, that he could not have a son like that. As usual, he made it about himself."

"Did he ever say anything about Alan, after you told him about your admiration for him, and him being gay?" asks Baldwin, holding his breath.

"He just said something like 'I always knew it. I just knew it.'"

Baldwin believes this is a key piece of the puzzle. Here is someone who knew about Alan's homosexuality and who cared one way or the other: Brian McGee.

"Did he say anything else?"

"Mumbled something about straightening Alan out."

"How did that sound to you?" asks Baldwin.

"Ominous," says McGee, as he looks back at Baldwin, again with a tear rolling down his cheek.

"When was this?"

"January."

"Eight, nine months ago. Any change in his attitude towards you since then?"

"Stopped calling, stopped coming to my meets. Then, he calls me when they found Alan's body, when it was in the news. He told me to stay away from the funeral.

Baldwin will write all of this down as soon as he gets back to his car. Brian McGee is shaping up as a potential suspect based on motive, means and opportunity.

96

"Is your father capable of harming anyone?"

"You mean, could he have killed Alan? Gone after him for being gay, for being my boyfriend?"

"Yes."

"I always thought he was just a narrow-minded blowhard, but now, I think, maybe it is possible. The two events are just too close together to be unrelated, you know what I mean? He finds out about me and Alan, then Alan is dead. I can't get the idea that my father might have killed Alan out of my mind."

Baldwin puts his hand on McGee's shoulder.

"This was difficult for you, Michael. Thank you," Baldwin says.

"Where is he buried?" asks Michael.

Baldwin tries to remember, then does. It's appropriate. "Saint Michael the Archangel Cemetery, in West Seneca."

"I'll go there," says Michael.

It has turned out to be a blessed day, thinks Baldwin.

On Wednesday morning, after he had taken a brisk walk in his neighborhood, checked in with the detachment, answered some phone calls and left some instructions for his men, Inspector Henri Paquette drives up to Toronto to speak with Quincy Taylor, the draft dodger. Taylor had agreed to meet him at a coffee shop on Baldwin Street, just a block from his job at Mount Sinai Hospital. They'll have an hour or so together before Taylor starts his shift in the radiology lab.

It's a two-hour drive through St. Catharines, then Hamilton, Mississauga and past the airport. Nearly all of it industrialized. Ships are lined up behind locks in the Welland Canal, the one that put the Erie Canal out of business once and for all. Railroad lines choked with freight trains, warehouses, medium-sized manufacturers and weedy lots filled with tractor trailers line the route. The final few blocks are a misery of cars and buses headed for downtown or flooding up towards the University of Toronto, but he gets to the coffee shop early.

It's crowded with young people, leaning over their espressos and inhaling their cigarettes. Everybody seems to have a book or two in front of them. A few are open to a page. Conversations are lively, peppered with laughter or well-aimed intellectual jabs. Everybody seems to be talking about important issues. World affairs, politics, scientific discoveries. Two young men with coke-bottle lenses argue about the best way to code something for a computer and draw flow diagrams for each other on a napkin.

Just as Paquette walks in two women abandon their table, which is actually a large wooden industrial cable spool, and he grabs one of the seats and puts his briefcase on the other. Most of the patrons ignore him, but a couple look at him as though trying to place him. Physics? Intermediate German?

A waiter takes his order, which includes a croissant with elderberry jam. Pairs well with French roast. A few minutes later, a young Black man in hospital scrubs pokes his head in, looks around, and zeros in on Paquette, who gives him a little nod towards his briefcase.

Quincy smiles and walks over, offers his hand. "Quincy Taylor," he says. He's about twenty, medium height and build, a light-skinned Black. Besides his hospital scrubs, he's wearing a hair net, probably to contain an afro. Paquette notices he has tiny earrings. Itty bitty pearls. He smiles easily and looks relaxed and at ease. Paquette gets it. He's eight hundred kilometers from Fort Dix and they can't touch him.

"Henri Paquette, Mr. Taylor. Thank you for taking the time to meet me." He discreetly shows Taylor his credentials. No need to freak out the other guests.

Quincy looks at the waiter and points to himself. The server nods and puts in an order for whatever is Taylor's regular.

"I hope this is alright, Inspector, but I asked someone to join us."

"Who?"

"He's my sponsor here," says Quincy. "That's not an official title or anything like that, It's just that he helps me get through the settlement issues. Where to live, work, do the paperwork so I can stay."

"I suppose that would be fine, then," says Paquette. "He might have some other answers for me. Is he on his way?"

Quincy smiles and turns towards a group of young men huddled around another table, sipping coffees. He crooks a finger and a tall, thin, long-haired thirty-year-old rises and walks over, carrying his cup. He extends a hand to Paquette.

"Rory Temple," he says, and Paquette introduces himself. Temple borrows an unused chair from a nearby table and sits on it backwards, arms leaning on the back. His knees almost reach the top of the spool, and one of them bounces up and down with that nervous tiptoe tik that some people have. When he sees Paquette watching it dance, he looks embarrassed and puts a hand over it. *Stop already!*

"Can you tell me a little about yourself, Mr. Temple?" asks Paquette. "It'll help me know what I can ask of you."

"I'm a doctoral candidate at the university, in philosophy," says Temple. "I am a member and volunteer with TADP. That's how Quincy and I became acquainted." He looks at Taylor and smiles.

"What's that?" Paquette thinks he has heard of it, but his work rarely gets him to Toronto, and so far, has not involved this mass migration of Americans. Maybe he saw it referenced in a police report or the news but didn't pay any attention.

"Toronto Anti-Draft Program. We are Canadians, mostly, who help men like Quincy acclimate to their new surroundings. We publish the Manual for Draft-Age Immigrants, a kind of how-to for men contemplating the move. I work on that when I can."

"I read it," says Taylor. "It convinced me I could do this and that's why I'm here." After a moment of contemplation, he adds, "And not wading through a rice paddy in Vietnam."

Paquette nods, asks if they mind him taking notes and they say no, go ahead. He reaches into his briefcase and removes a composition notebook and a pencil. He spends a minute scratching in what's happened so far.

"I appreciate both of you taking the time to speak with me," says Paquette. "I want to start by assuring Mr. Taylor that he is not in any trouble with the law. Not here. I am assisting an American investigation of a murder, of a young man from Lackawanna. There may have been two others. All three deaths involve men who may have been attempting to immigrate to Canada for the same reason you did, Mr. Taylor."

At the mention of murder, Temple's knee begins bouncing again and at the mention of Lackawanna, Taylor's eyes expand to the size of cup saucers. He may have thought, could that have been me?

"Murder?" asks Temple.

"Yes, I'm afraid to say," says Paquette. "No doubt about it. His body was found in the Niagara River, and the other two dead men as well. We don't know if they, like you, were resisting the draft and attempting to immigrate. We are checking on the third. Two came from distant states but died in the river. You may have some information that will help us solve the murder case, or at least give us a better understanding of the world in which this victim worked, people he may have known."

Temple says, "Quincy?"

Taylor nods and so does Temple. "Ask us whatever you want."

"Let's start with our victims," says Paquette. "All three are Americans, in their twenties, all found in the river below the Falls. In fact, all three went over the Falls. If they were known to you, that would be one more."

"What were their names," asks Temple.

"Dominic Styron, Jaime Roesler and Alan Crowe." says Paquette, and he studies their faces to see any sign of recognition.

Temple shakes his head at the cable spool, but Quincy looks at Paquette with those saucer eyes.

"Alan," is all he says.

"You knew him?"

"If you're Black in Lackawanna, you know Alan," says Taylor. "He was working for us on the housing project and everything else. Voting, education, criminal justice."

"Did you know him personally?"

101

"I shook his hand, made some small talk. He came to our church with a few other white kids who talked to us about what we could do, how we could organize, like that."

"About the draft?"

"No sir, about civil rights."

"Do you know if Mr. Crowe was active with draft resisters, helping them get across the border?"

"No, no idea. I didn't ask him for help and he didn't offer any."

"What about Styron and Roesler? Know them? Hear about them?"

"Nope," he says, shaking his head. "I got a ride across the bridge, said all the right things to the badge at the border, wound up here. Thanks to the manual." He glances at Temple and actually winks. "I didn't see or talk to any other Americans before or during my trip. Nobody doing what I was doing. So no, not those guys."

"But someone drove you across?"

"Yes."

"Can you tell me who?"

Taylor looks at Temple who gives the slightest head shake.

"Sorry."

"When was that?"

"January."

"What about you, Mr. Temple?"

"I don't recognize the names, but I'm just one of dozens of people who assist men who intend to cross," he says. "I could check with the office and call you. Somebody might know them."

"How exactly do you help draft resisters who cross the border? When and where does your help begin?"

"I assume that this information does not reach American law enforcement?" asks Temple.

"It won't," replies Paquette. "I want to know what Styron and Roesler might have experienced crossing the border, if that's what they were doing when they died."

"If they were trying to cross, and had done their homework, they would have known that they would not have been denied entry into Canada by Canadians," says Temple. "Answer a few questions at customs the right way, and you're in. However, the Americans have set up a net on their side of the border to interdict draft dodgers, those who have been drafted but do not intend to report. They rely on people to inform on draft dodgers, their own surveillance, stop and question procedures. Anything that works."

"Where do you come in?" asks Paquette.

"We advertise our services in campus newspapers, even radio, in the U.S. I heard that our phone number has turned up in lids of pot. Word of mouth works as well. Quincy here has already contacted a few of his friends who may come up here and join him," explains Temple. "Generally, they contact us and we coach them on what to do at the border, what to say. We can provide them with transportation to Toronto if they need it, arrange for a pickup in Canada. Usually, Niagara Falls."

"They get across the border on their own?"

"We can't help with that, but there are groups on the American side that help when necessary. We are allied with the Popular Democratic Movement, PDM, over there."

"They might provide transportation?"

"Yes, they probably do when somebody asks," says Temple. "But, Inspector, a draft resister could just take a tourist bus to get across the border."

Paquette looks at Quincy. "Mr. Taylor, somebody gave you a ride across the bridge. Then what?"

"My ride took me to Niagara Falls and left me with a man there." He looks at Temple who shakes his head slightly. "I can't tell you where that was or who that was, but I went there and he picked me up. He drove me to Toronto and he brought me to the people who have helped me ever since."

Paquette processes all of this. American draft resisters and dodgers get across the border in a myriad of ways, and the smart ones connect directly with the TADP people who guide them here.

"What happens to men who don't know about you," asks Paquette. "The ones who just cross the border with their fingers crossed?"

"In my experience, ninety percent of the time, they luck out," says Temple. "They ask around in Niagara Falls, to young people who look like them, and they get directed to here."

Quincy nods, but Paquette wonders about the other ten percent.

Paquette slides business cards across the spool to both of them. Temple clicks a ballpoint and writes Crowe, Roesler and Styron on the back of the card. It looks to Paquette like he'll check on those men.

"Are there other Canadian organizations or individuals who might be assisting immigrants? Anybody else who these men might have contacted?" Paquette asks.

"Yes," says Temple, "on both sides of the border. All kinds of ad hoc groups, activists, people who make one trip over the border with a war resister in the back seat."

"Any of these groups have a name, or a contact person? Maybe a phone number?"

"I can help you with the Canadians, but I'm sorry, not the Americans. They could get in very big trouble down there," says Temple.

"I fully understand," says Paquette. He spins his notebook around and pushes it towards Temple, who jots down the names of three organizations in Toronto that help resisters. He looks to the ceiling in thought, then adds a phone number to one of them.

"If you walk around this neighborhood, you'll see many American newcomers," says Temple. "They've settled in for good, bought houses, opened businesses, started classes at the university. It's regarded as an American ghetto. There are message boards everywhere with those groups offering help, and individual Americans looking for each other. It's probably what you would have found in European cities after the war ended. You might find something."

"That's an excellent idea," says Paquette.

"Four block radius," adds Taylor. "I search around myself."

Temple agrees to check the victims' names with others at the TADP office. He knows that everyone will be shocked and on high alert about the possible murders. Everybody will be more vigilant about who they communicate with and share information. Taylor checks his watch and gulps his coffee. Off to the radiology lab. Paquette pays the tab for everybody, gathers his things and decides to walk around a little, look for those message boards.

Like Temple said, the neighborhood is bustling with the new arrivals. They appear to be mixing with and blending in well with the longtime residents, who are mostly aging Jewish merchants and young Asian families. They are bringing businesses back to life, rehabbing older houses, opening craft and art galleries. Paquette passes three different publishing establishments with their products displayed in the windows. Young men, whom he supposes are Americans, quickstep past with places to go, Army surplus ammo bags slung over their shoulders, now holding books. A small group of them press by carrying musical instruments in cases. By the shapes, two guitars and a violin. One of them laughs and shakes a tambourine.

Paquette sees that there are message boards on almost every main intersection, and he stops and scans them. Apartment rentals, job postings, legal assistance, teach-ins at the university, items for sale, items needed. Somebody is starting a farming commune north of the city and is looking for joiners. And here and there a personal message: Davey T, contact your parents, GP sick, or Barbara the blond looking for hunk from LA. Contact me at Amex.

Three long blocks later a message stops him cold. Stapled to a telephone pole and partially obstructed by other postings is a handwritten note: *Jaime R where are you? Come to the yellow ford truck. Grant.* The note looks forlorn, like it could be weeks or even months old. Rain has caused the "i" in Jaime to become a teardrop. He doesn't know if that's Jaime Roesler, and he doesn't know what or where the yellow ford truck is, but he knows he better find out.

He decides to call his office and tell them he's going to spend the day in Toronto, but when he does, they tell him he should hurry back. Another body has washed up in the Niagara River, just below the Falls.

Inspector Paquette drives back to Niagara Falls in a daze. He can't remember what he saw or did along the way. His mind is riveted on the fact that after twenty-five years as a Mountie, with not a single homicide, he might now have four. Constable Papineau back at the detachment had little information about the new body, except that it is a male, white, and about twenty-five. The body was found in the gorge below the Falls. He hadn't been given any other information from the recovery team or the coroner's office. Paquette heads straight for the morgue and arrives at four.

Silas Griffin again meets him near the back entrance and escorts him to the examination room. As before, the body is on the stainless-steel table under bright lights, except this time he is naked. Griffin has not started the autopsy, but has cleaned the body, revealing the myriad of bruises, scratches, gouges, and broken bones the young man sustained while hurtling over the Falls and then driven with enormous force into the rocks below.

He and Griffin stand next to each other, looking at the mangled mess on the table.

"Every time I examine a body that has gone over the Falls," he says to Paquette, "I hope he or she was dead already."

"Why's that?"

"It takes about five seconds to hit the rubble at the bottom, propelled into it at eighty pounds per square inch. About the same as getting hit by a bus at fifty kilometers per hour. I cannot imagine the horror of those last five seconds, knowing what they would know."

"What do you know about him?" asks Paquette.

"My assistant went through his clothing," says Griffin. "No identification at all. Everything we know about him is from what we see on the table."

"His belongings might tell us something," says Paquette. "Where he shopped, what his style was, sizes, like that."

"I'll have my assistant do that," says Griffin, and he walks over to a side door, peeks his head in and says something to whoever is on the other side.

He comes back and says, "In progress. Ten minutes tops."

"And the body?"

"Dead about two days."

"Drowned?"

"Yes, there is water in his lungs. Just about all the damage we see is post-mortem. He drowned, then went over the Falls."

"What do you know so far?"

They both can see the man had longish hair and a mustache.

"Twenty to thirty years old. You can see he's white. He wore glasses, you can see the indents on the bridge of his nose. Perfect teeth, not even a filling, which would suggest some privilege. Maybe dental records will identify him. He was about five-ten, one-seventy-five. While I was cleaning him, I did find this," says Griffin, as he rolls the body slightly to expose his upper left arm. On it is a small tattoo, maybe the size of a coffee cup. It's a peace symbol with the letters R, C and T, O in the four pie slices. "Does this mean anything to you?"

Paquette does some quick processing. That inner light goes on.

"Yes, maybe," says Paquette. "I was just up in Toronto, near the university. I was exploring the neighborhoods and saw many references to Rochdale College fastened to telephone poles and hung in windows. Based on the nature of the postings, it is a new-age student enclave of some sort. This ink might have something to do with the college: Rochdale College, Toronto, Ontario. Perhaps he was a student or faculty."

"Could be. I wonder what he was doing down here?" adds Griffin.

"I'll have to find out who he was, first. Can you make his face somewhat presentable? Have a picture taken?"

"I can take one right now. I use a Polaroid. Standard practice these days," says Silas.

"Take one of his face and another of the tattoo, please."

Griffin cleans the face again and combs the hair back. There are deep abrasions that he can't do anything about and one cheekbone is higher than the other in a disconcerting way, but anyone who knows this man will probably recognize him. Griffin takes the photos, including one of the man's face wearing Griffin's glasses. He and Paquette each fan the Polaroids in a useless attempt to speed up the developing process. They both stop now and then to see how it's going. Finally, Griffin looks at the photo of the face and says, "It turned out good."

At that moment the assistant, a young man who is probably doing his residency here, emerges from the back room. He has a clipboard and he is pulling his glasses down as he approaches.

"Here's what I found among the deceased's belongings," he says, and proceeds to list each item and its size, color or pattern, brand, and level of wear. He was thorough.

The information doesn't distinguish the victim from anybody else his age in the U.S. or Canada. Levi jeans, a flannel work shirt from Sears, one Converse sneaker, a gym sock, a garden variety braided leather belt. He wore white Fruit of the Loom underwear. Paquette thinks to himself, *like me*. But what is telling, to Paquette, is that he didn't wear a watch or any jewelry. Unusual for a generation that often wears beads, friendship bracelets and so forth. Paquette thinks the boy may have been murdered, then stripped of identifiers to make his job tougher, if not impossible. If he was killed, the murderer didn't see the tattoo under his sleeve. That tattoo might be the only clue they'll ever have. Unless the teeth have a story.

Paquette leaves with the Polaroids. Griffin will take many more as the autopsy progresses. Or maybe that's the assistant's job.

Paquette drives to his detachment office, pours himself a cup of day-old coffee, which smells like charcoal and tastes worse, and settles in behind his desk. He finds the contact information for Rory Temple and dials him up. He doesn't know how late the activists work in Toronto but imagines that they don't wait very long before lighting a pipe of something. Surprisingly, a young lady picks up after one ring.

"I'm calling for Rory Temple," he says.

The line goes quiet for a couple seconds and he can hear her call out, "Rory, it's for you!"

Paquette can hear some mumbling and what sounds like feet clomping hard on a wooden floor approaching the phone.

"Hello?"

"Rory? It's Inspector Paquette. Do you have a minute for me?"

"Yes, sure, I was going to call you," says Temple. "I checked on Styron and Roesler."

"And?"

"So far, no one here at TADP has heard of either one," says Temple.

"What about Crowe?"

"Same. But someone in the Buffalo area, Lackawanna, who might be PDM, is actually a resource person for us across the bridge."

"What does that mean?" asks Paquette.

"It means that if we get contacted by a man who wants to immigrate, we might have them contact that person for any assistance he may need on the U.S. side of the border. Like a ride across the border, money, brief housing stay, bus ticket. Whatever."

"I assume the resource person was not Alan Crowe, and that you cannot provide me that person's name?"

"I am afraid not, Inspector. We must keep those people secret. They could get into big trouble in the States," says Temple. "But I'm telling you this in case Mr. Crowe was somebody else's resource person. In case he was killed because he helped war resisters immigrate."

Paquette imagines Temple is sitting there, rapidly bouncing his knee up and down.

"Thank you, and you're right. The police down there are trying to find a motive for someone to kill him, and that could be one. Did any of your people ever meet your resource face to face?"

"No," says Temple. "He or she was just a voice on the phone to us. But several arrivals mentioned them to people here, saying they did this or that and helped them get to Canada."

"Interesting," says Paquette. "Can you continue to ask around about Crowe? Can you ask the resource person if they knew Crowe, the next time there is contact with them? And Styron and Roesler, for that matter? Call me if anything comes up."

"Yes, I will," says Temple. "We all will."

"I called with something else," says Paquette, gravely. "Bad news, I'm afraid."

"Oh?"

"Another body was recovered under the Falls," he says. "Another young man."

"Oh my God," says Temple.

"We may have trouble identifying him, because he carried nothing," says Paquette. "But we have his picture and he had a distinctive tattoo." Paquette goes on to describe the body and the tattoo, and his hunch that it might have some connection to Rochdale College.

"I know a lot of men who look like that. I'll have to see his picture. And you may be right about Rochdale being the inspiration for that tattoo," says Temple. "Rochdale is a brand-new college housed in a single building that all its students and most of the faculty live in. It is a giant communal living and educational experiment. They are all politically and socially active."

"A place where someone would tattoo a peace symbol on his arm?"

"Absolutely," says Temple. "I wouldn't be surprised if they all did."

"If I drove up tomorrow with the pictures of the victim, could you show me to Rochdale and introduce me to the people there?"

"Yes," says Temple. "Meet me at the coffee shop and we can walk up from there. Noon?"

"Yes, noon. One more question, Mr. Temple, do you know anything about a yellow ford truck in the Baldwin Street area?"

Temple says, "It's an art and craft store and head shop. Features local artists and First Nation's handicraft."

"Can we go there, too?"

"Yes, of course, it's along the way."

After they hang up, Paquette studies the photos of the new victim and wonders, *what did you do to deserve this?*

On Wednesday evening, James Plishka transforms himself from police chief to WWII veteran. He dresses down, jeans and a polo, and drives his '65 Ford Galaxy instead of the official LPD Buick to the VFW Post in East Aurora. From his home in Orchard Park, it's a straight shot east on 20A, a two-lane highway dotted with farms between the two villages. Here and there a harvest stand featuring cabbage, carrots, apples and other late summer crops. He tells himself to make this trip again, when he can shop.

VFW Post 947 is housed in a turn-of-the-century, Craftsman-style, former funeral home on Main Street in the quaint village. A large, three-story affair with massive shaved-stone pillars holding up the wrap-around porch. It's a handsome old mansion on a street lined with them. Most have been converted to commercial purposes. A restaurant, an art gallery, a furniture store. But here and there the original owners are still nursing the rhododendrons and hostas. Some of them using walkers or wheelchairs to dribble water on the seedlings.

Plishka parks among the couple dozen cars and pickups, and one motorcycle, in the rear lot. Every night at the Post is happy hour, but Wednesday is also bingo, and there's prize money at stake, so the crowd is healthy. He hopes Harry Johnson and Daniel Fredricks are part of that.

The game started an hour ago. This is probably the fifth round. It's held inside the main viewing room from mortuary days. Most of the thirty or so guys and their wives are seated four to a table, which on many nights are for poker or bridge. Four men with cigars are filling the room with secondhand smoke. Several others are chain smoking Marlboros and Lucky Strikes. No one seems to mind. The place has twelve-foot ceilings and the blue fumes curl to the upper reaches, then dissipate.

Off to the side is a platform, which at one time propped up a coffin, now with the game host. Tonight, it's somebody's wife who pulls a ping-pong ball out of a big bucket and calls the letter and number into a microphone. She tries a joke or two between calls. "I 21" would be followed by "I only wish I still was, boys, you'd all be buying me a drink."

Each player has three or four bingo cards in front of them with two or three letters on each already dabbed in blue. Somebody will win soon and use the five bucks to treat his table to a fresh pitcher of Schlitz. Plishka buys three cards for a quarter each from the octogenarian out front, whose name tag says Benson. Benson winks at him and wishes him luck. Plishka fills out a name tag and sticks it to his shirt. He'll play next round.

He scans the hall and finds a table with only three players and joins them. Everybody spares a second to nod hello. One says, "What's up?" Another says, "Evening."

The housewife up on the dais says, "B 14." A moment later a goofy-looking guy across the room yells, "Bingo!" followed by a rumble of good-natured moaning from the rest.

"Second time he won tonight," says a tablemate, a wiry fifty-year old whose nametag says Trance. He pours himself another beer from the pitcher. "What are the odds?"

"Well, so far, one hundred percent," says a twinkle-eyed Irishman named Devine. He is a septuagenarian, could have fought in the Great War or the second, or both. "You look familiar," he says to Plishka. "Or maybe your name is."

"I've been in the paper a few times," says Plishka, as he spreads out his game cards. If they don't know why, he'll be happy with that.

"That could be it," says Devine, "but your name goes back a ways. Were you a ball player, back in the forties?"

"St. Stan's," says Plishka. "Shortstop."

"I was the coach at St. Mary's in Lancaster," says Devine, with a big smile. "I remember you now. How could I forget? You hit three homers off three different pitchers against us in the championship game. 1941. War Memorial Stadium. Seven thousand fans for a high school game, most of them to see you. You were like what, sixteen?"

"Seventeen," says Plishka. He squirms a little in his seat, slightly embarrassed. "We had a good team, top to bottom," is all he can say. He clears his throat, takes a sip of beer, stares at his bingo cards.

Recalling it brings up mixed memories. Plishka was All State, Mr. Baseball, batting champion, golden glove, could've gone pro. Was offered a contract by the Cleveland Indians after that game but got maimed on the beach at Normandy a few years later. He could barely walk for three years. He is a cop by default. The missed opportunity still haunts him.

Devine studies him for a second and senses Plishka's discomfort. "Listen, one of my players, from my team, he's here tonight. Maybe I can introduce you later," he says.

"Sure," says Plishka. "That would be nice."

At that moment, the microphone lady says the next game is about to start, and a second later says, "O 66." Plishka has that on two of his cards and dabs them with blue watercolor.

The third player at the table is named Boyle. Wide red face, waist pours over his belt in every direction. He reaches across the table and introduces himself to Plishka. "Army," he says. "You?"

"Same," says Plishka. "Europe?"

"I 19," says the mic. Plishka marks one card, then another. *I may get lucky.*

"Oh yeah," says Boyle. "Toured the continent with Patton. Got winged in Palermo in '43…"

"I 22," says the mic. Eyes go down to the cards. Trance got one. Devine, too. They dab away.

"Go home?" asks Plishka.

"Nah, patched up and sent back in time for the Bulge."

"B 4." Plishka has that twice. Dab. Dab.

Plishka looks at Devine and Trance. "What about you guys?"

"AAF," says Trance. "Pacific. Mechanic." He holds up his fingers to show a lifetime of grease under the nails. "Nobody flew without me," he adds.

"Navy," says Devine. "Bubblehead, Atlantic."

Plishka knows he was a submariner, and always wondered how those men survived the cramped, damp, claustrophobic life a hundred meters below the surface. He plans to ask Devine about that later.

"Nice to meet you all," says Plishka, and he means it. These are his people.

"G 60." All four are dabbing.

This goes on for several more bingo calls. More card dabbing. More dribs and drabs of service records, musters, discharges, decorations. Plishka decides it's a good time to segue into police work.

"I was hoping to see a friend of mine. Kevin Crowe? You might know him, Devine. Navy guy," says Plishka.

"N 42." More looking down, dab, dab.

"Crowe was on the surface," says Devine. "He was everybody's ride."

"Took Marines around," says Trance. "Dropped 'em off on atolls and islands."

"Sad thing," says Devine. "His son got killed." He looks around. "He's not here tonight, and I don't blame him."

"I heard about that," says Plishka. "That's why I was hoping to see Kevin."

"Murdered," says Devine. "Found in the Niagara River, crushed skull."

"O 71." Dab…dab.

"They were close, Kevin and his son. I wanted to offer my condolences," adds Plishka.

"It turns out the kid was a lefty," says Trance. "Antiwar, anti-establishment, you know the type. A radical. Probably a druggie. He must have broken Crowe's heart."

"N 35." Dab, dab...dab.

"So, maybe somebody killed him for his politics?" asks Plishka.

"If they did, they have a few million to go," says Boyle. "From what I see on TV, he wasn't a whole lot different from everybody else his age."

"B 11." Dab.

Plishka nods, takes a healthy swig of beer and wipes his lips. There's a bowl of chips on the table and he helps himself. *Where do I take this*, he wonders.

"N 43." Dab, dab. And Plishka realizes he just won.

"Bingo!" he calls out, and Devine reaches over and pats him on the back.

"You'll bring some luck to this table," he says.

"Or a pitcher of beer," says Boyle, looking at Plishka hopefully.

Plishka carries his card up to the dais and the VFW wife, whose nametag says Doris, checks it. Sure enough, he won, and she waves at Benson, who holds up a five-dollar bill. He summons Plishka over with an index finger. Plishka takes the cash and saunters over to the bar, where another wife is already pushing a full pitcher over to him. He slaps the five on the bar. He grabs the ice-cold jug with both hands and returns to the table. Waiting for him at his place are three more bingo cards and a hot dog. "Well, thank you, gentlemen," he says to the rest. "No, thank you," they say almost in unison. They all refresh their glasses.

The rest of the evening continues like this. Trance and Boyle have winners, too, and the lager keeps flowing. Plishka learns more about the Post, about a few more men, but not about Fredricks and Johnson. Whenever the conversation turns to the Vietnam war or the antiwar protests, his mates come across as patriotic and supportive of the war and conflicted about the antiwar movement.

They fought to defend everyone's freedom, including their right to be against the war, even to march and protest it. But disrespect those who go? Label them as murderers? Baby killers? Burn the flag? Vandalize government offices? They don't know where that kind of behavior comes from. "Who raised those people?" Trance asks. Kevin Crowe comes to mind, and Plishka has no answer. Then he asks himself, *where is Robert on all this?* His son must have an opinion, and they never talk about it. Maybe they should.

At around nine, bingo is over and everyone is packing up, saying final goodbyes, at least for tonight. Workday tomorrow, or maybe eighteen holes of golf for the retirees. Plishka thinks he'll come back just for the socializing. The room is filled with great stories and he only heard three of them. There are conversations, laughter, handshakes. Plishka can hear the Harley Davidson roar to life out in the parking lot. He sees Doris lean down and kiss a man in a wheelchair and swing around behind it to glide him out. Benson is counting the proceeds, making neat piles of twenties, tens, fives and ones. A woman whose hair looks like a Q-Tip, and who might be his wife, is counting up the change. There is a tap on his back and he turns.

"Plishka, this is your opponent from nearly thirty years ago," says Devine, with his hand on a guy's shoulder, gently guiding him towards Plishka. "My catcher, Dan Fredricks."

Lieutenant Abe Zubricky of the Buffalo Police Department had promised Detective Tom Baldwin down in Lackawanna that he'd put eyes on the mobster, Vincent Falco, on his behalf. What he didn't tell him is that he'd do it himself, since he had no budget or personnel to spare. Baldwin had told him that mafia types who may work for Falco have been interfering with city council decisions in Lackawanna. Attending meetings, controlling discourse, threatening attendees, one of whom turned up dead. Baldwin is looking for confirmation that they work for Falco.

So, on Wednesday evening, after a ten-hour shift during which he investigated a burglary, a car theft, two domestic abuse cases, another burglary and a hit and run that left a man in critical condition, Zubricky prepares to stakeout the Falco home. Maybe the mafia types will show up.

Zubricky is forty, short and round with curly black hair. Never married, but the shadchans at Temple Beth Israel were always trying to make a match for him and didn't give up even when he asked them nicely to please stop. He's married to his job, he told them. He's not good material for a traditional Jewish union. What he couldn't tell them, because they would never understand, is that he is hopelessly in love with Grace Slick, female front of Jefferson Airplane.

They thought that his devotion to work was even more reason to find him a wife. He could provide for her and the children. So, he threatened to stop attending services and they moved on to younger, more eager men. Zubricky reasons that there is plenty of time to have a family, but very little to catch all the criminals who are terrorizing his hometown.

Vincent Falco lives with his wife and two children in his father's former mansion in Elmwood Village, Buffalo's version of Beverly Hills. His father, Carmine Falco, as well as his mother, sister, the cook and a bodyguard had all been murdered there last year, and Zubricky had investigated. All the evidence pointed toward certain members of the Maglione crime family, the most powerful in Buffalo.

At the time, Stefano Maglione was expanding his operations and eliminating weaker rivals, including his own lieutenants, like Falco. Carmine became expendable. Maglione is still on trial, along with a half dozen associates, for these and other crimes, and his absence has allowed Vincent to assume his father's business operations. While he expands his control of drugs, prostitution, and loan sharking, the young Falco is also focused on dismantling the King Homes project in Lackawanna. Like his father before him, he considers it a threat to his legitimate home construction empire. Word on the street is that Falco has been recruiting new muscle from out of town to help.

Zubricky figures that all he really needs to do, at first, is monitor who comes and goes at Falco's house. Watch traffic in and out, jot down make and color, plate numbers, if possible, descriptions of occupants if he can see them. Relatively non-obtrusive and unnoticed.

Elmwood Village homes are huge, set way back from the winding streets, with manicured lawns, hundred-year-old elm trees, tall privacy hedges, stone walls. He parks his car two houses down, on the opposite side of the road. All he can see is the end of Vincent's driveway, which is flanked by tall stone pillars.

A few other parked cars are scattered on the block, so he doesn't stick out too much. Except the other cars, BMWs and Mercedes Benzes, look like they belong and his ten-year-old Rambler American does not. On his lap is a pair of large, powerful binoculars, the kind used by ships' captains during the war. In this case, a German U-boat. He can read the numbers on Falco's mailbox from a hundred yards away, but only one at a time. They completely fill the viewfinder. There's a streetlight right above the driveway. That'll help after the sun goes down.

He had brought along a thermos of coffee, a chicken salad sandwich, a box of raisins — which he is addicted to — and an empty liter coke bottle in case he has to pee. And he will. Like every other man his age, he has a prostate on a growth streak. On the seat next to him is a dog-eared novel he's been reading, a newspaper, and a notebook and pencil. He settles in at six sharp and waits.

Over the next two hours, eleven cars pass him going one way or the other, but nothing headed to or from Falco's house. These are mostly neighbors, in big new cars. Nobody takes notice of him, that he can tell. He manages to read several chapters in the book and all the sports pages before the sun goes down. At eight-thirty, an ice cream truck slowly creeps along the street with a calliope playing a loop. A Disney tune he can't quite place but won't be able to get out of his head. *Crap*, it will annoy him for days.

When the truck is one house away from Falco's, a large man whom Zubricky doesn't recognize walks down the Falco driveway holding the hands of two children. They look about six or so. Zubricky pulls up the binoculars to get a close look at the guy.

He zeroes in on the stranger. White, thirty-five, slicked-back black hair and long sideburns. Six-two, about two-twenty, muscular build. His nose looks like it was broken more than once. If the screenplay calls for a bodyguard or an enforcer, central casting will send him up. He could also play linebacker for the Chicago Bears. Zubricky does his best to memorize the face and promises himself to bring a camera next time.

The big babysitter buys the kids overloaded cones and gets one for himself. He then does his real job. He looks up and down the street that Zubricky is parked on. Luckily, he looks in the opposite direction first, and Zubricky is able to pull down the glasses and slouch out of view. He waits ten seconds, then inches up to watch the guy walk behind the kids back up the driveway. When Zubricky gets back to the station, he'll study the mug shots they keep and see if the giant was ever arrested in Buffalo for anything. Then he wonders if the FBI has his portrait. He's jotting down some notes and reminders to himself, when a black-and-white pulls up next to him.

Zubricky glances over and recognizes both Buffalo patrolmen who are looking at him: Mason and Schmitt. Mason rolls down his window and Zubricky does the same.

"Fancy meeting you here, Lieutenant," says Mason, grinning. Zubricky always disliked him. Snarky, lazy, corner-cutter.

"Likewise," says Zubricky. "What brings you to this country club?"

"A report that a possible pedophile is parked right where you are."

Zubricky is surprised. He thought he was pretty good at surreptitiousness, but he can understand why a citizen might have wondered about a middle-aged white guy with binoculars watching kids get ice cream. He glances around to see whose line of sight he might be in.

"I'm doing some surveillance," says Zubricky. "Done for the night. We should both vacate the premises. Don't want to get made."

"Maybe you already were," smiles Mason, and he and Schmitt burst out laughing. Mason rolls up his window and Schmitt pulls away with a bit of tire squealing.

Zubricky starts his Rambler and drives very slowly past the Falco estate. Standing on the driveway, twenty feet from the street under a lamp, is the babysitter. Arms crossed, eyes narrowed, lips pursed. He flips Zubricky off and holds the finger up until he's out of sight. *Well, my cover is blown*, thinks Abe. *I need a plan B.*

But just at that moment a black Cadillac passes him going the other way, towards Falco's house, and in his rearview mirror he sees it slow down, use its blinker, and pull in. He checks the time. 9:30 pm.

It takes him twenty minutes to reach the station, which is almost as busy as it was at noon. Buffalo comes alive after dark, with nocturnal bad guys and gals the predominant species. Night shift officers are either headed out or back in with a victim or a suspect in tow. You can't tell which because they are all bloody. Booking is busy with two scantily clad hookers, who are on a first name basis with the officer who brought them in. Both interrogation rooms are occupied. The staccato sound of typewriters, conversations on top of each other, phones ringing, doors clanging shut. The klezmer symphony of a chaotic law enforcement agency. Everybody manages to shut it out and get their jobs done, which is priority one. Done right is a bonus. Zubricky heads for the records office down in the basement.

"What do you need, sweetie?" asks Cheryl, the grandmotherly file clerk. She's been here, what, fifty years? Sixty? Must be. She is the corporate memory of every file of every crime and every criminal in Buffalo since Woodrow Wilson. She's a wispy, white-haired chain smoker. Rheumy eyes, false teeth that she clicks. A cigarette is always glued to her lower lip, off to one side. Nobody knows what she looks like or sounds like without it. And they don't know what they'd do without her.

"We have booking photos of known mafia?" asks Zubricky.

"Booking and surveillance. Organized by date, and then alphabetically."

"Can I have both, going back three years?"

"Who are we looking for? Got a when or a name? Would simplify things," she says. "Otherwise, you'll be looking at thousands of pictures."

"Nope," says Zubricky, "I just spotted this guy at Vincent Falco's house and want to find out if he has a history with us."

"What does he look like? Describe him to me."

Zubricky describes the babysitter/bird flipper as best he can, which is pretty good. A sketch artist could capture him perfectly.

"Three possibilities," says Cheryl. She turns and walks down an aisle between two rows of shelving. They're twice as tall as she is. Three-ring binders, cardboard file boxes, index cards with notations taped to empty spaces. She stops, takes two steps backwards, shrugs at something on a shelf, and keeps going. She reaches down and pulls a file box off the bottom shelf and carries it back to Zubricky.

"In this box, 1968, pull the file for Johnnie Tambourine. Not his real name, but the only one anybody knows him by, including us. I'll get the others."

Zubricky takes the lid off and sets it aside. The box is packed with people arranged in alphabetical order, last names first, first names last. These are all "T's," so Johnnie is right at the front. Zubricky pulls the file out and opens it on the countertop. Johnnie Tambourine is not his man, but damn close. Same size, same broken nose, but his hair is too thin and he's not as muscular. Looks flabby. He returns the file to the box just as Cheryl appears with another.

"Pull the file for Robert Golicki," says Cheryl, and she retreats back for the third candidate.

Golicki is halfway back in the box for "G's" in 1969. Again, the similarities are extraordinary. Cheryl has a gift. But it's not the babysitter. Golicki is a bit too short and his nose is jammed, but only once, up near the bridge. In the surveillance photo, he is busy punching out a rival in a parking lot somewhere on the westside. The Italian neighborhood, near the river. Some local hoods are watching appreciatively, like they're winning a bet. Zubricky wonders who the photographer is but knows why he didn't intervene. They all look like they'd kill you just for sport.

In Cheryl's third box, "C's" from 1967, she tells him to look for Dante Caruso. He pulls the file and looks at a picture he could have taken earlier tonight. That's him, that's the babysitter. No question. It's a photo taken of Caruso standing next to his car, looking off in the distance. The file has about a dozen surveillance photos, but no booking photo. He's never been arrested. But he isn't local, either. The notes say he appears now and then, apparently does some work for the capo, then returns to Atlantic City, where they imagine he comes from.

The organized crime unit, which has the highest turnover rate in the department, hasn't been able to associate his visits with any major crimes. Of course, if the mob thinned the herd or disciplined somebody in its ranks, nobody would complain or know about it. And that's what they usually bring outsiders in to do. Zubricky wonders if Caruso hit the Falco family last year, and if he did, why is he working for Vincent Falco today? *These people have no shame*, thinks Zubricky. Or maybe it's that *Art of War* thing: *Keep your enemies closer.*

At the bottom of the report are the names of Caruso's known associates. There are nine names, but two have been crossed out with the word "deceased" next to them. Three others have the word "Incarcerated." Zubricky jots down the names of the other four. He shows them to Cheryl.

"Got these boys in your collection?"

She looks at the list, spins around and heads down the aisle again. Returns with a fat three-ring binder.

"We got mug shots of them. They're local and have records," she tells him. "But two of 'em are in jail right now, awaiting trial. You want to look at these two. They're still doing crime out there." She underlines their names. Richard Paglia and Paul Stayton.

Zubricky finds them in the book. Both are in their forties, weather-beaten faces, hooded eyebrows, random pock marks, a scar, bored expressions. Stereotypical thugs.

"Can I have these?" he asks Cheryl, holding up the photos. The two mug shots and the cameo of Dante.

"Just sign these little releases," she says, sliding over slips of paper. Her cigarette bounces up and down on her lower lip while she says this.

Zubricky scribbles something on the papers. Cheryl slides them into some abyss under her counter. The twinkle in her eyes says that the paperwork is now nowhere.

Zubricky will show the photos to Baldwin, and he will see if these are the mafia types who attend and control the city council meetings in Lackawanna. But all he wants to do right now is get home, put on some Jefferson Airplane, listen to *White Rabbit*, and adore Grace Slick on the album liner notes.

At the VFW, Plishka and Fredricks shake hands with firm grips after Devine introduces them. They had probably shaken hands like this twenty-nine years ago after that championship game at the War Memorial. This time it's different. They aren't naïve, teenage baseball players competing for laurels, they're middle-aged husbands, fathers, war veterans. They have both been through a lot of life and their rivalry in 1941 is both a distant past and, in some ways, the fondest memory.

Fredricks is a little shorter than Plishka, maybe five-ten, and still has the athletic build of a high school jock. Muscular chest and biceps, flat stomach. Looks like he plays golf or tennis. Tanned arms and neck. He keeps his brown hair short and his facial hair shaved close. If Plishka had to guess, he spends a lot of time meeting strangers, whom he has to impress.

"Three home runs," says Fredricks, smiling. His teeth are perfect, and Plishka wonders if he had braces as a kid, or dentures now. "I was crouched down behind you for all of them. Watched them sail over that right field wall."

"It was the short end of the field," says Plishka, shrugging.

"Three different pitchers," says Fredricks, shaking his head in amazement. "And three different pitches. A fast ball, a slider and a curveball. You whacked them like they were teed up for you."

"Now you're embarrassing me."

"I heard back then that there was a Cleveland scout watching the whole thing. They offered you a contract right on the spot," says Fredricks. "What happened after that?"

"Normandy," says Plishka, pointing at his leg. He'd taken shrapnel while sprinting across the beach through German fire, and almost lost his leg. It took years to rehab.

"Well," says Fredricks, "you came home at least."

"That's how I see it, too," says Plishka. "Wanna sit down? Looks like the bar is still open."

"Till eleven," says Devine, the now overlooked coach. "I have to go home, take some meds and get some sleep. Deer season starts at dawn tomorrow. I'll catch up with you next week. Might have a twelve-point-buck story for you."

They all say their goodbyes and Devine heads for the door. Plishka and Fredricks grab a couple of stools at the end of the bar. There are three other vets leaning on the copper further down, watching a baseball game, probably the Yankees. The volume is low enough for everyone to carry on a conversation if they want. The three sports fans aren't, they're drinking boilermakers. The late-night bartender, Benson, raises his chin to inquire what they want. Fredricks orders a ginger ale and Plishka holds up two fingers.

"Where did you wind up, after high school?" asks Plishka.

"I graduated in June, after that game, and took a job at the Ford Stamping Plant. Five months later was Pearl Harbor and I enlisted, wound up in the AAF."

"In the air?"

"Tail gunner on a B-17," says Fredricks. "I invaded Europe feet first and on my belly when you were down below, on that beach."

Plishka laughs at that. It makes him remember that even though there were machine guns rattling away, bullets whizzing past, smoke and explosions and men screaming, and the sounds of the diesel engines of the Higgins boats motoring in, dropping troops, and pulling away, he did hear planes up above. He remembers looking up and seeing what looked like a thousand bombers heading inland over France. He remembers whispering, "Bomb the living fuck out of them." Now he's talking to one of the guys he sent that message to. *What a world we live in.*

"That was my twenty-fifth mission, so I was rotated out and spent the last year of the war doing mostly paperwork."

"Sweet," says Plishka.

"It got me started on my career. I liked it. I was in procurement, ordering supplies, working for the quartermaster," says Fredricks. "I got good with numbers, inventory, keeping books. When I got discharged, I tried to find similar work and did."

"What do you do now?"

"I sell Fords. Have my own dealership and repair garage. Ten employees."

"Wait a minute," says Plishka, "Do you own Fred's Fords, right down the street here?"

"That's me," says Fredricks.

126

"I bought my Galaxy from you five years ago," says Plishka, unable to control his grinning. "What are the chances? I mean, what a coincidence! Geez!"

They both laugh about that.

"Who was the salesman?" asks Fredricks.

"Bald older guy. Nice, soft-spoken."

"My father-in-law, Benny Toler."

"Yes, that's the one," says Plishka. "I don't want to rat him out, but I think he overvalued my trade-in."

"Happy with the car?" asks Fredricks.

"It's right out back," says Plishka as he thumbs towards the door.

"If you want to trade it in for a new one, we'll do the overvalue thing again."

They both laugh together. Plishka can sense a new friendship developing. He hopes so, because his life consists mostly of ordering one group of men around and arresting the other ones.

"So, you're married," says Plishka.

"Twenty-two years," says Fredricks. "Her name is Jan. She's the light of my life." He beams while saying it. Plishka can see that she is.

"Kids?" Plishka already knows about one.

A pall falls over Fredricks' face, and he glances quickly down at the bar. "We lost Dan junior in 'Nam. Six months ago."

"I'm so sorry to hear that," says Plishka softly.

"He was a beautiful kid," says Fredricks. He turns his head towards Plishka. "His picture in on the wall out front, along with all the others from this Post who have passed on. You'll see what I mean."

"I glanced at the board when I came in and noticed portraits of two young men, but I didn't look at the names."

"One is my Daniel, the other is Ron Johnson. Ronny. He's Harry Johnson's son."

"I didn't meet Harry, did I?"

"He's on a job right now, out of town. Probably back next week."

"Maybe then," says Plishka, hoping to meet the other possible suspect. Then he adds, "How old was Daniel?"

"Going on twenty."

"Drafted?"

"Yeah. Really low number in the lottery. Got called up almost immediately, went through boot, shipped out," says Fredricks. "Before we knew it, he was shipped back in a box. Everything happened so fast." He takes a sip of his ginger ale. The two men are silent for a minute.

"My son is still in high school," says Plishka, hoping to keep it going. "Robert. He's seventeen."

"Baseball player?"

"No," says Plishka with a small chuckle. "He takes after his mother. More the sensitive artistic type."

"What's her name?" asks Fredricks.

"She was Susan," answers Plishka. "Died of cancer nine years ago."

Quiet time, again. What can anybody say?

"We've both lost loved ones," says Fredricks. "To them!" He raises his glass to Plishka and they tap brims, guzzle them down. Benson appears and refills their glasses with Schweppes. Plops in a couple of ice cubes.

"I came here tonight hoping to see Kevin Crowe," says Plishka. "He just lost his son."

"We all heard about that," says Fredricks. "Murdered."

"Did you know him? He'd been about the same age as your boy."

"Same age but completely different, from what I heard."

"You mean, different towns, religions, circles of friends, like that?"

"Well, yeah, that stuff probably, but my Daniel was patriotic and brave. Crowe's kid not so much."

"I don't follow," says Plishka, though he most certainly does. In fact, he's leading this discussion.

"While Dan was in the Army, training, shipping out, getting shot to death in Vietnam, Crowe's boy, whatever his name, he was protesting the war, dodging the draft, insulting veterans, disrespecting the flag, and giving comfort to the enemy in the process. That's what I heard, anyway." Fredricks sounds bitter, but not full of rage. He doesn't sound like the guy who bashed Alan's head in, but who knows?

"I had no idea," says Plishka, shaking his head. From what he had learned about Alan so far, from his parents and from Baldwin, none of that was true. "I guess he made some enemies."

"There are guys here who say a fucking traitor," says Fredricks.

"Kevin Crowe's son? Do you think so?"

"If what they say about him is true, then, yeah. I can't stand watching the news anymore, seeing college kids with deferments marching around, safe and sound, while our boys go off and sacrifice everything to keep them safe."

"You don't think somebody from here, from the Post, would harm Crowe's boy, do you?"

"A lot of the men here would hate to be in the same room with any of those antiwar hippies. Me included."

"But murder one of them? A friend's kid?"

128

"I know some guys who say we need a few more Kent States," says Fredricks. "But to answer your question, no. Nobody here is crazy, insane. Nobody here would actually act on those feelings. We've all seen enough killing."

Plishka nods his agreement. *It's true, we have.*

Plishka has taken it about as far as he can on the first night. He has made contact, developed a rapport, learned a little about his possible suspect, and most of it points in another direction. But you never can tell. He looks down at his watch and expresses surprise.

"Oh geez," he says. "I gotta run. I'm sorry, have to pick up my son." He reaches out and shakes Fredricks' hand. "See you next week."

"Let's talk about you, next time," says Fredricks.

"We will! Lots to tell," says Plishka as he rushes out the door. *Like, for example, I'm a cop looking for Alan Crowe's killer.*

As he drives away, Plishka is conflicted. He thoroughly enjoyed socializing with his new brotherhood. It had been a very long time since he'd felt that close to men who were, for all intents, strangers. But they had all shared a common experience that altered the course of their lives. And even though they had wound up in different places, they all carry a gene that is awakened in warfare and nowhere else. The virtuous traits of that gene are brotherhood, loyalty, a sense of duty, a willingness to self-sacrifice, even the ultimate one. The recessive traits are anger, retribution, vengeance and a desire to cause the other guy to sacrifice. He resolves to find out if any of his new brethren exhibit the latter.

Gem awakens on Thursday morning to the sounds of Jamal snoring, a baby crying, Crosby, Stills, and Nash singing softly on a turntable next-door and the smell of coffee wafting up from the kitchen. She rubs the night crust out of her eyes and sits up. Looks around. *Oh yeah, this place. And I am Gemini, hitchhiking peacenik.*

She crawls off the mattress, throws the blanket over the sheets and pillow, and stretches. Bends left, then right. Touches her toes, leans back as far as she can, twists at the waist, does it again. She looks at Jamal. He's lying on his back on top of the bedding, mouth agape, fully clothed, still cutting Zs. She decides she can safely change out of her PJs. She digs around in her backpack and finds clean undies, fresh jeans and a tee, slips everything on and pulls up her high-tops. The fragrance of brewing coffee is a powerful, invisible siren, luring her down to the kitchen.

In the living room, bodies are strewn around haphazardly on mattresses or each other, like pins hit by a bowling ball. Snores, heavy breathing, an occasional cough or a humming sound assure her that they aren't dead. The detritus from last night's partying is everywhere. Wine bottles with cigarette butts floating in the remains, empty potato chip bags, candles burned down to a pool of wax, incense ashes forming long gray lines along a tabletop. A giant green glass hookah stands alone in the middle of the room, like an idol they had been worshiping. She creeps past and heads for the kitchen.

Aries is breastfeeding the now contented Arwen, sipping coffee, looking out at the daybreak through a dirty window. Gemini would like to get the house pressure-washed.

"Hi," she whispers, and Aries turns slightly to smile and nod.

"Morning, Gem," Aries replies, and turns back to her contemplation, while Arwen suckles contentedly.

Gem pours herself a cup of coffee from the percolator, lifts the cup with both hands and sips the magical juice slowly. She needs some enchantment this morning. Last night was intense. She replays it now that she is mostly sober.

The group had its gathering after dinner, reporting what they did, what they accomplished, what their plans are. It was impressive, and Gem actually felt a sense of pride for her new friends. She kept reminding herself that she is a cop, investigating a murder, and somebody here might have done the deed. And somebody else is FBI. She began to wonder, *what do I do if they're the same person?*

Jim, Amber and Amy had distributed a thousand fliers during an antiwar rally at the university. The college kids carried antiwar posters, chanted slogans into megaphones, lit candles, marched around the quad. Professors stood by appreciatively, giving thumbs up and flashing peace signs to their students. Two guys burned their draft cards to loud cheers. A girl exposed her boobs to them in gratitude. The cops rambled in after a while, swinging their batons but not actually hitting anyone, trying to disburse the crowd. That just made the kids more resolute and stupidly too brave. "Pigs!" people yelled. "Up against the wall, motherfuckers!" The cops made an example of a couple boys, threw them to the ground, cuffed them. Everybody got the message and most left quickly, some running. The cops didn't chase, it was lunch time for them, too. When the dust cleared, a few students strayed back to talk to Jim and Amber and Amy and wanted to get involved, maybe take a leadership role on campus. Adrian accepted their contact info and was very happy.

Ira, who presents as a cross between Jerry Rubin and Abbie Hoffman and is certainly the most militant, did a solo act in Allentown. He single-handedly preached the peace gospel to whoever would stop to listen. Even those who didn't. He had borrowed a bullhorn and made sure they could hear him several blocks away. Some merchants called the heat on him, he had to move on, but stayed just out of reach. It was hide and seek for about thirty minutes. By the end, he had about five young people following him like he was the Pied Piper, sneaking around, laughing, punking the cops. He got their contact info and they want to join the movement.

Peter, Sue and Ann had attended the school board meeting and spoke up about the need for a new elementary school for the Negroes in the First Ward. They presented a mountain of data and study results showing how new school buildings improve outcomes, including lower crime rates, increased graduation rates, and a more skilled workforce. They were mostly ignored by the board members, who are all white and acted like they could care less, but the Black folks applauded and thanked them.

After the meeting two more women from the community signed up for their taskforce that will work on getting a Negro elected to the board. A Black businessman volunteered to make his store a place where they can register voters. He surreptitiously pulled back his suitcoat to show that he carried a gun. "It's legal, and we won't have none of that deep south voter suppression shit here," he said, smiling. Again, Adrian was elated.

Jamal, Aries and a guy named Greg, who Gem has to admit is drop-dead gorgeous and who kept looking at her, had worked on the King Homes Project. They reported that they spent the day reviewing Alan's casework files and making sense out of it all. They were very excited. Greg is a second-year law student at Buffalo, so he was able to determine what Alan was putting together and what his logic was, where he was headed. Greg said that Alan had a gift and had found case law that everybody else had missed, including the city's lawyers. He said that he and Jamal and Aries should be able to piece it all together and hammer the daylights out of the city's position. They will be ready for the city council meeting on Thursday evening. Everyone applauded.

There were more reports from other small teams working on community service projects, all just getting started. Nothing huge, nothing earth-shattering, but Gemini was touched by the generous spirit behind the ideas. For example, Tedra proposed a clothing drive for little Black kids just starting kindergarten. The idea is to approach department stores that switch out what they carry on their shelves as the seasons change and get them to donate unsellable items for these poor ghetto children to begin their educations in style. Her father is an executive at Sears, and she convinced him to be the first in. Others will follow just for the PR.

It went on like that, lots of happy faces, clapping, encouraging words, congratulations. Gemini got the sense of family that develops among such people. Especially since all of them had left their real families behind, back in suburban Connecticut or New Jersey or in one case, Los Angeles, to do this work. This is their new adopted family and though they all know it's temporary, they cherish the moment. When the meeting officially ended, the partying officially began, and the sense of togetherness and shared commitment, one might even call it love, was the perfect starting point. Three joints were lit simultaneously.

Someone uncorked a two-liter bottle of wine, which got passed around in the opposite direction of the hooch. Gemini discovered the hard way that someone else had dropped in a tab of acid, at some point. She found herself sitting on the floor next to Greg, whose last name is Phelps, and whom she found almost irresistible. He could be John Lennon. He has an angelic face framed with long hair, bushy sideburns, a beard and mustache. Sensitive, dark brown eyes behind round, wire-rimmed glasses, an aquiline nose, puffy lips and perfect teeth. She could tell because he laughs a lot, at everything. She found herself doing the same thing, especially when the ecstasy nibbled at her brain.

The rest of the evening was swimming music, breathing walls, black-light waltzes on neon posters, and pairing off. Over the course of what might have been several hours or just a few minutes, she can't tell, nearly everyone found someone to love and wander off with. Sometimes just to a darker corner of the living room. Gemini snapped out of it long enough to realize she was making out with Greg. She was overcome with grief about it momentarily, her loyalty to Jack and all, but she just kept kissing him back because the chemicals had taken possession of her body and her body had taken over her mind. Or maybe the other way.

Greg seemed to sense this, and to his credit he backed off from what would assuredly have become serious nakedness, groping, and the exchange of bodily fluids. "I'm hungry," he said. "How about you?" Gem mumbled something that might've been yes and he jumped up, disappeared for a minute, and came back with a half-gallon of chocolate ice cream and two spoons. And that was that. They spent the next hour eating, laughing, and sharing lies. She knows she did, it's her job, and she's pretty sure he made up shit too. That's what boys do.

Gem learned this: Greg Phelps, which may or may not be his real name, is in law school and is helping to reconstruct Alan's work on the King Homes project. He grew up in Buffalo's most affluent neighborhood, went to private schools, wanted to go Ivy like his dad, but eventually decided to stay local and work in the community. When Gem asked him why, he hedged a little but after a while, after more probing, he hinted that he needs to make amends for his family's misdeeds. He never went further, so the Sam side of Gem will have to do some research and find out what the malfeasance might be.

By the time they both acknowledged that the evening is done, it was actually 2:00 am. They shared a last, long kiss that involved the tongue, looked at each other for what seemed like ten minutes, and separated. Greg actually drove home, wherever that is, and Gem somehow managed to get upstairs to her room. She doesn't remember changing into night clothes, brushing her teeth, or climbing onto the mattress where she stared at the ceiling, working past the hallucinogens. Last night, before conking out, she sensed that Greg is an enigma of some kind. Her intuition told her that he is even more complex than she imagined, but her brain was totally, chemically compromised.

So now, at 8:00 am, sipping coffee with Aries, Gem thinks it might be an okay time to ask about Greg. Everybody saw them together last night, so it'll come across as just checking on a guy she might screw. But before she can initiate, Aries does.

"You and Greg," she says, "an item?"

"I don't know much about him," says Gem, which is true. "I have been burned before by getting romantically involved with men before really knowing who they are, what they stand for," which is not true, but creates an opportunity to ask.

"I'm the same," says Aries. She repositions Arwen so the baby has the other breast. "Maybe I can fill in some gaps, if you want."

"Mmmhmm," mumbles Gem.

"He's from wealth, has some of his own, but wants to do good with it," says Aries. "I know this from personal experience."

Gem nods and encourages her to tell what that was.

"When I got here, I was eight months pregnant and hadn't had any prenatal care. He took care of it, made appointments, drove me to the OB/GYN. Took me to the hospital when my water broke, stayed for sixteen hours of labor."

"Who does that?" asks Gem.

"I know, right? He stopped by every day until Arwen got past the jaundice and we were both released," Aries says. "And you know what's the kicker? He picked up the hospital bill. Just paid it in full."

"Wow," says Gem, and she means it. Then she asks herself again, *who does that*, and she transitions into cop mode. What's his motive? There are any number of reasons why someone might help out a vulnerable stranger like that. On one end of the spectrum is saintliness and pure altruism. In the middle is creating a debt to collect on. On the other is guilt, penance and recompense. That misdeeds thing, again?

"Does he do that sort of thing all the time? Donate his time and money to help the needy?" she asks.

"If he does, he doesn't talk about it," says Aries.

"What was he working on before he started helping you on the King Homes?" asks Gem.

"He is with a legal clinic at the university that helps men apply for conscientious objector status or get other deferments legally. A law professor runs it. They don't get paid but pick up a ton of experience, and probably good grades," says Aries. "Alan was one of his clients."

"And he does all this good and doesn't expect anything in return?"

Aries nods. "So, what do you think? Nice enough guy for your high standards?"

135

"Well, yeah," says Gem. "I mean, I already have a boyfriend, but like the song says, 'If you can't be with the one you love, love the one you're with.'" But what she's also wondering is if Greg Phelps also had Dominic Styron and Jaime Roesler for clients. Is he the missing link?

Sam won't rest until she finds out more about the law student, Greg Phelps. Alan Crowe, who was attempting to get conscientious objector status and avoid military service, was one of his clients at the legal aid clinic up in Buffalo. He may have met and worked for two other victims of the Falls, Jaime Roesler and Dominic Styron, who could have been trying to buck the draft as well. He had helped Aries, Styron's girlfriend, through her pregnancy and childbirth. Even paid for it. And he really got her attention when he mentioned that his family, whoever they are, had committed "misdeeds" that he is somehow atoning for. Where to start?

She walks a few blocks away from the Swan Street commune to a payphone she uses to call Baldwin. It's on a busy corner and it's well used, not just for phone calls. She keeps the folding door open because some drunks must use it as a urinal. The floor is littered with the worst kind of trash: a used condom, a used needle. The handset is sticky. She holds it with a hanky away from her face, plunks a dime in and calls the station. Decker answers.

"Simpson here," she says. "Detective Baldwin, please."

Decker explains that Baldwin isn't in yet, but Chief Plishka is, and she asks to speak to him, instead. Plishka picks up after one ring.

"How's it going in Shangri-La?" asks Plishka.

"I am a member of the household, already, learning about their activities, a bit about the individuals," Sam replies. "I may win the chess championship."

"Anything illegal? Any top-ten most wanted?"

"Well, plenty of dope, of course," she says, "but for the most part, they're good kids trying to do good in the world. Very idealistic, bordering on unrealistic."

"Where did Alan Crowe fit in?"

Sam explains Alan's outsized role in fighting the City of Lackawanna over the King Homes. Alan had been the legal strategist, and after his death, nobody could make sense of what he had been doing. Whatever it was, it had the city lawyers scrambling. The PDM people were stuck with recovery work after his death. They were getting help with that from a law student named Greg Phelps. She tells him what she knows about Phelps, his philanthropic assistance to Ashley Lange, known as Aries, who also happens to be Dominic Styron's girlfriend, and his connection to Alan with his CO status.

"There's this web of intrigue surrounding this guy," says Sam, "I need some help, Chief, some investigative help."

"You want a background check on the Phelps character?"

"Yes sir, I'd like to know who I'm dealing with. He said something interesting to me. That his family had committed some unspoken transgressions that he is trying to make amends for."

"You said he's from Buffalo?"

"Yes."

"We have sources up there. Lieutenant Zubricky at BPD and Reynolds in the FBI. I can make those calls and get back to you one way or the other. If Phelps is a real name, and they broke laws, there might be files on them."

"Can you do that right away?" she asks, "I'm going to spend the whole day with him, and then go to the city council meeting with him and the others tonight. It would be good to know who he is."

"You're calling from a payphone?"

"Yes."

"Give me the number, I'll call back in half an hour with whatever I find out."

They agree, hang up, and Sam is free to head back to the commune or do whatever for thirty minutes. She decides to take a walk around the neighborhood, get some exercise.

The First Ward is what everybody calls the ghetto, on the western fringe of Lackawanna. Five thousand people crammed into ragged, sagging, aging houses. Fifty years ago, it was Polish, but they started moving out when the Black migration from the south started in the twenties. The Ward is completely hemmed in by the Bethlehem Steel plant on the west, five railroad lines on a wide bed of stone on the east, Smokes Creek on the south and the shipping channel and grain elevators on the north. There might as well be a wall around it.

The smokestacks of Bethlehem belch black soot from the blast furnaces twenty-four hours a day, seven days a week. On those rare occasions when the wind is easterly, it carries the pollution out over Lake Erie and away from the residences. Otherwise, it rises, cools, then crashes down on the First Ward. Today is one of those days, as Sam strolls through the neighborhood. She glances up at the stacks, and watches the smoke curl up, then bend horizontally over her head, and dissipate over the houses and businesses nearby. It smells like sulphur.

Sam imagines how horrible it would be to live here. To live in this industrial sewer every day. To breathe this air, wipe the soot off your house and car, try to raise a baby. She wonders what the life expectancy is of someone who lives here. And after a while, she begins to appreciate the righteousness of the King Homes project. It wouldn't be a lifeboat that can hold everybody, but a hundred and thirty-four families would be healthy. She begins to look forward to the meeting this evening. She wants to see who is standing in the way.

A quick glance at her watch tells her to turn around and head for the telephone booth. It's ringing when she's fifty feet away and she sprints for it, picks up.

"Sam?"

"Yes, sir," she says.

"I talked to both Zubricky and Reynolds," says Plishka. "Just our lucky day, I guess."

"They help?"

"Yes, indeed," he replies. "The Phelps Law Firm has represented the Maglione crime family for decades. Two generations so far. Two generations of attorneys and two generations of mafia. It's representing Stefano Maglione right now, in his ongoing federal trial. When that trial ends, they'll defend him in his city and state trials. Unless he gets the chair."

"Lawyers," says Sam, as though the word tastes bad. "Have they ever been accused of anything themselves?"

"No. It's not a crime to defend criminals in court. I mean, we actually assign public defenders to do that. And the Phelpses seem to have kept their noses out of the mafia's business. So far, anyway." Plishka pauses for a second, then adds, "But they apply all of their talents to getting killers, drug dealers, pimps and thugs out of jail and back on the streets. So, their noses are right up the mafia's you-know-what.

"Greg Phelps, the wayward son, seems very embarrassed about his lineage," says Sam. The thought crosses her mind that he might be seeking redemption. He might be trying to break away from his heritage. If he is, she wouldn't mind being part of that.

"Well, keep some distance from him if you can," advises Plishka. "If he isn't legit, he'll be a problem for us and if he is, he'll be a problem for his family. You don't want to be too close to that flame."

"Yes sir," says Sam, though she is already thinking about Greg Phelps in ways that she shouldn't.

139

Baldwin awakens on Thursday morning to find that Sandra has already left for work. The night before, she said there had been a terrible accident at one of the grain silos at the inner harbor, and that the press could enter the property at 6:00. He resigns himself to making his own coffee and preparing his own breakfast. She did leave him a very nice note and a wish to have a date night this evening, at the Lackawanna City Council meeting. "Wouldn't it be nice," she writes, "to watch them all change their minds about the King Homes and approve everything?"

He's half through with his morning routine, about to do some pushups, when the phone rings. He checks the time: 6:35. Must be important.

"Detective Baldwin, this is Inspector Paquette. I hope you are awake."

"I am, and this is the best time to reach me, I'll be running around all day."

"I'm calling with disturbing news," says Paquette. "We have another body in the river. A young man."

"Oh no," says Baldwin. "What we feared. Do you know who he is?"

"No, we don't. No identification on him. He did drown, and went over the Falls, according to the coroner," says Paquette. "He doesn't know what happened first."

"Any similarities to the others?"

"Approximate age, he was white, he dressed like a typical student. But no ID."

"Alan without my business card," says Baldwin.

"That's right," says Paquette. "But he did have a tattoo on his arm, and it could represent a college up in Toronto. I'm driving up there today to show his picture around and speak with some people. It's all I've got." Paquette goes on to tell Baldwin about his conversation with Quincy Taylor and Rory Temple, and spotting a message that may have been left for Jaime Roesler. "It's a long shot that the message was for our Jaime, and that I'll find the writer, but if it was and I can, we'll have some idea about Roesler's friends and plans, perhaps his whole itinerary."

Baldwin shares what he found out about Alan, his homosexuality, his former boyfriend and that man's father, who may now be a suspect.

"I got the impression that Jaime Roesler may have been a homosexual," says Paquette, "but no one told me that, and at the time, I didn't think it relevant. We thought Roesler was an accident."

"It might be relevant now, if both Crowe and Roesler were targeted for being gay," says Baldwin. "But there are other motives, as well." He then tells Paquette about the other investigators, who are talking to suspects and poking around Alan's former community of like-minded, antiwar activists.

"An important piece of information about that," says Paquette. "Apparently, someone at your PDM might be working with an organization up here that assists draft resisters. The Toronto people would call them up and connect them with a potential immigrant, someone who needs help getting to or over the border. Somebody down there drove Mr. Taylor over the bridge."

"Holy cow," says Baldwin. "The PDM folks insist that they don't do that."

"Well, at least one of them might. I suppose it could even have been Crowe. The Canadians have no reason to make this up and they say that several new arrivals shared what kind of help this person gave them."

"What do you know about them? A he or a she?"

"Nothing. The young people up here are very keen on not identifying Americans who help draft resisters. They would not tell me anything except they might belong to the PDM. I suspect it's your group, since they are right there on the border."

Baldwin decides that Sam will have to find out who it is, or was, and make that a priority. Paquette and Baldwin sign off and agree to talk again tomorrow. Both of them will know more.

Baldwin drums his fingers on the breakfast table, glances at his watch, and decides to try the Roesler family in Baltimore, to check on two details: Had Jaime been drafted and was Jaime gay? He flips open the files from Paquette and locates the Roesler number, dials them up.

"Hello?" says a woman's voice on the other end. She sounds a little tired.

"I'm sorry if I called too early," says Baldwin. He explains who he is and why he's calling, to get some additional information about Jaime. She introduces herself as Jaime's mother, Irene Roesler, and tells him it's not too early, she was just doing the breakfast dishes.

"I didn't know there was any kind of investigation going on," she says. "Why are the police involved? Wasn't it an accident?"

"Jaime's death may very well have been an accident, but we are trying to find out why he was in Niagara Falls in the first place. You helped rule out suicide for the Canadian authorities. So why was he up there?"

Baldwin then explains everything about the other young men, one certainly murdered, the effort to find any connections between the victims.

"The other victims," says Baldwin, "both had been drafted and were attempting to avoid induction. Both were applying for conscientious objector status and were, maybe, ready to run to Canada if that didn't work out. Can you tell me if Jaime was in the same boat?"

There is a long pause.

"Yes," she says. "He was. The Canadian police didn't ask about it, and we didn't volunteer this. Jaime had a very low lottery number and had been called up. We were all terrified of him going in the army. He told us he knew about someone who could help him get CO, conscientious objector status. He was excited about it, was in contact with the legal people, but then he just disappeared." She begins to sob.

Baldwin knows that young men who want to cross the border usually do, and don't die in the process. What happened to Jaime?

"I am so sorry," says Baldwin. He waits a beat or two. "Did Jaime tell you who was helping him with the CO status?"

"He said it was a legal clinic in Buffalo. When his body was discovered up there, we made that connection, but it also occurred to us that he was just trying to get to Canada."

"Did he talk about emigrating?"

"He considered it 'plan B' and he had a contact, an old friend, in Toronto."

More similarities, Baldwin writes all this down, actually starts drawing his own thought diagram. Circles connected to circles.

"Do you know who it was?"

"No."

"There is something else that I have to ask you, because it might be a commonality with at least one other victim," says Baldwin.

"Okay," she replies.

"Was your son gay?"

This is also followed by a long silence, then a sigh.

"No, he wasn't," she says, as though explaining this for the umpteenth time. "Some people thought that because he was always small, fragile, mostly interested in art things. In grade school he caught a lot of flak from the other boys. Meanies. But he was a premature birth, only weighed two pounds. We almost lost him. He was just starting to bulk up a little at the time he got drafted."

Baldwin takes note of that, scratches something out on his notepad. He thanks Irene Roesler for her help and promises to keep her in the loop.

"I dearly hope it was an accident," she says.

"Me too," he replies.

Baldwin drives to the House with everybody on his mind. The dead men have something in common besides their ages. Three of them, it turns out, had been drafted and all three were attempting to avoid induction using a legal maneuver: conscientious objector status. It still isn't certain that Roesler and Styron had been killed, and the one who most certainly was, Alan Crowe, had several dangerous people targeting him. And now there's a fourth victim?

He's anxious to speak with Chief Plishka about the VFW suspects, Fredricks and Johnson; with Zubricky up in Buffalo about the mobsters; and with Sam about anybody and anything at the PDM headquarters. He hopes he hears something from the FBI about their photo collection, but they were not reassuring about that. A quarter-million photos?

He arrives in his office at 8:00 and Decker hands him messages. Right on top is a call from Abe Zubricky in Buffalo, asking for a callback. Important, it says. Next is a message from Sam, who says that she may have some pertinent information and that Plishka knows what it is, too. She says it's about Alan's lawyer. And finally, a message to call someone named Beth Egan at the FBI. She says it's not important but wanted to keep him apprised of her work on the bridges photo survey. Baldwin decides to call her first, since it'll just be a brief how-ya-doin'.

"Egan," she says as she answers.

"This is Detective Baldwin returning your call."

"Thank you, sir," she says. She sounds delighted that he called back.

"You're studying the photos? Looking for our victim, Alan Crowe? Anything on that?"

"Only that I've looked at thousands of photos and neither he nor his car are in any of them on July 27, at least so far," she says. "But I am seeing many young men who could be crossing the border to escape the draft. Nervous-looking twenty-somethings, white knuckling the steering wheel."

"We aren't interested in that," says Baldwin, "but I know your bosses are."

"They did not order me to look for anything but your man," says Egan. "However, something is nibbling at my brain about something else. Just a hunch it might be important. Relevant."

"Like what?"

144

"I've only finished studying the first morning of traffic, tens of thousands of cars, but I've been developing this film since April and began seeing certain patterns almost right away. For instance, I've seen the same car with the same driver routinely, during the past five months. Usually the same day of the week. There isn't anything crazy about that all by itself. She could be going to work, could be running the same errand. But every time I see this woman, she has a different passenger. I saw her again today, crossing the bridge on the morning of July 27. A young male passenger. Not Alan Crowe, though."

"She?" asks Baldwin.

"Yes. A woman. The men are always in the same age range, about twenty or so. She might be older. Thirty? The two don't look animated, friendly, just staring ahead like they have a finish line to cross."

"Why do you think this is germane to our murder investigation?" asks Baldwin.

"Well, it's just that I'm scouring the photos looking for your victim in his own car, but what if he was driven over by somebody else, like these other guys?"

Baldwin ponders that. Egan is right. It's a needle-in-the-haystack problem and they aren't going to solve it with one FBI agent looking at a million photos. But what if she's the PDM helper Paquette told him about? What are the chances?

"You've got a point, Agent Egan," says Baldwin. "If Crowe was driven across the border in another car, we will never know or find out by studying your photo collection. I mean, maybe you already missed him in the thousands of pictures you already looked at. All we can do is hope you find him in his own car. Can you just carry on with that?"

"Absolutely."

"Thank you. But out of curiosity, I'd like to know more about this female chauffer, because she might be a person of interest," says Baldwin. "What does she look like, what kind of car? Got a plate number?"

Egan describes someone who could easily be the woman named Amber at the PDM commune but could also be any of hundreds of females with the same color hair, with the same braids. If it's Amber or anyone else associated with the PDM, this could be the person that Paquette told him about this morning. He now knows he's looking for a dark gray Chrysler with Massachusetts plates, and he knows the plate number.

"Agent Egan," he says – Beth likes the sound of that and doesn't correct him – "can you please send me one of the photos of the female driver?"

"I can do better than that. I can blow it up so you can see more clearly what she looks like."

"Wonderful."

"Do you want to see her passenger?"

"Um, that's not a bad idea. Just in case."

"I can drive the photos down to you at the end of the day, on my way home," she says. "I have a few thousand more photos to inspect today. I'll ask my da..., my assistant to make the blowups when he comes in."

Baldwin can't imagine how mind-numbing that job must be. He feels both sympathy and respect for Agent Egan.

"Many thanks," says Baldwin, and they sign off. Baldwin gets right back on the phone with Sergeant Decker at the front desk and asks him to find the registered owner of the Chrysler.

Then he calls Lieutenant Zubricky.

"I've got some pictures to show you," says Zubricky.

"My mobsters?"

"Could be yours, but definitely ours. And I have their names for you in case they are on your radar, too."

Zubricky gives Baldwin the names and brief histories of Caruso, Paglia and Slayton. Baldwin copies it all down in his notebook.

"I'll send you their portraits. One of our patrol cars will swing by later this morning with them."

"Perfect," says Baldwin. "I'm going to a city council meeting this evening and I'll see for myself if these are the guys who have been haunting it."

"There's one more thing," says Zubricky. "Dante Caruso is a known hitman, though never arrested. He is from Atlantic City and shows up now and then in Western New York. After he leaves, we usually find a dead person. Never the same MO, so we can't develop a routine or a profile. Unless you consider creativity as a routine."

"Do the dead people have anything in common?"

"They all made Stefano Maglione angry. One of them was that receptionist who used to work for him. Got suffocated in her hospital bed last year."

Baldwin immediately pictures the mob boss whom they brought down in '69, and who is fighting for his life in federal court. The receptionist worked for him and might have turned against him. She knew too much. He had her killed.

"You and me are on that list," says Baldwin.

"I thought of that, too."

"Now this Caruso works for Vincent Falco," says Baldwin, wondering who might be in the man's crosshairs on this visit.

"Yes," says Zubricky. "And we've made him angry, too."

That gives both of them pause.

"Falco's real estate interests in Lackawanna, Caruso's occupation, and Alan Crowe's murder. Motive, means, and opportunity. I think we have a solid lead," says Baldwin, "but we need proof and time to figure out what our next move will be." Baldwin tells Zubricky that he will call him tonight, after the meeting, and verify that Falco's crew are, in fact, the city council intimidators. "Without that, we don't have much to go on."

Baldwin walks to Plishka's office. The door is open and Maureen, Plishka's secretary, is walking out with some paperwork. They pass each other in the doorway, and she says, "We were just talking about you."

"Nice things, I hope," says Baldwin.

"I've got some intel to share with you," says Plishka.

"Sam left a message that you would," says Baldwin as he sits down and opens his notebook. "A lawyer?"

"Not just any lawyer. She met Alan's lawyer, or rather law school student, who was helping him file for conscientious objector status, keep him out of the military."

Baldwin shrugs. All it does is verify that Alan was, indeed, taking a legal path to avoid Vietnam. He may have changed his mind or run out of time, though, and headed to Canada. It's something he or Sam could check on.

"There's more. His name is Greg Phelps."

"Means nothing to me."

"The whole Phelps family are attorneys and they work almost exclusively for Stefano Maglione. They defend the mob and do a very good job of it. But this young man isn't going that route. He's working for the PDM. Right now, he has taken over Alan's role on the King Homes conflict."

"Then I'll likely see him in action tonight, at the city council meeting." But Baldwin just doesn't know how to process this new bit of information. Alan's lawyer, or legal advisor, is related to the lawyers who represent the mob that had reason to kill him. He looks perplexed to Plishka.

"I know," says Plishka. "It's complicated."

"Baffling," says Baldwin, as he shakes his head. A moment passes.

"I have information about our VFW friends."

Baldwin looks up, refocuses, and is ready to take notes.

"I met one of the men that Kevin Crowe told you about, Dan Fredricks, and I think he's not our man. Just a sense."

"And Harry Johnson?"

"I haven't talked with him yet, but I did some digging, found out who he works for, where he's been for the last eight months. He's a plumber, or master pipe fitter, who supervises big jobs all over the east coast. Hotels, apartment complexes. He's gone a lot."

147

"So, he may have been out of town, far away during Alan's demise?"

"Out of town, and right in town," smiles Plishka. "He's been working in Niagara Falls for months. Canadian side. I may meet him tonight. He's home."

Inspector Paquette gets an early start on Thursday. After calling Detective Baldwin with news of the fourth body found below the Falls, he performs his morning ritual of a brisk walk around his neighborhood, an hour reading the newspaper, a light breakfast at home with madame, and a brief drive to the detachment to check on his mail and phone messages, meet with the men, plan the rest of the day. Paquette is a man of routines, a trait that he believes has kept him fit and alert, even-tempered and dependable. He does not like surprises and does not want to be one, himself. His wife of fifteen years, Eloise, has told him that his constancy has made her life easy: no shockers. She knows exactly where he is, what he is doing, and when he'll be home.

Paquette was born in Montreal and speaks French with a slight Irish accent and English with a slight French one. His mother was an Irish woman whom his French-Canadian father brought back to Quebec after the First World War. Both parents were strict Catholics who kept him on a short leash. Parochial schools, fish every Friday, Sunday Mass, weekly confession, all the sacraments, a bit of nudging towards becoming a priest, which didn't take. Like everyone else with the same upbringing, he memorized the catechism in Latin. When he was twenty, in 1940, he enlisted in the Canadian Army to fight for the Commonwealth. At the time, he thought it would be refreshing.

He was put to work as a translator, helping the British interface with the French resistance. That involved receiving and interpreting codes, hidden messages, intelligence reports, and now and then desperate appeals for assistance from fighters deep behind Nazi lines. He got very good at extracting and processing all the pertinent information smuggled to him from the French and making sense out of it, and then making suggestions, when asked. How to proceed: To drop supplies and what, where, when, and how to communicate back to the senders. He did well, was recognized for his ability to analyze, comprehend, recommend. British intelligence offered him a full-time job after the war, but he declined. He returned home and joined the RCMP. Outwitting the Nazis had prepared him well to outwit the typical Canadian criminal.

The Niagara Falls killer is not typical, Paquette thinks, as he drives back up to Toronto, but he is reliable. So far, he's left behind a body during the first week of every month. Paquette makes a mental note to discuss that with Baldwin.

His drive to Toronto is much like yesterday. Same route, same traffic patterns, and he arrives at the coffee shop at about the same time. Rory Temple is there already, sitting at a table that he's saving at the window and bouncing his knee. Paquette shakes his hand, then excuses himself to order another wonderful French roast, another croissant with elderberry jam, and to use the toilette. After a minute or two, they are both settled across from each other. Temple sips dark, thick Turkish coffee from a tiny espresso cup with a little lemon wedge stuck on the rim.

"Thanks for meeting me," Paquette says. "I am sorry that it's under such unpleasant circumstances."

"If I can help..." and Temple shrugs.

"You may be able to identify the most recent body we recovered at the Falls. Do you mind?"

"Not at all," says Temple, though his expression of dread says otherwise.

"Know this man?" Paquette asks, fanning out the Polaroids that Griffin had taken at the morgue. There's no hiding the fact that the man is stone-cold dead and took a horrible beating under the Falls. Even Paquette can't more than glance at them.

Temple takes a quick look and turns away, puts his hand to his mouth as though he might barf. Paquette gives him some time to collect himself.

"I'm sorry," says Temple. "I don't recognize him."

"Would you please look at the tattoo on his arm, in this picture here?" asks Paquette, as he stealthily scoops the other pictures, the ones of the man's face and torso, like a Vegas blackjack dealer. He points at the tattoo, to give Temple something to focus on. Polaroids are small, and usually kind of fuzzy, but the tattoo takes up the entire image.

Temple leans over, holds his glasses, and takes a close look. Paquette watches him swallow hard, watches his Adam's apple bob up and down like his knee. The young man is powering through a very distressing moment.

"I haven't seen anything like it," says Temple. "But your instincts might be right. Those letters could stand for Rochdale College, Toronto, Ontario. Assembled the way they are in a peace symbol also makes sense. The college is ground zero for antiwar activity around here." He sits back and turns away again, stares out the window, tries to focus on the signage across the street or a passing car. Anything to take his mind off a dead guy.

"Where would a young person go to get a tattoo like that?" asks Paquette, as a waiter delivers his coffee and croissant. He takes a sip and a quick bite.

150

Temple is quiet for a moment, as though he's dwelling on something else, not the answer.

"Mr. Temple?"

"I'm sorry, sir," he says. A moment later he seems to have gathered his thoughts, or his feelings, anyway. "I'm not familiar with death like this."

"Nobody is," says Paquette. "You aren't alone."

"Not even you?"

"Not even me."

"How do you...how..." and Temple points at the picture.

"Justice," says Paquette. "I just want justice. It's how I was raised. So somehow, I find the strength to look at these pictures and process it all, try to find a motive for it and a person who'd have that reason to kill." He pronounces *reason* like *raison*, like he would in French.

Temple nods, and leans forward again, looks at the tattoo.

"There are three or four tattoo parlors here in the neighborhood, close to the university and Rochdale. What do you want to do next?" asks Temple.

"We visit them." He says *visit* like *veezeet*.

Temple leads the way. They walk together through the Baldwin Street enclave, past the many new storefronts and shops, sometimes stopping to greet an acquaintance or friend of Rory. They had decided not to show the murder victim's picture to just anybody. Too graphic, too depressing. But when appropriate, they show the picture of the tattoo. A few people admire it, want to know where to get one like it. Temple promises to let them know when they find out.

They visit two parlors within a few blocks of each other. Both artists admire the ink but say they didn't do it. One asks if he can have the picture, add it to his offerings.

On the way to the third tattoo parlor, which Temple says is on Baldwin Street, they run into a lithe, dark-haired coed named Solange, whom Rory knows from his antiwar work. She seems to have appeared out of nowhere. He turns to Paquette and says, "If anybody knows this tattoo, she does." And Paquette believes it. She's got a million of them.

Rory and Solange exchange cheek kisses, he introduces her to Paquette and shows her the picture of the dead guy's tattoo.

"Seen this before?" he asks.

Solange looks at it, then leans down and pulls up her pant leg, revealing the same tattoo just above her ankle. "Yes, indeed," she says. "I have another peace symbol right below my navel, if you'd like to see it." She looks right at Paquette when she says it, with a slightly evil grin. Paquette coughs into his fist and turns slightly, embarrassed.

"Where did you get this one, Solange?" asks Temple, pointing at her ankle.

"Toni's place," she says. "She's my favorite. Know where she is?"

Temple does. Toni is an artist who owns the parlor next to the Yellow Ford Truck, the art shop that Paquette asked about. He turns to Paquette. "We're close."

Rory and Solange exchange cheek pecks again, and she fades into the ether where she came from.

They march two blocks to Toni's tattoo parlor but it's closed up tight. Probably too early. They decide to check next door, The Yellow Ford Truck. The sign hanging over the sidewalk is large and swings back and forth with the slight breeze. It's all yellow and shaped like a pickup truck. Sitting in the driver's seat is a cartoon character who looks like he was drawn by R. Crumb. No lettering, suggesting that if you don't know what we do, you should just keep on trucking. Paquette is surprised he missed it. Probably walked right under it twice.

They enter and disturb a bell on the door, but nobody responds. Maybe the owner ran an errand. The shop is filled, floor to ceiling, all four walls, with shelves displaying books, earthenware, paintings, carvings, sculptures, weavings, baskets, and woven rugs. You could spend days here and not see everything. In fact, if you remove anything from a shelf, there's something right behind it, doubling the time it would take to see it all. Paquette is mesmerized. He's there to solve a murder but he is swept up by the finest examples of First Nations art and crafts that he has ever seen in one place. He might pick something up for Eloise, who is part Tuscarora.

"Hello!" Paquette calls out.

From the back a woman responds, "Coming!" and appears a moment later wiping her hands on an apron. "Firing a pot out back," she says. "Sorry. What can I do for you?"

Paquette extends his hand and introduces himself. She says her name is Madeline. Temple and the woman recognize each other, exchange hellos. She's about fifty, gray-haired, slim, face lines that confirm a life of smiling, a twinkle in her eyes that hints she's probably a little smarter than you, or at least three thoughts ahead.

"Can you help us identify the person who got this tattoo next door?" Paquette asks, holding out the picture of the dead man's bicep. She studies the tattoo for a moment, nods, "I've seen this before, I know I have. Hard to tell whose arm this is. Looks like a man, most likely."

"It's the arm of a dead man," says Paquette. "We are trying to find out who he was. This is the only identifying mark that we have."

"A dead man?" She is shocked, takes a breath, looks at the photo again. "Got anything more than this?"

"The other photos we have, of the victim, are disturbing," says Paquette. "Fair warning."

"I was a nurse during the war, close to the front," she says. She tips her head to the side, and Paquette interprets that as her own fair warning, and willingness.

Paquette produces the photo of the man's face, wearing Griffin's glasses. He holds it out to her.

"That's Grant," Madeline gasps. "He's dead? How is that possible? He was just here a week ago! Dropped off some more paintings."

"Grant," says Paquette. He remembers the note left for Jaime R that he saw yesterday, on a light pole a block away, left by someone named Grant. "Do you happen to know his last name?"

"Harel," she says. "Grant Harel. He's a magnificent artist whose work is right here." She gestures to one of the shelves crowded with small paintings, miniatures, depicting early meetings between First Nations people and French and English explorers and traders. Paquette picks one up and studies it. An Algonquin is presenting beaver pelts to a European trader, who appears to be offering a musket in exchange. Eloise would like it. She is also a history buff.

"Was he a student? At Rochdale College?"

"He's faculty there. The Art Department."

"We'll go there next, talk to the administrators, but is there anything else you can tell us about him?" asks Paquette.

"He's American," says Madeline. "Arrived here in Toronto two years ago. Like all the other young American men arriving every day, he was avoiding the draft, the war.

"Do you know where he came from?"

"Yes, because he spoke about it often and missed it dearly. Baltimore, Maryland."

Roesler was from Baltimore, too. That might be how they knew each other, thinks Paquette.

"Have you heard the name Jaime Roesler?" He asks.

Madeline puts her fingers on her brow, gives it a thought.

"Grant mentioned a Jaime. Asked me to watch for him, to call him if a young man named Jaime shows up."

"How long ago was this?"

"At least two months. Reminded me twice more, but nobody named Jaime ever showed up."

"Where did Grant live?"

"He lived where his students do, at the Rochdale College. All in one big building," she says, pointing generally north.

"I can take you there," says Temple.

Before they leave, Paquette buys the painting by the late Grant Harel. He turns it over and sees that Harel had signed and dated it on August 18, two weeks before his deadly tumble over Niagara Falls.

Gemini, Jamal, Aries and Greg Phelps meet for lunch at the commune. Someone had made a huge pot of spaghetti sauce and boiled up some pasta. Someone else had made a salad. Aries had baked a loaf of bread, and Greg had picked up a bottle of wine while driving down from Buffalo. A large two-liter bottle of merlot. They gather at the table, pass the dishes and wine around with laughter and goodwill. Aries nurses Arwen and wisely opts for a glass of milk.

"This is a wonderful way to kick off the day," says Greg. "But we do need to get to business right after lunch, get prepared for this evening."

"Something I want to know," says Gem. "What's the history of this fight with the city? How long has it been going on? I mean, I just got here and I think that context would help."

The others agree and look to Greg. Three pairs of wide eyes.

"Alan never told us," says Jamal. "A little like skipping to the middle of a book."

"Okay, I can give you the executive summary now, and more details later, after we clean up and we can use the table for documents," says Greg. "I agree. It's important that you know the background, how we got to where we are. None of you are from around here, so this is all news to you. You deserve to know the backstory and decide if you want to continue."

They all look startled. *If we want to continue?*

Greg begins with the events of late 1968, when the Catholic Diocese of Buffalo announced that it would sell its vacant property in Lackawanna's Third Ward, a solid, middle-class and very white part of town. It was a large rectangle of land right in the heart of the Ward. Prime real estate. Developers and builders had lusted after it for decades.

But the church had no plans or use for it, which surprised the neighbors. They had hoped the church would build a school or hospital, maybe an old folk's home. Build something and create some good jobs.

But the Bishop and his advisors had made up their minds. What was even more shocking to the neighbors, and the city government, was that the diocese decided to sell the land to a "Negro and Puerto Rican" nonprofit, which announced its plan to build over a hundred housing units, designated for families living in the First Ward. Negroes and Puerto Ricans would move in.

"That's the group we're working with. Mr. Jakes and them. They'd be able to leave the crappy shithole we are in right now," says Greg. "Brand new houses for brown people, far away from the stacks, surrounded by Europeans. The white community went ballistic."

"Violent?" asks Jamal.

"I'll get to that," says Greg.

He goes on. The Lackawanna City Council, pressed by the then-mayor, Angus Brophy and some pretty shady and powerful characters, condemned the land. It passed an ordinance that said the land could only be used for a public park or left vacant. They justified it by saying the sewer system could not handle more residences. It already overflowed and backed up during rainstorms. They added that the area desperately needed a park for recreation, ballfields, a pool, and like that. It became a done deal.

"Then what happened?" asks Aries.

"The diocese, to its credit, sued," says Greg. "It claimed that the ordinance was in violation of the Civil Rights Act, the one that had just passed Congress."

"The Catholic Church took Lackawanna to court?" Aries smiles and leans back with Arwen. "I'm a Catholic and I never expected it to ever do something that progressive. Some Catholics still do the Latin Mass."

"It wound up in federal court," says Greg, "and it was joined by a dozen Protestant and Jewish denominations. It dominated the news for months. Imagine the anger the white people had towards their own churches! The letters to the papers, the shouting matches at meetings, outside the courtroom. This town was like a bad day in Mississippi."

"So, who won?" asks Gem, playing the part of the outsider.

"Pretty soon, the Justice Department, the federal government itself, joined the case, and the city found itself fighting a losing battle. The judge found the city in violation of the Civil Rights Act and ordered it to rescind the ordinance, and to issue permits for construction of the housing development. But it's been over a year since the case ended. Still no houses. The city and the white folks have found other ways to delay it."

"With violence?" asks Jamal, again, nervously.

"Now we are there," says Greg, and leans forward, narrows his eyes. He taps the table with his finger as he spells it out.

"The lawyer representing the diocese was a priest named Martin Goezina. He was a brilliant litigator, beating the crap out of the city lawyers in every court appearance, every filed motion. His work led to the final verdict."

"You said 'was.' What happened to him?" asks Jamal.

"He was murdered," says Greg, who sits back and crosses his arms. Looks from one to the next.

The group grows quiet and still.

"Now I know why Alan never told us this stuff," says Aries.

"Do they know who did it?" asks Jamal quietly, after a moment.

"The cops were closing in on a mafia underboss, a guy named Carmine Falco, and then all of a sudden, he gets murdered along with his wife and daughter and a couple of other people. In their own home."

"Why was the mafia involved with the King Homes?" asks Aries, growing even more concerned. *We're the ones on the front lines, here.*

"Falco had a lot to lose if the housing project got built. He owned legitimate businesses and had already built subdivisions all around the site, and he would have had an impossible time trying to sell them if a Negro neighborhood suddenly sprung up next door." Greg points his thumb at the wall.

"So, then, who murdered the mafia guy, and why?" asks Gem.

"The law thinks he was whacked by the mafia kingpin around here, Stefano Maglione," says Greg. "Maglione controls the whole region. They think it was because Falco killed a priest, something even the mob doesn't do. Maglione's on trial now, for a bunch of crimes, including for hiring the hitman who killed Falco."

Gem knows how it is that Greg knows all this, and that it's accurate. She doesn't wonder why he's ashamed of his family business.

All of them sit motionless, lost in their own thoughts, which are pretty much in sync. They have watched enough movies to know that crime syndicates can be run from prison. The mob may still be working to stop the housing development, and perhaps Alan is another casualty of that. He was doing the same work as this Goezina guy. Now it's their job. One by one, they look at each other, searching out their friends' thoughts and feelings.

"Are we in any danger?" asks Aries quietly, hugging Arwen a little closer. Jamal nods, seconding the question.

"Alan is dead," says Greg. "If he was killed for the same reason that the priest was, then we may not be safe. We have to be very careful, stay close."

Gem decides to carry her .38 a lot closer. She wonders where she could conceal it. She's small, the gun is big. She also wants to calm everybody down a little. Panic doesn't help.

157

"The police are investigating Alan's murder," she says. "That Black detective. He seems competent. Like he's on it."

"What cop?" asks Greg.

"His name is Baldwin," says Jamal, and he takes out his wallet, pulls out Baldwin's card and hands it to Greg. "Gem is right. He's working the case. Asked a lot of smart questions."

Greg studies the card and hands it back to Jamal. "One Black Lackawanna cop investigating the mafia?" he asks. "Looking for the murderer of one of us? Doesn't give me a lot of confidence."

Gem knows there's more going on, more soldiers, more firepower, but she can't say anything about that. "Well, it's better than nothing, and I vote we help him out any way we can. He might be the guy who can keep us safe. Never underestimate a Black guy with a gun." She points in the direction of the Huey Newton poster.

Everybody nods, and even Greg agrees, hesitantly, yes.

Gem adds, "We know what we're up against. We should probably have plans, precautions. Like you said, Greg, staying together, never alone."

They all agree and discuss security measures. Jamal and Aries will always be together outside the house and especially at those city council gatherings, and Gem and Greg will do the same, when possible. Greg has classes and lives in Buffalo, so he can't be around all the time. Gem promises to be extra careful, especially after she makes her appearance at the meeting tonight. But she is more worried about Greg than herself. She'll be packing heat and channeling her inner cop.

By now they have finished eating, have cleared the table and dumped the dirty dishes in the sink for somebody else, later. Eventually, everybody gets stuck with it, and the gang imagines it will probably be Peter, whenever he wakes up. His favorite mug is at the bottom somewhere.

Greg makes a few piles of papers on the table and goes through them in chronological order. He begins with the case that the government brought against the City of Lackawanna last year, walking them through the entire file to highlight the important findings and judgments. To the other three, it's all a lot of legal jargon they don't understand, but they are impressed that Greg does. He talks about charging the City of Lackawanna with violations of the equal protection and due process clauses of the Fourteenth Amendment, the Civil Rights Act, and the Fair Housing Act of 1968.

Greg takes them through minutiae of the original case and the final determination: The City of Lackawanna was forced to rescind the original ordinance, the one that condemned the land and restricted its use to a public park. That ruling freed the diocese to dispose of the land to the nonprofits, and for the nonprofits to begin applying for the necessary permits to begin building. "But then it got interesting," says Greg. "It's a technicality that was overlooked by the judge. It made it possible for the city – the mayor, really – to screw the diocese and the Negroes."

"What happened?" they all ask at once.

"The court ordered the city to rescind the ordinance and allow the nonprofit to apply for permits. But one of the permits has to be granted by the county health department, and the request for the permit has to be signed by the mayor. He simply refused to sign the request. It was a very clever, passive-aggressive move. He wasn't required by the court order to ask for a permit, only to grant them. So, the nonprofit never got the sewer permit because the request was never submitted."

"Can't the court order him to?" asks Jamal. "I'm no lawyer, but the spirit of the court order…"

"No, it can't order him to do anything because he disappeared. Everybody knows he's in a witness protection program. Could be anywhere in the country. It turns out he was tight with the mob. He might resurface to testify against Stefano Maglione and then dive back down under a rock, but that's it. No mayor, no permit request, no housing development."

"That explains why the city hasn't had a mayor for over a year now," says Jamal. "It was in their own self-interest to keep the post vacant."

"You told us that Alan found something nobody else had, something that could break it in our direction," says Gem. "What was it?"

"He found out that Angus Brophy, the mayor who refused to sign the request for a sewer permit and who disappeared? He's legally still the mayor for two more years," says Greg. "It's in the city charter. They can't replace him unless he officially resigns. So, if he signs the permit request, the county will permit it, and the housing development can go forward."

"But nobody knows where he is," says Gem.

"The FBI does," says Greg, smiling shrewdly. "And I just might have something to offer them if they agree to help us."

Gem knows that Greg's family is as tight as can be with the mob, and that he has insider information that could break this and a dozen other cases. She surmises that the FBI informant, whoever that is, will probably tip them off that Greg's coming with a deal. She is also terrified that Greg is about to have a target on his back.

159

Baldwin takes his own car down to the wastewater treatment plant in Orchard Park. It's across from the high school, down a dirt road, past the Little League baseball diamonds. Two of them are tiny, for the beginners. One has solid plywood walls in the outfield and covered bleachers. It even has dugouts for the major leaguers: twelve-year-olds.

Brian McGee works at the sewage treatment plant. Opening valves, checking levels, moving black water through the various purification stages until it can be dumped into a concrete channel that flows into Green Lake. People actually swim in Green Lake, where there is a public recreation area with picnic tables and grills, a ball field, and a beach. During the forties and fifties, its nickname was polio pond, which may have been founded on solid evidence. It was and probably still is segregated.

Baldwin had rehearsed what he was going to say and how he was going to explain his visit to McGee, the homophobic and possibly homicidal alpha male. He'd learned from his psychology professor up at Hillcrest that people like him respond well to praise, flattery, admiration, high regard. Anything that lifts them up on a pedestal. When Baldwin learned that the man works all alone at a sewage treatment plant, he knew he would respond well to some lifting-up.

The plant consists of several rectangular concrete pools, connected with large cast iron pipes, sliding gates that look like locks on a canal, various catwalks and elevated tanks, and a few block buildings with steel doors. One of them looks like the office. It has some windows and the path to the door is well-worn asphalt. There are diesel pumps making a racket behind a chain-link fence and water is shooting out of a large-diameter pipe from one pool into the next. Oddly, it doesn't smell all that bad, maybe slightly of chlorine.

Nobody is around when he parks the car and shuts the door. There's one other vehicle in the gravel drive, a newish red pickup truck with a rack on the bed and a tow hitch in the back. Baldwin heads for the office building, but McGee steps out before he gets there. Stands about ten feet away.

"You gotta leave," says McGee, shooing Baldwin away with his hand and then crossing his arms across his chest. "Restricted area."

Baldwin looks around. *Restricted to what?* he wonders.

McGee is about the same size and build as Baldwin, maybe early forties, same auburn hair as his son Michael, but not nearly as good-looking. A lifetime of manual labor around some pretty nasty chemicals has taken a toll. His face features a lot of red splotches and pockmarks. He's wearing a sunbaked baseball cap, denim overalls and a dark green work shirt, all of it drenched in sweat or, possibly, regrettably, wastewater.

"Are you Mr. McGee?" asks Baldwin cordially, holding up his badge.

McGee squints and leans forward to see the badge but guards his territory. Feet planted. Body language says tense.

"Who's asking?"

"I'm Thomas Baldwin, a detective with the Lackawanna Police Department. Can I have a word with you?"

McGee looks confused for a moment. *Why Lackawanna?* He seems to be mulling this over.

"What about?" He still hasn't uncrossed his arms. Still seems wired.

"I'd like your advice about something. My investigation. Your name keeps coming up, I thought you could help," says Baldwin. "But if it's inconvenient, then okay, sorry to bother you."

"Let me see that badge again," McGee says as he steps towards Baldwin. Suddenly, he seems relaxed. Baldwin holds it out for him to take and examine. It isn't protocol to hand somebody your ID but it has the desired effect. McGee can feel the warmth of the leather holder, look closely at the brass insignia, see the embossed "Detective" on it. Feel the heft of the badge. It's the real thing. Baldwin is a Negro, but he has some sort of authority. *And he wants me to help.* McGee hands it back.

"Advice about what, Detective?"

Baldwin has won him over.

"Is there a place we can sit down?" asks Baldwin. He wants McGee to be comfortable, relaxed.

McGee smiles and waves his hand in the opposite direction. He leads Baldwin to a picnic table nestled in a little grove of trees behind the building. Looks like his lunch spot or maybe has a cigarette, sips his coffee here. The diesel engines are muffled in this little piece of heaven. He motions for Baldwin to join him at the table, which he must have heisted from Green Lake Park. "How's this?" he asks.

"Nice," says Baldwin, "thanks."

They sit opposite each other.

162

"You want my advice about something? An investigation?"

"Yes. A number of people said you'd be the one to ask," says Baldwin, and he can see that McGee likes the sound of that. "Are you okay with me asking questions?"

"Sure," says McGee.

"Let's start with you," says Baldwin. "If I take this to court, I want to establish your expertise."

McGee practically glows. "Makes sense," he says.

Baldwin proceeds to ask about McGee's background, his job, his personal life, family. His profession, which turns out to be Senior Engineer, Health Department. He already knows that McGee went to high school locally, no college, divorced, has a son who's an All-American swimmer. He knows that "Engineer" is a fancy title for opening and closing giant faucets. McGee tells him he's active with the volunteer fire department, Boy Scouts, coaches a Little League team, passes the collection plate at church. Baldwin tells McGee that he understands why so many people recommended him. McGee looks tickled.

"So, what are you needing my help with?" asks McGee.

"I'm investigating Alan Crowe's murder."

McGee suddenly looks uneasy.

"I heard about that, but I don't see how I..."

"I'm looking for suspects," Baldwin gently interrupts. "I want to look at his competitors, guys that he beat in swimming meets. I think there might be a motive there. Everybody says you know everybody in the sport."

McGee brightens up again, looks to the side, rubs his chin like he's thinking about it. "Well, you might be right about that," he says. "It was dog eat dog during those meets, especially when it got to sectionals and state. I was always watching my own son but saw a lot of Crowe and the boys he beat. You could just feel the hate they all had for Crowe."

Ah, thinks Baldwin, *the old misdirection play.*

"Why did they hate him?" asks Baldwin.

"Because he was so arrogant, high and mighty. He rubbed it in when he beat them. You should have seen the way he strutted along the pool, chest out, swinging those arms, smiling at the guys he just destroyed." He lets that hang in the air. "Any one of them could've killed him, ask me." He says ask like ax. '*You ax me.*'

Baldwin makes a show of writing all this down in his notebook, and McGee points at it and says, "I'll give you some names."

For the next ten minutes or so, McGee gives Baldwin a few names from competitors in other schools and describes them, their physiques, events, swimming styles. He spends three minutes on each one, giving the reason why that particular high school athlete would want to kill Alan Crowe two years after graduation. Baldwin writes it all down, and even asks McGee to repeat things, "To get it right." When McGee is done, Baldwin asks him if there were any parents he should investigate. McGee actually licks his lips and smirks.

"Yeah," he says.

Five more minutes on a bunch of parents, Baldwin scribbling away. McGee can't see this, because it's upside down: Baldwin is jotting down some ideas for a present for Sandra. She has a birthday coming up. Yoga mat, halter top, Jimi Hendrix album, new Selectric typewriter?

"You got all that?" asks McGee.

"Yes sir, I do, Thanks for all your help," says Baldwin. "Just one more thing, if you don't mind, if you have the time."

McGee smiles and puts out both hands, palms up, as if, whatever you want.

"How did you and your son Michael get along with Alan Crowe?"

McGee's smile disintegrates, becomes a tight angry glare. A switch has been thrown. For a second, Baldwin foresees a fist headed his way. He actually gives his gun a thought. Where is it, is it loaded?

"What do you mean?" asks McGee. Every word on the same low note.

"Well, from what you said, the only boys with a nit to pick with Crowe are on this list. Boys who he beat. But I did some research and Michael and Alan swam against each other six times in high school. Michael won once and Alan won five times. No animosity? Did Alan ever rub it in?"

"Every time," says McGee. Same low note. Maybe lower. "He was a prick."

"But no hate or anger from you or Michael?"

"Well, of course. How could there not be?" says McGee. "We both hated the guy."

"That's odd. I heard that they were friends," says Baldwin, calmly.

"That's a lie."

"They weren't friends? Were they enemies? Should Michael be on this list?"

"You fucker," says McGee. He stands up and glowers at Baldwin, looks like he could explode. "What are you sayin'? That my son is a queer?"

"Why would you assume that Mr. McGee?" asks Baldwin. "We're talking about murder suspects. How did queer come into this?"

McGee looks frazzled, like he just got punked. He realizes he inadvertently opened a whole new line of questioning. *Why didn't I just play it cool*, he thinks. He sits down and stares defiantly at Baldwin, who is jotting something down in his notes: *Supremes' new album*. He underlines it twice.

McGee watches him do this, looks concerned.

Baldwin glances up and asks, "Well?"

"Crowe was a homo," says McGee. "Everybody knew it."

"Do you think that was a reason for somebody to kill him?" asks Baldwin, as he poses his pencil over the notebook, ready to record his answer. Baldwin is still acting like he's looking for expert advice, but McGee doesn't look ready to answer that. "Do you think any of the names you gave me, would any of them kill Crowe because he was a homo?"

McGee nods his head, yes. "Nobody wants to get beat by a faggot."

"Would you?" asks Baldwin. "Your son got beat by a gay man. Five times. Would you harm him for that? Would you harm him because they remained friends?"

McGee has had enough. He doesn't answer, just purses his lips, stands up, and marches back to his office, slams the door. On his way back to his car, Baldwin can't help but notice all the heavy pipes and steel tools lying around. All of them look like heavy, indestructible baseball bats. He jots down the license plate number and a brief description of the red pickup. He'll ask Beth Egan about it.

Abe Zubricky has a light day, all things considered, so he sits at his desk at the downtown headquarters and opens the files on his three mafia soldiers: Caruso, Paglia and Slayton. He pulls out the carbon copies of their records and slips them into another file folder, to be sent down to Baldwin. He studies their photos for a moment before slipping them in the Baldwin folder as well.

Richard Paglia, it turns out, is the same age as Zubricky and grew up in the same neighborhood, just a few blocks away on Buffalo's west side. They could have been friends in high school, or classmates at least, and Zubricky will dig up his yearbooks from back then. He looks up at the ceiling and tries to remember somebody with that name, but the only one who shimmies into view is Carlene Paglia, a dark-haired, flirty beauty who started wearing C-cups in eighth grade. Every pubescent boy had wet dreams over her. She got pregnant in eleventh grade and disappeared forever. What a shame, thinks Zubricky, but it explains why he can't recall Richard.

The male Paglia has a criminal record that dates back to just after graduation in 1948. The economy was starting to bounce back after the war and people had decent-sized, union-negotiated, disposable incomes. Employment was practically one hundred percent. Most of the recently discharged soldiers spent their windfall on homes and cars, marriages, children, dinner dates and stuff manufactured by General Electric. Others visited prostitutes, gambled, drank to excess and engaged in other vices, like drugs, which made the mob very happy and very rich. Paglia helped that along.

As a teen, Paglia worked for the mob's numbers racket, picking up bets, collecting debts, occasionally snapping a bone or knocking out a tooth when called for. He graduated to extortion of small business owners and seemed to have specialized in new immigrants, particularly from Eastern Europe, who poured in as the Cold War heated up. If you were a shoemaker from Hungary who wanted to open a shop in Buffalo in 1956, you had to get permission from the mafia, in the person of Richard Paglia. He would stop by every week and you would pass him an envelope full of twenties from under the cash register.

From 1960 on, it was mostly the recreational drug trade. At first it was heroin and cocaine in the ghetto, which was violent and dangerous even for Richard, but then it got safer, more lucrative, and a lot more fun when white folks, particularly the hippie crowd, started consuming pot, acid and hallucinogens.

Instead of selling the stuff out of the trunks of cars on dark, dead-end streets, he sold it in nightclubs, at fraternity parties, and even a few country clubs. He got caught more than once and the Phelps Law firm got him off, but he still had a thick record book at BPD. Now, it looks like he's muscle for the mob, intimidating Negroes who want better housing.

Paul Slayton, the other Caruso colleague, is more mysterious. No one knows where he is from, originally, but when he was first arrested in Buffalo in 1964, he had a Texas driver's license. He had no paper trail of any kind in Texas, or anywhere else that the Buffalo police inquired. He had no birth certificate, no social security number, no property, bank accounts, military service record, credit cards, magazine subscriptions, or parking tickets. There are more than three dozen other Paul Slaytons who aren't him. In fact, he could be someone else entirely, but there is no way to prove it one way or the other.

One interesting note in Slayton's file says that he was once in jail in Texas for a short time, awaiting arraignment on a minor charge, when his cellmate begged to be moved to another cell, even solitary confinement if possible. He said his life was in danger, which jail officers assumed was because of Slayton. Slayton's cellmate was being held because he was a known associate of Jack Ruby, the guy who had shot Lee Harvey Oswald, who had assassinated John F. Kennedy a week earlier.

Slayton's police record says he'd been arrested six times over the last six years, each on charges of assault. He always uses his hands, which the report says are as big as Easter hams. All of his beating victims refused to press charges, sometimes from hospital beds.

He moves around a lot, never has a permanent address, no job, no family, not even a girlfriend. But somehow, he has a car, appears well fed, is nattily clothed, and healthy. And then there are those hands.

Finally, there is Dante Caruso, the babysitting, ice-cream-buying bird-flipper. Zubricky decides this is the ringleader, whom he has to take down if only because he's the one who made him and embarrassed him in front of Mason, of all people.

Caruso is the out-of-towner who shows up just before a homicide. Zubricky surmises that he was brought in for some special assignment, probably involving death, and that he is staying in the Falco compound up in Elmwood Village. If he was flown up from New Jersey just to kill the Crowe kid, then he'd be back in Atlantic City by now: mission accomplished. But he's still around, so what's the deal? Since this is mob-related, Zubricky decides to call the local FBI for some guidance.

"Reynolds," says the voice when the phone is picked up. Agent Reynolds is currently one of the few still working at the field office in Buffalo. Everybody else is scattered about, rounding up draft resisters.

"This is Zubricky at BPD," says Abe. "How are you holding up, Doug?"

"I'm surrounded by more criminals than fellow agents," says Reynolds. "So, it's a little like the Alamo."

"Is one of them named Dante Caruso?"

"He's in town," says Reynolds. "He's been around for months now, which is unusual. Almost a permanent resident at the Falco compound. Luckily, he's been quiet far as we know."

"Any idea why? What's he up to?"

"I told our CIs to tell me what they heard, and nobody heard nothing so far. And that's unusual, too. I would have expected a body to turn up somewhere," says Reynolds.

"So, a button man has been around for months, and no dead people yet. Could he just be on call? Insurance? Waiting for the right moment?"

"Those thoughts crossed my mind," says Reynolds. "I can't think of another explanation. You called me about Dante, so what are you thinking?"

"Well, first, a body did turn up. A kid down in Lackawanna who was working on a housing project that is probably pissing off Falco."

"I know all about it," says Reynolds. "That Black guy in Lackawanna won't leave me alone about it."

"You heard about the dead priest lawyer thing last year?" asks Zubricky.

"Of course."

"This is the same story, maybe. The kid was working on getting that same housing development built, the one they snuffed the priest over. Fighting the city council, making progress and enemies. Then he's floating in the river."

"Classic," says Reynolds.

"There's more. I'll find out for sure tonight. It's possible Caruso has been a figure at the city council meetings, sort of stage managing, keeping it going in Falco's favor."

"Also classic," says Reynolds. "Are you attending?"

"He knows I'm nosing around, but I don't want him to know I'm close. So, no, not in person. The Lackawanna detective, Baldwin, he's working the case, he will be there. He'll see if Dante is the enforcer of record."

"And if he is?"

"Then we should all watch him and see if he has another target. From what Baldwin says, there are a whole gaggle of hippie do-gooders helping the Negroes get their housing development. Any one of them could be next, but most likely, whoever is the biggest threat to Falco."

"I don't really care about them, but pretend I do. Any idea who that would be?"

"Whoever takes the dead guy's place, would be my guess."

Paquette and Temple make the six-block walk up to Rochdale College. They pass most of the University of Toronto's main campus, which has the architecture and gravitas of Oxford. Large granite buildings in the Romanesque and Gothic Revival styles, lots of ivy, sprawling yards walled in with stone, wrought iron gates. Serious-looking students sitting cross-legged under hundred-year-old trees, books open, penciling notes. Overhead, frisbees fly around. The more athletic students dive for them, making acrobatic grabs, while the others just chase them down and try to get there before somebody's unleashed dog does. Paquette wishes that he'd had the opportunity to study and play for four or five or six years like these young people.

"This is your world, Rory," he says. Their walk has turned into a sight-seeing stroll. Tie loosened, jacket open, hands in pants pockets.

"Yes, it is for now, and I love it," says Temple, with a bit of melancholy. "But I'll soon write a dissertation. I defend it, and then who knows where I'll be."

"Teaching somewhere?"

"That's the dream," says Temple. "I'd love to go to Europe. England or Scotland would be ideal, but more likely I'll wind up in Saskatchewan."

"Teaching Philosophy," says Paquette.

Temple looks askance. "Everybody needs some."

"They do," says Paquette. "They do, indeed."

After a few more steps, Temple asks, "How are you going to handle the inquiry up at Rochdale? I mean, Grant Harel was a member of the family there. It'll be like telling his children, his siblings, his wife or lover, that he'd been murdered. How do you do that?"

"We don't actually know that he was murdered," says Paquette. "But that's what I was wondering myself," says Paquette. "I've done death notifications more times than I can remember, but this will actually be my first time, ever, notifying family members that their loved one is dead, and might have been *deliberately* killed."

"I wish I could help you, but there's nothing in the philosopher's handbook that addresses that."

Paquette nods, "I'm not surprised. Maybe you can write that part."

Temple's face lights up, as though he might have a research topic for his dissertation. "Hmmm," he says.

Five minutes later they are standing across the street from Rochdale College, an eighteen-story apartment tower built just a few years ago. Temple had explained that the college is a giant cooperative, run by students who try to live communally, sharing space, chores, responsibilities and everything else. Students and their professors are together almost constantly, and the jury is still out on whether that is a good idea or not. There have been almost as many folderols as love affairs between them.

"This is as far as I go," says Temple. "I have a class in fifteen, and I have to go. I'm the instructor." He waves towards the college. "Walk in, ask around, I'm sure you'll find out who to talk to first."

They shake hands, and Temple adds, "Good luck, sir."

Paquette looks both ways and dashes across the street, just avoiding a motorbike with two people on board. They honk at him with what sounds like a clown nose. He dodges a small group of students who are squeezing through the door on their way out, and when he's in the clear, in the lobby, he's met by a middle-aged man and a younger woman whose arms are crossed, and whose expressions are sorrowful.

"Are you the Mountie?" the man asks.

"Yes," replies Paquette. "I'm Inspector Henri Paquette, RCMP. You were expecting me?"

"Madeline Shelby at Yellow Ford Truck called us, told us to expect you. Told us about Grant," says the woman. She touches her eye with a Kleenex.

"I'm Alejandro Ayala," says the man. "This is Marsha Drake. We are faculty here, in the art department. Grant is our friend and colleague." Both of them are dressed exactly like their students. T-shirts, jeans, sandals, leather friendship bracelets. They're maybe twenty years older, though, and a bit grayer, flabbier. Paquette can tell that Ayala is the painter. His tee is covered with haphazard blobs of random colors.

"Let's not do this out here," says Ayala, looking around. There are people coming and going, elevator doors opening and closing, somewhere a baby is crying. "Please follow us."

They lead Paquette down a hallway papered with advertisements, proclamations, announcements, protest posters, news clippings, and portraits of this generation's heroes. Mostly rock stars, but here and there an artist, an author, a poet, all of them contemporary Canadians.

172

They reach a door and slip into a small office with a few chairs, a couch, a turntable, bookshelves and more portraits. These are all painted on canvas: Fidel Castro, Che Guevara, and a few other Latin men and a woman, all wearing fatigues, berets. All with resolute expressions. The portraits are very good, featuring strong brush strokes and color combinations that enhance the bold, brave faces of the revolution.

Ayala sees Paquette studying them all, trying to drum up their names. "I'm Cuban," he says. "These were my heroes growing up."

"I see," says Paquette. He leans into a painting of Isabel Rielo, a lieutenant in Castro's army, its only female officer. She's holding a pistol flat against her face, caressing her cheek with it. Paquette remembers reading about her, not sure where or why, just that during the revolution she led an all-woman platoon against Batista's army and prevailed.

"Your work? It's excellent," and he means it. To Paquette, it's a travesty that such talent is unlikely to have any audience outside this tiny office in Toronto, while pop artist Andy Warhol is making millions and mesmerizing art aficionados in New York with pictures of soup cans.

"Yes. And thank you."

They all take seats. Paquette hands them both his card. "What did Miss Shelby tell you? About Mr. Harel?"

"That he is dead, that you are investigating. That's it. She doesn't know anything else. She just thought it would be better for her to tell us than you, a policeman."

"She is right about that," says Paquette, quietly grateful that she did the job he was worried about. "I'll tell you what we know so far, and then I hope you will answer some questions for me, to help with the investigation."

"What exactly are you investigating?" asks Ayala. "Wasn't it an accident?"

"We aren't sure. The coroner determined that he drowned," says Paquette, "but we don't know why he was in Niagara Falls. So, we are treating it as an inquiry for now. Will you answer some questions?"

They both agree.

Paquette spends the next ten minutes telling them everything: How Harel was found, that other young men were found in the river as well, what those three had in common, one was certainly murdered, what the American police are doing. He doesn't see the need to show them any Polaroids.

"The other young men, now deceased," says Paquette, "their names are Dominic Styron, Jaime Roesler and Alan Crowe. Do those names mean anything to you?"

Drake sucks in her breath, sighs. Ayala purses his lips, shakes his head, leans forward, elbows on his knees. Paquette can tell that they do. He waits.

After a time, perhaps five seconds of silence, Ayala says, "Yes. We know those names. Styron and Roesler were supposed to arrive here but never did. Months ago. We had no idea what happened to them. They are dead?"

"They drowned," says Paquette, avoiding the word murder, for now. "I take it there was a direct connection, between them and you, or with Grant Harel?"

"Grant was an American expat. He came here a couple of years ago to resist the draft, to not fight in the war in Asia. We here at the college helped him. We got him over the border, helped with documents, getting settled, and getting a job here as an instructor," says Drake, between tears.

Ayala picks it up. "He got active with the resistance, helping other Americans get here to safety. He had contacts with other Americans, and they all coordinated their activities, bringing men across the border and up here to Toronto."

"He personally assisted, maybe, eight men?" says Drake looking at Ayala, who nods.

"Styron and Roesler?" asks Paquette.

"Roesler was one of Grant's students back in the States," says Ayala. "Grant and he had stayed in touch and when Roesler got drafted, Grant arranged for him to come to Toronto."

"Arranged how?"

"Not sure, exactly," says Ayala. "He worked with people on the American side but kept their identities mostly secret, to protect them. Like I said, they communicate, cooperate, but I don't know who Grant was in contact with."

Drake shakes her head. She doesn't know either.

"And Styron?" asks Paquette.

Ayala takes this one, too. "Styron had gotten in touch with Grant. I don't know how. He was having difficulty getting a deferment from the draft, and Grant was facilitating getting him up here. When he didn't show up, we just thought he might have been stopped at the border or changed his mind. It's a thick fog down there until people suddenly emerge."

Drake agrees.

"Have there been others who you expected to come over, but who never showed up?" asks Paquette, hoping the answer is no.

"Almost certainly," says Drake. "It's a crap shoot down there. But I can't think of anyone in particular. If you had a name, we might recall."

"I don't have any other names," says Paquette. "Do you know the name Alan Crowe?"

They both shake their heads.

"So, Grant Harel had provided some kind of advice or help to Styron and Roesler, and they both fail to reach Toronto, both die at the border, and then he dies there as well," says Paquette. "Did he make trips to Niagara Falls? Maybe to meet people? Help them the rest of the way?"

"Not that I'm aware," says Ayala. "He didn't own a car."

"Would he have spoken to anybody here about going to the Falls?" asks Paquette.

"It's possible, but he had many, many friends. You'd have to ask dozens of people," says Ayala.

"Did he live here?" asks Paquette.

"Yes," says Drake. "He had one of the bachelor apartments."

"I'd like to see it."

The three of them take the elevator to the twelfth floor and walk down the hall to Grant's room. Ayala opens the door — Paquette notices none of the rooms have locks — and they walk in. It's a small studio apartment, with a single bed, a desk, bookcase, dresser, reading chair and light, a closet and a private bathroom. A tiny kitchen area. He can see why Grant painted miniatures. One corner of the room is his studio. A canvas covers the floor. On it a table is littered with his paints and supplies, and a small easel holds a work-in-progress the size of a postcard. Paquette sees that it's just a sketch but would have become a painting of a First Nations family in a canoe, pushing through a river. Mother and infant in the bow, muscular father behind them, driving his paddle into the water. The dead artist had a talent for bringing people to life in his work.

Paquette removes a pair of latex gloves from his pocket, snaps them on as he says, "Please sit and watch, perhaps on the bed. Don't touch anything, please." They do as he suggests.

Paquette starts with a scan of the whole room. He's trying to get a sense of orderliness, and does anything look askew, disturbed, missing, out of whack. He looks in the closet and bathroom. There are just a few dress shirts, trousers, and winter gear on hangers in the closet, and toiletries in the bathroom, a used towel slung over the shower rod. No drugs in the cabinet.

He looks through the dresser. Only the usual. Socks, underwear, t-shirts, a tie. A drawer with sweaters, winter socks, a knit hat and gloves.

Then he moves to the bookcase and studies the titles. All but three are large-format art books, the masters. There's a copy of the book Temple and Taylor told him about, the *Manual for Draft-Age Immigrants*, a phone book for Baltimore, Maryland, and another for Buffalo, New York, which actually includes all of Erie County. He opens it and finds several dog-eared pages and names underlined. He places both on the bed. He'll be taking them back with him.

Then he inspects the desk. There is a pile of paperwork for the courses Grant taught. Lists of students, notes he jotted down for some of them. After one name, Linda Shatek, he wrote, "Promising." *She'd probably like to know that,* Paquette thinks.

There is a calendar where Grant wrote down appointments, meetings and such. Nothing for the dates he would have traveled to or been in Niagara Falls, or the day he died. Paquette takes the calendar as well. Maybe he can establish a routine of some kind.

He checks the desk drawers and finds the usual stuff. One is full of pens and pencils, paper clips, a magnifying glass, office gear. Another has stationery and envelopes, some stamps. In another drawer Grant stored cards and letters that he had received. They are held together with rubber bands, so Paquette decides to take the whole bunch. In the last drawer he hits the jackpot: Grant Harel's address book and his diary. The diary is held shut with a tiny lock, which he'll have to crack, and he decides to take it back to the detachment and get a professional to do it.

He turns to the bedmates. "Do you know his next of kin? Did you ever meet them?"

"His parents came up here from Baltimore a couple of times," says Drake.

"Very nice people," says Ayala.

"I suspect I'll find them in the address book," says Paquette. "Please let me make the notification. I'll work with them to return his body. If you choose to call them, please wait two days, and tell others to wait, as well."

They nod their understanding.

"Should we plan on boxing up his belongings, sending them back to his family?" asks Drake.

"Wait on that, as well. I or other officers might be back to gather other evidence. I'll let you know."

"We'll make sure the room remains undisturbed," says Ayala.

"I'm grateful," says Paquette, as he gathers up the things that he'll take with him.

"I dearly hope this turns out to be some kind of accident," says Drake. "If someone murdered Grant, who was the most perfect human being..." She breaks down in tears and Ayala puts his arm around her. "Who would do that?"

As far as he knows so far, Paquette thinks, all four young men were perfect and who, indeed, would kill them?

Chief James Plishka drives himself to the VFW in East Aurora, hoping to introduce himself to Harry Johnson, the murder suspect. It's Thursday evening at the Post, nothing special going on, but he had checked with his new friend Dan Fredricks, who said Harry would be there. They usually meet on Thursdays to watch a baseball game, he said, and Harry has a four-day weekend before heading back up to work nonstop on a new hotel in Niagara Falls.

Like before, the parking lot behind the Post is nearly full. It includes the Harley Davidson, and Plishka pauses to admire it. He always wanted to ride a motorcycle, but Susan had discouraged him, said it scared her, she didn't want to scrape him off the pavement or pry him out of the grill of a tractor trailer. Now, it just seems kind of late to start, and there are a million other ways to die, especially in his line of work. Still, he thinks, look at all that chrome. He can see his distorted reflection in ten places at once. This bike has some kind of Indian tasseled leather and gemstone decorations that demand the machine must cruise Route 66, through the New Mexico high desert, past the red mesas, into the Arizona pines. It smells like hot oil and wax. He's not sure he likes the ape-hanger handlebars, though. He'll have to meet the owner and ask him, "What's that all about?"

Inside the Post, behind the bar, Benson is filling another pitcher of beer that will be slid down the copper-covered hardwood slab from man to man until he has to fill it up again. In about a minute. Ten guys watch the game intently and somehow manage to pour a new one without looking down or spilling a drop. There are three black-and-white TVs suspended above the shelves of bourbons, gins and ryes, all tuned to the Red Sox–Yankees game, the greatest rivalry in the American League. It's the bottom of the third, tied two-up, when Plishka gets there and takes a seat next to Fredricks.

"Culp is pitching tonight," says Fredricks without looking away. "He has Munson with a full count and Murcer is on second."

"A hit?" asks Plishka, as he points at the jug of Schlitz, and Benson puts a glass in front of him.

"Culp walked him, then he stole second." says Fredricks, and he holds his breath as Culp winds up, fires a fastball, which Munson fouls off into the first-base stands. Some kid snags it bare-handed. The fans around him slap his back. He'll get it signed and that ball will become an heirloom, everybody knows.

The score is still tied in the top of the fourth when Harry Johnson arrives and sits on the other side of Fredricks. Plishka steals a look. The consummate Marine, with buzz cut, muscular jawline, a neck that looks like he'd be impossible to hang. When he puts his forearms on the bar, it looks like he might bend those pipes to his bidding bare-handed. He lights a cigarette, a Lucky Strike, by flicking a wooden match with his fingernail. This guy, thinks Plishka, is one giant blob of testosterone.

Between batters, Fredricks introduces Plishka to Johnson. They reach around behind Fredricks to shake hands, and it's then that Plishka sees that Johnson has a prosthetic leg from the knee down. He sits on the very edge of his stool so it can extend to the floor. Johnson follows Plishka's eyes as they study his appendage, and when they meet each other's, Johnson says, "Okinawa. Two days later, the whole shit storm was over."

Plishka points to his own leg, which took shrapnel on Omaha Beach. He still has it, and it reminds him all day long with a dull ache. "I got to keep mine."

They shake hands again, firmer.

"Dan tells me you were a ballplayer," says Johnson. "A good one."

"Those were the days," says Plishka.

"What do you do now?" asks Johnson.

"Besides being a loyal Fred's Ford customer," says Plishka, smiling, "I'm a cop."

That turns some heads. Three guys down the bar glance at him, one gives him a thumbs-up.

"So, still in uniform," says Fredricks. "We have a discount on a new Mustang for men in blue, or any other color."

"Tempting," says Plishka, pauses and asks, "Convertible?"

Fredricks bobs his head and adds, "Fire engine red."

Plishka narrows his eyes and says, "Oooo."

"What department you in?" asks Johnson. "Not out this way?"

"I'm the new chief in Lackawanna," says Plishka. "Been there for more than twenty years."

A look of recognition passes over both of his new drinking buddies. Fredricks nods and Johnson says, "I saw you on television last year, I think. You solved the priest murder, the mob hit. Sonofabitch. I didn't make the connection. You put, like, a dozen wops in jail."

A moment later a shot of Irish whiskey lands in front of Plishka, and Benson points down the bar. Three Yankee fans are pointing at him and one mimics pounding it down. He does, and waves at them, smiles his gratitude.

"Just six. They're on trial and they got good lawyers, so we'll see how that turns out," says Plishka.

The crack of a bat on TV gets everybody's attention. A Red Sox is rounding third, hard to tell who it is, but the right fielder, looks like Jim Lyttle, rifles a throw to home. The ball gets to Thurman Munson on a bounce and the sliding Sox gets to the plate at what looks like the same instant. A moment passes, everybody holds their breath, there's some dust that blows away, and the ump finally, overly dramatically, signals out! It's a Yankee crowd here in East Aurora, and the place erupts. Now Benson is pouring everybody a shot of the Irish.

Ninety minutes and a lot of drinking later, the game ends with a Yankee W. The three of them had talked about baseball, the mob, high school sweethearts, baseball again, the mob again, the drug problem among college students and teenagers, color television, the space race, civil rights – Johnson comes across as kind of racist – and finally cars. Then Benson turns the channel to the late-night news.

The scene is the aftermath of a firefight in Vietnam. Viet Cong bodies are lined up on the ground, row after row, some in grotesque, mangled states. What looks like a charcoal roasted arm sticks up from under a body bag. An American general, the caption says it's Creighton Adams, looks on approvingly, surrounded by subordinates who might be explaining things to him. Pointing one way, then the other, then up. Smoke rises from various places in the field behind them. Soldiers are carrying more bodies and adding them to the macabre collection.

In the background, other soldiers are carrying weapons and throwing them on a pile. In the foreground a reporter, wearing fatigues and a field hat, holding a microphone, describes the battle that had ended a few hours earlier. He has to stop briefly when he is drowned out by the sound of a helicopter thumping away overhead. Nobody at the bar listens to him, anyway. They have all seen this and heard this before, in person.

Plishka, Johnson and Fredricks watch the war quietly, each lost in his thoughts. Plishka is thankful that his son Robert may never be in a place like that, and he's keenly aware that he sits with two men whose sons died there. Without a doubt, they're thinking about their boys. Johnson takes a long pull on a bottle of Schlitz and smacks the empty bottle on the bar.

As if they were communicating telepathically, Benson pours him a shot, which he downs immediately. Benson shows the bottle to Fredricks, who declines with two hands up in surrender. Plishka does the same.

When that segment ends, the news switches to a college somewhere stateside. A long line of antiwar protesters, about fifty-fifty men and women, march with candles, chant slogans: "Hell no! We won't go!"

They're all wearing their own kind of uniform: bell-bottom jeans, high-top sneakers, rock-band t-shirts, long straggly hair. Most of them are smiling, probably stoned. The news reporter this time is a woman standing in the same spot as the guy in 'Nam, holding a microphone the same way, thumbing over her shoulder the same way. She describes what's going on behind her, and this time the men at the bar are listening.

"I'm here at Columbia University in New York," she says, "where more than five thousand students from all over the city have gathered for this protest march and demonstration, which will stretch well into the night. Speakers will include Abbie Hoffman of the Chicago Seven, and actress Jane Fonda. Similar demonstrations are happening simultaneously in Chicago and San Francisco..."

Benson appears again with the bottle of whiskey, and this time all three of them accept a shot.

"Turn it off, please," says a veteran at the end of the bar. He looks like he might have been in the First World War. Very gray, stooped, sad eyes that have seen it all. His hand, wrapped around a bottle of Gennie, trembles.

Everybody agrees. Benson pulls the plug on the TVs; they all go blank.

"I can't imagine what it's like to see that, for you two," says Plishka.

Johnson and Fredricks look over at him. Fredricks swallows hard and nods. Johnson's eyes are narrowed, he's grinding his teeth. "I can't tell you how much I hate them," he says.

"I get it," says Plishka. "I'm sorry for you both."

With the game over, and the televisions off and the evening ending on a flat down note, men begin to peel off, head for the door. Fredricks slides out of his chair, slaps Plishka and Johnson on the back and says he's tired, a little drunk, maybe, and has to move some cars tomorrow. He flings his jacket over his shoulder and leaves with the crowd. Johnson starts to do the same.

"Stay a minute, Harry, I'd like to talk to you about something," says Plishka.

Johnson is a little surprised, and glances down the length of the bar at Benson, who is busy cleaning up, carrying glasses back to the kitchen. "Okay," he says. "What about?"

"I'm investigating a murder," says Plishka. "Maybe more than one."

"Do say." Johnson's eyes narrow again. His jaw moves back and forth.

He tenses up. Plishka tries to read the body language, and if he's right, this could get ugly.

"Alan Crowe," says Plishka. "Know him?"

"I know he's dead," says Johnson.

"You also know that he's Kevin Crowe's son, right?"

"Yeah, so what? Lots of people know both of them. What are you getting at?"

"And you know that he was one of those antiwar protesters, and a draft resister, am I right? Like the ones we just saw on TV?" Plishka can see that Johnson knows where this is going. Johnson shifts around in his seat, looks off to the side.

"Everybody here at the Post knows that. It's no secret. We all felt bad for Crowe, about his son being a deadbeat hippie, commie freak," says Johnson. He looks around like he's trying to find a place to spit.

"People here heard you threaten to kill one of them, then Alan Crowe is dead. Did you have anything to do with that?"

That gets Johnson's attention. It looks to Plishka like Johnson is trying to figure out how much he knows, and therefore how to play this. Johnson is taking too long to answer.

"Here's what I got so far, Harry. Here's why I am asking you these questions," says Plishka. "First, you know who the victim is and you threatened to kill someone just like him. Second, you knew where to find him. Third, he was murdered in Niagara Falls, and that's where you been working for most of this year. And fourth, there are other victims just like Crowe, and they all died up at the Falls. Where you have been working."

"You got nothing," says Johnson.

"I got more," says Plishka. "Crowe was murdered with a heavy instrument, like a pipe. You work with pipes all day long. If I have your truck impounded, would my techs find Crowe's blood on a pipe rolling around in the bed, or on a wrench?"

"We're done," says Johnson, and this time he does spit, on the floor.

"I'm not done, Harry," says Plishka. "I got motive, means, and opportunity." He holds up three fingers. "You check all three boxes. All you need to do is give me a reason to believe you didn't do it. An alibi? Someone else to look at? If not, I have to come right at you, frontal assault."

"The Japs tried that and we mowed them down like bottles on a fence." He slides off his stool and walks out the door, pretty smoothly for a guy with an artificial leg. You'd never guess he had one. Plishka waits a moment, then follows him out to the parking lot. He sees Johnson standing next to his pickup, looking over the side, into the truck bed, pushing things around. They sound round and heavy.

181

There had been a day, not that long ago, when a Negro would never attend the Lackawanna City Council meeting. You weren't welcome, and they made sure you knew it. This is a white town and you are an unwanted interloper. Keep your distance. Go away. This was before the Civil Rights Act, The Voting Rights Act, the march on Washington, King's assassination, RFK's assassination, before the *Lackawanna Beacon* had a Black reporter, and the police department had a Black detective. Before a federal district court ruled against the city in a civil rights trial fourteen months ago.

The city council used to meet in a small conference room that might accommodate ten or twelve people, max. Most of the time it would be empty except for the councilors and a few petitioners. But ever since the King Homes project became the main agenda item, they had to move it to the largest public space in city hall, ironically called Fellowship Hall. The city even had to buy fifty more bridge chairs for the overflow crowds.

At tonight's meeting, more than half the citizens there are Black, a few are Puerto Ricans, the rest are white. They crowd into Fellowship Hall, but there is no mixing. All the Black folks are on the left, all the whites on the right, and even though there's a few empty seats in the white section, the slight overflow of Blacks stand against the left side wall. They leave the front row empty. It's reserved for their allies, the hippies, who haven't arrived yet.

The five members of the council are already seated at the slightly raised table up front, facing the crowd. They are talking quietly, straightening out piles of paper, poking the microphones in front of them – *dump, dump* – killing time. They don't look at the audience but steal a glance at the doors now and then, as though anticipating the grand entrance of some special guest. Or the grim reaper.

Tom Baldwin and Sandra Moore are having their date night in the back row. Sandra has a notebook on her lap and a pencil poised over it. Baldwin scans the room, looking for the three mobsters. He had gotten their photos from Zubricky just before lunch and had memorized their portraits. They haven't arrived yet, but there are five minutes to go. If they are who Zubricky thinks they are, they probably won't recognize Baldwin, though they might remember Moore. Everyone does. She's a beauty who everybody compares to Diahann Carroll.

Just as he was leaving the office earlier, Beth Egan had shown up and handed Baldwin an envelope with photographs of the woman who made a habit of crossing the Peace Bridge with young male passengers. They were both in a hurry and they promised each other to reconnect tomorrow. He tucked the envelope in his jacket pocket and now he has a moment to look at the pictures. He slips them out and takes a quick look. The driver is indeed the young PDM lady introduced to him as Amber, but the young man sitting next to her, looking nervous and twitchy, isn't anybody he'd seen before. Now he has a new line of inquiry. He slides the photos back in the envelope and back into his pocket.

"What was that?" whispers Sandra.

"Another complication," says Baldwin quietly. "Or, on the bright side, the answer to a question."

A minute before showtime, the trio of mobsters arrives through a fire exit on the white people side. Baldwin immediately recognizes them as Caruso, Paglia and Slayton. They're dressed in dark suits, open shirts, gold chains. Absolutely humorless expressions. Two of them take empty seats among the population, while Caruso circles around and stands in the very rear, behind Baldwin, obstructing but not blocking the main entrance. Thirty seconds later, those doors open and four PDM commune members push past Caruso, excuse themselves for brushing up against his massive shoulders. They walk single file to the front, to their saved seats that put them stink-eye-to-stink-eye with the city council. The Black people behind them pat them on the shoulder, whisper support.

Baldwin recognizes Jamal and Aries, and Sam, of course, and assumes that the new guy is Greg Phelps. He's carrying a fat briefcase that he places on the empty seat next to him and pops it open. One of the councilors leans way over the table to get a peek. It's hard to know what he expects to see besides paper. Gold bars? A weapon? He sits back down, bumping his microphone, which makes a loud reverb sound. It's the calmest noise the meeting will hear all night.

A tall, fiftyish councilor, whose name plate says Starzynski, calls the meeting to order and asks everyone to stand for the Pledge of Allegiance, which they do. Baldwin is a little surprised to see the hippies do it, but then again, they were in high school not that long ago and it's probably muscle memory. He can imagine Aries saying to herself, *wait, what?*

At the end of the pledge, a Black man in the audience says loudly, "Yeah! Liberty and justice for all!"

That causes a small chorus of 'Amens!' and, 'Say it!'

"We won't tolerate any disruptions," says Starzynski, as though he's addressing a kindergarten class. "You'll be removed. Got that?"

"White people, too?" asks a grandmother in the middle of the colored crowd. There's a lot of chuckling at that, most of it cynical, at least among the people on the left.

"Kick her out," mumbles a bald, fat, white guy in the middle of the right. There's a rumble of approval and what sounds like the "N" word.

"Wait, wait, wait," implores the lone councilwoman, whose name plate says Mrs. Jensen. "We have a full agenda, lots of important business. Let's not get started this way."

"They started it," says the fat guy. More rumbles, slurs.

"Just shut up, Gary," says Starzynski to fat man. They stare at each other like brothers-in-law, one or both of them angry that their sister chose such a loser.

Gary waves okay, and harumphs.

Starzynski waits a few moments to make sure everybody is onboard with what passes for decorum in a meeting monitored by the mafia. He looks prepared to tell others to shut up. Everybody clams up for the moment. Then he begins the meeting with reading the agenda. Fifteen items that various citizens have requested be addressed. Discussion about the King Homes project is last, as the most controversial, and the council probably decided to have the option to gavel it finished if it gets rowdy. Everything else will just fly by, they think.

For the next two hours, the council tackles one tiny tidbit of city business at a time.

There are several requests for zoning changes or code exceptions. One homeowner wants to build a backyard fence higher than the code allows because his neighbor's dog can jump up, get its head above the enclosure, and snarl at them while they are just sitting there, drinking a beer after work. It's approved. But then the neighbor complains that he shouldn't have to pay half the cost. There are arguments back and forth. Ten minutes later, he agrees to pay his share as long as they hire his nephew to build it. He assures everyone the kid will be the low bid, or he'll throttle him. Laughter, good-natured handshakes.

Another item is a zoning exception. A prominent businessman wants to open a liquor store less than five hundred feet from a church. In fact, less than four hundred feet. Three eighty-five, to be exact. This debate takes longer, because the original code was made back when bars were open at about the same time that Sunday Mass was going on. Lots of old-timers remember making their first communion with drunks stumbling past. The rule of thumb back then must have been that drunks can't walk five hundred feet. They question what the store hours will be, and will the owner close the place to accommodate a wedding, a funeral or a baptism. Someone jokes that those are the occasions when everyone is looking for a liquor store. It's the only time the Blacks and whites laugh together. The council tables it, possibly hoping the businessman will make it worthwhile for them.

On and on it goes. Every item trivial to the audience, crucial to the petitioner. That's until they get to the King Homes, which is emotionally charged, earthshaking, life-changing, heartbreaking, and temper-testing for everyone in the room. The hundred or so attendees transform from yawning, fidgeting, slouching, bored neighbors into fighting-mad contenders.

Gary the fat guy speaks first. "I thought this was settled."

"We all did, Gary, but the Negroes have another legal issue that must be addressed," says Starzynski.

"Oh, crap," says Gary, bored, despondent. Another says, "Can't you people just let it go?"

"Mr. Phelps? You're up. What do you have to say?" says Starzynski.

Greg stands up. Unlike his countercultural colleagues, he's wearing an expensive suit, silk tie, cufflinks. Looks like a high-priced lawyer. He surveys the audience, who are the jury as far as he's concerned, and notes the mafia guys. His eyes rest on Caruso a little longer. He clears his throat and begins. He took a course on courtroom performance, that's obvious.

From Baldwin's perspective, and from Sandra's as far as he can tell, Phelps is brilliant. Sandra writes shorthand notes as fast as she can, doesn't want to miss a thing. Phelps accurately summarizes the entire situation from its beginning to now. Nobody can dispute a single thing he says: The diocese did this, the city did that, the court ruled this way, the city was required to do that. He points out each of the areas of disagreement, from the point of view of both sides. He explains why the city is right on one count, why the Negro nonprofit is right on another.

Finally, he says that the one remaining issue preventing the construction of the King Homes project is the sewer permit, which must come from the county's health department, and what's holding it up is the absence of the mayor, Angus Brophy, who must request the permit. What goes unsaid, but what is known to all, is that Brophy has disappeared and is probably in some sort of witness protection program. When he is finished with his summary, he asks, "Do we all agree on this?"

The councilors look at each other, a bit dismayed. They seem to be disoriented by a lawyer presenting their point of view as well as his clients'. After a few moments, Starzynski says, "Yes, we think so."

Baldwin watches the councilman on the far right, who is taking minutes, writing something down. He looks to Sandra, who writes the response down in her notebook.

"Thank you," says Phelps. "In light of this, here is what will happen next."

Greg goes on to declare that the Popular Democratic Movement, in solidarity with the Negro nonprofit Better Homes Now, are working closely with law enforcement agencies to locate Angus Brophy and secure his signature on the required documents. He tells them that he expects this to happen within the next two weeks. He tells them that when he has Brophy's signature and has had it notarized, he will submit the paperwork to the county and city and they are required by the federal court to approve the sewer permit, and then the final building permits. He tells them that the Negro nonprofit has financing for the first stage of construction and expect to begin before winter.

The room is consumed in stunned silence. The only sound is the clock on the wall behind the councilors, which ticks off five seconds, then five more. Tick, tick, tick...

Then all hell breaks loose.

The Black people leap to their feet and cheer, laugh, exchange hugs and handshakes. Even Tom and Sandra embrace and manage a long kiss. It looks like the PDM kids might be carried out on broad, workingman shoulders.

On the other side of the room, the white folks are leaping to their feet, knocking over their chairs, shouting, pointing fingers, screaming at the city council and at each other. The council members are doing the same, shouting back. Starzynski is pounding his gavel into the table but nobody can hear it. Somebody in the audience missteps on a toppled chair and tumbles to the floor, taking a couple of women down with him. There's a scream.

Baldwin scans the room to see what the mobsters are doing. To his shock, two of them still sit in the midst of the crowd, calm as can be. Arms crossed over their chests, taking it all in as though it's a nice show. Caruso stands in the back, relaxed, smiling slightly. Baldwin looks to the front and sees Starzynski glance around frantically until he finds and locks eyes with Caruso. Starzynski looks a little surprised. Baldwin turns to see what he sees. Caruso is smiling and using his hands to signal calm down, calm down, it's going to be just fine.

Baldwin looks towards the front of the room again, makes eye contact with Sam. She raises her eyebrows and shrugs. *I see it too, what does it mean?*

After the city council meeting ends, after two Lackawanna policemen show up to restore order, after the white and Black folks have managed to leave for home without throwing a single punch, the PDM team piles into Greg Phelps's car for the brief, fifteen-minute drive back to the commune. Everyone is on cloud nine after Greg's performance and the message he drove home to the city: You can't stop this anymore. You are toast.

Baldwin had intercepted the cops when they arrived, and told them to ignore Sam, that she was on assignment, and they did. But they had to physically remove fat man Gary, who kept screaming at Starzynski long after it did any good.

The parking lot is slowly emptying. A couple of times, a Black attendee taps on the window and flashes a peace sign or a thumbs up in front of a big smile. A white guy pauses in front of their car, puts a maniacal look on his face and runs his finger across his throat. A white grandmother, dressed for Sunday Mass, stops, stares at them, then shouts, "Fuck you!" But this is clear: the Black folks float by in blissful happiness, the whites trudge along like Napoleon's army leaving Russia. Defeated. Ragtag.

"That was amazing," says Aries, breathlessly. "How did you arrange for all that? For the mayor to be located, to sign the documents, and for the financing?"

"Yeah," says Jamal. "Fucking great!"

Greg is quiet, a little fidgety. Gazes ahead, doesn't share their joy much. He hasn't started the car.

"Greg? What's the matter?" asks Gem. She sits next to him in the front seat and looks over at his profile, backlit by a streetlamp illuminating the parking lot. He's beautiful in that light and she wants to jump him, but it looks to her that he is deep in thought, or guilt of some kind. Unhappy, that's obvious. It takes him a minute to answer.

"I made it up," says Greg. "I haven't contacted the FBI or other law enforcement to find Brophy, to get the documents signed. That was bullshit."

He smacks his palms against the steering wheel.

The gang is stunned into silence for a moment. Eyes blink, mouths drop open.

"What?" they all say, almost in unison.

"Why?" asks Gem. "Why did you do that? Where does that leave us?"

"What's going on, Greg?" asks Aries, sounding a bit angry. "And what about the financing, is that bullshit, too?"

"No, that's real. I'm financing it," says Greg. "I'm ponying up the initial bridge loan to begin phase one of construction. Fifty grand."

"You're rich?" asks Gem, though she knows the answer and the probable source.

"Inheritance," says Greg. "I've been looking for just the right investment opportunity and this is it. It's not charity. I'll make some money. Once work starts, the banks will come crawling. They like money, too."

"Why make up the rest of it, what did that accomplish?" asks Aries.

Gem looks at his profile again. "Greg?" softly. She wants to reach out and caress his face.

"Alright," says Greg. "What I'm about to tell you has to stay in this car."

"What?" they all say again. "Why?"

"Because it could put us, or more like me, at great risk. We have to keep this quiet, even from Adrian and the rest. It'll just freak everybody out."

They squirm. Nobody is ready for this.

He goes on. "I am being set up. I thought I had it all figured out. What Alan was doing, why he was killed, why I'm here instead. Now I'm sure of it, because at the end of the meeting, when the white folks went ballistic? The mafia guys didn't. They were calm and happy. They acted like they got what they were after."

Gem channels her inner Sam, the cop. She sees it now, as well. They could only be happy about one thing.

"The mafia wants to locate the mayor, Brophy, for their own reasons and they want you to do it for them," she says quietly.

"Yes."

"Brophy is in witness protection because he is, in fact, a witness," she says.

"Yes."

"Their boss, that Maglione guy you told us about, the mafia boss, Brophy is a witness against him?"

"Yes."

"A dangerous witness?"

"Absolutely," Greg says. "He's the one person who can put Maglione in prison for a very long time. Maybe even the chair. They killed Alan to find Brophy."

"What do you mean by that?" asks Aries. "How do they find Brophy by killing Alan?"

"By getting me to do it. Alan knew we needed Brophy's signature but he had no idea how to get it," says Greg. "But the mob knows that I do. They must've figured that with Alan out of the way, I'd step in, and that's exactly what happened."

"How would you get Brophy's signature?" asks Gem.

"It's a long, complicated story, but basically, I have tons of valuable information that the Feds would eagerly trade for. They would give me Brophy, I'd give them about a dozen reasons to."

The other three glance at each other. Aries raises her eyebrows. Jamal nods his understanding.

"So, you trade your intel to the FBI, and in exchange, they give you access to Brophy," says Jamal. "All the mob has to do is tail you until you meet Brophy with the paperwork to sign."

"That's right," says Greg. "Then, I suppose, they'd kill us both."

"Oh my God," says Aries, terrified. "Now what do we do?"

"I hadn't thought that far ahead," says Greg. He smacks the steering wheel again. "The good news is that we are safe for a couple of weeks. We are an asset to the mob as long as they think we are going to lead them to Brophy."

"If you're right," says Jamal, "if the mafia guys killed Alan, we got to go to the cops. I mean, what else can we do?"

"He's right," says Aries. "I hate to say it, but we have to go to the pigs."

"What do you say, Gem?" asks Greg, turning to her.

"We have no choice," says Gem. She is answering as Gem, not Sam, but the answer is the same, either way.

Greg nods. He knows they are all right.

Gem says, "Detective Baldwin, the Black cop from Lackawanna, he was here tonight."

"I saw him, too," says Aries.

"You think he's the one we should talk too?" asks Greg.

"He's trying to find Alan's murderer, and we know who did it and why, so yes, he's the cop," says Gem. "I think we can trust him."

At that moment, maybe five spaces down in the same parking lot, under the lights, they all watch as Baldwin and Moore walk hand-in-hand to a Volkswagen Beetle, hop in, and drive out carefully. "That's him," says Gem.

"He looks familiar," says Greg.

"He's been around the house," says Aries. "Asking questions."

"No, that's not it," says Greg. "I think I saw him on the news or something. A while ago."

"We've got to help him catch Alan's killer," says Aries. "That's the priority. Not this Brophy guy or anything else."

Gem nods, then Jamal.

"Yes, of course, you're right," says Greg, "I'll call him tomorrow, see where that goes." He starts the car and slowly drives out of the parking lot. He stares ahead at the street, looks to the left, pulls out onto the highway, heading west on Ridge Road, back to the First Ward. Up ahead, the smokestacks at the steel plant are rumbling, belching smoke into the night sky. You can't see the stars. Gem watches Greg's expression, full of determination and resolve, as he drives along. He is risking his life to help a bunch of Black people build a housing development. Who does that?

"What you're doing, Greg, is brave," she says. "Righteous." She sees him blink a couple of times.

She decides to make love to him tonight. She can't help it, he's perfect.

Sitting in their car in a dark corner of the lot, Caruso, Paglia and Slayton watch them leave and finally have a chance to light their cigarettes.

It's early morning, and Sam is feeling pretty good about everything except, maybe, a little guilty about last night. She and Jack aren't married, or engaged, or going steady, but they have been a close couple for months now. He's been a teacher, a mentor, a boyfriend, and good at all three. What does she do now, with how she's feeling towards and acting with Greg? She wishes that her sister Sarah was still alive. She's the one she could confide in and Sam misses her dearly when stuff like this comes up. But she has a cop job to do, so she calls Baldwin from the smelly pay phone down the block.

"Ricky?"

"Good morning," says Baldwin. "Your boy Phelps was awesome last night."

In more ways than one, thinks Sam.

"He was," she says.

"The mafia thought so, too," says Baldwin. "Any idea why?"

Sam explains everything that Greg had shared, his suspicions, his confirmations, and Baldwin keeps saying "Yeah," and "Makes sense," and "Okay, good."

"He's going to contact you today, this morning, and tell you that they killed Alan and what their motive is."

"We'll need proof," says Baldwin. "Does he have any?"

"No, but he has a way to maybe get some," she says. Sam tells him about Greg's plan to set up the mob: Make a big show of connecting Greg with Brophy for the document signing, wait for the mob to act, and nail them.

"It all makes a lot of sense," says Baldwin. "But it may not prove that they killed Alan. Whatever happens next may not solve the Crowe murder, but it might nab some mafia hitmen."

"And get that housing built," says Sam.

"Two out of three ain't bad," says Baldwin. "One more thing before we hang up."

"Sir?"

"Amber."

"What about her?"

"She has been driving across the bridge into Canada often, over the last five months, with young men who were dodging the draft."

"I didn't think we cared about that."

"Two of them could've been Styron and Roesler. Maybe Alan."

"Ah," says Sam. "You want me to pry it out of her?"

"Yes," says Baldwin. "And since you are going to be her new best friend, maybe you can tag along on the next trip. It'd be nice to know how the system works."

His phone rings a few minutes later. "This is Greg Phelps," says the caller. "Can we talk?"

For the next twenty minutes, Baldwin listens while Phelps tells him who he is, what he's been doing to assist draft resisters, work on the King Homes, his connection to the PDM, and so on. Then he gets to talking about Alan, what he thinks happened to him, why, and what could and should happen next.

Baldwin acts as though this is news to him, but he has already thought through what to ask and do next. To pull it off he'll have to get the FBI, the Marshall's Service, and probably some federal attorney involved to make a deal with Phelps. That's a lot of organizing. He's glad Greg gave the city a two-week window. It could take that long.

"What is it you have to trade with the police, with the FBI, in exchange for approaching Mr. Brophy?" asks Baldwin. It's the thing nobody knows.

"My family, but not me, has been legal counsel to the Maglione family for many years. Since before I was born," says Phelps. "I grew up surrounded with my family's clients, the Magliones, at baptisms, marriages, funerals, holidays, dinner parties. They were like relatives. My older sister is married to a Maglione. That's how close we are. I'm a brother-in-law, which is ironic when you think about it."

"Go on."

"I know everything the Magliones have ever done and would like to do."

"Hearsay," says Baldwin. "Maybe privileged."

"Let the district attorney decide that," says Phelps. "But it may not matter whether what I deliver would hold up in court or not. The Magliones will assume that it will and they will act accordingly."

"They will stop you."

"They'll try to kill me." He sounds like he's willing to take the risk. "And Brophy, too, of course. Both of us are equally dangerous to them."

"I'll get the wheels in motion," says Baldwin. "It may take a few days to get everybody on board."

Phelps gives him his phone number.

"Mr. Phelps," says Baldwin. "You just told me that you help men get conscientious objector status at your legal aid clinic."

"Yes," says Phelps, "and that part is protected by attorney-client privilege." He thinks Baldwin wants some names, something to pass on to the feds.

"I understand that," says Baldwin. "But I have the names of two young men who are now dead. I know for a fact that they were seeking CO status. If I tell you their names, can you confirm whether or not they were your clients? They may have been murdered. It'll help the investigation."

Phelps is silent for a while, wondering perhaps what the legal ramifications might be, wondering if he should consult his professor. Finally, he says, "What are the names?"

"Dominic Styron and Jaime Roesler."

Silence. For a little too long. Did he hang up?

"Mr. Phelps?"

"I'm still here," he says quietly. "Yes, I was helping them with the paperwork." Another long silence. "They're dead?"

"Possibly murdered," says Baldwin. "When did you last see them?"

"Last I heard from them was months ago. May, June. I never actually met them, we worked over the phone and by mail. They were supposed to come here and finish the paperwork but didn't show. I thought they maybe panicked, went to Canada, or maybe just relented and showed up for induction. They would not have been the first."

"Maybe you should come in," says Baldwin. "I have many more questions. Maybe this afternoon?"

"Yes, of course." He's thinking. "Three?" asks Phelps.

"Yes, three. Between now and then think of everything you can about those men, especially anything they had in common... anything," says Baldwin.

There's another silence.

"Alan was one of my clients, too," says Phelps.

"We'll talk about him, too. I'll see you at three," says Baldwin, nodding because he knew about that, and they hang up.

Baldwin gets right on the phone with Reynolds at the FBI.

"You and I may have a way to get what each of us wants," says Baldwin.

"How so?" asks Reynolds.

Baldwin explains everything, and it takes fifteen minutes. If the ambush goes as planned, Baldwin will arrest the murderer of Alan Crowe, Reynolds will arrest an entire nest of mafia enforcers and the boss who hired them, Vincent Falco. And the government would get even more ammunition for

Maglione's firing squad: Phelps's inside information and an attempt on the life of a witness.

"Do you think we can get organized? Set a trap?" asks Baldwin. "Can we arrange for Phelps to meet with Brophy?"

"The U.S. Marshalls have Brophy, not the FBI," says Reynolds. "And his deal is with the U.S. Attorneys. They would all have to agree to this."

"I understand," says Baldwin.

"But I won't take the offer to them," says Reynolds. "Not on my watch, not in a million years."

Baldwin is shocked. "Why not?"

"Because they have Maglione by the short hairs, have Brophy in protective custody, and frankly, I don't give a flying fuck about your dead hippie and the Lackawanna Negroes."

Baldwin has had all he can stand of Reynolds and slams the phone down. *Plan B,* he thinks.

When Gem studies Amber Penrose closely, for what might be the first time, she appears older than the rest of the gang. Maybe thirty? She has reddish blond hair that she wears in long braids, one behind each ear, that swing loosely when she walks or turns her head, like Olive Oyl's arms. She's freckled, tall, big boned, curvy. The first time Gem saw Amber, she realizes now, her impression was Viking: strong, resolute, a fighter. But that was passing judgment on a physique. Amber has since come across as kind, warmhearted, and compassionate. A peacenik; a love child in a gladiator's body.

Amber is typically quiet during the evening group discussions, listening carefully to what others say, nodding when she agrees. She makes few comments during those family meetings, but when she does, it's usually in agreement with something someone else said, and it's always about the war. In her corner of a bedroom, co-occupied by three others, she has papered the walls with newspaper photos of Vietnamese villagers smiling toothlessly at the camera, fishermen pulling in nets, rice-paddy workers bending over their crop, children sitting in lotus position, staring down at open books. She chose the photos that depict a Vietnam at peace, perhaps to help her visualize the future. She sees them first thing in the morning, last thing at night. Looking at those pictures is for her like reading scripture is for a monk.

If only we were all like that, thinks Gem. But it's time to engage.

Gem watches Amber as she leans over the cutting board in the kitchen, drawing a long knife through a pile of collards that one of their Black neighbors had brought over from a backyard garden. Cutting them into strips, then into chunks. They'll get sauteed with some peppers, garlic and onions, chopped potatoes, maybe some pork sausage, and make a soul food dinner for the gang tonight. Gem thinks she should run out and get some cornbread. But there's that police work to do.

"I'd like to help," says Gem. "If I can."

Amber looks up and smiles. "There's a lot of chopping to do, grab a knife."

Gem finds a large bread knife, runs it through the wheel sharpener a few times and tests the blade. Good enough for defenseless vegetables. She reaches into the huge bag of potatoes – they eat a lot of these inexpensive carb-filled beauties – and begins her slicing and dicing. She quickly develops a routine. Cut the fruit lengthwise, put the two halves side-by-side, cut each half lengthwise, then slice the four slivers into half-inch chunks. Amber looks over and nods approvingly. "Brilliant," she says to Gem.

"I noticed that everybody here has some sort of a passion," says Gem, eyes on her knife and her fingers. "Something they spend all their energy on. Like me on the King Homes project."

"You're right, they do," says Amber cheerfully. "Everybody has a special power and they brought it along to Lackawanna."

"What's yours?" asks Gem.

"Oh, I do a little of everything," says Amber, "but if it has to do with ending the war, then I'm all in."

"What's behind that, do you think?"

"My dad died there. He was a doctor. The hospital was supposed to be safe, off limits, but it got attacked and we lost him." She says all this matter-of-factly, as though it happened a long time ago, she's all cried out and she's come to accept it. But she does wipe an eye with her sleeve. Maybe it's the onions that she's mincing.

"He was in the military?"

"No, he was with an NGO and was caring mostly for civilians caught in the middle. Fifteen of them died in the attack."

Gem doesn't want to know, so doesn't ask who did the attacking.

"I'm so sorry to hear that," says Gem. "I can tell you miss him."

They look at each other and Amber nods, wipes the other eye.

Gem decides to change the subject and asks Amber where she's from, about her family, has she ever had a real job. Amber is happy to move off topic, too. She grew up in Gloucester, Massachusetts, and her family traces itself back to the Mayflower. Her ancestors include soldiers who fought in the revolution, the Civil War, and all the rest of them, some writers, poets, abolitionists, preachers, and, of course, a doctor. Her mother's side of the family is the same, from the same part of the state. "I am most certainly inbred," she laughs. "There must be more than one great-great-grandparent who shows up on both family trees."

Amber went to Smith, got her degree in English, thought she'd become a writer or maybe work in publishing, but wound up writing copy for an ad agency.

"I sold chewing gum and cigarettes," she says. "Got paid well but I really, really hated it. Then the war happened and I quit to do what I'm doing. I probably have a pacifist as an ancestor. He or she is definitely on both sides of the family. I got a double dose of antiwar DNA."

They laugh together. The huge pile of chopped veggies is growing, and they are slowing down, not wanting to finish and break off their conversation. Amber asks about Gem, who is tempted for about one second to come clean. Instead, she does her job and lies through her teeth. At least, most of it is a lie, but Gem does tell Amber about losing her sister, Sarah, and how heartbroken she has been ever since. She tells Amber about her addiction to romance novels, Camel cigarettes, which Amber did not sell, her boyfriend "Ricky," and her attraction to Greg Phelps. Amber raises her eyebrows at that and says, "I approve!"

After twenty minutes of this kind of chatter, they develop a bond, Gem thinks, and she feels bad about it. She had lied to her.

At last, the mountain of veggies is ready for the sauté pans, and they cover it with a few sheets of foil. Amber washes up and Gem says she's going to have a smoke out front. Amber joins her. They sit on the porch floor and drape their legs over the side. Somebody is playing music down the block at a volume that makes you wish it was either lower or louder. It just sounds like noise. A few blocks west, the steel plant makes a continuous baritone growling sound while it belches smoke, like a giant snoring dragon.

"What's new on the antiwar front?" asks Gem as she lights up and draws on her smoke.

"We've been planning to leaflet at the steel plant, actually," says Amber. "Informing the workers there that they're contributing to an illegal, immoral war. We asked the national to send us the leaflets, they might arrive next week."

"Does that work? Do you see results?"

"You can't look into a man's heart, you can't tell what they are thinking," says Amber. "You're pretty sure it doesn't when they tell you to fuck off. But when they glance at the pamphlet for a second or two before crunching it up and tossing it back at you, it makes you think that maybe they thought about it." Amber shakes her head, a little glum.

Gem takes another pull on her cigarette. "Have you ever done anything that, you know, actually works? Something gratifying? Where you see immediate results?"

"I have," says Amber. "Kind of on my own." She looks over at Gem, pleased with herself. "Adrian probably wouldn't be happy with me."

They share a conspiratorial smile.

"Hmmm," says Gem. "Sounds naughty. Anything I can help with?"

Amber gives it some thought. She seems to be pondering whether or not to share what it is, not whether or not she actually needs any help. She hems and haws for a minute.

"It's a little risky."

"I take risks," says Gem. "For a good cause."

Amber hesitates some more, then relents to her new confidant.

"I take draft dodgers across the border. To Canada. It's a great cause."

"You mean, guys who got drafted but won't go?" asks Gem.

"And they can't get any kind of deferment," says Amber. "They're physically fit, not in college, don't have some essential job, like that."

"Somebody told me that Alan was trying for conscientious objector status," says Gem.

"Nobody ever gets CO status," says Amber. "He never would have gotten it."

"Why?"

"Not a Quaker or a Mennonite, and his only other choice was to come out of the closet, and he wasn't going to do that."

Gem reacts as though she didn't know that Alan was gay.

"How do you find them? The guys who want to cross?"

"They find me," says Amber. "I'm part of a network."

"Did you help Alan cross the border?" she asks gently. "Is that how he got to Niagara Falls?"

"I offered to, and we talked about it, but he decided to drive himself across when the time comes. I gave him somebody to contact in Toronto, but I don't know if he ever did. A week later we heard he was dead. Murdered."

Gem is surprised. This is brand new, maybe it can break the case somehow. Maybe Alan did contact that somebody in Toronto who might know what his plans were. Alan's car is still missing and it could be in Canada. Baldwin needs to know.

"Amber, this information could help the police. They're looking for his killer. What if this is relevant?"

"If I go to the police, I'd be turning myself in," Amber answers. "And, of course, Adrian would find out. I'd have to stop this important work, probably get told to leave this place. I gave this a lot of thought, and I decided to keep quiet about it." She looks at Gem imploringly. "You won't tell, will you?"

Gem shakes her head no, which is another lie. She'll call Baldwin as soon as she can. She wonders if Amber had driven Styron and Roesler across, and how to find that out. Does Amber remember everybody? Keep records? Stay in touch with them? Check up on their welfare? Who on the other side does she coordinate with? How does she ask Amber these questions without sounding like it's a cross examination? She decides on one question only and see what blooms.

"Think about this, Amber," says Gem. "The piece of information that could help the police solve Alan's murder."

"What would that be?"

"Whether or not he tried to get to Canada."

"I told you, I don't know."

"But what if he called your friend in Toronto, what if they arranged to meet or something, or what if Alan told that person what his plans were?" asks Gem. "They might have important information and would want to help. Can't you call them?"

Amber nods, agrees that asking can't hurt and might help depending on the answer. And she makes a slip. "I'll call Grant tonight," she says.

Baldwin sits in his office, feet up on the desk, staring at the ceiling, pondering which of his three primary suspects in the Crowe murder is guilty, and how to prove it. It's a perplexing task. And more troubling, is there somebody else out there?

One by one, he reviews the men in his crosshairs. The three most common murder motives are sex, revenge, and money, and with these men he has all three. McGee the homophobe had a strong motive, the opportunity and the means to kill Crowe, but has no obvious connection to Roesler and Styron. If all three deaths are related in some way, McGee could be in the clear. If they aren't, then McGee could be Crowe's killer. Johnson, the angry superpatriot, had opportunity and the means to kill all three, but the motive to kill any of them? Murder a draft dodger? The son of a colleague? It's a stretch. And the mob, in the person of Dante Caruso, has motive, opportunity and the means to murder Crowe, but not the other men. Phelps presented a compelling argument that Caruso is the Crowe killer. If that's the case, then who killed the others, and why? Are there actually two, and perhaps three different killers?

The only things that connect the three men right now are Niagara Falls and Greg Phelps, who was helping all three to get a draft deferment. Baldwin takes out Sandra's thought diagram and draws a few more circles with connecting lines. It's an incomprehensible geometric mess.

At that moment his phone rings. It's the Mountie, Inspector Paquette.

"I have the name and occupation of the fourth body," says Paquette.

"Another American?"

"Until a couple of years ago, when he immigrated from Baltimore to Toronto to evade the draft," says Paquette. "His name is Grant Harel, and he was a friend of Jaime Roesler, and was assisting both Roesler and Styron to get to Toronto, but, of course, neither one made it."

Baldwin writes the name down, and while he's at it, adds another circle to the diagram with the initials GM in it. He connects it to the JR and DS circles. "Anything connecting him and Alan Crowe?" asks Baldwin.

"I'll go through his things, looking for that," says Paquette. "I've got a lot of written materials to pore through. Diary, correspondence, address book. There are phone numbers in the Buffalo area code. I'll call them, see who answers. The phone companies will help, too."

Paquette adds all the other details he has about Harel: his job, friends, and his preoccupation helping other men to defect. He even tells Baldwin how talented a painter the man was, and that his wife agrees.

"I notified his parents in Baltimore, and they were terribly shocked. They were a close family and they were aware of his vocation helping young men defect. They didn't think he was in any danger up in Toronto doing that. Despite that closeness, they didn't have any other names to share. They said that the last time they talked, he was very content."

Baldwin and Paquette are quiet for a moment, both wondering suicide, accident, or murder?

"We may know who his American contact person is, that 'resource' you told me about. We have somebody looking into it," says Baldwin.

"Have a name? I can look for it in Harel's incidentals."

"Amber," says Baldwin. "That's all I have so far, and it might not be her real name."

"I may have seen that name, or an initial," says Paquette, "I'll look again. Or maybe she's one of the phone numbers I'll call."

A few minutes later, after they hang up, Sam calls.

"Hi, Ricky."

"Mr. Phelps and I have a meeting today, at three," says Baldwin. "It turns out he was assisting Roesler and Styron, as well as Crowe, to get CO status."

"Amazing," says Sam.

"He's the connection," says Baldwin. "But something tells me he's not the killer."

"He's not," says Sam, definitively, though she is emotionally compromised.

"He and I will have a conversation this afternoon," says Baldwin. "Why did you call?"

"Amber and I have become more acquainted, and she shared."

"What do you know?"

"Amber's last name is Penrose, and she's from Massachusetts. She ferries men across the border when all hope is lost. She offered to drive Alan Crowe, but he told her maybe later. Next thing she knows, he's dead."

"We have pictures of her doing that, driving across with men in tow."

"There's more," says Sam. "She is part of a network that includes people in Canada, and she gave me a name. Somebody she told Crowe to contact in Toronto. She's going to call him, check and see if he did. I thought it would help the investigation."

"What's the name?"

"Just a first. Grant."

Baldwin sighs, shakes his head.

"She's wasting her time. He won't answer," says Baldwin. "Grant Harel is dead. Just like the others. Over the Falls."

"Fuck," says Sam.

"Yes," says Baldwin. "What you said."

"What do you want me to do?"

"Keep doing what you're doing," says Baldwin. "Find out if she knew Styron and Roesler. Did she drive them across the border? I could come and question her about that."

"Don't blow my cover," says Sam.

"It's also important to find out who Amber actually delivers these draft dodgers to in Niagara Falls. That's who the mystery man, or woman, is right now. The missing link."

"Amber on one end, Grant on the other, mystery man in between," says Sam.

"That's what it looks like," says Baldwin, as he works on Sandra's chart again. More circles and a square.

At three sharp, Greg Phelps appears at Baldwin's office door. He taps it with his knuckle and Baldwin gestures towards the chair opposite.

"Thanks for coming in," says Baldwin, as he reaches over the desk and offers his hand. They shake. "Water? Maybe a coke? The coffee is terrible."

"No, thanks, I'm good," says Phelps as he plops down. He has his briefcase with him, sets it down next to his chair.

"I'm not going to make any headway with the FBI," says Baldwin. "They don't need you, they say."

"I thought so," says Phelps.

"But I may have another way to do it, so keep the faith," says Baldwin.

Phelps nods but looks discouraged.

They study each other for a few seconds. Each thinking, *you come from such a different place.* Phelps is a twenty-five-year-old white male, born into privilege and surrounded by family friends who are criminal-clients. Baldwin is a thirty-year-old Black, born into a lower-middle working-class family, surrounded by Missionary Baptists. Here they are, trying to solve murders together.

"I did what you suggested," says Phelps. "I tried to find any similarities between Crowe, Roesler and Styron, and there just aren't any. I went over their paperwork, their petitions to be granted conscientious objector status, and there's nothing there. They could not be more different."

"So far, the only thing they all have in common is you," says Baldwin.

"That crossed my mind, too," says Phelps, dejected. "I wracked my brain for a clue as to why that would be. Zero, nothing."

"How did they find you?" asks Baldwin. "They came from different states. Different times. Do you advertise?"

"Mostly word of mouth. Our law professor, David English, is well known, has a large network, the word spread about his clinic. He wrote a book about draft deferments, how to get them. It's just out there. We get calls all day long."

He explains to Baldwin how he happened to be working the phone when Roesler and Styron called, months apart, and how he worked with them long distance before arranging to meet them.

"They were supposed to come to Buffalo, to meet, get their applications finished. We had dates set up. They would have had to return to their hometowns and petition the draft board that called them up." He takes a piece of paper out of his briefcase and slides it over. It has the two victims with the chronology for both. When they first called, letters that went back and forth, the days they were scheduled to arrive here.

"But they never showed up?"

"No, so I thought they took the alternative, and headed for Canada, or maybe just showed up for induction."

Baldwin looks at the dates they were expected at the clinic. In both cases, a few days before turning up under the Falls. "You could be right about Canada," says Baldwin. "Have you ever heard the name Grant Harel?"

"No."

"He's dead too, same circumstances, and he knew both Roesler and Styron. We are trying to determine if he knew Crowe."

"A draft resister?"

"He emigrated to Toronto a couple of years ago and began helping others do the same. He was up there waiting for Styron and Roesler but they never showed, so he and his friends up there thought they gave up."

"And I thought they made it," says Phelps, exasperated.

"Are you aware that Amber, at PDM, moonlights as a chauffeur, driving draft dodgers across the border to Canada?"

"How do you know that?" asks Phelps.

Baldwin doesn't mention Sam but slides the photos that Beth Egan had printed for him across the desk. Phelps studies them, nods. "I heard that the Feds were surveilling the bridges, I guess it paid off. Is she in trouble?"

"Not with me, but I'd like to know if she transported Styron, Roesler and Crowe, wouldn't you?"

"Yes," says Phelps. "It would fill in the gaps."

"And there would be somebody besides you who connects the victims together."

Phelps looks at him with alarm. "You don't think Amber is involved in the killings, do you?"

Baldwin shrugs. "I don't know what to think."

There's a moment of silence while both of them consider this. Phelps shakes his head almost imperceptibly. Baldwin's expression says anything's possible.

"I think the time has come to show these photos to Amber," says Baldwin. "And ask her if she knew any of our victims who were found under the Falls."

"I'd like to be there," says Phelps, "in case she needs legal advice."

Baldwin is aware that showing Amber the photos and questioning her about Harel, Roesler, and especially Styron might be the unfortunate way that Aries finds out about her lover's fate. But he has to move forward with the investigation, and the puzzle pieces seem to be locking together. A picture is emerging, and Amber seems to be in the middle of it.

"There's more to share with you, I'm afraid, because it'll come out soon, when we talk to Amber," says Baldwin as he opens his file drawer and pulls out the Styron folder. He hesitates a moment before handing Phelps the picture of Ashley Lange, Styron's lover in Akron, Ohio. "Does she look familiar?"

"Why am I looking at a picture of Aries?"

"This was in Dominic Styron's file, sent over by the Mounties. Her real name is Ashley Lange. She was Styron's girlfriend, and Styron is most likely Arwen's father."

"Oh my God," says Phelps, as he stares at Ashley. "What…how…"

"That small world thing," says Baldwin. "Amber may need a lawyer; Aries will need a good friend. So, yeah, you should come along."

"When?"

Baldwin nods. "We could do it now, if you're free."

When they drive to the commune in their separate cars, one behind the other, they are followed by a nondescript brown Chevy. Paul Slayton is behind the wheel.

Baldwin and Phelps arrive at Swan Street right behind one another and slam their car doors in unison. One of the men, Peter, is still puttering with the engine of a VW van, swearing under his breath. Aries and one of the other ladies are on the front porch with their children. They both wave enthusiastically at Phelps, less so at Baldwin. But they aren't unfriendly, maybe just curious, or cautious. The homey smell of southern cooking comes wafting out of the house and almost bowls Baldwin over. He subconsciously hopes that no matter how this questioning goes, he gets invited to dinner.

Two blocks short of the house, Slayton had pulled over and watches what he can. None of the hippies notice him but about a half-dozen neighbors do. White men in their neighborhood are either undercover cops or drug dealers. Sometimes, but rarely, they are there to fix a broken utility or check on a stopped-up sewer. The mothers keep their kids indoors.

Baldwin and Phelps didn't discuss how and when they'd tell Aries about Styron, and Baldwin wishes that they had. He glances over at Phelps as they approach the women, and he sees that Phelps has the same concern. Baldwin gives him the tiniest head shake, and Phelps gives him the same size nod.

"Are we on?" asks Aries, a little excited. She's obviously referring to the sting operation, the one where the mobsters try to kill Greg and then Baldwin and the entire FBI step in at the last moment and either arrest or shoot Alan's killers in a hail of gunfire.

"Not yet," says Phelps.

"We're working on it," adds Baldwin.

The look on the women's faces asks, *so what are you doing here?*

"Is Amber around?" asks Phelps.

Aries and the other woman, Ann, mother of the two-year-old whom she named Elrond, look at each other a little surprised. Nobody ever asks to talk to Amber.

"Inside, making dinner with Gem," says Aries. "Just walk in, we're occupied." She gestures towards the children.

The aroma of the dinner prep is luxurious. Baldwin's mouth waters involuntarily. He has to stop a few feet in and concentrate on cop mode. He looks over at Phelps who is doing the same. *I know,* he seems to say.

Adrian appears, seemingly out of nowhere, and extends his hand. "Good to see you again." He turns to Phelps and says, "Hi Greg." Then he looks at Baldwin inquisitively. Puts both palms up.

"Likewise," says Baldwin, "but I'm here to speak with Amber."

"What about?"

"Police business," says Baldwin, politely, and he tries to pass by Adrian. But Adrian puts out a hand on his chest, gently, and says again, "About what?"

Baldwin considers, for one second, pushing the hand away and becoming the belligerent cop who doesn't put up with any kind of shit, but instead he says, "Nothing to do with your work here. Nothing, I hope."

Adrian looks at Phelps, who lowers his eyes and nods. He's telling the truth.

Adrian steps to one side and says, "Kitchen."

In the hot kitchen, Amber and Gem are cooking the veggies and sausage chunks in a medley of pans on the four-burner gas stove. Steam rises from all of them, and from time to time there's a little crack and sizzle from the sausage. Gem sees them first, and smiles at Phelps with what can only be described as affection, maybe laced with lust, and she nods a hello to Baldwin. Amber is bent over the stove stirring the collards and seasonings, focused on soft not soggy. She's concentrating on the food.

"Amber?" says Baldwin. He has a sad expression that says bad news.

She turns, comprehends the situation, perhaps she relents. She lets out a sigh and wipes her hands on her apron. She looks at Gem and says, "Take over?"

Amber leads them through to the back of the house, where there is an infrequently used back porch. It's where they stack the garbage bags until collection day, which, in the ghetto, is unannounced and sporadic.

"This is kind of private," she says. The three of them stand in a small, somewhat tight triangle. There's only one chair. A small dog yaps nonstop in the neighboring yard. They all wish it would just shut up.

Baldwin holds up the photo of Amber in the driver's seat, some random draft dodger next to her, taken on the bridge. "There are more like this," says Baldwin.

"That's me, alright," she says, and puts her hands out as if expecting to be cuffed.

"That's not why we're here," says Baldwin. "Not my jurisdiction."

She puts her hands down. Relieved. "What then?" she says.

"Two other men, besides Alan, have been killed at the Falls, all about a month apart," says Baldwin. "I need to know if you drove them across the border like this guy." He waits for a reaction, and Amber hesitates before nodding and biting her lip. "One is Jaime Roesler, from Baltimore, the other is Dominic Styron, from Ohio."

Amber's face melts. She chokes up and puts her hand to her mouth. Her eyes well up and she nods her head vigorously. "Yes," she struggles to say through a low moan. "Yes."

"Can you tell me how they found you?"

She's still in shock, but manages to say, "I get names of men and meeting places from a contact in Toronto."

"Grant Harel?" asks Baldwin.

She nods and looks surprised that he knows the name.

"I sorry to tell you that Mr. Harel is dead, too, also at the Falls."

At that, Amber's knees give out, and both Baldwin and Phelps reach out and catch her before she collapses. They help her sit on the wobbly old chair, the only one on the cramped porch.

"I'll get her some water," says Phelps, and he disappears into the house.

Amber puts her elbows on her knees and her face into her hands. Her braids droop down on either side. She sobs, her back heaving. Baldwin puts a hand on her shoulder.

A minute later, Phelps appears with a glass of water with Adrian, Gem and Aries close behind him. They stand crammed in the open doorway. Aries carries Arwen, who naps on her shoulder. Amber takes a sip.

"I didn't know," she finally gets out, in a mousy whisper.

"I know," says Baldwin. "Can you tell me where you take the men? Who you meet with?"

She looks at him through her fingers, probably wondering if she should tell or not.

"Whoever it is might know what happened next," says Baldwin, not allowing that whoever that is might have determined what happened next.

"I drop them off with a man at a hotel they're building in Niagara Falls," she says. "Then he takes them the rest of the way, up to Grant, to Toronto."

"What hotel?"

"It's called the Exeter," says, Amber. "It's a big construction site, right beside the river, above the Falls."

"Always the same man?"

"With Jaime and Dominic, it was somebody different, but he knew the routine and seemed nice," says Amber.

She appears to be recovering a little from the shock, and she seems to understand the importance of these questions.

"Dominic?" asks Aries from the doorway. Everyone looks at her; Baldwin, Phelps and Gem concerned. "Did you say Dominic?"

Gem puts her arm around Aries and pulls her tight. Phelps steps over to her and puts his hands on her shoulders.

"Is Dominic in Canada?" Aries asks.

"I am so sorry," he says softly, "but Dominic is dead. He drowned in the river."

"No," she says. "You're wrong." She holds Arwen a little tighter. "You're wrong!"

"The Canadian police found his body, and he was sent back to Akron," says Baldwin. "Three months ago. We are all so sorry to tell you this."

Aries shakes her head, pulls away from everybody and hurries away into the house. Adrian, Gem and Phelps follow her. She's the important one now.

Baldwin watches them disappear into the house, can hear some voices, can hear Aries say "No" one more time, and then they are too far away. He turns his attention to Amber.

"Dominic and Aries were…?" she stammers.

Baldwin nods.

"Oh no," she says and buries her face in her hands again.

"None of this is your fault," says Baldwin. He gives her a minute. Then another. Slowly she lowers her hands and looks up at him.

"What can I do to help?" she asks.

"Tell me what you can remember about the man you left Jaime and Dominic with."

She proceeds to describe a man who could only be Harry Johnson, master plumber.

"This is important, Amber, so try to remember," says Baldwin, a little panicky, "Did you leave anyone else with this man?"

She bursts out crying. "Yes, I did."

"When? When?"

"Yesterday," she says.

"What's his name?"

"Thomas Jordan, Thomas Jordan!" she stammers.

Baldwin knows who killed Roesler and Styron. Maybe others. Maybe yesterday. He rushes back to the House to find Plishka. Phelps stays behind at the commune to comfort Ashley Lange, and Sam continues to play her part as Gem, consoling Amber. Both women had been gobsmacked.

"Sir, we have a breakthrough," he says breathlessly at the chief's office door.

"On Crowe?"

"No, on the others," says Baldwin. "It's Johnson, it's got to be him." He explains everything to Plishka, who reacts to each alarming detail with a nod, a quick note to himself, a to-do list.

"Johnson is in Niagara Falls," says Plishka. "And you're saying that Amber delivered another draft dodger to him yesterday?"

"Yes sir."

"Did she tell you his name?"

"Thomas Jordan," says Baldwin. "She dropped him off with Johnson at about ten yesterday morning."

"Call Paquette immediately, then get up there and this time, take your gun," orders Plishka.

His call to Inspector Paquette takes five minutes, and Paquette tells him he can be at the hotel in five more. He says he has seven Mounties who will accompany him, and they'll secure the scene until Baldwin arrives. They agree on a meeting spot. Nobody will go in or out without their notice.

Baldwin races up to the Peace Bridge and is flagged through customs on the Canadian side. Paquette must have called ahead. A motorcycle cop leads him up the QE Way at twenty mph over the speed limit, straight to where Paquette waits for him: a command post under a pergola a half a block away from the hotel.

The Exeter is partly complete on the outside, with curtain walls installed all the way to the top. The ground floor is surrounded with material stockpiled and needed to finish the inside. Cranes lift pallets of drywall to upper floors, men in yellow hardhats direct the operators, who skillfully guide their loads into openings or drop them on scaffolds. Baldwin notices large bundles of pipes waiting to be hoisted up for the plumbers. Johnson is up there somewhere, probably waiting for the supplies, and hopefully not for the police.

"We checked with the construction managers, and Johnson is working on the fourteenth floor," says Paquette. "Also, we have teams searching the gorge and downriver, in case he's done away with Mr. Jordan."

"He has no way out?" asks Baldwin.

"No, we have men on all sides and as you can see, the site is surrounded with chain link fencing. The only egress from the site is through three gates, north, south and west, or straight down into the river on the east side. Certain death."

Baldwin wonders if that is how the victims met their end. Tossed through a window or off the superstructure and into the water. It's possible they were lured to their deaths with the promise of a million-dollar view of the Falls, only to be pushed. It wouldn't take much, if you trusted the man standing behind you.

"How do we play this?" asks Baldwin.

"I suggest you and I go in together with backup and make the arrest."

"Up to the fourteenth floor?" They both crane back and look up. There are no glass windows, just the openings for them. Instead, clear plastic sheets billow out from the empty rectangles with the breeze.

"Safer for all concerned if we summon him down," says Paquette. "Maybe have the supervisors send up a messenger, tell him to come look at some new plans or something."

"I'd like to be that messenger," says Baldwin. "If he senses something is off, he may panic, do something stupid. We don't need a hostage situation."

Paquette nods, "Good thinking."

"We need him alive," says Baldwin. "We need him to tell us if he killed the men, all four, and if there were others. We need to know what happened to the latest."

"I'll make sure my men know that," says Paquette.

It takes ten minutes to get Baldwin looking like an engineer, and for Paquette to coordinate his men. He talks with the construction managers, who quietly move their men out of the ground floor, where an elevator containing a murderer may soon land. Baldwin confers with them, too, getting some advice about what to say and how to say it, to get Johnson to descend with him. A few minutes later, they're ready to move.

214

Baldwin takes the temporary lift up to the fourteenth floor. It's an open affair, just a platform running up and down through what will one day be a closed shaft along the exterior wall. He can see in every direction, and notices that with every floor upward, less has been completed. Men are at work on each floor, bent over some project, looking at plans, pointing at some detail. He looks like them: yellow hardhat, safety belt, steel-toed shoes that he borrowed. They're a little uncomfortably tight. The lift comes to a bouncy stop on the top floor. He sees Johnson immediately.

Johnson is looking over a set of plans on a makeshift table. Two other men, much younger, hover nearby as he explains something to them. He stabs his finger at something on the drawing, scowls, turns to one of the apprentices and points at something on the other side of the room. The guy jogs over for it. Baldwin feels for his weapon, tucked behind his waist, gets accustomed to the clothing he'd have to work past to pull it out in an emergency.

He walks towards Johnson. "Mr. Johnson?" he says, smiling apologetically.

Johnson looks up and scowls again, like he's expecting bad news.

"I'm Billy Shields with the HVAC team," says Baldwin. "They sent me up to see if you have a minute to come down and look at the new units that just arrived. Somebody down there isn't sure that they're to spec, that you'd be able to make the connections. One guy thinks that they aren't."

"Well fuck," says Johnson. "We been waiting three weeks for that stuff and it might be wrong?" He rolls up the plans he's been looking at, hands them to the other assistant without looking at him. Just stabs them into the guy's chest.

Baldwin shrugs and puts his hands up. Not my fault.

Johnson says something to the two young guys, waving his finger around, then looks at Baldwin. "Let's go."

The lift moves slowly on the way down and they're both able to see everything inside and outside the building. Nothing holding them in the thing but some homemade pipe railings at waist height. Down below, a hundred-fifty feet, they both see a small cluster of project-manager types in hardhats and suits staring up at them. But there is something else painfully obvious. They can both see two groups of three uniformed cops, one to the left, one to the right, also staring up at them. One of them is holding and talking into a handheld radio, another actually has binoculars.

"What did you say your name is?" asks Johnson.

"Billy Shields," says Baldwin.

"Why haven't I seen you around before?"

"I just came on the job, now that the HVAC units are here."

"Here, where?" asks Johnson. "I don't see them."

"They're still on the truck, other side of the building."

Johnson slaps the emergency stop button. The lift jerks to a halt between the tenth and nineth floor. "Bullshit," he says. "There's no truck over there, I was just looking down at that landing a minute ago."

Baldwin has no answer for a second too long. Johnson moves close in and grabs him by the shirt with both hands. Baldwin instinctively grabs his wrists.

"Who the fuck are you and why the cops?"

Baldwin can feel Johnson begin to lift him off the ground. He's pushing him towards the railing. Baldwin steals a glance at the crowd below and he sees a lot of scurrying around, cops beginning to draw their guns. He forces himself to relax, to melt, to become dead weight. Johnson is freakishly strong but still struggles to keep Baldwin upright. Baldwin is mostly on the floor. Getting tossed out is no longer in the cards.

"Give it up, Johnson!" It's Paquette on a bullhorn. "There's nowhere for you to go, nothing you can do! Let the man bring you down!"

Johnson still has a grip on Baldwin's shirt. He stares into Baldwin's eyes, trying to decide what he'll do, and to Baldwin it looks like giving up isn't it. He pushes Baldwin away. With acrobatic agility, Johnson slides off the lift and drops onto the ninth floor.

The men working there had become aware of trouble and had moved away, as far away as they can, off to the fringes. With them watching, Johnson runs for the east side of the building overlooking the river and stops at the edge of a window opening. It's the size of a garage door. Baldwin gives chase. He's twenty feet behind Johnson and stops. He has to talk the man out of what he clearly intends to do.

Down below, a hundred feet, the Niagara River roars past at twenty-five mph and ninety decibels. Nobody can swim against that current. A hundred yards downstream, it's flowing close to seventy mph as it rushes over the Falls. If Johnson jumps and hits the water, he's doomed.

"What you did was wrong!" shouts Baldwin. "But this won't make it right!"

"What I did was right!" shouts Johnson, without turning. "This is necessary!"

"Don't take your life!" says Baldwin, as he steps closer.

"I don't have a life," says Johnson, turning slightly to be heard. "This is my only option."

Baldwin tries to conjure what his psychology professors would say in this situation. How to touch this man with something both logical and emotional. He doesn't have time, says the first thing that comes to mind.

"Your son, Ronny, he admired you so much he followed in your footsteps! Is this how you'd want him to see you?"

Johnson freezes, turns slowly, it struck a chord. Behind him, Baldwin can sense more people arriving, probably law enforcement. Whoever they are, they stop well short of the two main actors. They don't want to change whatever the dynamic is.

"I can't promise you anything if you turn yourself in," says Baldwin. "Except you'd keep your honor, and that's what Marines swear to do. Ronny died honorably. Please, Mr. Johnson, do what is honorable. Do one more thing that he would admire."

It works. Johnson, whose jaw was clenched and determined, suddenly collapses emotionally, his body goes slack. He takes ten steps towards Baldwin and turns around. He puts his hands on the back of his neck and kneels down. Two Mounties rush forward and put him in cuffs. One of them says to Baldwin, "Good work, sir."

Paquette's men march Harry Johnson away after informing him of his Charter Rights. They tell him why he's being arrested — for the murder of two men — and inform him that he can remain silent, and that he is entitled to counsel. Baldwin catches a few more rights as the cadre steps back to the lift, but he's got other things on his mind: What happened to Thomas Jordan, is he still alive? And who killed Grant Harel and Alan Crowe? While he stands at the window opening, watching the river rush past below, Paquette shows up at his side.

"The Canadian Government owes you a debt of thanks."

"There are a lot of people who deserve thanks," says Baldwin, "but we aren't done yet, are we?" He turns to Paquette, who is nodding. "Any sign of the Jordan person?"

Paquette shakes his head.

"I don't know whether that's good or bad," says Baldwin.

"We'll be interrogating Mr. Johnson, maybe he'll tell us, and I'd like you to be there," says Paquette. "We will provide him with a solicitor, which may take a while. My guess is late tomorrow morning. You can stay here at our expense, or come back at eleven?"

"I need to report back to my chief," says Baldwin. "And my wife."

"There will be an escort at the bridge for you," says Paquette. They shake hands, and Baldwin takes another look at the river, and shivers. It's dark, deep and fast. Powerful and unstoppable. Once that thing gets hold of you, you're done. *What a horrible way to die*, he thinks.

217

On his way back to the bridge, Baldwin uses his radio to reach Plishka, who is just getting ready to leave for the day.

"Johnson is in custody here," he says. "The Canadians have him for two murders, Roesler and Styron, and maybe there'll be evidence or a confession for the others."

"Was there a shootout?"

"No, almost a suicide," says Baldwin. "I had to convince him to surrender. I got lucky. Pressed the right buttons."

"I'm proud of you," says Plishka. "Good job. Alive, maybe he'll tell us more."

"I'm coming back up here tomorrow," says Baldwin. "If he does, I'll hear it."

Sandra has dinner ready for him when he arrives home. He locks up his weapon, takes his have-a-blessed-day note out of his pocket and kisses it, puts in a jar with hundreds of others, and joins his wife at the table. He tells her everything, and like a good wife and a good reporter, she listens intently and writes it all down.

"Can I go with you tomorrow? To report on the rest?" she asks.

"Better if we don't travel together, in case I get sent off to investigate a new lead or follow up on something he tells us," he says. "But follow me closely and you'll get the same police escort I did."

They spend the rest of the evening talking about the people and events that led to the arrest, and Baldwin is reminded to call a few people. One of them deserves a big thanks. He looks at his watch, holds up a finger, like excuse me, and calls Reynolds at his home.

"It's late," says Reynolds. "What now?"

"Not too late for good news," says Baldwin, and he tells him how the day went, leaving little out except Amber Penrose's name. He doesn't think Amber will be doing any more deliveries, so why complicate her life?

"So, what you're telling me is a war hero, a Marine, is going on trial in Canada for chucking a couple of draft dodgers in the river," says Reynolds. "I'm supposed to be happy about that?"

"He murdered them," says Baldwin. "I thought maybe you'd like to call their parents and tell them the man's been caught. The FBI played a huge role in that."

There's a long silence, perhaps because Reynolds, himself, was caught off guard.

"I told you going in that you could take credit for it. Do you want it or not?" asks Baldwin.

More silence. When he finally speaks up, Reynolds sounds a tiny bit less confrontational, a tad more professional. "So, our photography project paid off," he says. "Just not the way we thought it would."

"Agent Egan," says Baldwin, "If it weren't for her keen eye on photos that she developed months ago, we'd be nowhere. She broke the case."

Baldwin can't see him, but Reynolds is shaking his head, thinking *Agent Egan.*

"She'll be very happy to hear that," he says.

"My wife wants to interview her for her story, for the paper," says Baldwin. "Will that be okay with the bureau?"

Reynolds says, "Absolutely. Why the fuck not?"

Early in the morning, as he expected, Gem calls him from the filthy phone booth.

"Somebody puked in here last night," she says, "so let's make this very quick, how did it go?"

Baldwin tells her everything and tells her that he's headed back up to the Falls and will learn more. She tells him that Greg and the rest of the PDM people spent the entire evening and most of the wee hours consoling Aries and Amber, and they both finally fell asleep surrounded by their "family."

"It was so tough on both of them," says Gem. "Amber unknowingly drove Styron up to his death, and here she is, living with the man's lover and child. It's killing her. She'll never live that down."

"She'll be asked to testify at Johnson's trial, most likely," says Baldwin. "She'll have to relive it."

"Hopefully, she'll see that as a chance for redemption," says Gem.

"And Ashley?"

"She doesn't blame Amber, but she's in shock that he was so close, and neither of them knew it. He passed right on by, then ended."

"Too many secrets," says Baldwin.

"I know," says Gem. "I'm one myself. I am not looking forward to the day that I come out of the closet with these folks."

"I can't tell you when that will be," says Baldwin. "We still have one, maybe two more mysteries to solve."

Baldwin drives up to Niagara Falls, followed closely by Sandra. He takes it slower than the escort would like because her VW Beetle has a top speed of fifty on the flats, forty-five tops uphill. The motorcycle cop keeps waving him on but he maintains a pokey slog. Finally, the cop just waves goodbye and takes off. Not doing any good here. They arrive at the Justice Center at 10:45, which happens to be two floors above Silas Griffin's morgue. Baldwin hopes that Thomas Jordan isn't down there.

He finds out immediately that he isn't.

"Mr. Jordan is probably having a cup of coffee right now with Quincy Taylor," says Paquette. "They're friends from Lackawanna."

"Oh, thank you Jesus," says Baldwin, lifting his eyes to heaven.

Paquette smiles at Sandra, who's standing next to Baldwin, then adds, "Right after he was met by Mr. Johnson, one of the other Rochdale College people appeared to carry him off for Toronto. It was just a case of very good timing."

"This story keeps getting better and better," says Sandra, and she reaches over and introduces herself to Paquette.

They exchange pleasantries, she asks if she can observe the questioning. Paquette tells her no, not allowed, but since she's here, she can interview some of the men who were involved in the arrest, and she can visit the site, "To get a true sense of the drama that your husband was involved in." She's delighted with that, and pinches Baldwin on the elbow. Paquette assigns one of the constables to be her guide, and they leave together, talking animatedly. She's already got a notebook out, jotting things down.

The interrogation room is arranged with the two parties facing each other, about eight feet apart, each with their own table, a space in between. Paquette, Baldwin, a representative from the Crown Attorney's office, and another official sit at one table. Johnson and his legal counsel, a man named Jeffrey Childs, sit across from them. A stenographer sits off to one side, two uniformed policemen stand against the wall behind Johnson.

Johnson wears a tunic and baggy pants that are a little too short, provided by the jail. You can see his prosthetic leg at the ankle. He's muscular, quite fit looking, and dwarfs Childs, whose name fits. He's on the short and frail side. Baldwin was told that he's an excellent barrister.

After the formalities, after everyone is introduced and Johnson is once again told of the charges against him and reminded of his rights, the questioning begins.

"We'd like to begin by telling you why you were arrested, what evidence we have against you and then we'll move on to hear your statement," says Paquette.

Johnson nods.

"Our case rests on these facts: American law enforcement found witnesses who will say that you threatened to kill American men who attempt to avoid military induction. Shortly after you made this threat, two men who immigrated to Canada for that reason, who were in fact on Canadian soil, were found dead in the Niagara River. Another witness will say that they delivered these men into your hands immediately before they were drowned. Yet another witness will say that they were supposed to meet these men, but you agreed to meet them instead, because they were unable to do so. We believe that you used the opportunity to murder the men by forcing them into the river, above the Falls, leading to their deaths.

"Lastly, your behavior when confronted by police yesterday, your instinct to take your own life, suggests to us that our theory is correct. Your own words to Detective Thomas Baldwin, seated next to me, confirms this."

Paquette then asks Childs if his client would like to respond or remain silent and wait for a trial. The representative from the Crown Attorney chimes in, saying that if Mr. Johnson cooperates fully, it will determine whether he is charged with first- or second-degree murder, and that would affect his ultimate sentence if he's found guilty. Childs knew that this was all coming and says that Johnson will respond and cooperate fully.

Baldwin relaxes. He didn't realize how wound up he was. This whole nightmare might be over.

Paquette looks at the accused. "Mr. Johnson?"

"Everything you said is true," he says. "I did throw those two men into the river from the building. I did intend to kill them."

The room goes silent. Less than a few minutes into the inquiry, a full confession. Paquette and the others were unprepared for this, they all appear surprised, relieved. The other official at the table looks over at Paquette, smiles and shrugs. That was easy.

For the next thirty minutes, Paquette and the other Canadians question Johnson about the murders: where, how, why. Johnson tells them how this all came about. He tells them the why, first. He tells them about his patriotism, his son's death in Vietnam, and his animosity towards the antiwar hippies. Then, the where: His job put him in the perfect place to target men who evaded military service by coming to Canada.

Finally, he describes how he murdered the men. He says that he has a coworker at the construction site, who he watched meet a woman there. It would happen fairly often, at least twice a month. She was a hippie, maybe thirty years old. Red hair. She would always show up with a young man in tow. He was twenty, twenty-two maybe. Nervous, twitchy. The guy carried luggage or a duffel bag. They would then park the newcomer somewhere nearby; she would take off. And at the end of the shift his coworker and the traveler would pile into a car and disappear.

It didn't take a genius to realize that they were taking American draft dodgers to Toronto. Johnson saw an opportunity and told his coworker he would be happy to help. At first, the guy thought he was kidding, or maybe he didn't trust him. But on two occasions he was desperate, and he asked Johnson to fill in because he couldn't make it. Johnson agreed.

Styron was the first. The woman delivered him to Johnson at the appointed time. Johnson lured him to an upper floor when everyone else had left for the day, to see the Falls from an excellent vantage point. Shoving him through the opening into the Niagara River was trivial. The first guy cartwheeled into the river and disappeared. He says he did the same with Roesler a month or so later. Roesler was so small, that Johnson was able to pick him up by his belt and heave him into the river, like a bag of laundry. He says he forgot their names and didn't really care.

"Were there any others?" asks Paquette.

"No," says Johnson.

Baldwin whispers to Paquette, "May I ask a question?" and Paquette nods.

"What about Alan Crowe?" asks Baldwin.

"No," says Johnson. "He was the son of a friend."

"What about Grant Harel?"

"I don't know who that is," says Johnson, and he scans the faces looking at him, questioningly.

Baldwin, and he thinks probably everybody else, believes him.

"Are you remorseful?" asks Paquette softly. It may make some difference during trial and sentencing. Johnson gives it some air, then speaks.

"At the time I did it, no. I didn't enjoy it but I had no regrets. But now, I wonder what I was thinking?" He looks at Baldwin and directs his words at him. "I don't know you. I don't know who you are, but you made me think about honor." He looks at his hands, folded on the table in front of him, stares at them. "What I did was dishonorable. I am ashamed. If my son was alive today, I would not be able to look him in the eyes. Ronny would never have done what I did." His voice cracks and Childs puts his hand on his shoulder.

Paquette looks at everybody else, and they all nod at him.

"Thank you, Mr. Johnson, I believe we are done here." He says a few more formalities for the stenographer to include, time stamps, attendees, like that.

Everyone pushes off the table and the two uniformed officers step forward to escort Johnson back to a cell somewhere.

"We've still got two unsolved mysteries," says Baldwin to Paquette when the room is cleared. "What's your instinct about them? About Crowe and Harel?"

"Johnson isn't involved," says Paquette. "But that's just what you asked for, my instinct."

"Yeah, me too. He doesn't know who Harel is. Or was."

"A copycat?" suggests Paquette.

"Nobody knew about the murders," says Baldwin. "There wasn't anything public to copy. No, I think Alan was killed by one of our other suspects, but Harel? I dunno. The first time we talked, didn't you say there are a number of suicides at the Falls?"

"Yes, there are. Eight or ten a year."

"Maybe we should look and see if Harel had a reason to kill himself," says Baldwin. "It's something we should rule in or rule out before chasing murder suspects."

"I'll pursue that," says Paquette. "I'm in touch with his closest friends, and I spoke to his parents. And I have some personal papers, including his diary. There might be some indication he would do something like that."

"I have an idea, a plan, to put in motion back in the states that could lead to Crowe's murderer," says Baldwin. He spends the next few minutes explaining it, the Phelps sting operation, and Paquette is impressed.

"And there's another suspect, a guy named Brian McGee," says Baldwin. "I'm not sure how to nail him. Plenty of motive, from what I've been found so far, but no evidence."

"Let me know if I can assist with either of those inquiries," says Paquette. "Meanwhile, I'll notify Roesler's and Styron's families about how they died, why, and who did it. The man will be brought to justice."

"It may bring them some relief," says Baldwin. "Thank you for doing that. I'll do the same with the women back at the commune in Lackawanna."

As they part ways, Baldwin thinks about human nature, and how incongruous it is that capturing the killer, knowing his motive, even his methods, may be a balm for the sorrow felt by a victim's loved ones.

40 NOTIFICATIONS

Tom and Sandra Baldwin meet at the same pergola that had been the command center when Johnson was arrested, near the hotel building site. Amid the sounds of workers back on the job and the Niagara River roaring past, they discuss the arrest and the inquiry that Baldwin had just witnessed. Sandra takes notes as fast as she can. She can't wait to report on the sensational capture of a double murderer – by her husband – and the man's confession. She already got backstory and terrific anecdotes from other officers who were on the scene. This is a scoop, an exclusive, and the *Lackawanna Beacon,* itself, will once again be in the news. Not to mention Sandra Moore, reporter.

"Can I quote you on all that?" she asks.

"Of course, but not on the rest of what we talk about," says Tom. "Totally confidential."

"Ongoing investigation?"

"Yep," and he proceeds to tell her that they now think that the mob murdered Crowe to position Phelps right where he is: Trying to locate Brophy to get his signature. Law enforcement is going to take advantage of that. "The plan is to give Phelps access to Brophy and watch the mob follow. Then drop the net on them."

"You'll be there?" she asks, hoping not.

"I hope so," says Tom.

Sandra feels a shade of dread. Those men make a living killing people and have no conscience. She remembers the movie *The Brotherhood* with Kirk Douglas, where they went around killing *each other.* She shivers, and Tom senses her anxiety.

"The arrests will be well planned and managed. Nothing to worry about," he adds.

She has her doubts. Not about Tom, but everyone else.

225

"This is the same FBI that got Martin Luther King completely wrong, and now he's dead. Not to mention Medgar Evers and dozens of other civil rights activists," she protests.

"The FBI isn't part of this," says Tom. "They don't want to help. Risk averse and lack of interest."

"Don't want to help the Black people?" she asks.

"Or the antiwar kids."

She falls silent, shakes her head, still worried about Tom.

"What's next on this case, the double homicide here in Niagara Falls?" she asks.

"It's in the hands of the Canadians. I'll have to return to testify," says Tom. "The only thing left for me to do is tell Aries…Ashley Lange…that her boyfriend's murderer has been apprehended and has confessed, and to tell Amber that she has crossed the border for the last time."

"I'll write about Ashley Lange," says Sandra. "A human-interest sidebar. But Amber Penrose?"

"She'd get in some kind of trouble," says Tom. "Possibly with the law, definitely in public opinion." He waits for her to decide. She shakes her head, no, not worth it. Another reason to love this woman.

On his way back to Lackawanna, Baldwin radios the chief and tells him how it all went, what his next steps are. Plishka tells him that he will break the news to the men back at the VFW Post. They should know what the cost is of an overheated reaction to the antiwar movement. He volunteers to call the Crowes, too, and tell them that they are still looking for Alan's killer. Baldwin agrees. They should know.

At his detachment office, Henri Paquette phones up the Styron family in Akron, Ohio. He tells them that their son was actually murdered while trying to emigrate to Canada, and that they have arrested the culprit, who has confessed. He does this with both professionalism and compassion, a rare combination. The Styrons, for their part, react with the rare combination of shock and relief. For months, the idea that Dominic had died by suicide or accident had been nagging them as unbelievable. Now they know. They can seek closure.

Paquette also tells them that Dominic left behind a child, a two-month-old girl named Arwen whose mother they know, Ashley Lange. He can tell from their reaction that this is news and it is joyous. They ask how they can contact Ashley to meet their grandchild and he tells them, hopeful that a reunion will soon heal other wounds.

Then he calls the Roeslers with essentially the same message and gets the same reaction: closure. They ask some questions about their son's murderer: Why did he kill their boy, was he remorseful, what will happen next. Paquette

226

explains what he knows. But something unexpected happens after that.

Mrs. Roesler tells him that Jaime's former art teacher had called a week or so ago and asked about Jaime. He did not know that Jaime had died at the Falls and was shocked, crestfallen, when he learned of Jaime's fate. He said he had expected Jaime to join him in Toronto months ago and wondered what had happened. He never expected this.

"At the time, when he called, we all thought it was a suicide or an accident. That's what we told him it was," she says. "He was very distraught, really upset. Now I have to call him and tell that Jaime was killed on purpose, and that they caught the guy."

"What is the man's name?" asks Paquette, predicting the answer.

"Grant Harel."

"They were close?" asks Paquette.

"Like brothers," says Roesler. "He was Jaime's teacher and mentor. Jaime wanted to be just like him. I can understand why he tried to get to Toronto."

"I'm sorry to tell you that Mr. Harel is deceased," says Paquette, piecing together what may have happened, what probably did happen.

"Oh my God," says Roesler. "How? Where?"

"He drowned at the Falls," answers Paquette. "Like Jaime."

Baldwin drives straight to the commune. It's late afternoon now, a couple of PDM males are on the front porch, as usual, smoking home-rolled cigarettes and passing a bottle of cheap Ripple. Someday in the future, when the resistance isn't necessary, when Yale is behind them, when they are fully integrated back into society, when they are investment bankers or corporate execs, that will be a pair of Cuban cigars and two Hendricks martinis. They barely look up when Baldwin walks up the steps, but one of them points with his thumb toward the door and says, "They're inside."

He finds Aries, Amber, Adrian and three others sitting around a table, sipping coffee or tea, a block of cheese in the middle of the table with a knife stabbing it, a bowl of crackers nearby. They all look up at him, cow-eyed, waiting for the results of his trip up north. He looks from one to the next, takes a breath.

"The man named Harry Johnson is responsible for Dominic's and Jaime's deaths," he tells them. "He confessed today, faces justice in Canada."

Amber hangs her head, covers her face with her hands and weeps.

"Why?" pleads Aries. "What reason did he have?"

Baldwin explains it all to them, and Johnson's motive clearly makes them all uncomfortable. They look at each other timidly, trying to read each other's reaction, and none of them seems grounded. The man's son died in Vietnam, fighting for what he believed in, and we are on the other side, trying to prevent people like him from doing that.

"What will happen to him?" asks Adrian.

"That's up to the justice system in Canada," says Baldwin. "Life in prison, most likely. They took the death penalty off the table."

Once again, the antiwar comrades at the table appear flummoxed. Two draft evaders were murdered, and their killer will live to a grand old age. The concept of upside-down justice seems to be challenging all of them, including, Baldwin notices, Gem.

"We talk about a lot of things at our evening meetings," says Adrian, "but nothing quite like this. If my animal instinct kicks in, I'll be disappointed if that man gets to live." The others are a mix of nods and head shakes, and they all look surprised that Adrian suddenly doesn't sound like a guru. He sounds, for a moment, redneck.

In what can only be described as understatement, one of the other young women says, "It certainly will be thought-provoking."

The first person Baldwin calls when he gets back to the House is Greg Phelps. He tells him about the proceedings up at the Falls.

"As a law student, I wish I was there," says Phelps, "but as a long-distance friend of the victims, I'm glad I wasn't. I don't know how I would have reacted to that man." He pictures himself leaping over the table to strangle him. Drawing a hidden gun and shooting him. And then, just as quickly, he regrets the violent reaction. *Don't reflect the very person you hate.* "Maybe what I'll do is visit him in prison and talk to him some day, try to understand his anger, or whatever it was."

Baldwin can understand what Sam sees in Greg. This guy is special.

"That would be good for both of you, I think," says Baldwin.

There's a brief silence.

"There's something I have to tell you, Detective," says Phelps, "about our other thing."

"Oh?"

"I'm being followed," says Phelps, "everywhere I go."

"That's not us," says Baldwin.

"I know. I catch a glimpse now and then. It's always one of the men from the city meetings. Different cars, sometimes on foot, sometimes just watching me from across the street. One of my co-workers at the legal clinic noticed one of them and it creeped her out, the way he just stared."

"What did you do?"

"I told her he must be working for the government, maybe the FBI, watching who comes and goes. She agreed."

"Well, they are doing what we hoped they would," says Baldwin. "Tailing you until you meet up with Brophy. Get used to it. The Feds turned us down, so we have to go to a different plan."

"I just hope the thugs don't get impatient," says Phelps. "You know, let's just whack this guy and move on…"

"Maybe you should keep somebody else close to you," says Baldwin. "Safety in numbers."

Both of them think of one person: Gem.

Baldwin calls Abe Zubricky up in Buffalo with an offer he can't refuse.

"How would you like to personally arrest Vincent Falco and a squad of his soldiers for attempted murder?"

"Yes," says Zubricky. "What's the play?"

Baldwin explains it all to Zubricky, highlighting that the FBI declined to participate.

"We don't need a real Brophy to pull this off," says Baldwin. "And we could do it tomorrow."

"You want we should choreograph something that looks like a meet between Phelps and Brophy?" asks Zubricky.

"Yes, and it shouldn't be hard," says Baldwin. "Especially because there will be no federal marshals, no federal attorneys, and no protected witness. Just a lot of good guys with guns."

"Absolutely," says Zubricky. "We'll meet tomorrow at our place at BPD headquarters. If they're watching, and we know they are, it'll be convincing. Get Phelps here."

On the following day, after Baldwin had convinced Phelps to play along, even though he would not get Brophy's John Hancock on the sewer permit request, they drive to a meeting up in Buffalo. Phelps was convinced by the argument that they might catch Alan's murderer. One win is better than none.

The Buffalo police headquarters at 74 Franklin Street is four stories tall and takes up an entire block. It was built in 1936, like a fortress. Zubricky and a cadre of plainclothes cops with bulges at their pecs, which aren't muscles, wait for them in a conference room on the top floor.

"Falco's boys are out on the street, watching us in here, thinking we are making a deal," says Zubricky. "We'll stay here for thirty minutes or so to make it authentic."

"What's next?" asks Phelps.

"You and me pop out of here. We'll make a show of handshaking and agreement-making down on the street, outside the building," says Zubricky.

"We'll both smile and pose for them. We have to convince them that the next time you and me are in the same place, Brophy is there as well."

"Where will that be?"

"We'll find a location where the Feds would keep Brophy. A hotel, maybe. Or a safe house somewhere," says Baldwin. "They'll be following both of us after today."

"When?" asks Phelps.

"We'll make them wait. Get anxious, hopefully careless. A few days, a week?"

"Okay," says Phelps. "What do I do between now and then?"

"Your daily routine. Don't make them suspicious about anything. Keep doing whatever radical leftist shit you usually do," says Zubricky, smiling congenially.

Phelps nods. He has three new CO status cases he's working on. He'll focus on those.

Zubricky snaps his fingers. "We have the perfect place for this to play out in our favor. It's a house on the west side, in the Irish neighborhood, where they'd expect it to be for a guy named Brophy." A couple of the other cops nod, smile, they know what he's talking about.

"Why perfect?" asks Baldwin.

"The houses on either side are owned by Buffalo cops. There's a huge brick church across the street. It's a one-way street. No alley behind. Once they're in range, they're screwed. We close the top and the bottom, and they're in a bottle."

"I like it," says Baldwin.

Everyone is in agreement. They decide on one week later at 9:00 am, so kids are in school. Baldwin will pick up Phelps at the commune to drive him to his rendezvous with the virtual Brophy. Buffalo cops will be in position, and the street out front might be the killing field.

Before they break up, Zubricky turns to Phelps. "I'm curious why it is you are turning on your own family," he says. "I mean, I'm glad you're doing it, but why? What happened to you that didn't happen to everybody else named Phelps?"

Phelps looks at Zubricky for ten silent seconds, maybe asking himself the same question. "I'm a product of my times, I guess," says Phelps, finally. "My parents and my older brother and sister, they were all a product of theirs. All the social upheaval going on around us? That's what's shaping me. Civil Rights, women's rights, an unjust war. One trial after another." He stops for a moment and then adds, "I'm just trying to do the right thing."

The other men in the room are a bit embarrassed. In their macho world, nobody is ever honest about their feelings. It's like pointing to your heart and saying to an adversary, *here, hit me here.* Zubricky purses his lips and nods. The others move off towards the doors, heads down, confident that he probably is trying to do the right thing.

On the drive back to Lackawanna, Baldwin tells Phelps that he will ask Gem to come along next week to the end game with the mobsters.

"Whoa," says Phelps, turning towards Baldwin. "Won't that be dangerous?"

"I'll make sure she knows that it's dangerous," says Baldwin. "She can decide whether to come or not."

"Why bring her along?"

"If she's in the car with us, the goons will be even more convinced that we are not aware of them. They have already seen her with you and they probably expect another hippie to come along." Of course, Baldwin also wants another cop with him, especially one so deep undercover that the element of surprise will be like having five cops.

"She'll be safe?"

"The meeting place will be crawling with law enforcement. Yes, she'll be safe."

Ten minutes later, they pull up in front of the commune, slam their doors, and are met by Gem and Aries, who's holding Arwen in her arms. They all greet each other, and Phelps and Aries walk off together up the steps to the house. Baldwin and Gem overhear Aries tell Phelps, excitedly, that Dominic's parents are driving up from Akron in a few days. She's happy that her daughter will have grandparents to dote on her. And with the love of her life now out of her life, she might be considering that it's time to raise her daughter back in civilization. You can see it in her eyes.

When they are out of earshot, Baldwin says, "Get ready for some police action a week from today." He tells her about the trap they're laying for the mafia, and the role she'll play. "It's dangerous, and you will be charged with protecting Phelps until he's within the law enforcement perimeter."

"At the moment, he and we are within the mafia perimeter," she says.

"Oh?"

"I took a walk through the neighborhood, spotted them a block away on each side of the house. They didn't give me a second look. No threat." she says.

"In cars?"

She describes their nondescript, boring, older model Chevys. "They blend right in with all the other cars parked around here, but not the other drivers."

"They'll be following Phelps wherever he goes, and I want you with him always," says Baldwin. "Find a way to carry your weapon."

"I have an Army surplus ammo bag," says Gem. "Fits my new persona."

"Good idea. Keep up with the make-believe," says Baldwin.

To Gem, however, there's nothing play-acting about spending the next week with Greg Phelps.

At his desk back in Niagara Falls, after his conversation with Irene Roesler in Baltimore, Henri Paquette studies the pile of documents that he brought back from Toronto. Grant Harel's paper legacy. Somewhere in there may be something that confirms his suspicion that of all their dead boys, Grant was the suicide. One of the constables with lockpicking credentials had opened Harel's diary; his calendar lay open; a collection of letters held together with a rubber band on top; his phone books with dog-eared pages and underlined names and numbers are stacked on the corner of his desk. He decides to start there, with the Baltimore phone book. Perhaps there is a confidant, maybe a best friend or a counselor, whom Harel contacted to discuss his thoughts and intentions.

He calls the first number he turns to, someone named D. Fontaine, in Baltimore. The phone rings a few times, and a man picks up, says, "Hello?"

"I'm calling from Ontario, Canada, for someone who may have known Grant Harel. Someone named Fontaine?" says Paquette.

"Yes, that's me, who's this?"

Paquette introduces himself and tells him why he's calling, that D. Fontaine was an underlined name in a phone book owned by a man now deceased, Mr. Grant Harel. Paquette tells the man he's trying to piece together Harel's final days.

Fontaine is a little slow to respond, probably shaken, but finally says, "Grant was my roommate in college. We talked for the first time in quite a while last week. He's dead?" Fontaine sounds stunned, but not completely surprised.

"Drowned, I'm afraid," says Paquette, withholding his suspicion about how. "May I ask you what you two talked about? And for my report, what is your full name?"

"Donald Fontaine," he responds. "Grant called out of the blue a week or so ago. He wanted me to remind him who our religion professor was at St. Johns College."

"Did he say why?"

"Only that he remembered the man for a lecture he gave about guilt and forgiveness," says Fontaine. "I didn't remember that lecture, but I told him it was Father Damien Engle."

Paquette turns to the E section in the phone book, and quickly finds Engle's name, underlined, checked off.

"Grant seemed very depressed," says Fontaine, also out of the blue.

"Did he say what he was depressed about?"

"No. But, I mean, why try to track down your old professor to talk about a lesson on guilt?" He lets a moment go by before asking, "Did Grant kill himself?"

"That's what I'm trying to find out," says Paquette.

"Grant was a very empathetic guy," says Fontaine. "Way more than regular people. When someone was hurt, or something disastrous happened, he felt it. He mourned for days when my mom passed away, and he had never met her. He could feel my pain, though. He was like that with all kinds of bad news." Fontaine pauses briefly. "Did he get really bad news?"

"Yes," says Paquette, "I think he did. Very bad news."

"Then the worst happened," says Fontaine, resigned.

Paquette finds himself nodding, also resigned. "Thank you for this bit of help. I'll call Father Engle and see where it leads," he says.

Engle sounds ancient when he finally answers his phone, after maybe eight rings. He's slightly out of breath when he struggles to get out the "Hello?"

"Father Engle?" asks Paquette.

"Retired, thankfully," says Engle, "so call me Damien. Just Damien."

Paquette responds, "Please call me Henri, which is what every priest who ever whacked my knuckles with a ruler called me at Sainte Jeanne d'Arc Catholic school in Montreal." They both laugh, but Henri has serious business to do, and he jumps right in. He tells Damien who he is and what he is trying to establish: Did a former student named Grant Harel commit suicide? Damien is shocked, but eager to explore that with Henri.

"Grant called me about a week ago, maybe more," says Damien. "I had not heard from him in about seven years. It began as a casual reacquaintance and catching up. He told me about his work up in Canada, as an artist and teacher. I told him about my retirement, books I have been reading, one that I wrote. And then he told me about his other work in the antiwar effort."

"What did you think of that?"

"I was very proud of him and told him so. Catholic social teaching is against war, especially for what is so clearly a political end. I told him he was saving lives. Not only the young men who don't go off to Vietnam, but the

Vietnamese who they don't kill."

"Then what did you talk about? He must have had a reason for tracking you down."

"He had a question. He recalled a lecture I had given in a course about the desert fathers, about mysticism in Christian thought. The topic is a little weighty, but in that particular lesson, I talked about forgiving yourself as a necessary step before asking for forgiveness from God. This has to do with enabling God, who is always inside of you, to speak to you. You have to make room for God."

"He wanted to know more about that?"

"Yes, and I was very pleased. When he first heard that lesson, he was probably about nineteen years old. Nobody at that age has lived long enough, has had enough experiences, has made enough bad decisions to ever consider seeking God's forgiveness for anything. The very idea of it is foreign, off in the distance in time and place. But here he was, wanting to know about it again."

"And you obliged."

"Yes, we discussed it for an hour. In the end, he thanked me for clarifying it for him, he said he was greatly relieved, and he sounded it."

"Did you ever find out why he sought you out? Why this was important to him?"

"No, and it wasn't for me to ask. We weren't in a confessional," says Damien. "But now that he has possibly taken his own life, I wish I had. Are you trying to find out why he might have done that?"

"Yes," says Henri. "So far, the only person with motive, means and opportunity to take Grant's life was Grant, if I'm right about his motive."

"I'll pray that he didn't," says Damien. "It's a mortal sin."

Paquette makes a couple more calls to underlined names and numbers in the Baltimore book. An old friend, a draft dodger's parents – he made it to Toronto – and the Roesler family, whom he chose not to call. He knows how that went.

Next, he flips through the letters and postcards that Grant had saved in a drawer. All the postmarks were from months ago, and he pulls out several from Jaime Roesler and one from Dominic Styron. The last ones he received from both boys, a month or so apart, were confirmations that they were on their way, and would meet with Amber in Lackawanna. As far as Harel was concerned, both men were headed to Toronto and had arranged things with a reliable resource, Amber Penrose, to get as far as Niagara Falls. But then they just disappeared.

Paquette picks up Harel's calendar, pages back a few months and sees that he had penciled in dates for Styron's and then Roesler's arrivals. Here and there are other names and their safe arrivals, but not for Styron and Roesler. He had put question marks next to their names. Paquette opens Harel's diary and checks to see if he had anything to write about that.

May 31, 1970
Dominic was supposed to arrive today but wasn't at the pickup spot in NF. Jerry came back empty-handed. Called AP and she said she did the drop-off. Don't know where he is. Maybe went to Montreal or headed west. Good jobs in Edmonton.

There are other entries for that date, mostly related to his students, a faculty meeting, and talking with his parents. He pages forward a month.

July 2, 1970
Still waiting for Jaime. NF contact said he was waiting at the drop-off point and then just vanished. That's just like Jaime, playing games.

Paquette flips pages to the end of the diary, the last entry before Harel's tragic end.

September 11, 1970
I can't believe that Jaime is dead. It just seems impossible. Why would he do that? Could it have been an accident? He was such a daredevil, I'm thinking he walked along the top of the wall, hit a wet spot, slipped and fell in.
I am filled with guilt. I convinced him to come here, then sent somebody else to collect him. I should have been there the minute he arrived. I could have prevented this. He's dead because of me. Mea Culpa! I have to ask for God's forgiveness for what I've done, and what I plan on doing.

Paquette is convinced that Harel planned to take his own life for causing Roesler to lose his. He believes Harel's logic was terribly faulty, but we can't go back in time to straighten him out.
Harry Johnson's actions led to the suicide of Grant Harel, and Paquette will make sure that Johnson, his attorney and the prosecutors know about it. He readies himself to call Harel's parents and his colleagues at Rochdale to share his conclusion, and finally Baldwin, to close the case.

The week rushes by. Greg Phelps moves into the commune and takes up residence across the hall from Gem, sleeping in a claustrophobic, smelly room co-occupied by Peter and Sue. He and Gem eat together with the others, communally, in the dining room. Gem goes to work with him every day at the legal clinic, bringing along her ammo bag full of paperwork, a romance novel, and her .38.

The clinic is up at the university, a thirty-minute drive in good traffic and weather. Along the way in both directions they talk about life goals, ideal lifestyles, model life partners, and so on. Three days of that is like six months of dating, only better. Instead of the endless, silly fun that defines casual dating, she and Greg are facing a showdown with armed men and are deathly serious about getting this right or not at all, and they have a deadline. Three days of that intensity, and Gem knows that she's hopelessly falling in love. Greg shows all the signs that he is, too. The car they share is like a space capsule on its way to Mars, possibly not returning.

Watching him work for eight hours in between each date seals the deal. The legal clinic is in a windowless basement room that might have been the janitor's office back when the building had one. Above them is one of those huge red brick campus structures with classrooms, labs, faculty offices, and an eight-hundred seat auditorium. Their space is the one that has the nuclear war triangle on the door, so far underground it's where you'd go if the Soviets got nasty.

Greg fields calls and opens mail from all over the country: Young men looking for some way to avoid military service. He spends an inordinate amount of time asking the men about themselves, drilling deep to uncover that one thing that might be an out for them. Are you gay? Do you have young children, is your job indispensable, are you the sole provider for a handicapped person, are you a Quaker?

When he's not on the phone, he's typing letters to those who mailed the clinic. He personalizes each letter, signs it with a flourish, licks the stamp. He works pretty much nonstop, except to look over at Gem from time to time and smile, or shrug, or comment on the chances for the last caller. The most frequent prescription is, "He should go to college."

While Greg busies himself with his job, Gem busies herself with hers. As Sam, she had scoped out the whole basement, noting access points, escape routes, hiding places, likely danger zones. She preprogrammed her response to any sound, warning sign, or intruder, from any direction. If this, then that, times twenty. She always keeps the ammo bag with her piece in it close by, but she isn't satisfied with how long it would take to reach for it and pluck it out. Officer Samantha Simpson is ready to defend her ward.

After a few days, she contacts Jack Weidner, and he brings her a Beretta 70, a much smaller weapon, and an ankle holster. She can wear it all day long under her bell-bottom jeans. And she'll have twice the firepower. She's ambidextrous and could fire a ten-round barrage at the bad guys, all within about five seconds, if it came to that.

On the same day that she gets her preferred weapon, Dominic Styron's parents arrive from Akron, and spend the day at the commune. They meet everyone, get into polite debates with Adrian and a couple of others, hold and cuddle their granddaughter, and help her open a ton of presents that they brought her. Mostly onesies covered with Disney characters, some picture books, plastic rattles, a mobile for over the crib featuring Bugs Bunny, stuffed toys and a playpen. They stay for dinner and promise to come back the next day. As they're leaving that evening, Dominic's father says cheerfully, "Think about packing your bag." Aries says, "I already have."

Ashley and Arwen Lange-Styron depart the next day, for good, to Akron, Ohio. Two more hippies arrive in the early afternoon from places unknown and undeclared. Since both are cute girls, Adrian doesn't care. In they come, opening their backpacks, spreading their clothes on the beds, picking through the laundry, prepping to occupy the space of the recently departed.

Adrian and the rest of the PDM have no idea what has been planned for Greg, Gem, and the entire law enforcement community of Western New York. It wasn't necessary and it was probably a risk to share it with them. So, when the day arrives, those who are awake to see it are surprised when Detective Baldwin drives up, and Greg and Gem walk out to his car and climb into the backseat. Off they go without so much as a goodbye.

Just to make absolutely certain that the mobsters have no trouble following them, Baldwin wears his uniform and drives a black-and-white. Just to convince them that they are headed to some sort of meeting with important people, Phelps wears a suit and carries his briefcase.

At this point, Gem transforms mentally entirely into Sam. She's dressed more or less like she usually is, looks like a hippie flower child. But she's armed to the teeth carrying the ammo bag containing her .38 and wearing the ankle holster with her Beretta. Her eyes dart around, scanning, picking up the visuals if not the scent of the bad guys. Like a baseball player imagining what he will do with the ball if it comes at him, she rehearses what she'll do if bullets start flying.

They drive right at the speed limit through Lackawanna. Baldwin gets on the radio and says, "LPD Unit 12 to BPD HQ, over."

A voice comes back, "BPD HQ, we hear you LPD 12."

"We are on our way with Mr. Phelps, should make it to the rendezvous in fifteen."

"Roger that," says the voice. "Confirm the address."

"We're headed for 312 West Randle Street."

"That's correct," says the voice. "Drive safe."

They click off.

"What was that all about," asks Phelps.

"The mob has police scanners and we just gave them the address where this will all go down. They will try to position people there before we arrive, and follow us in. They behind us?" asks Baldwin.

"Yes, sir," says Sam. "Four cars back. Tan Chevy. Dirty windshield."

Phelps looks at Sam with a curious expression. Like, *you sound a lot like a cop.* Sam sees this, shrugs, and says, "I watch a lot of television."

"I see them now," says Baldwin, glancing into his rearview. "Most likely, there's another that we don't see."

Five minutes later, Sam spots another vehicle. "A black caddy with tinted windows just fell in behind the Chevy."

"That could be Vincent Falco, himself," says Baldwin. "He couldn't stay away. Maybe wants to personally shoot Brophy."

"And me," says Phelps. Sam reaches over and squeezes his hand.

Ten minutes later, they arrive at the house on West Randle. On the street outside is a Buffalo police sedan with two plainclothes cops, Zubricky and Merritt, who specializes in organized crime, though the mafia doesn't know that. They step out of the car and welcome Baldwin and his companions. The five of them climb stairs into the clapboard house, where the mob now believes Brophy awaits.

What the mob doesn't know is that there are ten other Buffalo police undercover officers stationed nearby. Three inside the house at entry points, two in the steeple of the church with a sniper rifle, and five more in deep undercover: posing as a newspaper salesboy, a homeowner raking his yard, and two neighbors chatting on the sidewalk two houses down.

241

A handful of civilians are nearby, walking a dog, pushing a baby carriage and just strolling along. Several are kids. They're supposed to be in school.

Three minutes after Baldwin arrives with his people, two minutes after they and the cops disappear into 312 West Randle, the brown Chevy and the black caddy arrive on the street from the south, and two nondescript older model cars from a side street. They double park, leave the motors running, and eight men emerge with guns drawn. It looks like they have automatic weapons and handguns. One of them is Vincent Falco. He stands back against one of the cars, directing traffic. The others seem to have orders. Three rush up to the entry door and push right in. The law enforcement officers outside, raking a lawn and talking about the weather, hold their fire. But inside, it sounds like a war.

Paul Slayton becomes the first and hopefully only man Sam shoots dead. He charges into the house, bent on killing everybody as long as one of them is Angus Brophy. He immediately opens fire with an automatic weapon with a thirty-round clip. Bullets tear through the air and smash through wood, glass, and people. Detective Merritt is caught in the chest. Greg Phelps instinctively slides over to protect Sam, to get in front of her. He is hit in the shoulder and falls back on her.

It looks like Slayton is taking a keen interest in finishing off Phelps. When she feels his weight push back on her and tastes his blood, Sam bends her knee, brings up her ankle, pulls the Beretta from the ankle holster, flicks off the safety and fires one shot as she swings the weapon up, completely on instinct and muscle memory. She hits Slayton right between the eyes. He looks surprised, and crumples to the floor. Nobody timed it, but it took about one second. For some reason, she thinks of how proud Jack would be of her. *One shot, dead center.* Baldwin throws himself on top of both Phelps and Sam.

The rest of the indoor shootout lasts about ten seconds. Zubricky and his men blast away with Caruso and Paglia. Boom, boom, boom, pop, pop, boom. One of the cops has a pump action shotgun and every time he fires, chunks of wall explode. Back and forth. After a hundred rounds are fired and no one seems to be moving, after the smell of gun smoke, blood, and something burning starts to clear, the cops get up to inspect the carnage.

Caruso's chest is pock marked with at least five bloody holes. Blood is running out on the floor in every direction. Paglia is still alive, somehow, and begs for help. "It hurts!" he cries. His right ear was shot clean off. Doesn't look like he was hit anywhere else.

"We got a live one!" shouts a cop.

Good, thinks Baldwin, *we may find out if they killed Alan.*

Outside, things are a little different. It's where the upper crust of the underworld and middle-class law enforcement interface. Slightly less loss of life, slightly more deal-making. It begins when everybody can hear a firefight inside the house, and Falco's bodyguard pulls his gun and rushes toward the front door. The police sniper in the church belfry blows him away. The man's head vaporizes while the rest of him divebombs to the ground. After that, it's a lot of shouting, get on the ground, drop your weapons, don't move. Cops rushing forward from every direction, handguns poised to blast away. That sort of thing. The mob concedes. Four guys are face down on the pavement...check that...three guys are face down and the fourth is simply down. The fifth, Vincent Falco, just stands there, shifting his weight from one foot to the other.

Falco, who actually wore an expensive suit to the intended massacre, coolly tosses his weapon far enough away to claim he never had it, kneels on the ground, has a 'bad day at the office expression,' and probably expects an apology from the Buffalo police, because he really liked that driver. The cops cuff him and the others, tell everybody not to move, collect weapons or kick them aside, and start the ID-ing process. Back at headquarters, Cheryl will have to start a whole new file box. Zubricky comes out of the house and personally does Falco. Top dog to top dog.

Two ambulances were staged a block away and siren-in on command. Medical personnel dressed in white scrubs dart out and start checking on everyone's well-being. Not much they can do for the headless bodyguard, so they're waved into the house to care for the wounded. Almost immediately, Paglia is perp-walked out, palming his now unoccupied ear-space, and is told to lie down on a gurney. A medic tapes a huge gauze over the wound and the cops cuff both his wrists to the piping. He keeps crying like a baby.

Zubricky walks over to the gurney with Paglia stretched out on it, ambulance guys running around, getting him ready for medical attention.

He leans over Paglia, who is still whimpering about his ear, and whispers into his remaining one, "What ever happened to Carlene?"

Inside the house, EMTs rush to help Merritt, who was shot twice. They think he'll survive. Both bullets missed his heart and exited cleanly, but not before shattering some ribs and mowing through his lung. He'll never serve in the field again, will have a long recovery, will probably retire. But boy, what a story to tell his grandkids.

Another EMT attends to Greg Phelps. The bullet pierced his shoulder and shattered a clavicle, but missed any vital organs. After surgery to repair the damage and remove any bullet fragments, he'll be okay. Okay to be a lawyer, but probably not an intramural softball player, and he may have to learn how to write left-handed.

Sam had started some first aid even before Baldwin got off them, stuffing her hippie bandana into Greg's bullet hole to stop the bleeding, and caressing him to keep him from passing out. She kept whispering, "Stay with me, stay with me." When a paramedic starts examining him, cutting his clothing away and applying a real bandage, he turns his attention to her.

"You're a cop?" he asks, awestruck.

"My real name is Samantha Simpson," she says, as she massages his arm. The medic keeps telling her not to, but she keeps doing it and Greg seems to like it.

"You saved my life," he says. He shakes his head at her with profound admiration.

"You saved mine first," she says, and kisses his hand.

Baldwin examines everything, taking it all in. A war zone. As he's wandering around in the house, inspecting walls and furniture pockmarked with bullet holes, the air thick with the smell of gunpowder, here and there blood spatter on the walls, a pool on the floor, he spots a bloody, flesh-colored blob wedged into the corner. He takes out his hanky and picks it up. It's an ear.

Three dead mobsters, two wounded good guys, and hopefully somebody remains who can tell him who killed Alan Crowe. He tries Paglia first, he has a bargaining chip. Paglia is strapped down there in the gurney, still moaning, probably more about how deformed he'll be than how much it hurts. A BPD officer stands guard over him and steps aside for Baldwin.

"Richard?" he says and points at his shield.

Paglia looks at him like he's the dishwasher. "I don't talk to darkies," he says to Baldwin, then turns his head away and says, "Fuck off."

"I just need an answer to one question, maybe could help your cause," says Baldwin.

"You don't hear so good," says Paglia.

"Without your right ear, Richard, you're the one who won't hear so good, but I can help." Baldwin holds up the bloody hunk of flesh by the lobe and wags it at Paglia. "They will sew this back on if you answer my questions. If not, try to imagine what your nickname will be in Attica."

Paglia tries to grab for it, but he's shackled. Baldwin continues to display it, just out of reach. Paglia curses in Italian, utters oaths, threatens Baldwin's family, but finally relents.

"What's your fucking question?"

"I want to know if you guys did Alan Crowe."

"Who's that?" asks Paglia. "Never heard of him."

"He was the smart guy at the city council meetings. He was the guy who backed the city into a corner. He pissed off your boss."

"Alls I know is one day he's gone and the other one is doing the business. Made no difference to me."

At that moment the EMTs are pushing past and getting ready to haul Paglia into the ambulance. Baldwin hands Paglia his ear and asks the EMT if they might be able to stitch it back on if they get him to surgery fast enough. The EMT shrugs and says, "I guess so," and they load him onboard.

Paglia shouts back to Baldwin, "Never heard of the fucker!" and the rear door slams shut.

Baldwin has no reason not to believe him. So now what?

Baldwin studies the street scene as the ambulance pulls away. He sees Vincent Falco in the back seat of a black and white, a cop on each side. The other mafia soldiers are being herded into a paddy wagon, the dead one is covered with a coroner's sheet. Blood has leaked out and runs into the gutter. Technicians are taking pictures, making diagrams. On the opposite side of the street, in front of the church, cops are slapping the back and congratulating the sharpshooter. "Whoa," says one of them happily, "What a shot!"

He sees a housewife emerge from the house next door with a tray of coffees and what might be cookies. She must be a cop wife, because three of the undercover cops come over and one of them kisses her.

Zubricky spots Baldwin and walks over to him.

"Falco lawyered up."

"I was hoping to ask about Crowe," says Baldwin. "Not that he'd admit anything or confess, but I thought, maybe there would be some kind of tell, some flicker on his face."

"We may never know," says Zubricky. "But Vincent will go away for a very, very long time, and we probably saved Brophy's life, at least long enough for him to testify against Maglione, start a new life in Wichita. This is going to go very good for all of us. I mean, you know, politically."

"Now that the threat is gone," asks Baldwin, "and that we deserve some thanks, do you think the Feds will get us Brophy's signature?"

Zubricky smiles. "Already got that in motion. One of our city attorneys will get the documents signed and will turn them over to Phelps. A matter of days."

Baldwin extends a hand and thanks Zubricky. He's looking forward to telling Phelps and Sam, Sandra, Mr. Jakes, everybody. Their time has come!

One day following the shoot-out on Buffalo's westside, Sandra Moore submits her second spectacular true-crime exclusive to the *Lackawanna Beacon*. Not only does she scoop the Buffalo papers but she gets interviews with participants and eyewitnesses no other reporter even knows about. She gets quotes from the sniper and what he saw from forty feet above street level; a personal account from the undercover Lackawanna cop who shot one of the would-be assassins at close range; and a graphic, surgical description from the doctor at Buffalo General who reattached an ear on one of the mafia gunmen. The story is syndicated and picked up by papers all over the country.

She also writes a sidebar about Greg Phelps, whose courage and willingness to act as bait for the sting led to the mass arrest. He even took a bullet for the cause. She uses the opportunity to write about the King Homes project and the great assistance that he provided to that effort. He'll be a hero to some, not so much to others, but he's okay with that.

Somewhere in Buffalo, the attorneys at the Phelps Law Firm, including Greg's father, brother and sister, are scrambling to do damage control. A mafia underboss and a whole passel of hired guns are killed or captured while trying to assassinate the primary witness against their client. If the police can connect them with their client with so much as, or little as, a phone call or note or a visit to the prison, this will doom their defense. Stefano Maglione is a goner. His final breath might be taken in a seated position.

Somewhere in Lackawanna, members of the city council have mixed emotions. Each of them is probably reading the story at home while sipping morning coffee, scratching their dog's head. None of them enjoyed being choreographed and manipulated by the mob. Those guys were scary, and now they know just how much. Three of them dead? One lost an ear? Geez, they are all thinking, that could have been us! On the other hand, now they are gone for good. Or, conversely, gone for bad. Now the Negroes will build their goddam houses! They are probably thinking, *we just can't win.*

Two days later, Samantha and Jack Weidner have a heart-to-heart about their relationship. She tells him how she's feeling about this other man, and to his credit, Jack understands. He's fifteen years her senior and, although flattered that she chose him for a while, he knew they would not make a go of it. He tells her he'll step aside with incredibly fond memories. She will always be special, stuff like that. They will back off the romance, but continue to be partners, training buddies, and expert shootists together, but Sam wonders if she shouldn't introduce Jack to Amber.

Three days later, Vincent Falco and four mafia soldiers are arraigned on multiple charges stemming from the deadly skirmish. They are all remanded without bail and will likely spend eternity in one jail or another, some of it before and most of it after trial.

Four days later, SAC Doug Reynolds at the FBI field office in Buffalo takes a call directly from J. Edgar Hoover. Nobody ever gets a call from the director, who wants to know why the fuck his FBI was not involved in the biggest shootout with the mafia in decades. He says he's reading about it on the front page, the goddam headlines, of the *Washington Post*. What Reynolds hears has some of these words: **Goddam girl cop, Jew cop** and **Negro** (he doesn't say Negro) **cop** shoot gangsters **in face** blow away a **gangster's head** arrest a dozen mafia **hero cop** shot in chest **hero Negro cop** (he doesn't say Negro) saves life of **hero hippie lawyer.** All that bloodshed and heroism and the FBI had no role in it. He's livid, and Reynolds is certain that his next assignment will be somewhere northwest of Fargo. His plane ticket arrives later that afternoon. It's worse than he thought.

Five days later, a sealed envelope is delivered to Greg Phelps, recovering from a gunshot wound at Buffalo General. Inside is a notarized request for a sewer permit, addressed to the Erie County Health Department and signed by exiled Lackawanna mayor Angus Brophy. He puts it back in the envelope and tucks it under his pillow. The only person he will trust it with is Officer Samantha Simpson.

Seven days later, sequestered in her photo lab in the underground garage of the Federal Building where she has been studying tens of thousands of photographs but looking for just one, FBI clerical assistant first-class Beth Egan hits paydirt.

"Dad!" she shouts. "Come look!"

There's some knocking around in the darkroom next door, where he's been developing film for the past month. Probably putting things away safely. Then Bruce Egan finally appears behind her.

"What's up sweetie?" he asks.

"Look," she says, and hands him the loupe.

He bends over to study the image on the contact sheet that she excitedly points at. He examines the front grill of a beat-up maroon '62 Pontiac Tempest. Inside, behind the windshield, are two men.

"Okay," he says and looks over at her. "What am I seeing?"

"Does the driver look like this guy?" she asks, and hands him the eight-by-ten of Alan Crowe. She can't wipe the smile off her face.

He looks at the portrait, bends over the contact print again and says, "Yep. That's him alright. Who's the other guy?"

"I dunno," she says. "We have to make a blow up of this picture, Dad, can you get right on that? We may have cracked another case! I'll call Detective Baldwin!"

An hour later, Baldwin arrives at the lab and is greeted by the Egan family. Dad and daughter are seated on folding chairs at Beth's workspace, smiling like Cheshire cats. Bruce holds up the enlarged portrait of Crowe, and Beth holds up two enlargements. One is of the front of the car showing two men inside, and the other one a blow-up of the mysterious passenger. The array stops Baldwin cold.

"Lordy, Lord!" says Baldwin, shocked and delighted. "A break! This paid off!" He drops into a chair and stares at the pictures, one after the other.

"Good work, Egans," says Baldwin glancing up at both of them. "When was this taken?"

"The time stamp is July 30, eleven-fifteen a.m." says Beth.

"Peace Bridge?"

"Yes sir," says Beth. She hesitates before asking, "Do you know this other man, sir?"

Bruce looks at him with the same question.

"I do," says Baldwin. "His name is Michael McGee."

"That doesn't mean he did it," says Plishka when Baldwin shows him the photos. "But it does make him a suspect. Last guy he's with before his death?"

They're in the chief's office. Sam sits quietly next to Baldwin, learning more about investigations. She doesn't know it, but Plishka is grooming her to become a detective in a few years, just like his chief did with him. He loves crashing glass ceilings. First a guy with a handicap, then a Black, next a woman. *There are people who will hate me for this, but fuck 'em.*

"I know," says Baldwin. "I'm missing that motive thing."

"You told me about your interview with McGee," says Plishka. "He told you that he still loved Crowe, missed him and all that. He hinted that his father could have done it because he hates homosexuals."

"Yeah."

"Misdirection?"

"If it was, he's really good at it. His father tried the same thing when I talked to him. Gave me a dozen other people to look at. Not subtle about it, though."

"Family trait?"

Sam coughs, more to draw attention than clear her throat. They both turn to her with the 'what?' look.

"What if they did it together?" she asks.

Plishka's eyebrows pop up. He holds up the photo of Michael McGee and Alan Crowe in the car together. He squints and tries to peer into the backseat. "I can't see if there's a third person in the car. Bad camera angle."

"Why would they do that?" asks Baldwin, though he has his own theory.

"What if Alan decided to avoid Vietnam by coming out?" she says.

"Okay," says Baldwin. "Keep going."

"What if he called Michael to tell him they could be together again. Or maybe needs someone to verify that he's gay for the draft board? What if he asked Michael to help him?"

"And?"

"What if the shoe is on the other foot now?" she says, on a roll. "What if it's Michael's career that would be screwed if their affair came out?"

"He'd be off the swim team, no chance for the Olympics. Probably thrown out of the fraternity. Friendless," says Baldwin, agreeing with her.

"Dig into this," says Plishka. "It sounds like a pretty strong motive if that's what Crowe planned to do, and if the McGees knew about it."

Greg Phelps is the first one they call. He's still at Buffalo General, healing, getting pain relieving drugs that make him a little loopy, feeling pretty good. Even better when Sam calls.

"Hi handsome," she says, "How's the patient?"

"As of this moment, excellent," he says. "Coming over?"

"Soon," she says, "but I need a quick answer."

"Yes," he says, "I love you." It's not the loopy drugs.

Sam is struck, in a good way, almost cries, glances over at Baldwin who's watching and hearing Phelps' side of the conversation. Baldwin raises his eyebrows. She smiles and says, "Baldwin is on the call, he can hear you."

"Get the rest of world on, I'll tell them, too," he says.

Sam blushes, smiles, wipes a tear. "I'll come over today, but we have an important cop question."

"Okay."

"Alan Crowe. Was he ready to declare that he's a homosexual, to get CO status?" she asks.

"I wasn't positive, but he was leaning that way. He said he had people to talk to about it. I assumed parents, friends, confidants. It would have been a big step. His whole life would have changed."

"Would he have stayed out of the Army any other way?"

"No, I'm afraid not. He'd be walking point right now, in a jungle somewhere in 'Nam."

"Did he consider going to Canada?"

"He was considering that, too," says Phelps. "Both choices were bad, for him, but Vietnam was worse. It was tearing him apart."

"You said leaning toward coming out, why?"

"He said it would be liberating to just be himself, finally and forever. In Canada, he'd be in a gilded cage forever."

Baldwin jumps in. "Greg, it's Baldwin. Did he mention anybody at all, a name, who he wanted to talk to?"

Phelps is quiet for a moment, replaying their conversations. "He said something about somebody special, that's all, no name."

Baldwin and Sam exchange a glance and she mouths the word, "Bummer."

A moment passes and Phelps says softly, "Come visit, Sam."

Baldwin nods at her and mouths the word, "Go."

Baldwin needs more, so he drives to the PDM commune, hoping to see Adrian, who said something important on day one of the investigation. As always, the drive is disheartening as the environment changes abruptly from agreeable middle-class to devastating poverty the closer he gets to Bethlehem Steel. He always thought that that was an unfortunate name for a steel plant, especially one that hovered over so much destitution.

The commune is decrepit as ever, except the VW vans must be working now. Nobody cursing under the hood and they seem to have switched places. The duplex looks deserted. No dope smokers on the front porch. He walks right in. Same concoction of acrid aromas greets him, and he can hear a one-sided conversation down the hall in Adrian's office. He peeks around the open door and sees Adrian on the phone. The boss holds up a wait-a-minute finger and waves Baldwin in.

After he hangs up, Adrian invites Baldwin to sit down, offers him a cup of coffee or tea. Baldwin declines.

"What's up?" asks Adrian.

"Things seem different around here," says Baldwin.

"Turnover. It happens. Aries and Jamal are gone, two newbies just moved in. Amber is so depressed I'm not sure she'll last. Gem was a surprise nobody expected or liked much. And our lawyer is in the hospital."

"I'm sorry about Gem," says Baldwin, "but she solved the murder of two young men and helped arrest your nemesis. She's a good cop, with the emphasis on good."

Adrian concedes the point. He gestures toward a backpack near the door. "That's her stuff, if you want to take it. But you didn't come for her laundry, did you?"

"No," says Baldwin. "I'd like to show you something, but I need your assurance to keep it quiet."

"Okay, I guess."

Baldwin shows Adrian the photo of Crowe and McGee in the car, then the close-up of McGee. "Do you know this man?"

"Nope. Never saw him before."

"When we first met, you said that you were sure that Alan would get CO status, that he'd be mopping floors somewhere. What made you say that?"

Adrian leans forward and rests his chin in his hands, elbows on the big desk. "Alan was a gay man, and he was going to admit that to the draft board. It's not CO status, exactly, but it is a get-out-of-Vietnam card. Who's the guy in the photo?"

"A former boyfriend."

"Maybe he's the guy that Alan told me he was depending on," says Adrian.

"Depending on for what?"

"I don't know. Corroboration, maybe? Emotional support? I don't know."

"Did he mention a name?"

Adrian looks to one side, trying to scratch his brain, dredge it up. Then a light goes on. "Micky? Marty?"

"Michael?" asks Baldwin

"That's it," says Adrian.

Baldwin holds up the photo again. "Meet Michael."

Back again to the House and a huddle with Plishka.

"Michael McGee knew what Crowe was going to do," says Baldwin.

"Bring him in for questioning," says Plishka.

"Arrest warrant?"

"I think that's premature. At this point he is a material witness," says Plishka. "He doesn't have to cooperate at all, but he will."

"He'll want to help if he's innocent," says Baldwin, "or keep up the charade if he isn't."

"Exactly," says Plishka. "Call him and ask him to come in, tell him it's urgent, new evidence, whatever you can think of."

"The father?"

"We could question both of them at the same time, but not together." says Plishka, liking the idea. "I could have a couple of uniforms pick him up when we know the son's arrival. If they tell him we need his expert advice, he'll come here on his own."

Back in his own office, Baldwin calls Michael McGee at his fraternity house at Cornell. One of the pledges assigned to answer the phone runs off to find him, and McGee picks up a minute later.

"Hello?" he says.

"Detective Baldwin here, how are you today?"

"I'm fine, thanks. What can I do for you, Detective?" says McGee.

"We've had a break in the case," says Baldwin, "Alan Crowe's murder."

There's a longish silence on the other end before McGee says, "Good, I've been wondering how that was going."

"Are you free to talk to me about it?" asks Baldwin. "Not on the phone. I have physical evidence to show you."

"I'm driving up to Buffalo tomorrow," says McGee. "I'm going to visit his grave. Finally have a weekend off."

"Oh, I'm happy to hear that," says Baldwin. "I wouldn't mind going there, myself. Never had the chance after the funeral. We could meet at the gravesite."

They agree on the time, noon, the following day.

Baldwin tells Plishka the plan. Plishka will arrange for a couple of officers to collect McGee senior and bring him to the station at about the same time. Then they choreograph their questions so they can compare answers and test Sam's conspiracy theory. Whether the McGees were working together or not, they feel confident that they are close to closing this case, with one McGee or the other. Maybe both.

The next morning, something occurs to Baldwin, and he calls Beth Egan at the FBI photo lab. She has stopped looking for the Tempest, and her father is back into retirement. She is alone again in the darkroom, developing film of yesterday's bridge crossers: nosepickers, peeing babies, newlywed smoochers. The photos are still technically terrible. For FBI agents, it's obvious that practice does not make perfect, at least where a camera is concerned.

"Did you catch your killer?" she asks.

"Maybe, thanks to you," says Baldwin. "Can I ask another favor?"

"For sure, what do you need?"

"Can you look at the bridge crossers maybe a half hour before and after the Crowe photo? I have a hunch you may find another person of interest."

"No problem," she says. "Make, model, plate number?"

He gives her a description of Brian McGee's pickup and tells her what he looks like. An older, raggedy version of Michael.

"Give me an hour."

"If you find the truck with that driver, can you make another jumbo print and bring it to the station right away? Bring it to Chief James Plishka."

"Roger that," says Egan. She had always wanted to say, 'Roger that.' It's so law enforcement. And she's excited that for the next hour or so, she's in the game again.

At about the same time, Chief Plishka calls his counterpart at the Orchard Park PD, a golf buddy named Carl Bonner. They exchange a couple of pleasantries and one or two lies about their last golf scores, then Plishka tells him that this is a courtesy call. A couple of his uniforms are coming to collect a material witness in his town and bring him up to Lackawanna for questioning. "He might be a suspect," Plishka adds. "Murder."

"Who is it?" asks Bonner.

"Brian McGee," says Plishka.

"No shit," says Bonner, only a little surprised. "I can't stand that guy. Mind if I tag along? I'd love to take a picture of it."

"It's your town," says Plishka. He tells him when and where – the treatment plant – and then they make a date to play a round for a dollar a hole.

The investigation into Alan Crowe's murder has taken so long that there is a carpet of grass growing on his grave. Somebody will have to mow it in a week or so. Michael McGee is standing at the foot of the emerald rectangle when Baldwin arrives. He's right on time, he realizes, because the siren at the firehouse a block away sounds the twelve o'clock whistle. Back in the day, everybody set their clocks to it. It's an accompaniment as he approaches the grave.

Crowe's stone is a short marble marker with his name, birth and death dates, and the engraving, 'Taken Too Soon.' There are quite a few older flower arrangements, as though someone has been coming often, and a new fresh one. Probably from Michael.

It looks to Baldwin that McGee had been crying. His hands are at his sides and one clutches a handkerchief. His cheeks are rosy, eyes puffy. He stares ahead at the marker when Baldwin sidles up beside him.

"I wish I knew him better," says Baldwin. "He was just one of group of students with information I needed to solve a crime a year ago. I didn't make an effort to get to, you know, to get friendly."

"He was special," says McGee.

"That's what I'm finding out. Perfect inscription. He had a lot more to do."

"Yeah," says McGee. "Perfect."

"Want me to leave you alone here for a while?" asks Baldwin. "I can wait over there." He points at a bench under a pine tree.

"No, that's okay. I'll go with you." McGee takes a last look at the grave and the two of them stroll over to the bench. They sit. "You have something to show me?"

Baldwin takes the Peace Bridge pictures out of a manila envelope and hands them to McGee, then waits for a reaction. McGee stares at the pictures. Spends almost a full minute on each one. He doesn't register anything, as far as Baldwin can tell. No emotion at all. He finally hands them back to Baldwin and leans forward, elbows on knees, hands clasped.

"Care to comment?" asks Baldwin. He just wants to hear the first thing that McGee has to say no matter what it is, especially an answer to the question, 'Why did you lie to me?'

Silence while McGee gathers his thoughts.

"He got in touch with me, so I came up. He wanted to talk."

"About?"

"About us. Things were coming apart for him. He was called up, was supposed to report, go to boot camp, Vietnam. He had no good choices. But…"

"But?" asks Baldwin

"But he had one good choice, or he thought so."

"Which was…?"

"Finally coming out as a gay man and reuniting with me, if I was willing to do the same thing."

"Were you willing?"

"It was a case of very bad timing," says McGee. "Two years ago, no question. It's what I wanted. We broke up because I wanted to be out. Now it was role reversal. I have a life. I'm in college with the deferment. I'm an inch away from All-American, two years away from the Olympics. I could win a gold at Munich. I hesitated to say yes. I needed more time, but we both knew the answer would be no."

"Why didn't he just declare his homosexuality and not get inducted?"

"He would have lost everything, he thought. Even his family. I thought he'd be okay, that his mom and dad would accept it, so would his friends. Most of them knew anyway."

"Why were you two going to Canada that day?"

"I talked him into just going. Go to Canada, don't report for duty. I could cross over and visit anytime. It was the only solution left for him. Like I said, no good choices, but that one seemed like the best one."

"When was the last time you saw him?"

"We drove up to Niagara Falls, spent the day together there, then I took a bus back to Buffalo, got my car and drove back to Ithaca. That was about six in the evening. I thought he continued on to Toronto or somewhere."

"Why in heaven's name didn't you tell me all this before?"

"I thought I'd be a suspect. I thought my homosexuality would come out. My life would be ruined. Maybe it already is," says McGee. He looks up at Baldwin. "I didn't think this part of the story would help you find his killer. If I did, I would have told you."

"I wish you could prove to me everything you just said," says Baldwin.

McGee fishes around in his pocket and produces one of those strips of photos that you get from a booth. The kind you sit in with your girlfriend and it takes a series of pictures with the two of you making weird faces and maybe, if you're lucky, kissing. The strip McGee hands Baldwin shows him and Crowe pressing their faces together, hugging, and finally kissing. They both look genuinely in love. No way McGee caused any harm to Crowe.

"We both had pictures like this," says McGee. "Look at the back."

Baldwin flips it over. Crowe had scribbled, 'With love always, until we meet again.'

"I wrote the same thing on his," McGee says.

Two Lackawanna police officers show up unannounced at the sewage treatment plant in Orchard Park. Chief Bonner follows them in his car with an instamatic camera on the seat next to him, a silly smile on his face.

McGee is tight-roping from one concrete pond to another on a steel catwalk. The diesel pumps are clamoring away so he doesn't hear them approach and looks startled when he sees them waving him over. He holds up a finger, does a few more work things like tightening a valve and checking a gauge, then climbs down.

He walks over to the cops, who have been joined by Bonner. They're standing by the black and white, arms crossed.

"What's going on, Bonner?" he asks. Sounds annoyed.

"These men are from Lackawanna," he says. "They want you to accompany them to answer some questions. Seems like you're some kind of witness."

"Witness to what?"

"A material witness," one of the cops says. "We were sent to bring you in. You are not under arrest, you can refuse, but we would appreciate your cooperation."

Bonner chimes in. "A material witness! That's a big deal, Brian. You should go. And here, let me get a picture of you with these men in blue…" Bonner swings his instamatic up and the two cops crowd in closer to McGee. McGee even drapes his arm around one. All three of them smile. Click.

McGee is actually excited. "Let me batten down the hatches and I'll be with you in a minute." He turns and rushes off towards the collection of pipes and valves. Bonner grins at the two cops and winks.

A little before noon, Beth Egan appears at Plishka's door and hands him a file folder. He takes it, thanks her, looks like he might just set it aside. But she wants to see him open it. She stays put. Plishka looks inside and there are two eight-by-ten photos. He shakes them out. A shot of a shiny red pickup driving towards the camera on the Peace Bridge and a closeup of the driver, who Plishka recognizes as the scout leader, church deacon, water department engineer, loud-mouth homophobe Brian McGee.

"When were these taken?" he asks.

"11:21 am on July 30," Egan says. "Eight cars behind the Pontiac Tempest. It took me one minute to find him."

"I wish we had proof where he went from here, when he returned, what he did in the time in-between."

"Sorry," says Egan. "I do have a suggestion about that, if you plan on questioning this man."

"What?" asks Plishka.

"Tell him you do have that information."

Plishka sits back, nods understanding.

"You could tell him almost anything and he'd think you were telling him the truth. Cops don't lie. Back him into a corner," she adds.

"Genius, Agent Egan," says Plishka. He looks at his watch, sees that his patrolmen will be walking in with McGee any minute. "Why don't you stay and help me out with that?"

"Would love to, sir. Good cop or bad cop?"

"Bad cop," says Plishka. "Let's really throw him off his game."

Egan sets her purse down and takes one of the chairs. About three minutes later, McGee and the two cops arrive at the door. Plishka thanks them and sends them on their way. He stands up and shakes McGee's hand and introduces Special Agent Beth Egan of the FBI. McGee looks a little perplexed but generally proud to be a material witness. It looks like he did his best to clean up before taking the ride up to the House but missed a few spots. There's some oil on his shirt, some dirt, something that looks like tar on his shoes. Plishka hopes that's what it is.

"Thanks for taking the time from your busy day to help us out," says Plishka.

"Not a problem," says McGee. "What am I a witness to, do you think?"

"A murder," says Egan gravely, replete with hooded eyes. To McGee, her expression is accusing.

"What!?" says McGee, surprised. He twists in his chair nervously.

"Well, we aren't certain you saw it, but you were in the right place at the right time," says Plishka softly. Sounds consoling. McGee nods and calms down a little, but shoots a glance at Egan, who stares at him, expressionless.

"Where was I? When?"

"Niagara Falls, Ontario," says Egan with a tone that sounds challenging, like, *try and deny it.* "On July 30th, this year."

"No, I don't think so," says McGee. "That was a workday. I work. I can't just go for a joyride to the Falls."

Egan and Plishka create a dramatic moment by staying silent, then looking at each other, then back at McGee. He's anxious, looks from one to the other. "I wasn't there! I didn't see no murder. James, you know me, I'm telling the truth!"

"You're right, Brian, I do know you," says Plishka in a soft, reassuring voice.

"Do you own a late model, red Ford pickup, with license plate number ECC 2946?" asks Egan.

"I think that's right. Yeah, so?"

She hands him the bridge picture, the long shot of the truck. You can't see the driver very well. "This one? It's on the Peace Bridge. It's going to Canada."

"Looks like mine, but I might have lent it to a friend."

She hands him the closeup, and when he sees it, he knows that he's toast.

Michael McGee agrees to follow Baldwin back to the station where he can make a statement, explain his actions on July 30, provide whatever evidence supports his story. Baldwin is certain he's innocent, didn't murder the love of his life. This is all a formality. What Baldwin really wants is for Michael to witness his father's third degree. Fifteen minutes later, they're in a small dark room looking through one-way glass at Brian McGee, who fidgets nervously.

The interrogation room is a windowless, claustrophobic cell that one might find in a psychiatric ward. Painted a nameless shade of green, scuffed everywhere as though people have walked on the walls. The table and chairs are bolted to the floor. There's a metal pipe running the length of the table where prisoners who have been arrested are usually cuffed. McGee's on one side of the table and Chief Plishka and Beth Egan face him. He hasn't been arrested for anything yet, hasn't been Mirandized, so his hands are free. He's gesturing with them. Baldwin throws a toggle switch in the observation room and McGee's voice comes through at the end of a sentence.

"...treat a material witness?" He sounds upset and defensive.

"You weren't truthful with us, Mr. McGee, so we just want to know why?" says Egan.

"What she's saying is we just need you to clarify your statements from before," says Plishka a little more gently and understandingly. To McGee, it sounds like Plishka is saying, 'You didn't lie, you just weren't clear.'

McGee nods. Takes a deep breath. "Yeah, I forgot, I did drive up to the Falls that day."

"Can you tell us why?" Egan again.

He hesitates, looks to one side, which is often what someone does before lying. Plishka and Egan look at each other for a moment, then back at McGee. Finally, he says, "I had an errand. Something I had to pick up for the plant. Um, chemicals."

"Okay," says Plishka, "That explains it. Luckily there'll be some receipts or a reimbursement check that we can get from the town, to back you up."

McGee takes out a hanky and wipes his face. "Hot in here," he says.

Egan positions her pencil over an open notebook. "Can you tell me the name of the vendor?" Egan is good at sounding doubtful, suspicious. It makes McGee twitch.

"I'll have to think about that," says McGee, looking off to the side again.

"Maybe we should get to the reason we asked you in," says Plishka. To McGee, it sounds like a reprieve.

"Yeah," he says. "The witness thing."

In the observation room, Baldwin and Michael watch the interview and both feel the tension rising. "What have you got on him?" asks Michael.

"If I had to guess, we have pictures of him following you and Alan into Canada," says Baldwin. "Did he know that you were in town, visiting Alan?"

Michael puts his hand up to his brow and nods. "Yeah, it's possible. I told him I was coming up, needed something from my room. He wanted to know how come. I told him for a friend. He probably suspected something and followed me around."

"What is it you needed from your room?"

"The medal that I won for the one time I beat Alan in the pool. Sectional championship, freshman year. I wanted him to have it. For me, hopefully for him, it would be like an engagement ring."

In the interrogation room: "Since you were in Niagara Falls at exactly the same time that Alan Crowe was murdered there, and you knew him, we thought you probably saw him there," says Egan, again with the hooded eyes, arms crossed.

"There's about a million people there," says McGee.

"I should tell you that we have many more photographs," says Egan. "Would you like to see them?"

"Of me?" asks McGee, alarmed, disbelieving.

"Some," says Plishka. He sounds a bit remorseful, as though they have something that actually ties McGee to the murder, and he doesn't want to incriminate a friend.

"Take a look at these," says Egan, and she shows him the pictures of Alan and Michael in their car, crossing the bridge a minute ahead of him.

McGee studies the prints. "Michael," is all he says.

Egan leans forward and points at the picture. "Right in front of you, Mr. McGee. As of this moment, Michael is our primary suspect in the murder of Alan Crowe, and we believe that you saw it." This time, Egan actually slaps the table. McGee jumps.

Plishka reaches over and puts his hand on Egan's and says, "Let's not get ahead of ourselves, Agent." Egan plays along, pulls her hand back and leans back in her chair. Crosses her arms. Stares angrily at McGee.

McGee is so consumed with the scene of his son with Alan, he may have missed that part. His eyes drill into the picture and his face reddens with every passing second. Plishka is beginning to worry he'll have a heart attack. Then, just as quickly, he deflates. A long exhale. He coolly hands the photo back.

"It's obvious to us that you were following your son and Alan Crowe. This photo and others prove it," Egan says. "We believe that they had an argument that got violent, Michael killed Crowe and dumped his body into the river. We believe that you saw this and you are trying to protect him. As I said, we have more photos."

McGee takes another deep breath and lets it out slowly, using every second to ponder his response. He surprises them.

"If you have more photos, then you know that's not what happened," he says calmly, completely out of character.

"What happened, Brian?" asks Plishka. "Will you need a lawyer?"

"I won't need one for Michael, because he's innocent."

"Do you want an attorney? We can get one for you," says Plishka.

In the next room, watching and listening to this, Michael's heart is breaking.

McGee refuses a lawyer, waives his rights, and tells them the story.

He did follow Michael from their house to his rendezvous with Alan Crowe. They had met at a public pool in South Buffalo where they competed during their early teens. He watched them sit next to each other closely, touch each other now and then, put their heads together in a way that made him feel sick. Then he saw Michael give Crowe something. It looked like a swimming medal, and he knew that it was, and it made him furious.

After a while, they got in Crowe's car and he followed them. Up into Buffalo on the expressway, then over the Peace Bridge and up the QE Way to Niagara Falls. He stayed back so Michael wouldn't see him, but Crowe was driving and probably didn't think much of a red truck a half mile back. He said he thought that they were running off together. He was getting more furious as the miles ticked by, as he thought of them together, maybe forever, in Canada. All that work in the pool, raising an athlete, an All-American, gone. No Olympic glory. Just shame.

He managed to stay with them when they got to the Falls, then followed them on foot, watched from afar as they walked side by side, took in the sites, dined outside at a café. They looked like honeymooners and he was sure everybody else thought so, too. A homo couple on honeymoon. It was disgusting. At one point they got into one of those photo booths and spent several minutes in there. He didn't want to imagine what they were doing.

In late afternoon, they walked to the bus station and he watched Michael buy a bus ticket for Buffalo. He saw them slide into a dark corner between some concrete supports, and embrace. He was sure they were kissing. He wanted to throw up. Michael boarded the bus and quickly took a seat at the window, smiling at Crowe. Crowe blew him a kiss. They waved to each other as the bus pulled away.

Then he followed Crowe, who was heading back to his Tempest.

He had parked his car in a long-term lot right along the river about a quarter mile from the Falls, and McGee had parked his truck not far away at a spot on the street. As it happened, they both walked right past McGee's truck. First Crowe, then fifteen seconds later, McGee. He reached into the bed of his truck and grabbed a length of one-inch pipe as he walked by, and then carried it like a cane.

Crowe never saw it coming. When they reached a remote stretch of sidewalk, shielded by trees and parklike underbrush, McGee rushed forward and brought the pipe down on Crowe's head with all his might. He says he heard it crunch. He reached into Crowe's pockets looking for the medal Michael had given him. He found it and took his wallet and keys, too. He's not sure why. The sidewalk was right along the river. It roared past just feet away. He threw everything into the river with the pipe, but he kept the medal. His adrenaline was so high he had no trouble lifting the body and dropping it over the stone wall and into the torrent. It was swept away immediately. The whole thing took about ten seconds. Maybe less.

When McGee is finished, he has a weird, diabolical smile on his face.

"Is that everything?" asks Plishka.

"Yeah," says McGee, nodding. "That's what happened."

"Where's the medal now?"

McGee reaches into his pocket, digs deep, and plucks it out, holds it up proudly. "It's a souvenir from Niagara Falls," he says.

Plishka and Egan in the room with him, and Michael and Baldwin watching, are dumbstruck. Egan excuses herself and rushes out of the room, manages to get to the ladies' room down the hall before retching. Plishka, who had seen every manner of death in North Africa and Europe during the war, is nonetheless shocked by the cold-blooded, gleeful brutality. He can't move for a minute. Michael drops to his knees in the tiny observation room and weeps uncontrollably, giving Baldwin something to be useful for. He drops down next to him offering comfort.

When he gathers himself, Plishka pushes a button on an intercom and asks the officers standing outside to come in. He orders them to place Brian McGee under arrest for the murder of Alan Crowe, to read him his rights, to take him to holding. Plishka makes a mental list of everything that must follow: McGee will need a lawyer; Have him write his statement; Wait. Should he do that now? Schedule an arraignment; No wait, is this our case or should he be tried in Canada? Notify the parents, the Canadians. Mixed in there is some dumb stuff, like, did the murder weapon just sink, can they recover it? Is Crowe's car still at the Falls? What first? What else?

EPILOGUE SIX MONTHS LATER

After their trials in Canada, both Harry Johnson and Brian McGee were given life sentences and are serving their time in the same prison. They will never be paroled. Nobody knows if they are acquainted or what they would think of their mutual connection to Niagara Falls. No one ever visits either one. No one writes.

Hanging on the wall in Detective Lieutenant Tom Baldwin's office is a framed, completed thought diagram of the Alan Crowe murder investigation. All of the known unknowns and unknown unknowns had been uncovered and discovered. No more squares and triangles. The diagram consists entirely of circles – everything is a known. All the criminals have been sent to jail if they had it coming. Baldwin got the promotion that he had coming. He has been taking photography classes with his new Nikon, a gift from Kevin Crowe.

James Plishka became a regular member of the VFW Post in East Aurora. In fact, he was recently voted in as a Post Trustee. He drags along his mate-for-life, Jennifer Simon, and she often fills in behind the bar, helping Benson draw the beer. Plishka plays bingo every Thursday there with his new best friend, Dan Fredricks, who sold him a cherry red Mustang convertible with an overvalued trade-in.

As a result of her extraordinary work on the case, Beth Egan was awarded a new job title at the FBI: Director of Forensic Photography. She now spends all of her time taking and evaluating photos for the bureau. No more file clerk work. They hired her father as a part-time assistant. Hanging in her office is the news clipping that Sandra Moore had written, describing her work cracking the murders at the Falls. It's from the *New York Times* and includes a flattering portrait of her studying a photo with a magnifying glass. Two other dark government agencies that do supersecret, clandestine operations have reached out to her, trying to lure her away.

Officer Samantha Simpson is now called upon to do undercover work regularly, sometimes borrowed by the FBI. She has successfully infiltrated a sex trafficking ring, a teenage drug clique at a local high school, and a car theft squad. But she has steadfastly refused to imbed again with the antiwar movement. She tells them that she can't do it, that she's a conscientious objector. On a personal note, she moved in with Greg Phelps to test out what might become a lifelong partnership. So far, it looks good.

For his part, Phelps did indeed obtain all the necessary permits to proceed with the King Homes development. He personally financed the first three phases of site development and found private equity to build the homes themselves. The investors remain anonymous, smartly unwilling to expose themselves to the vitriol of the white folks. Even though he and his family are estranged, there are rumors that they are, in fact, also seeking redemption.

Abe Zubricky got married, but not to Grace Slick. It happened quite by chance. *The Buffalo Courier-Express* ran a piece on him highlighting the role he had played in bringing down the Falco Flunkies, as they were christened by the media. A divorcee named Carlene O'Malley got in touch with him to congratulate him on capturing her cousin, Richard Paglia, whom she had always hated. She also asked if he could help get her son into the police academy. After long conversations on the phone, they discovered they had been high school classmates, that they are both single, and have something in common: They both love Jefferson Airplane. Next thing they know, they are dating regularly and boom, fall in love. His stepson, Anthony, is a state trooper.

Inspector Henri Paquette of the RCMP was honored twice for his work on the Falls murders and suicide. One honor came from the Canadian government at its annual law enforcement appreciation day in October, up in Ottawa. Parades, a plaque, a serenade by a pipe and drum corps, a bunch of speeches. But the one that meant the most to him was a quiet affair in Toronto hosted by the Toronto Anti-Draft Program and the faculty and students at Rochdale College, thanking him for solving the murder of three boys and the suicide of their friend, Grant Harel. It was personal, for them.

In Lackawanna, as at PDM chapters all over the country, Adrian Foster's group of activists continue to work and play together. The war in Vietnam grinds on, their protests follow suit. Just about everyone who knew Alan Crowe has moved on, replaced by fresh, excited, energized blood. Except Ira is still around, and still can't beat Adrian at chess. Amber Penrose returned home to Massachusetts, is taking some time off and is applying to medical schools. She now wants to complete her father's work.

Jamal is back in DC, working on his degree and thinking about running for office someday, in the future. Or maybe law school, followed by a judgeship. He can't decide. Ashley Lange is raising her daughter in Akron, Ohio, surrounded by doting grandparents, aunts and uncles, cousins. A real family.

Ten million people visited Niagara Falls, Ontario, since the three murders and the suicide that entangled all these people. There were three suicides and one fatal accident at the Falls during this period, none involving young men dodging the military draft.

ABOUT THE AUTHOR

Larry Elin is Professor Emeritus at the Newhouse School of Public Communications at Syracuse University, where he taught in the Television, Radio, Film department for 20 years. Prior to that, he worked for 24 years in the entertainment business, notably in computer graphics, animation, visual effects and interactive games for children. He created much of the computer animation for the Disney feature film *TRON* and won the first Clio Award ever awarded for computer animation. He can be found in Wikipedia and IMBd. He is the author or co-author of three non-fiction books (also available on Amazon), the author of the crime novel *The Cinder Drop* (available on Amazon), and the producer, director and editor of numerous films, documentaries, television commercials and interactive products. Much of his work can be found on Vimeo. He is the father of two, grandfather of one and lives with his wife, Katy Benson, and pets Reesa and Scamper in an off-grid yurt in Fabius, New York.

ACKNOWLEDGEMENTS

I am forever grateful to my wife, Katy Benson, for all her moral support, as well as grammar, spelling and punctuation expertise. She edited the entire manuscript. Several friends and relatives read the manuscript and provided terrific creative feedback: Beth Egan (who has an important character named after her), Tim and Kathy Downey, Bill and Kathy Kita, Rosemary Graham, Carole Holtz, Don Benton, Bob Foard, Laura Hegstetter, Don Peters, Peter Drake, Natasha Cooper, Virginia Harel, Sara Mastrangelo, Nelson Price, Jim Sweeton, Patricia Infantine, and Peter Moller.

They all provided valuable feedback on the reader's experience, helping me add more intrigue, realistic human encounters and feelings, and more page-turning mystery. They also found and pointed out a bunch of dumb mistakes which, thankfully, you did not see.

Although the crimes, the investigators and the criminals are completely fictional, the setting and many of the events and circumstances that form the basis for this story are true. Here are some of those whose work I made hay with:

Thank you, John Hagan, for your book *Northern Passage, American Vietnam War Resisters in Canada*. This book, published in 2001 by Harvard Press, tells the true stories of American men who avoided military service during the Vietnam war era by fleeing to Canada. It tells the stories of the Canadians who sympathized with them and helped them to resettle in their country. If I got any of that right in my novel, it is due to Dr. Hagan's brilliant and personal work.

In *The Falls*, as in my debut novel *The Cinder Drop*, I relied on information about an actual lawsuit filed by the Catholic Diocese of Buffalo against The City of Lackawanna in 1968 over its condemnation of land that the diocese planned to sell to a Negro and Puerto Rican non-profit to build decent housing.

The case can be found here: https://casetext.com/case/kennedy-park-homes-assn-v-city-of-lackawanna. Makes for some very interesting reading. I acknowledge Thomson Reuters for its website Casetext.com, where I found this amazing piece of history.

I owe the late Frank E. Hollins and his weekly newspaper, *The Lackawanna Leader*, (which went out of print in 1982) a debt of thanks. Archived issues of the paper provided valuable insight and coverage of events in 1968-1970, which I leaned on heavily to build the story of *The Falls*. Much of what you have read in this novel is based on actual occurrences.